THE CURSE OF PIRINI LILAPA
GUARDIAN OF THE CORE (BOOK 2)
MICHAEL E. THIES

 Writer's Block Press

WRITER'S BLOCK PRESS

Guardian of the Core

The Curse of Pirini Lilapa

For information please contact:

Writer's Block Press, 4266 Bonmaur Terrace, Slinger, WI
53086

Michaelethies@michaelethies.com

Printed and bound in PRC and the United States of America. Published by Writer's Block Press. All rights reserved.

Family Crests and Badges by Melissa Thies

Map by Ben Hying

Cover by Scarlett Wang

ISBN: 978-0-9895668-2-7

Library of Congress Control Number: 2018904668

CONTENTS

PROLOGUE

The strong breeze that had awoken the Guardian of the Core, Edwyrd Eska, died to sporadic, light strokes that massaged his neck. It was the grave of night, though the gloaming roamed, not willing to give another inch of territory to darkness. Sands glistened in the light, and Eska could still see the mountains off on the horizon from his perch on the veranda.

Wind slapped him.

This was how it always happened when she wanted to see him. Eska clutched the gray pendant on the necklace at his throat, remembering her present. She had given it to him at a time like this 150 years before, when the suns overhead converged to form an eclipse known as Pirini Lilapa, or the Great Inferno. It had marked the fourth remembrance of the Great War, a war that had been so violent and terrible that the Ancients themselves, the very creators of the universe, disappeared.

Another gust. Almost a howl now, as if she were growing impatient.

Why this night? Eska did not know. Perhaps it was the impending closeness of the suns. Perhaps it seemed only right after a day such as Coronation. The month and a half duration of the Trials had fulfilled the purpose of finding him an apprentice, someone who would take his post as protector of this system of Gladonus. A system that lay home to billions of people, all who looked to him and his position as Guardian of the Core, as their protection from what was about to come. Whether those people knew it or not, Pirini Lilapa would bring a Curse with it, and a beautiful chaos would ensue.

Eska turned around. Tundra's naked body, covered by sheets, lay in his bed underneath the dawning light. She wasn't pretty—pronounced wrinkles and a scar on her cheek took her beauty from her—but she was loyal, and to Eska that was beautiful. And even though their relationship compromised his vows, he had otherwise spent his life living within those confines. He had given his fullest to Gladonus when he saved the system from the terror that befell it during the last Pirini Lilapa—Deimos. He never allowed himself to be swayed by any one nation, not even when his home nation of Nova continued to shrink in size over his lifetime. And his affair resulted in no heirs; he took no hand in marriage, but who were the Twelve to say that he, too, couldn't have love? He maneuvered past his bed, dragging his gloved hand over the sheet, feeling the rise of her legs as he passed her to exit his chambers.

Outside his estate, he walked upon the vast empire of dirt terrain. Only the stars gazed down upon him; only they watched him skulk through the night, guided by the faintest breeze. In this midway between dark and day, the stars looked more like jewels. Out of the billions of stars, one was his. And from that star he could make a wish. Any wish. He had known which one was his for over fifty years now, but he had never called upon it. What could he wish for that he didn't already have?

When he took his eyes from the sky, he realized he was at the face of the Gamrol Cliffs. This was where the wind led him, where she had called him.

Eska jumped. The wind caught him and lifted him past the boulders concealing the entrance to the cave. Despite being isolated here at the base of the cliff, the breeze intensified. It billowed his cape and ruffled his silk clothes. The wind pushed him inside and heeded him down a path lighted with yellow moss and slimy with wetness.

"He's here. He's here," the wind seemed to whisper.

Eska knew it wasn't the wind, though. Windies floated by him, giving the illusion of wind. Berol, their leader, found him after he had traveled a quarter mile into the cave to a spacious dwelling with stalactites dripping cool blue in splats on the floor.

"He who can hold wind, what do you want on this late of night or early of dawn?"

The windy was one and a half times the size of the others, but Eska still had to squint to make visible the fairy-like creature. Translucent wings and the pale, blue body made him blend in with so much of the cavern. "She called me here. Let me see her."

"As you wish, Guardian Eska. The one who can hold wind."

Berol howled and soon the whole cavern echoed their leader. Windies flew all around him, creating a blue tornado of action. Anyone not used to it would have been thrown back by their raw strength, but not Eska. The man who could hold wind only stood and watched as out of the tornado stepped a translucent woman wearing a flowing white robe. Blue curls hung past her shoulders, bouncing with her every step. The cavern was almost a vacuum now. The sudden change left Eska breathless. Although not as breathless as the first time he saw her. All the air had been pulled into creating her—Zeph. She was wife to the Ancient, Bane, sister to Anemie of the Twelve and mother to Naydeia.

"Guardian Edwyrd Eska... It has been too long."

Her lips were lush with light blue, and her skin pale as moonlight. She was there, not physically, but through the Power of her windies. He did not have time to go to her floating isle in Mistral tonight.

Eska used his necklace to control what little air remained. Finding cadence to his breaths, he spoke. "Yes, much too long."

"I believe the last time we met under *these* circumstances was during Pirini Lilapa." Zeph shuffled around him, walking on air.

"I suppose that is the reason you called me here tonight?"

"Yes. In the coming months the suns will merge and when that happens Pirini Lilapa shall begin and surely the Curse will follow."

"Last time you called to me as I sat alone in my room, trying to figure out how to stop Deimos as he ravaged the land. I had been Guardian for only 35 years, and you called me to give me..." Eska pinched the pendant between his index and thumb to show her.

"And this time is not so different. Except for your age and experience. Deimos came into the world during that time... I only gave you a tool to stop it." She walked around him, her white robe dragging on the air as if it were earth.

"The other Guardians... Have you seen them as well?"

"No. My eyes have only laid sight upon you, Edwyrd." She stopped in front of him and looked at him with dark blue eyes. "And you wonder why that is?"

"Yes," Eska admitted. He stood, hands behind his back, not removing his gaze from hers until she started her circular path again.

"They did not need the help that I bestowed upon you."

"Why was I chosen, though?"

"The Other... the Third One himself birthed that demon, and only Ancient Power can fight Ancient Power, so I gave you the greatest secret that my husband ever told me."

The Other. The Third One—that is whom she had scantly referred to last time. Never once was the real name mentioned. Never once was it written in the history of books. Never once was it allowed to be said if myths were true. It referred to one being—the Third Ancient. Guardian Eska stood in silence as he processed her words.

"Some names are sung for sorrow. Others given for greatness. And yet there are those who are merely fit for fate," Zeph said.

"And which of those am I?" Guardian Eska did not like the question and knew he would like the answer even less.

"Fate," Zeph responded, cold and isolated.

"Is there any way someone can change their fate?"

Zeph laughed and twirled. Her gowns caught on her body, and before he knew it, she stopped in front of him. "You who says you must learn to accept death. You ask this?"

"Death is not fate. So I ask you again, is there any way someone can change their fate?"

"Everyone must die eventually, Edwyrd." Her smile fell to a grim line. There was tension. And pause. Just long enough for him to feel his own mortality in the rise of his skin and the lack of air. Then she continued, "Unlike death, however, every man can mold the clay of his fate. Nothing is ever set in stone. The question is, why would you want to?"

"My role began with Deimos then?"

"No, no it did not. Your role is just beginning, Edwyrd."

"And this?" Eska cupped the necklace in his hand, laying it out for her to see again.

Zeph laid her transparent hand on top of his. Somehow Eska felt her. Perhaps he was the only one that could. He saw through the ghostly white hand she offered. He saw straight through her eyes.

"The necklace will help you stop it once it begins."

"Help me stop what?" He spoke without thinking, lost in her trance and faint embrace.

Zeph smirked. "That you should already know."

PART 1: ZAIN BERRESE

RECAP:

Zain Berrese, a member of Gazo's Weapons' Academy, received an invitation to partake in Guardian Eska's Trials. He was not the only one, for there were seven other contestants chosen, one being his adopted brother, Zakk Shiren. Not wanting to be outdone by Zakk once again, Zain pushes him off the ship as it is leaving for the Central Core. It is this guilt of seemingly letting Zakk die which plagued Zain throughout the remainder of the time on the Core. It is there, in the midst of the Trials, he learned that Zakk isn't dead and that he is planning revenge on Zain's family. Zain's anxiety over this drove him to deny the offer of being apprentice to Guardian of the Core.

Now, he rushes home to save the family he nearly let slip away...

CHAPTER 1

A RIDE HOME

"**Y**ou in deep thought or somethin', Mr. Berrese?"

The question took Zain unaware. He looked at his taxicraft driver's face through the rearview mirror. A hint of intrigue hid in those amber-specked granite eyes. *Maybe he's never seen someone of my skin color before...* Zain crossed his arms over his broad chest, tucking his hands underneath, trying to cover as much of his smoky onyx skin as possible. The movement would have made his father ashamed. Being a jeweler, he had raised Zain to know all types of jewels, and to be proud of his color for it was much more elegant than the fair, howlite people in the south of Ka'Che or the citrine-colored folks in the nation of Chaon, even further south.

However, his father wasn't there now. To Zain's knowledge, he still worked for Lord Zigarda in Empora, fashioning a set of jewels so exquisite it had already taken countless months, and Zain wondered how much longer the project would last. No, what was there now was this man's continued stare and pearly grin that went with it, as if he had found something exquisitely delectable about Zain. Zain shifted in the back, trying to avoid it but to no avail. Even if he had been successful, he still wouldn't have escaped the metallic stench of blood that lingered in the air.

The odor had only come about after they stopped in Mox, two days after Gabrielle's mother dropped him off in Callumbra. They had stopped to break up the monotony of the airroads, to stretch their legs, and to have a more comfortable place to sleep. Luckily, he was almost home. *Only a few more hours.* To Zain it would feel like an eternity, especially since it seemed that, overnight, the man had changed from driver to reporter as the slew of questions had yet to cease.

In truth, though, Zain was surprised that the man had even agreed to take him to Konmer considering the two-and-a-half days it took to get there by hovercraft from Callumbra. However, the fee was reasonable and Zain couldn't see any other way of returning home. The only one with a license for flying a ship in Ka'Chean airspace was his brother, Jamaal, but he lived in Mistral with his family. Because the ship he arrived on was Emporian, it could only fly to port city hubs and then transfer from there, hence the reason Gabrielle's mother left him at Callumbra's hub as it regulated the air travel for the southern part of the nation. So, a taxicraft was his only option, unless if he had wanted to rent a hovercraft himself, but he was too tired to fly for such a long time.

"No, why?" He paused. "Do I look it?"

"You got that impatient look on your face. Trust me, I know people, especially impatient ones. I'mma taxicraft driver for cryin' out loud, I get 'em all the time. Besides that, I'mma good character guesser. Seen and been with 'em all, really."

"Oh..." Zain collected himself.

"You don't mind if I listen to some radio, do you, Mr. Berrese?"

"No, go ahead," Zain whispered. "And you can call me Zain."

"Thanks."

Zain leaned his head against the window, reacquainting himself with his home in the nation of Ka'Che on the planet Myoli. Once the cityscape of Mox became boring, he closed his eyes. *Zakk...* The cackle came back to him, the threat towards his mother, and finally... Zain opened his eyes and rubbed his jaw, swearing he still felt the pierce and the pain of the object, whatever it was, sliding into his chin while on Vatu Volcano during the last of Guardian Eska's Trials. It was clear that he wouldn't be escaping this problem anytime soon.

He heard the click of the radio.

A melody came on and a man's soft voice soothed the speakers. "*Your face is my face, your skin is my skin, and I want to be wherever you've been...*"

The channel changed.

"Greed. That is what is turning our society into the mess it is today."

Zain's ears twitched as a man with a deep voice talked, confident and knowledgeable.

"If we just learn to accept what we have, Gladonus would be a better—"

The radio shut off.

"No one wants to hear that rubbish. Everyone is greedy. We're human, after all. Eh, Zain?"

Zain caught the taxicraft driver's gaze from the rearview mirror. "We are. But, I think greed leads to problems."

"Nah, it leads to motivations. It gives us something to strive for. When our wants become our needs that's when we are most deadly 'cause we have boundless determination. We have freedom. And that's all that anyone really wants, right?"

This guy is giving me a lecture now? Zain exhaled. "I guess so."

"I can see you don't wanna talk. It's okay. Long day?"

"Yeah. Past couple of days."

"Where you fly in from?"

"The Core."

"Like Guardian Eska's Central Core?" The man flicked his gaze to the review mirror.

"That's the one." Zain smiled weakly and fidgeted with his fingers.

"Twelve take me now. I don't believe you! What were you there for?"

Does he not know the Trials were happening? Or is he just testing me to see if I was actually there? The man continued focusing on Zain through the mirror. "I competed in the Trials."

"That senator from Mistral... Numod... Numen... Noman..."

"His name was Senator Numos."

"Numos! That's it! Ah, I can't remember names. Been with too many. It's hard to keep track. Anyway, he was there too. I just saw him the other night on some show. Well, his picture, anyway. He'll be actually appearing later this week. Guess he interviewed the winners of the Trials. Did he interview you?"

"No."

"You lost then, eh?"

Far from it. He doesn't need to know that though. "Yeah, I lost."

Before Zain could say more, the taxicraft driver said, "The news be saying the winner of the whole thing has to meet all the lords and ladies from every nation. Not only that, but I hear he will be meeting the Twelve. The Twelve! Can you believe it? Nerve-wracking, wouldn't that be?"

"Yeah..." Zain lied. His uncle was actually one of those individuals who would meet the new apprentice, and his uncle had never been intimidating. Stubborn, perhaps, from the times Zain had been to the castle in Ka'Che's capital, Pelopon, but never intimidating. The Twelve, however, was a different story. One Zain had disavowed years ago before the Trials even began. *Maybe it's for the best that I said no.*

Zain flexed his hand and looked off into the distance. While in thought about the implications of his actions, he grew oblivious to whatever more the taxicraft driver was saying. And, eventually, there was nothing, only his reflection on the window and the reverie he slowly drifted into with the tapering of the cityscape into plains. Past the plains grew the Anga Mountains, which held so much history for Zain.

When the mountains finally came into view, so returned the taxicraft driver's voice. He tapped the glass with his knuckles and exhaled. *One last thing to do. I'll need to go there later.*

"... And that is why I never trust someone that I don't *physically* know. Anyone can verbally agree, but it takes a real man to shake on it, you know?"

He turned his head back to the driver and caught his errant gaze. "Listen, I'm tired. I would rather not talk."

"Sorry about the story. I'm just still amazed. A real-life Trials participant in my taxi. I'll be damned. Sure thing, Mr. Zain. I'll put the music back on. It'll help you sleep."

The calm blues lulled his senses but still couldn't put him to sleep. Not now. Not when he was so close to everything.

Two hours northeast of Mox, Zain arrived at a large driveway of paved stones leading to his two-story house. The taxicraft stopped in front of a black cast-iron gate. On the sides of the gate were stone pillars crowned with a light.

"I can walk the rest from here. Thanks."

"You sure? You got a lot of bags."

"Yeah, yeah it's fine. How much did we agree upon, fifteen bonds?"

"Bonds come in two, so why don't you just give me ten."

Zain scanned the man. "Are you sure?"

"Yeah, this way I have a bond for each finger. Lucky me." The man laughed.

Zain counted the coins and paid the driver. "Thank you."

"The pleasure has been mine. You kept me company." The driver cupped Zain's hand in both of his and shook it. "And now that we've shaken, I trust you. You remember my story, right?"

Flakes of granite invaded the man's eyes, overtaking the amber once present. They looked different from the ones he had seen before, but they probably weren't. Zain couldn't remember, for he was too tired after his time on the Core.

He shook his head and blinked. "Yeah." He tried to pull out his hand, weakly at first, but the man didn't relinquish his grip. *Does he not feel me?* Zain pulled harder, making it obvious with a polite "You're welcome." The man finally let go, pulling his head away once he noticed Zain's stare.

Zain slung his longsword over his shoulder, grabbed his duffel bags, and scrambled out of the taxicraft. Fresh air welcomed him home. After scanning his hand on the security box near one of the pillars by the gate, he walked in long, quick strides, ready to remove the weight on his back.

Chapter 2

REUNION

The brick façade of Zain's house seemed darker than the tan it actually was in the light of the deep-blue lapis lazuli sun, Lugh. Bushes and trees stood as the rear guard for the house; the long driveway and the gate before it had always been the first defense from unwanted eyes. Various places of the wooden roof sloped upwards into spires, almost like the top of cathedrals, marking the new additions to the already expansive house.

As Zain walked the cement path that led to the front door, he took a moment to stop and peer into a window next to a tree. His mother, Brisine, stood in the kitchen. He exhaled. *She's safe.* He walked further up to the doorstep and pushed the doorbell. Inside, he heard feet shuffle. Zain prepared himself; it had been a month and a half since he had seen her.

The door opened.

"Who—" His mother's sentence fell short. A cup fell from the drying rag in her hands. "Zain." The crack of ceramic.

Zain smiled. "Mom." He pushed forward, put his arms around her, and held tightly. Tears soon dampened the collar of his shirt, but he didn't care.

"Is it really you?" She pulled back and looked him over.

"Yes, it really is."

She closed the distance and squeezed Zain. Although it felt longer, a minute later, she pulled back.

"How clumsy of me." She sniffled and bent down to pick up the broken cup.

"I got it." Zain bent down to help.

"Thanks, Zain." She stopped another tear and asked, "How did you get back?"

"One of my friends, Gabrielle, got accepted to the Trials, as well. Her mom took me home."

She smiled and walked away to the kitchen, her hips swaying back and forth in a loose flowing black skirt that came down to her ankles. "A girlfriend of yours, is she?"

"Just friends for now." Zain finished putting the shards on the rag and carried it to the garbage in the kitchen.

"And how do you know her?"

"She trained at Gazo's sister school, Gracie's, on Empora. That's where she lives."

Zain entered the kitchen to the scent of honeyed ham and the dull but rhythmic chop of a knife to cutting board.

"Zain..." His mother sighed.

"Yah, Mom?"

She transferred the cooked food onto plates. "Let's go into the dining room. We need to talk."

"Oh no. What's wrong? Is it Dad?"

"Your father is fine. He is still in Mendeck with Lord Zigarda doing work."

"Still? It's been half a year now."

His mother nodded. "Yes, still. I haven't heard from him for a month. That isn't what I wanted to talk with you about, though."

Zain bit his lip. *What could it be?* Zain followed his mother to the dining room. She set out a plate of ham and potatoes and then sat down across from him with a plate for herself. She prayed; Zain followed her in mute devotion.

"What happened during the Trials?" Zain's mother folded a linen over her lap.

"What do you mean?" Zain cut into his ham.

"On your way back, you told me to stay safe? What's going on?"

Zain cut into his ham, trying to buy more time. From across the table, his mother put her hand on his. They locked eyes. A tear slid down his cheek. Zain recapped the whole ordeal with Zakk then, from the betrayal to the times Zakk taunted him throughout the Trials to the final confrontation with him on Vatu Volcano.

"'Don't worry about your mom . . . She'll be cared for. Very well.' And those were his last words."

"Zain Berrese, you tried to kill Zakk? He's practically family! Wait until your father finds out. Or your brother!"

"Jamaal *does* know," Zain muttered.

"What was that?"

"I... I told Jamaal everything when he saw me on the Core. I couldn't live with the guilt. I came back to make things right. I needed to know you were safe first though."

"I can't believe my son would stoop to such lows. We took Zakk into this family because we knew how much you had grown attached to him when you were a child. After you told us about how his parents died, what else were we supposed to do..." She hung her head and rubbed her temples.

"I..." *Damn.* Zain crossed his arms and exhaled deeply.

Silence.

"Lie down on the table. Now."

Zain's eyes widened as she came back with a couple of cloths and a large knife.

"Do it now."

"Mom, what are you—"

"Whatever Zakk put in your chin is still in there. I'm getting it out."

Zain crawled onto the dining room table, making sure not to put too much pressure on either side. His mother hovered over him, knife in hand.

"Chew on this and squeeze the table."

Zain tried talking his way out of the operation, but she shoved the cloth in his mouth, grabbed the back of his head, and pulled back. Zain squeezed the table and closed his eyes, waiting for the incision.

"Where'd he put it?"

Zain pointed to the spot and then returned his hand to the side of the table. His mother groped his chin. When the knife first entered his skin, he squeezed the table. After it dug deeper, he kicked his feet back and forth and bit on the cloth. Warm blood ran down his throat. He thought he could feel skin dangle from where it was peeled back. Fingers felt all around his jawline.

Then..., a yank.

Zain squeezed the table more tightly. He held his breath. Even through the dam his clenched eyes created, tears managed to escape and slide down his temples. Pressure pushed upon his chest. Tension intensified in his chin.

Then..., it was gone.

He breathed and opened his eyes.

"Put this under your chin."

Zain used his right forearm to wipe away his tears and took his left hand to grab the towel and place it under his chin. He blinked a few times, trying to see what she held. She twirled it around in her fingers. It looked like a thin needle, no longer than half an inch. A green light blinked on and off at the top of it, and it had a circular base.

"What do you think it is?"

"I don't know," Zain answered.

"We are getting rid of it, whatever it is." She let it fall to the floor and stomped it with her heels until the light no longer flashed. "That should do it, right?"

Zain wished he could answer her. He only nodded and with a weak voice said, "Yeah."

"Go get cleaned up. I'll clean up down here, okay?"

"Alright."

Zain got off the table. When he made it to the threshold between the dining room and the main entranceway that led to the second floor, his mother said, "Zain, it's nice to see you again."

Zain smiled. "You too, Mom. I'm glad you're safe."

Upstairs, Zain threw the duffel bags on the floor and unstrapped his longsword, leaving it on his bed. Blood wet his chin. *Time to examine this.* He went to the bathroom and looked at the inch or two of skin missing. Zain cringed. It bled, and would continue to do so until it clotted. He found another towel and held it to his chin. A picture of the Anga Mountains in the fiery light of the glowing garnet sun, Freyr, caught his eye, hanging up on the wall behind him. He sank his head in thought. Downstairs, he could hear the water running as she cleaned up his mess. But it was time for him to take care of his own mistakes. She would be safe for a few more hours; he was home now. He looked at the picture again and exhaled.

I need to go. One last time.

CHAPTER 3

THE SPOT

The mountain rose up another couple hundred feet or so, but Zain didn't care about making it to the top. It didn't happen there. It happened here. He stopped less than three-quarters of the way from the top. Aches and callouses had worked their way into his hands, and sweat gathered on his clothes. For only climbing this particular path once a year, he was surprised by how well he could still climb.

At this height now, on this ledge, he saw the expansive Krine Sea. Although he couldn't see the nation of Empora from his spot, he knew it lay there, and over there, Gabrielle. She played a role in him coming here. To this spot. Not because she suggested it. She hadn't. But he needed to tie up one loose end before he could truly move on. There were bigger issues now, and he didn't have room for ghosts.

He moved his gaze.

Every year it was the toughest thing he did.

His eyes retraced the cliff behind him. At the top, a large crack split the precipice like a basin. And by his feet he noticed tiny rocks and scars. His side ached. It always did when he thought of her and that day. It reminded him of the surgery, and the metal put into his side to repair and stabilize his body after the boulder had nearly crushed him completely.

He inched forward. When his feet got to the ledge, a rumbling came to his ears. He jerked. His side ached even more. From above he saw the boulder falling; the deafening crash that hit the ledge before it rolled onto his side; Ava being nearly swept away by it. She dangled there. Her eyes held fear. Uncertainty. Zain reached out for her. She latched on.

His fingers began sweating.

She fell.

Zain crawled back to the middle of the ledge, not wanting to see the aftermath. But he did. He always did whenever he returned. The screech. The sickening splat. The sudden shock. The tears that flowed after, too busy lost in his own loss to feel the pain in his side. Every part of that day a nightmare.

Zain scooted backwards until his back hit the rocky cliff. His breathing heightened. Tears still flowed. Zain yelled then. To no one but himself. He hoped the Twelve heard him and saw his anger and pain and agony. A part of him wanted them to recognize him on this day, the very day he stopped believing in them. *I didn't want your Power, anyway. I wouldn't have wanted to meet you.* He thought back to how he rejected Guardian Eska. He was lying to himself. Perhaps he did want the Power that came with being Guardian. Here, anyway.

His fingers trembled as they reached for his academy knife and unsheathed it. He rolled up his sleeve on his left arm. Would this be the time he would actually do it? He had cut himself once the first year he visited and another time a year after. Or was it two? Regardless, two scars still lingered there. He almost never saw them, though, for he wore a long-sleeved academy uniform. Then he saw his hand and the scars there from when his sword broke during the second trial on the Core.

"Why?... Why?...," Zain sobbed.

His hand shook as he thought about drawing the knife upwards this time instead of across. The tip of the knife poked against his skin. He began to drag it. It felt warm but wrong.

Overhead the suns watched him, curious if he would finish what he had started. He sat there, low and pitiful, blankly gazing across the sea.

That's when he saw beyond the sea to Empora. Not literally, figuratively. *Gabrielle...* The tingle came back to his neck as he remembered how she held her dagger against his throat during the first trial. *Pain... Hopelessness... Futility...* Her words returned. *Zere are zings worse zan deaz.*

Zain gasped.

He dropped the knife.

He leaned his head against the cliff. Without meaning to, he said her name. "Ava..."

"Zain..."

Zain jolted. He saw her there. In front of him. He bolted upright. He walked towards her, saw through her, saw the Krine Sea and everything that lay beyond. If only he could get past her.

"Ava, this is my last time coming here."

She didn't move. Didn't say anything.

"I can't live my life holding onto the guilt I have for you. Every time I come back to this spot, I remember you... and us. I can't afford to do that any longer." He regained his confidence. "I've learned that there are things worse than death... Things like pain... and hopelessness... and futility."

She stood there, face stoic, hands clasped together, intent on watching him.

"I can't continue to be a prisoner to those things. I know I promised I would always remember you... and I want to... but some things need to be forgotten... I can't hold myself accountable for your death any longer." Zain took a long moment to look at her. Her eyes had taken the color of the suns. "I am moving on." Zain turned around to face the rock cliff.

He hoped she would say something.

After a minute of clear silence, he spoke again. "Ava, I came to say goodbye." Zain turned back around and when he did, he noticed Ava fade from sight.

"Goodbye, Zain. I am glad you are moving on. That is what I always wanted." She smiled and then disappeared into nothing more than a gust of sea wind.

Another gust. It beckoned him to leave.

Zain gave a hefty sigh. He picked up the knife on the ground. Fresh blood coated it. He took one last look at the scars on his arm he made over the years. *It's over.* He sheathed his knife and rolled up his sleeve, keeping his eyes focused on the newest scar—the one on his hand. *It's time to find you, Zakk... and right another wrong.*

CHAPTER 4

GETTING TO SAFETY

H e had kept Gabrielle safe during the fourth trial on the top of Vatu Volcano. He had made sure his mom was safe upon returning home. And he had now just finished making amends to a past girlfriend he no longer could afford to mourn. Zakk now needed his attention, and Zain knew he had to oblige. He had to make things better because he knew his family wasn't truly safe until there was no longer a rift between them.

As Zain made his way back home from the Anga Mountains, he thought about what his next step would be. *How do I find him? How did he find me, even? Who is he working with?* There were many questions he needed answered, but silence wouldn't aide him; neither would the suns that dipped behind him. He would be home by the time the last of the light faded from view. But with the impending night and the sequential silence, Zain's eyes slowly became lead. He used whatever little energy remaining to return home.

He slouched to the door and on instinct began to ascend the steps on the right-hand side.

"Goodnight, Mom," he tried yelling, but a yawn stole his strength.

No response. He took a few more steps and noticed a splotch of red on the lobby floor. Then he noticed more.

"Mom?" Zain reversed his movements.

Silence. Dead silence.

He crouched down and put a finger in the warm, red substance. He didn't need to. He already knew what it was. But a part of him didn't want to believe it. That part of him wanted to pretend that he didn't smell or taste the metallic copper.

Zain drew the knife on his belt and followed the trail of blood into the dining room. Portraits lay dismantled and in disarray. His mother lay in a pool of her own blood, hand over her neck.

"Mom!" He kneeled beside her and pulled on her hair to raise her face. Red covered it, but she blinked, continuing to hold her hand to her throat. "I'll get you something!"

Zain rushed into the kitchen and grabbed a towel. He held it under her chin and looked at her eyes wide with fear. She cowered away from him, almost as if he were some unknown stranger.

"Mom?"

She glanced down at his hands.

Zain tensed his neck. He still held the knife.

She scooted back.

"Mom, it's me. It's Zain."

She closed her eyes and shook her head, as if trying to blot out her worst nightmare.

What is going on? "I'm letting go of the knife. See me." Zain set it on the ground next to the blood. She opened one eyelid. "What happened?" Her eyes widened as he crawled closer. "Mom, it's me. It's Zain. Your son? Little Bear."

Her shoulders slumped. "Zain?" She coughed blood.

"It's me."

She sniffed, and a tear rolled down her cheek.

"What happened? Was it Zakk?"

She shook her head. "You..."

"Me?" Zain said the words aloud that he meant to think. "I was at the Anga Mountains. I left." Zain put his head down. *I left. This happened when I left. Why did I—*

"Cab..." She pointed towards the kitchen. She coughed more blood.

Zain's eyes widened. *Cab... cab... cabinet! Cabinet!* He bolted to his feet and went to the kitchen, scouring in any cabinet he could find. To his dismay, he found nothing besides pens, memo pads, towels, and utensils. He returned to her side.

"Which cabinet?"

"Fridge..."

He repeated the word back to her. She nodded. He left. Yanking open cabinets in the refrigerator, he found vegetables, fruit, condiments and then stopped when he saw syringes. *What are these?* He picked one up and read the label. *Blood thinner.* Another one. *Fever reducer.* Another one. *Anti-in-flammation. A hah! Blood clotter.* He grabbed it and rushed back to her side, showing her the label.

After she nodded her approval, she tilted her neck away from him and pointed.

Zain assumed he should insert there, so he did. He pushed down on the plunger and waited. While he waited, he examined the portraits strewn about the table. He saw a safe, slightly ajar. *We were robbed?*

Standing, he moved away from his mother to the exposed vault. Although the chandelier over the table lit the room, it did an effective job of exposing the contents of the deep vault. With hardly any light to see, he pushed his face against the wall and reached blindly in the deep vault for anything leftover. There was nothing until Zain strained to push his arm back a little further. *What's this?* He stretched his fingers towards the object and inched it closer with the tips of his fingers until it was close enough to grab and pull out.

Suspiciously, Zain eyed a black plastic box with three buttons that would probably open it after a certain sequence was entered. *Is there more?*

Using the same method as before, Zain reached back inside the vault. This time he found a different object. It felt like an envelope. Zain pulled it out and opened it. *A telecard!* Zain pushed the black button in the center of the card, and a miniature hand-sized version of his dad, Laron, appeared and spoke:

If you are seeing this card, then that means I am probably dead, and you are looking for my will. I hope this is not the case, and that we are here as a family, together, ready to look upon the wonders I have gathered for you all during my travels. Here is my heart as I will spill it to you. Hopefully, I still have one to spill.

This is the last will and testament of Laron Sean Berrese. In my travels I have seen the world, outside and inside the deepest mountains. The most stunningly cut jewels I have presented to the wealthy and royal alike. If I ever were to die and leave a project unfinished, I left instructions on how to finish the current project in the vault. If this is the case, please hand over the documents to Simon Hosair, the current vice president of Berrese's Lapidary at the time of this recording. If no son of mine wants to take over the jewelling industry, then leadership goes to whomever may be vice president.

There is a black box in front of you with a three-key lock. The box represents my heart, and all of you are the key to opening it. Enter B-J-Z for the order you entered my world.

Zain's mother opened her eyes now, intently focusing on her husband's voice.

This is what I left for all of you. All of my family.

He pushed the entry code and inside found a golden feather that gave off a rainbow glow. Also, a large velvet sack securely tied sat beside it, along with a ring that shined as brilliantly as the chandelier above. Zain picked up the sack, opened it, and saw it held three charcoal-black rocks sitting amidst sand.

Brisine, my wife and my love of thirty-five years, I give you not only half of my wealth that I have accumulated but something greater. Inside the velvet bag is Vanishing Sand I received while on Acquava, finishing Marquis Axyel's staff. It was from a gypsy near the Scorched Desert on the island of Talyn. She told me that all you need to do is outline a circle with a little of the sand on the floor and throw one of the three stones included at your feet and you will be able to teleport anyone within that circle to anywhere within 500 miles. If you, Zain and Jamaal, are ever in trouble, I leave the way to get you out.

At the calling of her name, his mother stood and came to Zain's side. She still held the towel to her neck, but the fact that she stood meant that the medicine was working.

Jamaal, my first son. My married son. My brilliant son. To match your brilliance, I am leaving you a ring. Ever since you told me that your proposal to Reine didn't go as planned after seeing the rainbows, I wanted to give you a chance to redo that moment. This ring consists of a diamond and around it separate gems, one for each color of the rainbow. Give it to Reine someday and let it bring back any light that may have left. Bring light into her world since she has brought so much into yours.

Finally, Zain, my fighter and second son. In my time spent with you, do not think I have not noticed your want of travel. You were meant for something bigger than jewels, bigger than this place. While on my travels I found a vendor, and he sold me this feather. I admit, it seems rather a foolish gift for you, but the vendor said that out in the open air it points in different directions, regardless of the wind. He couldn't tell me where it came from, simply that it floated to him one day many years ago and after discovering its unique qualities thought it intriguing and mesmerizing. I have seen it point in different directions with my own eyes. My hope is that it points you in the right direction, son, and if you are ever in need of an adventure, perhaps this feather will guide you to one.

I will be waiting for all of you across the Field of Souls and on top of the tallest of mountains. In due time I will see you, and my hope is that it will be many years from now. Goodbye. I love you... always.

"You don't think Dad's actually dead, do you?" Zain shut the vault and picked up his knife on the floor.

"No... Zain... That look." His mother grabbed his arm, using the other one to hold her cloth. She coughed, but this time no blood escaped her mouth.

"What look?" He stared his mom down.

"No." She shook her head. "You are not..." She paused. "Follow... ing." She struggled.

Although not a complete sentence, Zain understood what she meant. He said, "But, you couldn't tell me apart from him?"

"No! Dangerous. He... he..." Tears crept from her eyes.

"Was *me*! I need to find him and see how he is me. I need to find out where he's going."

"May be more." The raspy voice strengthened her argument.

"All the more reason why we need to leave, and I need to follow. It may not have been Zakk, but what if he is connected to Zakk?" Zakk's last words prickled Zain's skin.

She slapped the side of his arm. "Where they meet?"

"I don't know. I... I just... It's not safe here. We need to leave."

"Leave? Where?"

"Your brother. His castle in the capital. It will be the safest place you can be."

"You?" She pointed.

"I'm going after him. As soon as I see you safely there."

She beat his arm again and slapped the side of the head. "No idea where." She slapped him again.

While cowering his head to lessen her blows, Zain noticed the telecard. *Dad must have left something.* He put his hand up, signaling for her to stop. Then he played the card again. His ears perked up when he heard, "*If I ever were to die and leave a project unfinished, I left instructions on how to finish the current project in the vault.*" Zain stopped and turned.

"There."

"What?"

"There must have been documents to finish a project in there. There was nothing else besides that box. Zigarda was Dad's last project. The man who did this to you has to be over in Empora."

She removed the cloth from her neck and felt her wound. It had completed clotting with the help of the medicine. She coughed and tried her first full sentence. "That isn't where Zakk is."

It wasn't, no, but Zakk would have to take another backseat. A different threat had come into his life. A threat he planned to eliminate. "No, it's worse... It's Lord Zigarda. What if Dad's life is in danger now that whatever it was has been retrieved?"

"Zain, I want to see your father, too." She paused, catching her breath. "You won't..." She coughed. "Not allowed entry. Just you." She left to retrieve a glass of water from the kitchen. The first sip she choked on, the second as well, but she managed to drink it all in time.

Zain sighed.

She put a hand on his shoulder. "Arrive at castle." She massaged her throat. "I will talk to my brother. Maybe he can..." She coughed and took another sip of water. "Do something."

"How do you know he will?"

"He's my brother." She took his hand and rubbed it.

Zain returned the gesture. "I hope he's still the brother you knew growing up."

He looked into her eyes. They held a vivacity to them now; one that had been close to perishing not even an hour before. He felt the wound on her neck, his fingertips sliding over the sticky red, the pungent smell wafting up from her clothes and the pool on the floor.

"What did I give you? Why did you have it?"

She drank more water. "Blood clotter. Worried for you and practice with sword. I always had one ready for either you or Zakk in case injury."

She spoke in broken sentences, but she spoke, and that is what mattered. Her want to keep her family alive had inadvertently kept her alive. Zain hoped that his desire for the same would do more than that; he hoped it would bring his family back together and leave no scars in the process as the wounds were finally mended.

CHAPTER 5

THE CONTACT

Zakk had been back in Mendeck for just under a week since his rendezvous with Zain on Vatu Volcano. His contact still had not called him, and that made Zakk worry. He installed the location device in Zain's chin well enough—what was taking so long?

After being picked up from Trent's Forest on the night he missed his flight to the Trials, Zakk arrived in the city of Mendeck, the capital of the nation, Empora. The ruler of Mendeck, Victor Zigarda, was known to have no love for the Central Core or of Guardian Eska. Zakk didn't see how such open animosity could exist, but then he thought back on his own relationship with Zain and saw they weren't so different, he and Zigarda. Perhaps that is why he embraced the man who gave him shelter and food, and most of all, family.

When he arrived in Mendeck, Victor Zigarda had pitted him against the head of Zigarda's troops. Zakk had taken that man's head, and, in the process, gained Zigarda's respect. He wasn't first in his division at Gazo's to lose. He meant to win, and that is what he would have done at the Trials if only he had competed. As head of the guard, he passed his time training the recruits and soldiers. Above all, Zakk excelled at training others—*fight for others, then fight for yourself,* as Gazo's taught.

It was during one of these sessions when his telecommunicator rang. With a quick downward slash of his sword and a fluid knife-check to the neck of his opponent, Zakk ended his training session. His opponent had been a man of mediocre ability and even that generosity only granted to him by the snakeskin suits Zigarda equipped his troops with. Suits designed by Zigarda's top scientist, Dr. Genus Cere. Scaled to the skin, the snakesuits allowed them to move faster, and with the increased agility, strike harder, although the suits sacrificed protection. Zakk didn't believe in the suits and their qualities because he knew Gazo's didn't. If he was to fight, then he'd fight with armor on his body and a sword in his hand.

"Is it done?" Zakk asked a man who stared back at him through his telecommunicator screen with a disfigured, wrinkly face.

"I have the rest of the documents. I slit the lady's throat to get them, though. I'm heading back to Callumbra Port. Arrange a ride."

Zakk paused for a moment, taking it all in. Then he said, "I will let Zigarda know."

The connection ended.

Zakk looked up at the red mist that hung over the city—the Red Cloud, as the civilians called it. *If I had gone, would the outcome have been as violent?* He gulped. A gust of hot wind slapped him. He looked back at the troops. "I need to leave. Francis, you're in charge. Divide the soldiers into pairs and give them sparring regulations."

A black man with cropped hair, a big nose and even bigger ears looked at him. The man looked comical, really, but he knew how to swing a blade and wield a knife, and that's all that mattered. "Of course." Francis stared at the troops. "Line up."

Zakk went inside the circular dome closest to the courtyard, not caring to note the names of the soldiers Francis was calling out into pairs. While he walked the interior of gray and blue tiles, he thought about Brisine. Just a little. *I wonder how Zain is coping with his loss.*

Zakk continued onward towards an egg-shaped elevator. He swiped a black card with ivory lines over the keypad and touched *Throne Room.* Zigarda would be there hearing the civilians and acting his duty of lord. He never really did much of anything about the complaints, though. Zigarda, for the worst, had a one-track mind, something Gazo's always warned against—*always see each brush stroke of battle, for it determines the war's portrait.*

"... doing about Pirini Lilapa? The Curse? Surely it will come soon."

The beep of the door closing behind him alerted the others of his presence.

From atop the ostentatiously tall throne, Zigarda said, "I am in constant contact with the Guardian of the Core. At any reports of danger, I will notify him directly. You have my word."

Zakk listened to the lie roll off Zigarda's tongue effortlessly.

"Yuan, lead this man out and notify the guards he is the last of my civilian hearings for the day."

With Yuan gone, only Edwyn Lyze, Zigarda's advisor, stood at the base of the throne.

"How does training fare?" Edwyn said.

"They are decent, but rely too heavily on that snakeskin suit."

"I believe you enjoy your own suit, no?"

As head of Zigarda's troops, he had received his own special coat, metallic onyx in color and made of hard and strong microfibers that were more durable than the snakeskin and lighter than steel. However, Edwyn's logic was flawed; Zakk possessed the skills to be formidable without the suit, and with the suit, well, competition didn't exist.

"When I wear it, it fits me well," Zakk responded. He then directed his attention towards Zigarda, who hid under his cloak of brown, not wanting to show the burned face Eska gave him during his own Trials 200 years previous. "My contact just told me everything is picked up."

Zigarda leaned in his throne. "Perfect." He grabbed a flask by his side and gulped the liquid inside.

"He will be at Callumbra Port in four hours. Someone needs to retrieve him."

Zigarda shifted his posture to note the returning figure of his receiver, Yuan Shimes. "Pick up our shapeshifter at Callumbra Port. He has the rest of the documents to complete Berrese's project."

"Which ship should I use?" Yuan tapped fingers studded with garnets against his arm. A half-hat covered the left ear, part of his left eye and the left side of his hair, leaving black bangs hanging down the other side.

"It makes no difference. Just retrieve him. And quickly. Dr. Cere is very busy as of late."

"I will leave immediately." Yuan bowed and left.

Zakk remained. Hands fisted, he looked at the floor.

"Is there something—"

Zakk shot his glance up towards Zigarda. "Why wasn't I sent?" Zakk interrupted Edwyn's question. He knew questioning the lord may have its repercussions but so did not sending him to Zain's home.

Edwyn stood shocked at Zakk's protest. He, too, looked at Zigarda, unsure as to what would happen next. Arms out to his side, chest inflated, Zakk stood his ground, looking up to the man until Zigarda finally removed the cloak over his head and peered down to Zakk from on high.

"You want to know why I didn't send you?"

"Yes," Zakk responded.

Zigarda stood and slowly walked down the throne, each step echoing a heavy thud, and giving time for Zakk to contemplate what would happen next. Out of instinct, he made sure to note Edwyn's position. The man was weak, with no muscle on a body fit with flab and curly hair that even more accentuated a pudgy face. But, as Gazo's said: *Even the weakest man is strong with a knife is his hand and knowledge of where to stand.*

When Zigarda made it to the bottom level, he stood eye-to-eye with Zakk. No hair covered his head and wrinkles drooped his skin, making the burns even more disfiguring. Zakk saw the tissue underneath. As they stood face-to-face, no talking occurred. Zigarda surveyed him, never blinking; at least, Zakk couldn't tell if he tried to or not, for Zigarda possessed no eyelids. He knew the move to show his face was meant to be a form of intimidation, but Zakk wouldn't cower, so he continued looking straight into Zigarda's lidless, charcoal eyes.

"You failed at the end of your assignment. That is why you didn't go."

"I traveled the Core from east to west and south to north. I told you everything I found."

"And what you found were windy cliffs, pyramids you couldn't enter and lakes. So far, none of it is what we were looking for."

"The pyramids were not a find?"

"Yes, well they are pyramids you could not enter, so I am unsure of their value yet."

Zakk bit back his tongue. His mission on the Core involved reconnaissance. Despite his lack of findings, that is what he did. There was nothing much on the Core. "I delivered the blood-recorder to the senator as you asked and put the tracking device in Zain as was instructed. It is because of that that your shapeshifter now has the documents. How is that failing?"

"You may have alerted Eska to my plan."

"And I also may have saved your plan. Zain denied the apprenticeship because of my interference."

Before he knew it, Zakk was on his knees with a pain in his stomach and ankles. Underneath him tiles wrapped around his feet, locking him in place. *Power.* Careful not to put either hand on the floor, he touched his cheek and felt a slight wetness. He pulled his hand back. Red.

Zigarda bobbed on his feet in front of Zakk. He clenched Zakk's jaw. "Do not think yourself a hero, boy. There was always another plan in case things went awry." Zigarda looked at the knife in his hand, examining its blood. Zakk's blood. He smirked.

"Is that what the shapeshifters are for?"

Zigarda sheathed the knife at a pocket on the side of his hip, one Zakk had not known was there, and redirected his attention at Zakk. Still squatting in front of Zakk, he asked, "And what is that to you?"

"Zain's mother died. I could have gotten those documents without any fatalities."

"What's one more life?"

"She was innocent."

"What is *innocence?* Everyone in Gladonus is culpable of something. Aren't *you* guilty of wanting that result?"

Zakk bit his lip and cowered his head. He knew what Zigarda referred to. It had been the day after he had been picked up from Trent's Forest and brought to Empora. They had asked Zakk what he wanted for payment and he had responded with "family and equality." He went on further to elaborate how Zain should know what it's like to lose family, as he had lost his.

"Besides, she was not your true family. Not like us. Not like now. Sometimes sacrifices have to be made."

"No, she wasn't." Zakk avoided Zigarda's gaze. Both of his true parents had been killed in an infamous killing spree, noted as the Konmer Killings when he was only six. But Zain's mother took him into her home after she found out about his situation and the other failed foster parents. That made her the closest thing to family he had.

"That's the reason you came with us the night your best friend betrayed you, correct?"

Zakk inhaled deeply. "It is."

"That is the reason you left Gazo's, correct?"

Zakk peered into Zigarda's charcoal eyes. He knew why Zigarda was lord and why his citizens believed him. The man, despite all of his lies, was well spoken, logical, and cunning. Overall, he was deadly now and Zakk could only imagine how lethal he was in his younger years. Before answering, Zigarda continued.

"How could you return to either of those when Zain is so much a part of them?"

"That..." Zakk almost didn't want to admit it, but he knew he should. "That is why I am here now."

"Precisely." Zigarda stood up. "My advice, boy, is to forget about your past. Cut ties with it. It will only hold you back. You are with your new family now. A stronger family."

The shackles of tiles holding his ankles in place were removed. Zakk was free to stand, but he remained kneeling until he no longer heard the mixed cadence of steps from Zigarda and his advisor leaving. With his right hand, Zakk checked the wound on his cheek; it was still fresh. Smearing the tiled floor with red, he pushed himself up and went back to the courtyard.

Blood. It was an interesting thing, and now that Zakk had encountered shapeshifters, it fascinated him even more. He had seen twenty of them change from deer to humans the night he was retrieved from Trent's Forest. And when Zigarda had first taken in Zakk, he had made it a point to show them off, saying that they had come from an old man's heeding. Zakk assumed that man was Dr. Cere as Zigarda talked with no other old people and he was the one most busy in the Blood Chambers or in a large obelisk that rose up from the Web's bowels, working on a project that even he didn't have access or knowledge to.

When he returned to the courtyard, he didn't return immediately to sparring. From one of the half-walls that led to a different section of the three-part dome structure called the Web, he let his gaze linger, watching as Francis still held command of the troops, new ones now, and others wandering to and fro throughout the complex courtyard the Web provided.

In time, he ended looking up at the large obelisk. As Dr. Cere wasn't in the throne room today, Zakk assumed the old man to be inside, working, like usual. In fact, he hadn't seen Cere since the ride from the southern nation of Chaon to Empora. "There is lots of work to be done" is all he had said, and then he disappeared. Like Zakk and Zain's friendship... it just disappeared.

CHAPTER 6

IN LORD'S COMPANY

F lying in their hovercraft, Zain and his mother passed the Crossing, a rather large and highly trafficked stone bridge that was the sole path leading across the Split River. From the Crossing, if one followed the Split River west, one would see mountains to the north and eventually the river would flow into Kilmer Waterfall. To the north, hovercrafts could pass, but that would lead them off the Traveling Road, which was how the capital of Ka'Che, Pelopon, stayed connected with the major cities. From the Traveling Road stemmed various highways, country roads and streets that tapered off to less important, minor cities. And even though the grave of night loomed, the Crossing was abound with air and ground traffic.

Traffic ceased past the Little Bend, where vehicles either went west towards the minor cities of Arwood or Hollan or the major city of Cotterall, or north to Pelopon. Leagues upon leagues of plains were the boring carpet they traveled on, often called the Long Stretch by many travelers. Some even thought Pelopon was chosen as the capital in early times before the Great War, when families of power still battled for leadership, because the army would get bored before reaching the capital and would turn back. Regardless of that reason, though, Pelopon was still closer than any other northern city, and Zain knew its proximity to the Krine Sea was the real reason that Pelopon was capital.

Most of the city faced the Krine Sea, where chalk-white cliffs stood sentinel to the beating tide. Houses and shops lined the base of rocky and grassy cliffs overlooked by his uncle's home, Castle Semson, located a few miles inland from the white cliffs. Any ship that meant to dock at the North Port would be seen coming leagues off, making it the perfect vantage point for attacks. Zain veered off the Traveling Road to a narrow, winding pass that led to the castle. Nearly a year had passed since they had been there last.

"How are we to get in?" Zain turned the wheel a little.

"The castle's guarded heavily. I've told my brother to keep watch for us—Look, someone is coming." The fluency in her voice had returned to her, although she still didn't sound herself, and every so often she would cough.

A long, rectangular hovercraft with two circular landings, like ears, approached in the moonlight. A metal railing ran along the front of the ship, enclosing a steering station. Soldiers, dressed in heavy shades of dark green, rode upright on the ears, hands on their hilts. Zain slowed, ready to make contact with the group.

"Identify yourselves."

"Brisine Berrese and my son, Zain. The lord knows of our coming."

"We have been notified to see you to the castle. Follow."

The ship turned around with ease, and Zain followed. The creaking cogs of the drawbridge crunched behind them once they passed. Around the gate, clusters of different-sized round towers outlined the castle—they seemed shorter and skinnier in the front and taller and wider in the back of the castle, near the location of living quarters. Guard barracks were to the immediate left of the portcullis. Led to the right, they deposited their vehicle in the garage that housed other hovercrafts and battlecrafts.

"Brisine—"

"Gerald?"

The man laughed a little and nodded. "Yes..." He squinted. "Zain? How you've grown."

Gerald Starshine was one of the lord's royal guards. In the years before becoming a royal guard, he had trained at Gazo's Academy. Zain heard feats of Starshine's impressive handling of a morning star there from his trainer, Baron Gaul, who had even fought him on occasion. He received the nickname Star Slinger while at the Academy, and it stuck ever since.

Zain cocked an eyebrow. "Grown?" He had finished growing during his seventeenth year.

"Your face has hardened." Save for a thin grizzle over the lips and chin, Gerald Starshine kept a shaved face and pate. "When do you finish with training at Gazo's?"

"I—"

"We need to speak to my brother. Immediately."

"Impossible. He's asleep, my lady."

"Wake him; these issues cannot wait till morning."

"I'm afraid they'll have to. It's the grave of night, and I am busy supervising the Night's Command."

Zain's mom stepped forward and removed the scarf from around her neck.

"You're cut." Gerald leaned in closer.

"Go. Now!"

Gerald's brows furrowed. "Follow me."

Up past the steps were two large wooden doors that led into a great hall grander than Guardian Eska's. It could seat 2,000 and nearly 5,000 if the great hall next to it was used as well. Music, food and bathroom chambers were found on either side. Most were little rooms, large enough for ten. Past the grand tables, where the non-royals would take their place, were three polished oak tables raised on a four-foot stone dais. They were for the marquises or barons who ruled the major cities and the surrounding minor cities. Even taller was a dais solely for the lord and his family and other high-ranked guests who came to visit. In the back left of the hall, stone staircases led to the dungeon below or upwards to another level. Zain and his mother followed Gerald up the staircase. At the top, they took a bridge over a grassy court centered with a water fountain surrounded by trimmed hedges. In the middle of the fountain, four falcons faced the four cardinal directions, and each spilled water from its mouth.

Past the bridge, they descended a staircase to the cobblestone road and took it to the hearing chambers. "Wait here. I will go get Lord Vangle."

When the door shut, Zain's mother walked to lean against a paned glass window, basking in the moonlight filtering through. Eyes closed, she held her hands to her lips.

"What are you praying for?" Zain sat in one of the many pews in the room that looked to the vacant throne.

"That my brother will listen."

He's not much of a brother if he doesn't believe you. Zain tapped his feet and crossed his arms. *I could be on a ship by now.*

Minutes passed.

Silence lingered.

A creak in the back of the room alerted Zain to a new arrival—his uncle, Lord Abraham Vangle. In his early fifties, he still had a full set of hair and a pair of sideburns that did all but connect at the chin. He was lean but not overly muscular and donned in a dark satin-red night robe, stitched with the lord's sigil of a falcon sitting and watching from a man's arm. He said something inaudible to Gerald, and the guard left.

Abraham turned his attention to Zain and then to his sister. "Bri, why do you drag me from my wife and bed at this hour?"

"I was almost killed tonight!"

The lord stepped back from the shout. As loud of a shout as it could be, anyway. The grittiness of it caused Lord Vangle to rub his temples. After a moment, he proceeded forward, taking his place upon the throne. "You sound awful. Killed? By whom?"

"My son." At this, the lord's mouth stood agape, and he surveyed Zain. Zain's mom continued, "But it wasn't truly Zain, it was someone who..." His mother erupted into a fit of coughing caused by the wound on her neck. Lord Vangle stood up but remained still, unsure if he should attend to her. When Zain approached her, she stopped and started speaking again. "It was someone who looked exactly like Zain." She reached out and put a hand on Zain's shoulder.

"I'm... I'm not sure I follow." Lord Vangle sat back down, hand under his chin.

When his mother tried to speak, Zain put a hand to her side and spoke for her. Although he didn't know the exact details, he relayed the story to his uncle through the details he had concluded based on what he saw. When he told of how he came home and found her in a pool of blood and how she didn't want his help at first, doubt showed on his face as clear as the moonlight now. After Zain finished, his mother went to Lord Vangle and showed him the wound on her neck.

"You are saying he switched from being your son to being someone else?"

"Exactly! He was... a... a... shapeshifter, skinchanger, whatever you want to call it."

"What did this *shapeshifter* steal?"

Zain spoke this time, letting his mother's voice recover. "I think he stole my father's project plans."

"And what makes you assume that?"

Zain took out the telecard they had previously discovered in the vault and let it play. When skepticism still controlled his uncle's face, Zain said, "My dad said he kept plans to finish projects in his vault. And most currently he was working with Lord Zigarda."

"Why would they need his plans if they have him?"

Zain didn't know the answer to the question. But something must have gone awry if they needed his plans. Struggling to come up with an answer, Zain said, "Perhaps he forgot. Or needs specifics."

"Someone sent a shapeshifter to my home. I nearly died, Abe."

Lord Vangle bit his lip and then brought a fist to his mouth. He glanced around the room, searching for nonexistent council. *Why don't you believe her? Would she lie? Would she cut herself?*

After the unabridged silence, Zain let his arms fall to his side once more and stepped forward. "Zigarda sent that man. And whoever he is, I plan to go after him."

"Easy, boy, easy." The lord stood up and walked to one of the windows. "Your father will be fine. You storming Empora's castle by yourself might endanger your life and his."

Silence.

Lord Abraham leaned his forehead against his arm that rested on the wall. He turned and said, "No. Absolutely not. I will not send your boy off with troops to make war."

"Not war. Just a visit. To make sure Laron is safe."

"Bri, even if I could, I wouldn't. Your story is... well... excuse my wording, hard to swallow... Shapeshifters were a race that died out after the Conquest four-hundred-and-fifty years ago. What's more is Empora holds ties, great ties, with Acquava, the sole source of our life. We have limited resources to clean water here; it's murky, almost all of it. If we wish to not pay any more on embargoes, neutrality with Empora must be maintained. One word from them and—"

"And neutrality will be maintained. I promise."

"Zain, you do not know Lord Zigarda as I do. If you so much as touch the hilt of your longsword, Zigarda will consider it an attack. If *any* of my men do, he will. He's grown senile in his old age."

"I won't, sir. I swear it by Tomahawke." Zain felt the lie come out of his mouth more quickly than he could stop it. He really wouldn't lift a sword if granted a peaceful visit, but he wouldn't pray to any god that he would obey if not.

"Please, Abe, for your sister and your nephew?"

Lord Vangle's eyes were wide open. "Bri, you realize the position you're putting me in?"

"Yes, and I'm sorry." After a brief cough, she continued. "But if you had not seen Shayna for half a year, what would you do to know she's alright?"

"I know your struggle... That is what makes this even harder. I cannot allow Zain to go."

So much for family. "I knew he wasn't going to help, Mom. Talks like a lord, not like any family member I know. I'll go by myself. I'll make sure Dad's alright. Lord Vangle... I hope your family is never in danger."

Zain turned on his heel, not wishing to hear the lord's response, slamming the wooden behind him.

A few stragglers still roamed the pier by the time Zain arrived. He didn't have an uncle as far as he was concerned, and he wouldn't stay at the home of anyone who didn't support family. *I'll just go myself.*

Zain bypassed the inn near the pier called The Ship's Station and talked with a man carrying a bucket of fish heads. "When does the next ship leave?"

"Soon as that red sun comes up."

"No one will leave now?"

"Not any smart fisherman." The man walked away, humming.

Others on the pier all said the same thing. After so much rejection, his eyelids shook and his hands quivered. *Perhaps some rest would do me well.* He turned back with slumped shoulders and proceeded to the inn.

The room Zain checked into had a window that overlooked the sea, basking in the moonlight. Light trickled in, landing on his bed. He didn't go to sleep right away; he lay there, thinking.

The rings around the planet divided the sky into quadrants. It reminded him of his family's division: his mom back at the castle, his dad overseas, his brother on a different planet, and his best friend lost. What he wouldn't give to have his family whole again. He went back and forth with himself as he evaluated his choice to reject apprenticeship from Guardian Eska.

If I were the apprentice, I could save Dad easily. No one could refuse me, besides Eska or his council.

You wouldn't have been able to save your mom.

Eska would've helped.

Why didn't you tell him?

Zain thought about his other side's logic. *Why didn't I tell Eska? It's not his family. It's mine...*

Then why would he care to help you? You would have had Coronation. And then training. He wouldn't have let you leave.

I... Zain didn't know anything else. He lost a little piece of himself as he realized his other self's logic. No path provided a solution. He was stuck. Stuck here. Here until morning.

CHAPTER 7

SIBLING LOVE

B risine couldn't sleep. Worry kept her awake. As she stood on the veranda with a stone railing, in front of a curtain of silk, she looked upwards and saw her family as lost and scattered as stars, as divided as the rings that split the sky.

What has my family come to? She laid her face down in her hands and wept. Her tears matched the cold wind flowing past her dress. She took her hands and laid them as support against the railing. Guards patrolled below, wandering through the grassy courtyard. Could they hear her weep? She broke out into more tears when she saw her wedding ring—a gold band with a large, blue diamond in the center squared in by smaller, yellow diamonds. It had been the most beautiful thing Laron had ever made. And it was hers. Laron gave it to her as a promise that he'd support her and their family. He did. He gave it to her, saying she would be his only love. She was. He told her he would always be there for her. But where was he now? Now, when she needed him most?

A knock came to her door. She almost couldn't hear it. Past the silk curtain, she walked beside two large, polished, rustic oak dressers that blended well with the grayer walls of stone and brick. In between the wall and a night-stand sat a hand-crafted wooden canopy bed with intricate leaf drawings that crawled up each post. White curtains hung over the sides for privacy and a little more protection against the cool air. Wooden falcons, perched on top of each post, displayed the sigil of her brother's house. Another knock ensued. *Who could it be?*

She opened the wooden door marked with cast iron locks and stared at her brother, still garbed in the robe he wore before.

"Abe—"

"Bri... Sis... Why do you do this to me?"

Searching his eyes as she had done the stars earlier, she found care. "Do what?"

"Ever since your boy stormed out it has left me with a sour taste. I can't sleep. Can I come in?"

She nodded and let her brother enter.

"Can we talk?"

With still no idea if it was the lord who came to scold her, or the brother who came to comfort her, she nodded, but held onto her silence. She followed him out onto the veranda. Together they stared out into the openness of the courtyard. Abraham's lodging sat at the back of it, enclosed by castle walls.

"I stopped the ships," Abraham said.

"You did what?"

"Your boy—"

"Zain... Please..."

"I'm sorry. Zain left the castle; a guard reported that he saw him leave. He didn't bother chasing, though. Instead he found Gerald, and Gerald found me as I was trying to sleep again."

"Where is he now?" Brisine clung to her gown, swaying in the light breeze.

"Pelopon, at this point I assume, trying to find a way to Empora himself."

"You have to stop him! If he boards a ship—" She stopped. She realized that this is why he stopped the ships. Perhaps it was her brother who came to speak to her now.

"No ships are to leave the North Port till I raise the ban. He will find no ships to sail with. And I doubt he will go to the cities with the Southern Ports by the Shrouded Gulf."

"And why is that?"

"He didn't take your hovercraft. He's walked... and even if he did it would still take him nearly three days to reach the port. Listen, Bri, I'm sorry about tonight. Dammit, I am. But my people look to me."

"And my family are your people. Your most important ones. We all miss Laron. In truth, I haven't been happy since he's left. I've been lonely." Her sentences came slow and labored, always fighting off coughs that gathered in her throat.

"That is something you never should have to deal with. My castle is always open—"

"Your castle is not my husband! Your castle will not hug me like he does! I do not want the stone kiss of your castle!" She broke out into a fit of coughs and sobs. She covered her mouth and moved past him towards her nightstand, where sat a glass of water. She swallowed some and noticed he had come inside as well. She cleared her eyes and walked towards her brother, taking his hand. "Abe... I saw two Zains... Two! How is that possible, if not for a shapeshifter?"

"You realize how impossible that sounds, right?"

"Maybe it has to do with the suns converging?"

"Pirini Lilapa?"

"Grandma always told us stories about her mother living through the wrath of Deimos. Maybe this is the Curse starting again."

"The suns are not converging for another two months, if we are lucky."

"Contact Guardian Eska; surely he would know." Brisine locked eyes with her brother.

"Guardian Eska is too busy readying his new apprentice for the Meeting of the Twelve. It hasn't even been twenty-four hours since I left the Core for Coronation. This *occurrence* would be seen as annoying and is too far out to be related. Eska won't have time to take a call from me. Bri, I want to believe you, I do—" He clasped his hands behind his back and went outside again.

"Then do it. When have I ever lied to you?" She followed him out onto the veranda. After a few moments, she said, "Remember when we were younger and Lukas told you he got an arm chopped off sparring with one of Father's retainers, and you believed him and were even ready to give your own arm so he may have one again?" When she spoke softly, the wound left her alone.

Abraham chuckled.

"It was me who told you not to. I pulled my arm inside my sleeve and claimed I lost an arm too. Lukas was just mad he couldn't cast Power and you could."

Lukas was the eldest Vangle. He would have inherited the throne from their father, Tyon, except he was Denied and not Blessed like Abraham had been. Lukas had thought that if Abraham lost an arm people would want a whole ruling rather than a cripple. Lukas had always been conniving, but that trick had gone far enough. Even Elorine, her older sister by five years, went along with it so she might become lady of the castle. Now Lukas lived to serve his younger brother as the head of the royal guard, and Elorine married the Marquis of Cotterall, Ramsey Sesso. She caught a glimpse of her brother feeling his arm.

"I was only nine. And just cast my first spell at that point."

"Or do you remember when Catherine told you that ridiculous tale about our race emerging from beneath the Krine Sea and that's why our skin is darker than others."

Abraham roared with laughter. "Yes, I do. I was scared to go swimming in lakes when we traveled to other nations like Acquava or Epoch because I thought the clean water might make my skin a different color. Gods be good, I was seven when I fell for that. You were barely five."

"But five I was. And—"

"Bri—Bri. Who is speaking right now?" Abraham chuckled a little.

Brisine stopped in mid-sentence. It wasn't the usual carefree, brash her—she spoke like a politician, building her argument so that her brother couldn't refuse aid. She talked like Laron and Jamaal. She smiled weakly. "I'm sorry."

"No, it's quite alright. I enjoyed it."

"What I'm trying to say is that I've never lied to you. So why would I lie now?"

A long silence followed. Long enough where Brisine had wondered if Abraham had forgotten how to speak. She saw the cogs turning in her brother's mind. She hoped the right levers would turn. When he did finally speak, her heart jumped a little.

"Alright. Alright. You've convinced me... In the morning twenty of my men will accompany Zain to Empora as envoys, and nothing more. Once there, Zain will meet his father, make sure he is okay, and leave. There will be no raising of any swords by either side."

It all sounded good on the wind, but she wanted reassurance. "But what if they do?"

"Then we will call our flags. The falcon always watches... You know the saying."

She did. And the falcon was aggressive. There hadn't been war on Ka'Che lands for centuries. Minor pillages that needed resolutions and that one scuffle in the Frozen Pass with soldiers from Lokigh, but never war. Had Abraham's soldiers forgotten how to fight? Had they forgotten how to *fly as falcons*, as the saying went? She hoped not, because if they had, Zain would be right in the middle of it.

"Thank you, Abe." She leaned over and hugged her brother tightly, hoping to do the same to her son and husband soon enough.

CHAPTER 8

SETTING SAIL

Z ain paced back and forth in front of his window at The Ship's Station, the inn that Zain had secured a room in overnight. Freyr crackled over the Krine Sea. Lugh would join it in time. *Should I check again?* When dawn hit the sea, he had searched for early sailors. Truly, he did. But they all gave him the same response, a different one from last time, however. This time, they curtly said, "Lord's orders." *Maybe it's been lifted by now. And if it's not...* Zain found his academy knife and slipped it into a small sheath on his waist, behind his back. With his bags, he left.

Outside, ships of red sails and gray sails racked the heavy, murky waves. Each was made of a gray wood and had names of the wives their captains would never meet while traveling the Krine Sea. Names like *Annabelle,* or *Alimrah,* or *Leona,* and pictures of half-naked mermaids to match adorned the bows; he heard that they existed in every major sea or ocean but Zain didn't think that possible. He had only ever heard of them showing on Acquava. Beautiful women, they were said to be, with comely breasts and fins of pearls and scales. And a kiss that would let you breathe underwater forever after.

As Zain walked along the pier, he sought out people who he had not spoken to yet. Most were people from the night before, but one group of men with red snakeskin vests and large tattoos stood around mumbling with one another, toothpicks bobbing in their mouths like a fishing bobber on water. Clearly, they were not from Ka'Che, and if luck would have it, they would be returning to Empora soon. Zain inflated his chest and swaggered over to them.

"What ye want?" A man in a red snakeskin vest asked. He had a long scar across his burly chest and a sword hanging by the belt of his shorts.

"A ship. A ride to Empora. I need to leave."

The man's contagious laugh soon caused the others beside him to laugh as well. An earring of an anchor dragged down the man's earlobe to nearly his shoulder. Zain grimaced in pain. "You outa luck, little laddie. Your lord ain't lettin' anyone leave this port." The man spat, nearly hitting Zain's foot, and turned away.

"I need a ride."

"And I need me a *krinka* wench right about now, but I don't see none of 'em round here, eh?" The man stared down Zain.

The others shifted their stances. Intimidation never fazed him, though. Gazo's had taught him better than that, and the Trials had pushed him further than he thought possible. He needed a ride. And he would get one. He reached behind him and felt the hilt of his knife.

"I need a ride," Zain repeated.

"Piss..." The man with the snakeskin jacket leaned in closer. "Off." The man's spit and stench hit Zain like a punch, but he didn't flinch.

Wrong answer.

Halfway through pulling his knife out, Zain heard his name.

"Zain Berrese, I wouldn't do that."

He spun around, knife in hand. A man wearing a flowing garnet robe slashed with black, and who wore a glass piece in front of his left eye, making the brown almost blue, stopped five paces in front of Zain. It was Errion Vesk, his uncle's advisor. Most everyone at the castle called him Eerie for short, though, partly because he knew about many queer things.

"Put the knife away. None of these men can help you."

Zain walked forward and sheathed his knife. "I need to leave."

"Yes. Well, you are to come with me back to the castle." Eerie moved forward and readjusted his glass piece.

Zain looked past the man to two royal guards standing behind, dressed in pressure suits of dark green. Shoulder pads attached to the chest overlaid material of the same fiber that slid down the back. A thin mesh of wires ran underneath to give more mobility while the thick pad covered the vital upper torso. Knives and daggers, attached to either side of the shoulder pads, could be drawn and thrown at a moment's notice, and the sigil of the overlooking falcon emblazoned brightly upon their chests in a field of red and brown. Tinted visors concealed their identity.

"Where are we going?"

"You will find out soon enough."

Past a road that went around the grassy and rocky cliffs, Zain followed Eerie to the royal docks. The lord's armada waited there, patiently, rocking on the waves. A palatial ship named the *Sea's Commander* floated by the lord's private pier in the white cliffs. Four large sails attached to masts with flags of white, each bearing the falcon sigil, were being raised as they pulled in.

The balance and coordination training at Gazo's allowed Zain to maneuver the narrow and rocky path into the cove with ease. Lord Vangle's family and Zain's mother waited for him. At the first possible moment he believed Lord Vangle to be within earshot, Zain shouted, "Why won't you let me leave?"

"Zain, your mother and I talked last night... and... although I'm not completely convinced of these skinchangers, I can understand what your family is going through. Your mother's pain affects me. I do not think I could go without seeing Shay for half a year." He spoke over the wind. With one arm he held down the dark trench coat he wore that would have otherwise flapped in the breeze. With the other, he held his wife, Shayna.

"Mom is he—"

"Listen, son." She brushed back her hair and crossed her arms over her chest.

Abraham continued, "Therefore I will allow you and twenty of my guards to take the *Sea's Commander* to go to Empora as envoys only. Am I understood?"

Zain widened his lips and nodded. Then he asked, "Why can't we just use one of your spaceships?"

"Do you want the truth?"

Zain raised an eyebrow. His smile faded.

"Because you are too brash. Getting you there faster would only intensify the meeting. You need time to mull over how you will handle it."

Zain's jaw dropped.

Lord Vangle continued, "Furthermore, there will be no fighting while you are there. I will notify Lord Zigarda of your arrival and discuss a few things with him as well. Gerald will be my contact while you travel there."

From behind him, one of the guards with Eerie pulled back his visor and laid a gloved hand on Zain's shoulder. "Aye, my lord."

"The ship will be ready to leave by noon. Make sure you have all your things."

Despite the rudeness in his comments, his uncle allowed him to leave. Zain stepped forward. "Abraham, thank you so much." Zain pulled him away from his wife for a brief second and hugged him, along with his mother.

"You are welcome, Zain. I am sorry about last night."

Zain nodded. "Mom," he whispered, "thank you."

"Zain... This is yours." His mother laid down the golden rainbow feather in his palms.

"The feather?"

"Your father gave it to you. This is a start of a new adventure after all, isn't it? It'll remind you of us." Zain's mom gave an awkward smile and her eyes watered.

Zain took the feather and hugged her again. When he pulled back, he looked at the feather. It pointed northeast. *What's there? The Frozen Pass?*

"I can see where you get your determination from. Just like your father. He would be proud. Bring him back safely for us. Promise me that. Okay, Zain?"

"I'll bring him back. I promise," Zain whispered, eyes focused on the feather, and wondered what kind of adventure would be in store for him.

CHAPTER 9

THE KRINE SEA

Z ain woke in the belly of the ship to the rocking of waves. The same waves he had fallen asleep to. For how long, he wasn't sure. Woolen sheets kept him warm. Oil lanterns, encased in glass, hung from his side of the room. Couches and tables large enough to hold fully spread maps sat along the wall, and plants basked in the sunlight by the glass window located behind. His quarters were in the stern of the ship, on the second of five levels.

While the ship rocked, he twirled the golden feather in his fingers. Since his mother had given him it, he had made it into a necklace by threading a strand of gossamer through the thickest part of the quill.

The feather was rather dull below decks as it wouldn't randomly move or twitch, so when boredom set in, Zain got dressed in a white undershirt with a golden vest over. His uncle's sigil of a falcon overlooking a sea, eyes red and ready, sat on the upper right of his vest. He slung his longsword over his back and trucked up the stairs in his leather boots. Men on board the ship had on similar vests except unlaced, some exposing hairy chests. The only ones who had not changed clothing were the guards, still dressed in shades of green padding with thin mesh-wire underneath. With helmets removed, the guards' identities were obvious, making Zain more comfortable because he knew with whom he talked.

Already on deck was captain of the sea, Aeneas Khréos, and his first mate, Bern Denardi. Both had sailed ships since their youth. Before boarding the ship, his mom had told him that Aeneas had never failed in his travels across the seas of the world and had even sailed the Ertich Sea in the frozen north of Sereya. And when she talked about Bern Denardi she said, "He is a man of little words, but every word holds a lot of weight. He is first mate after all. If he speaks to you, Zain Berrese, you better listen." Zain had nodded at that moment, and now, looking at him, he thought it better to not talk to him, but rather to see more of the ship. On deck were ten guards, five of whom were overlooking the wooden railing, helmets tucked underneath their arms, three of the other five were placed carefully on the yardarms of the mainmast, and the last two were perched in the crow's nest.

"Zain. You're awake." Gerald strolled over.

"How long have I been asleep for?"

"We've been on the sea for two days now. I was beginning to wonder if the seasickness got to you."

"Two days?" Zain couldn't believe it at first, but then he realized how little sleep he had received in the past week.

Overhead, the suns shone brilliantly on the murky waters. The band that encircled Myoli shot out from the northern horizon. In front of him lay the vast expanse of inky gray known as the Krine Sea, and behind, the city of Pelopon was already washed away by a blue horizon.

"Don't worry. I have made the necessary calls to Lord Vangle."

"And?"

"He wishes us the best of luck. Says I'm to keep an eye on you too. Personally make sure nothing happens to you."

"Best of luck? Against what?"

"There's krakens and octopuses in the sea. Why do you think it's all murky? They fight, and Aeneas will be the first to tell you..."

"First to tell what?" The sea captain had left the wheel upon seeing Zain on deck. Bern now took control.

The eyes of an eagle sat on the forehead of Aeneas's green bandanna, which pushed tresses of brown hair to his eyebrows. A feathered vest overlay a white shirt spun with threads of silk. Chains of various sizes and colors and jewels hung around his neck. Zain would have almost believed that it was the most jewels he had ever seen before, remembering the time he went down to an excavation site with his father at the age of thirteen.

Gerald continued, "I was just saying how guards always need to be present on deck to spot leg battles."

"Best not be gettin' caught in one of those," Aeneas said.

"Leg battles?"

"When kraken and octopus battle it out, the water erupts with slashes from their legs. Can't go runnin' as fast as them, now. Why we only got two, and them be havin' at least six or more."

Zain strained his ears in an attempt to understand Aeneas's harsh sea-slang.

"Tell them 'bout that one battle you seen?" Gerald smoothed a hand over his bald pate.

The guards by the railing had come to listen now, too. Nothing excited anyone so much as battles on the sea, or battles in general. No songs were sung about inland battles anymore; now they sang about sea battles if you were lucky enough to see one.

"Well..." Aeneas cleared his throat, and for the first time, Zain noticed a scar across the neck.

"Well, one day I was headed down to the southern port of Empora, on a trade with Rydel, the name of the first capital. I be travelin' down past the Thievin' Isles, men ready on deck for attack. Those sea pirates always attack down there.

"Anyways, I seen a geyser erupt out of the sea. And I'll be the first to tell ya, I was scared. Perhaps we had reached some unmarked hot baths out there. But then I saw tentacles come out of the water and I'll be damned as a kraken as bi' as this ship was flailin' around, slappin' the bubbly head of some octopus nearly three-quarters its size. They fought so hard my boat got drenched with water, and we were a league away from them, too. Anyways, I put my spyglass in after cleanin' it and I see the kraken start to lower its mouth on the brainy part of that octopus. And just when I thought it was over for the puss he holds it back and shoots a stream of ink the same color as this sea into that beast's eyes and mouth and swims away.

"Moments later I didn't see that kraken. Suppose it sank faster than a chest of gold. Vicious thin's, they be. Why, I bet they could break this ship in half if they thought us a threat, despite our steel sidin's."

After the story, the guards returned to their posts, and Aeneas back up to the bow of the ship, humming away. "That's why we need guards, my boy." Gerald slapped him on the back and went below deck.

They should be called watchers, not guards. Zain doubted that no matter the crew they had on the ship, if a creature like that attacked, they'd sink right down to the sea locker with all the others.

Zain spent a few hours on the bow of the ship, talking with the captain and first mate. He found out that Aeneas added a new necklace every time he completed a voyage. His count was going on fifty-three. He also learned the man had an eagle bonded to him. That's why he wore a leather glove that slipped up to his elbow and shoulder pad—so that Reyson could land. Zain hadn't noticed the bird until Aeneas pointed it out—far ahead, another pair of eyes for danger. Aeneas told him that Reyson couldn't even see land yet, so they were still at least a couple weeks or more away.

After he had talked to them for a little while, Gerald came to get him for supper, and at that point introductions were made. All names seemed fit for alliteration. The largest men went by the names of Broadened Barry and Giant Garie, and both were men near the height of Cadmar Briggs, a Trials participant, but much more robust. Then he met Nimble Nyrin, a small, stout boy of not even fourteen years if Zain would have guessed, but he knew that Nyrin had to be at least sixteen to be a castle guard. After, there was Quiet Quint, a man with black, curly hair, same as his goatee, who hardly said anything at all. Why, he hadn't even said his name; Gerald had to do that for him. He laughed all the same, though, as they swapped tales of ladies at sea, training stories, and places they'd been or would like to be. By talking with them so much, even Zain received a nickname—Zealous Zain, because he was so adamant about seeing his father.

"So, Z.Z..."

Zain looked up from the steel spoon he twirled in his empty bowl to Interested Isaac, a man new to battle, Zain presumed by the lack of muscles. In truth, the man reminded him of his most recent trainee at Gazo's. Zain didn't mind that he sharpened his mind and not his sword. Not all men were fighters; some were thinkers, others tacticians, and the few that established themselves as leaders by living to the Gazo's code: *fight for others, then fight for yourself.*

"You say you trained at Gazo's?"

"Trained and a trainer, actually."

"How is it there? I always applied but was never accepted."

Zain could see that being true. Gazo's didn't accept just anyone to the most prestigious academy in the system, an academy that held more titles than any other academy, even those on different nations like Pauana on Mistral or Timsons on Epoch. Zain remembered the day he applied and had to show his ability in front of Instructor Barrata. He showed his nascent ability through a series of slashes and strokes at ceramic plates. Zain didn't miss once, even the trick one that came from behind at the end. He had done it with Zakk's help, though. Zakk had told him the exact count he should keep before swinging behind him, and the tactic had worked. Something Zain had never forgotten, because Zakk had never let him forget.

"It helped me to be chosen to go to the Central Core and compete with others for apprenticeship to Guardian Eska."

"You've actually *met* Guardian Eska before?"

"Yes..." Zain could feel annoyance for Isaac rising in the room.

"Did you win?"

"Of course he didn't win." Haughty Hector spoke up from the end of the table, his loud voice booming across. "He'd be there now if he did."

"Oh... yah..." Isaac retreated.

If only you all knew. Zain fisted his hand and tapped the wooden table. *No need to tell them that.* "I lost to Gabrielle, a student at Gracie's Academy. But, she failed too in the end. Eirek, a man from Cresica, is Eska's apprentice now."

"You lost to a girl?" Hector exclaimed.

"She wasn't just any girl. She was as nimble as Nyrin... and as quiet on her feet as Quint... and as sharp-minded as Isaac..."

"I hear the girlies at Gracie's Academy can walk on water. That they're *that* quick and *that* light."

It was Nyrin who spoke. Although young, Zain could tell why he enlisted as a castle guard instead of a guard for a marquis. The boy had been doing tricks with some cups for ale on the table before speaking, making the man across from him, Stubborn Symón, guess where he had hidden the potato. *Quick with his hands and his feet. He could be deadly, even a royal guard in the years to come.*

"That's what Gracie's Academy was founded on, anyways. That's an old myth, though," Zain answered.

"Do you know the tale about Gazo and Grace?" Nyrin asked.

"Yah, do you?" Isaac added.

"Of course he knows the tale," Hector exclaimed. "He went to the damn school."

"Please tell. Old stories always fascinate me," Isaac said.

"First supper is almost over," Gerald said to his right.

"Well, then..." Zain tapped the wooden table.

"By all means tell it, just be quick with it. The stars are out, and I wish to join them."

Everyone chuckled at that.

"Alright, well, Gazo and Grace were husband and wife back in the times before the Great War occurred. On Ka'Che, Gazo had been an accomplished warrior, winning Pelopon for his commander, Pelop 'Frogsbane' Swander, against forces led by the southern army of General Empor Rydel. Instead of taking the head of the royal guard, Gazo decided he had done enough warring and returned home to his family.

"Gazo believed only men should be able to fight, not women. He saw no women on the battlefield before, so why should it be different? That is why, when he caught his wife, training their daughter Gracie, how to fight, he became infuriated and beat her. This happened numerous times. Still, Grace wanted to teach her daughter how to defend herself.

"One time the beating was so bad that Grace tried to kill her husband in the night by putting a sword through his stomach. But Gazo only laughed at the wound. This was a man, after all, that had seen more wounds and scars than the locks of her hair. So she stabbed him with a hidden knife in the upper chest region. Still, he just stood and laughed and smacked her with his hand, and said how fun it would be to kill her like she tried to do him. So she picked up her daughter and ran from him. Gazo chased after her, then.

"Grace ran all night and day, never resting, carrying little Gracie in her arms all along, and when they reached the Krine Sea, she ran all the way across it, as well. Gazo ran over the sea too but did not make it very far because he was much heavier than her and sank to his death."

"The wench could walk on water?" Haughty Hector slammed down his cup of ale.

Fingers were missing from the man's hand. And an ear as well. With an attitude like that, it was no wonder why he got into confrontation. It reminded Zain of Hydro Paen, another Trials participant whose skill could only be surpassed by the man's ego. *At least Hydro had the skills and the title to back his arrogance. What does this one have, fiery hair?*

"Nyrin, can you walk on water?" Hector asked.

"I dunno. I never tried. No one wants to go swimming in this murky water." Nyrin played with his cups, pushing his shoulder up against Quint's, motioning that he wanted him to pick.

"I have to give our day's report to Lord Vangle. All of you up at posts on the upper deck now. Tell the others they can come and eat." Gerald stood up and made sure everyone was out of the galley. His arm caught Zain, as he was the last one to leave. "Zain..."

"Yah?"

"You alright? You seemed a bit agitated back there. Listen, don't let Hector get to you. He's the loudest one here. Him and his buddy, Sheamus."

"Sheamus? He never talks. He just shifts his eyes back and forth like he's plotting something."

"That's cause he most probably is."

"What do you mean?"

"Sheamus is a scout. That's what he's trained to do. Also, he knows how to spot an advantage. That's why we call him Sly Sheamus around the castle; he's known for fighting dirty during duels, kicking up dirt, or using the terrain, but all legal and all brilliant tactics that many fighters forget to utilize."

"That's why he's here then? What about Hector?"

Gerald shook his head. "Actually, they volunteered to come."

"Why?"

"To prove themselves to Lord Vangle and others around the castle, I suppose. Want to move up higher in the ranks. And, well, they don't come from the best of backgrounds."

"What do you mean?"

"Sheamus's brother had been a cleric until a malpractice in medicine. Hector's brother a felon; his father a penalized black-market dealer in weaponry."

"You can't choose your family."

"No. You can't. But blood certainly does matter, your family of all should know that." Gerald clapped Zain on the shoulder.

Zain frowned. "Was my face that obvious?"

"It was."

"It's just that I've dealt with Hector's type before. They're never fun."

"No they're not... especially here out in the openness of the Krine Sea. Because they don't have castle walls surrounding them, they feel less regulated. You have to step up and take charge. It's not my place to. Yes, I may be a royal guard for your uncle, but you outrank me. Command them like you command respect at Gazo's and you'll get it."

"Why are you telling me this?"

"Cause I won't always be there with you on deck or in the galley. It wasn't bad tonight, but the sea is long and our voyage has just begun. You'll have to start being a leader and make decisions that will affect us all."

CHAPTER 10

BULLY

Z ain lost count of the days at sea. He twirled the golden feather by his fingertips. Even though the breeze went against them, it pointed north. *What adventure lies in the Frozen Pass?*

"The stars are abandoning us."

Zain tucked the feather back inside his shirt. He turned left. No one. The deck stood empty, except for him. When he turned back to gaze at the sea, he noticed Nimble Nyrin to his right. *How did he approach?* Zain hadn't even heard him walk. Did he walk on air like Grace walked on water?

Zain noted the clouds, blotting out the suns. "They'll come back to us."

"Hector told me they won't."

That guy. Zain clenched the railing. "Why does he say that?"

Zain leaned away from the railing to look at the callow man dressed in a seafarer's cloak slashed with white. Overtop were pads of armor patterned in thin mesh wires, much like chain mail except more lightweight and durable. A sword hung at his hip, the pommel shaped into the likeness of a falcon, signifying his fealty to Lord Vangle.

"Mendeck is called the Starless City. You've seen it haven't you, on your tournament travels?"

Zain had been to Empora's newest capital, Mendeck, but in truth he had never noticed if light shown from bulbs or the sky. He had never heard it called the Starless City, but he had heard it called the Red Cloud before. It was a large metropolis that never slept, and factories, purposed to make new inventions, let out red smoke to fuel their sky. From space, one could always point out Mendeck due to the infamous Red Cloud.

"Mendeck is full of light," Zain said.

"But not stars." Nyrin crossed his arms and exhaled. "I was always told that the stars are how Ancients watch you. How they guide, protect, judge and make your wishes come true."

If only, Zain thought. *No star has ever answered my prayer.*

"And who taught you that, Nyssy?"

Zain looked back. Hector approached from below deck. Muscles rippled through the tight mesh that encircled his body where pads of armor did not. A scar slid across one of his forearms and a stub stood in place of his left pinky. Larger than Zain and twice the size of Nyrin, Hector made an intimidating opponent.

"That's not my name!"

"Might as well be. Yuse haven't even hit puberty yet and not no speck of hair grows on that face. How do I know yuse ain't no girl?"

The shouting grew. Soon the confrontation became a spectacle.

"Hector, enough. Why are you doing this?" Zain positioned himself in front of Hector.

"He's a green boy. Never even been outside the city before. I don't need inexperienced fools like him getting—" Before Hector finished his sentence, a throwing knife soared through the air. He caught it. "Yuse little..." Hector groaned. "Tries that again." He dropped the knife to the deck, smearing the wood with red.

Hector swung his sword. *No!* Zain reached for the hilt of his blade. Before Hector's sword even got halfway, a spiked ball curled around it and snatched it from his grasp. Hector toppled to the ground. Nyrin laughed. Zain didn't. Everyone peeled back as Gerald, the Star Slinger, stood, arms crossed, his boot trapping Hector's sword underneath.

"There will be no fighting. Period. Not on this ship, not once we reach port, and not even if Lord Zigarda himself says you may freely kill him. We are envoys of Lord Vangle, honest men with honest words and hands. Is this understood?"

Zain looked to the deck. It was only halfway out, anyway. When Zain raised his head, he noticed Gerald glancing at all three of them. Gerald spat on the ground, turned on his heel and went below deck.

When the crowd cleared, Zain sighed. *Dammit.*

After supper, Zain stuck around to help with the dishes. When finished, he moseyed his way to the deck and peered out over the rail. Clouds still blocked any light, but it didn't stop the sea from glowing in patches like lighted lily pads on a pond. *What are those?*

"See ya caught a glance of the light lilies."

Zain craned his neck to see Bern Denardi. Smoke and the clanking of a wooden stub that replaced his left leg followed the man as he limped towards Zain.

"They're beautiful."

Bern stopped by him and took the cigar out of his mouth. "Then you must be blind. Nothin' but glow-in-the-dark fungi. Ain't nothin' special."

"But they glow when nothing else does."

"They glow when things get dark. Otherwise, you'd see them when the suns are out. They glow when they need to. If they shined when they didn't think they could, now that'd be somethin'." Bern took one last puff from his cigar, tossed it into the murky water on top of a light lily, and walked away.

Silence. Stillness. Wind. Not hot or cold, just humid. Zain remained hunched over the railing, thinking about Bern Denardi's words. The water rippled in the breeze, making the reflection off the light lilies sway like flickering light posts.

Footsteps clattered on the deck.

"Zain, you're still out here."

"I'm admiring the light lilies."

"Are you now?" Gerald stood next to Zain on the ship.

"First Mate Denardi doesn't think they're anything special. But I do."

"Bern doesn't like much. Lived in the castle long enough to know that." Gerald chuckled.

Zain stared at the lilies in contemplation. After a moment, he asked, "How do you do it?"

Gerald raised a nonexistent eyebrow. "Do what?"

"Lead."

"You need to evaluate every situation."

"How?"

Gerald's face shone in the pale glow of the light lilies. "Always see each brush stroke of battle, for it determines the war's portrait."

"The saying from Gazo's?"

"Yes. To lead a group, you must look at what is best for the whole company. Hector and Nyrin fighting is not productive; it'll create animosity. That's why I stopped it. You have to take charge."

"But how?"

"Sometimes to start, you just have to talk. I'm sorry I cannot help more. But authority is something you find, in your voice, the confidence in it."

"How will I know when I have it?"

Gerald chuckled. "Your crew will listen. I'll leave you with the light lilies. I'm going to report to Lord Vangle for the night."

He didn't follow Gerald to the telecom chamber, but wondered if he should. *What is he going to say? Something about me?* Zain didn't know, but communication bothered him the least. Respect lay on his mind, the kind that Gerald demanded. Because nights would come faster, and if Mendeck truly was the Starless City, then even the brightest stars wouldn't shine or be there to guide him.

CHAPTER 11

A NEW LAND

"Land ho. Land ho."

Zain awoke to shouts of Lord Vangle's envoys spurred on by the captain of the ship, Aeneas Khréos. Wooden footsteps ran rampant outside and above his room. Even below deck, Zain could hear Aeneas's eagle, Reyson, singing the song of land to the air. Pulling on a pair of trousers, he exited his room.

Above deck, the majority of the crew stood on the bow. Maneuvering his way past, he made it to where Bern Denardi held a large wheel decorated in gold and bronze. An eagle squawked up above, flew higher, and then dived to land on Aeneas's leathered arm as he stood leaning over the front of the ship. Bern yelled at the crew to get back to work, reserving the spot for Aeneas and himself. Gerald held Zain tightly when he turned to leave.

While Aeneas and Bern yelled orders, Zain said to Gerald, "I don't see any land."

"He sees with his eagle eyes." Gerald pointed to his eyes. "The Power of being bonded, I suppose... or curse, as some see it."

Curse, Zain thought. *How could bonding with an animal be a curse? They give you extraordinary abilities.* When still a boy, Zain heard that everyone, Denied or Blessed, had an animal that they could bond with. It was just the matter of finding it—a task in itself.

Dressed in a coat as vibrant as a peacock's tail, Aeneas turned to them. Plush feathers snaked around his arms and a ruched white undershirt held all of his jewelry, as extravagant as his coat. "We'll be docking at the northern port in Liom." Aeneas twirled his necklaces by his fingers.

"Midday, you say?" Gerald asked.

"If Anemie is good to us, even sooner. From there it's a two-day voyage to Mendeck by hovercraft and then perhaps even a few more hours once you reach the city traffic," said Aeneas. "Bern, more southbound. We'll miss it if we continue course."

"Aye, Captain."

Aeneas turned to Zain, his eyes as red as his eagle's. They changed to a dull brown that did not befit the lavishness of his coat or jewelry. "How long shall we dock for?"

"Lord Vangle is allowing us a week's time," Gerald said after Zain remained silent.

"Will that be enough time?"

"We will be back by then."

"And if you're not?"

"Send for us. You have my telecommunicator number?"

"Yes," Aeneas answered. "You will message me then when you are on your way back?"

"Yes," Gerald answered. "I will contact the ship's communication center midday everyday."

"Excellent. Bern, grab the map for Empora from the table in my chambers. I will take over from here. I have a reputation to maintain. I have never *not* docked a ship. As for you two, have your things ready. The land is approaching fast. Anemie is blowing us her luck."

At midday, they made port near the minor city of Liom. Seven ship houses of steel stood aligned like garage doors for boats, separated by piers of more steel. Deckhands helped tie the *Sea's Commander* in place.

Before leaving, Zain took the opportunity to talk to his crew. "Men, before we step onto Emporian soil, there are a few things I wish to mention." Zain looked at Gerald, who gave a subtle smirk and wink before returning to his stoic stature. Zain turned back to his crew.

"Firstly, we had issues with each other on board the ship; this will not be tolerated from here on out. Secondly, you are here together and we will stay together while in Mendeck. If you leave our group, you better take others with you. There is safety in numbers. Finally, we are envoys—remember that. Are there any questions?" Zain waited a moment, but no one said anything. "Then let's leave."

The others left the ship first before Zain followed Gerald. Bern and Aeneas trailed both of them and stopped at ramp's end.

Gerald looked back. "Are you staying at the inn then until we come back?"

"Yes. We have some tidying to do now, but I will look for your call each day. And to make sure our ship isn't ransacked whilst at the inn."

"Take care," Gerald said.

"Aye, you more so. Zain, you as well. You're in good hands." Aeneas smiled.

"Thanks."

Off the ship, black bear and white tiger furs garbed men and women along the northern port. Ship captains distinguished themselves from others by wearing vests of kraken or octopus skin, and some went as far as to have pieces of tentacle hanging from braids in their hair or as badges on their vests. A few inhabitants donned a sigil of a white tiger prowling an open field of snow stitched upon their garbs. A painted paw print on the side of the face marked most females who wore the sigil. Most men wore tinted, thin-framed glasses.

Yet, those were the few and the rich, Zain supposed. Most wore tattered furs with holes (if furs were worn at all). If not, doublets of white, stained with yellow piss and puke and liquor gave the poor their own sigil. They lay on the ground with not even enough energy to rattle the cans at their feet.

Zain and Gerald led the twenty men behind them through the seedy streets of slum and sea. Inns coupled next to whorehouses received the most attention. Street vendors sold octopus, fish, and some even rare kraken meat to all of those who had coin enough to pay. Past the city square where a giant metallic kraken poured water from its tentacles lay hills of white. *A recent snow?*

"Why do they wear such warm clothing?" Zain kept an eye with Gerald.

"They're tigers, Zain. They've come from the major city of Lokigh by the Frozen Pass bearing Pillian Desmier's badge."

He must be the marquis. Regardless of the sigil, though, all still remained steadfast to Lord Victor Zigarda in Mendeck. Zain himself recalled wearing the falcon of Pelopon in tournaments for Gazo's. Only those who served the house by blood or blade could wear a sigil though. Did these men and women all serve the city of Lokigh? If so, what were they doing here?

As if he had read Zain's thoughts, Gerald whispered, "They've heard of our arrival, I'm sure. They're scouting for Lord Zigarda, I reckon."

A few of them made no effort to stop staring. Some of Zain's men stared back, all the same. The fight for intimidation caused Zain to continue walking, sword strapped to his back, hand covering his knife handle.

They walked to the skirts of town and saw a group of hovercrafts large enough for fifteen people each, blocking the road out. A man in a red robe, studded with garnets and, underneath a black tunic, waited outside, tapping fingers plated in red metal against his arm. A half-hat covered the left ear, part of his left eye and the left side of his hair, leaving black bangs pushed down to the other side. An eye scanner attached behind the right ear guarded his brown eyes. Two guards in sleek, ruby-red, full-body snakeskin suits with spiked shoulder guards stood with lances drawn, tip into the ground.

"Who is that?" Zain whispered through tight lips.

"Yuan Shimes, the receiver for Lord Zigarda."

"Receiver?"

"Yes. He's to take us to Mendeck. And bring us back."

"I've received verd of your coming." Yuan's voice came off no louder than a whisper. "Gerald, is zat correct? And Zain, you have your fazer's face. I'm sorry about za predicament we've put him in. It shows great loyalty and devotion to family zat you've come such a vays." The lengthy man with a long face and sinewy arms rubbed the sleeves of his robe while talking.

Zain eyed him up and down. "How long before I get to see him?"

"Maybe half a veek. It vill take us a few days to reach Mendeck viz such a large party."

"And for the nights on the road?"

"Ve have arranged lodging in quainter towns along ze way. Ven ve arrive in Mendeck, you vill find a place near his lord's keep."

"Not inside?" Gerald asked.

"His majesty does not let large groups of outsiders stay inside his valls. Take it as no slight, it's only policy... Shall ve be off?"

With a snap of his fingers, the guards jumped in the air and landed in the hovercrafts, ready to steer the vehicles. *They must've jumped ten feet in the air at least to get past those railings. How is that possible? Can they use Power?*

Zain stayed with half of his men and Gerald with the other, making sure to separate Nyrin and Hector to avoid further feuding. As the crafts' engines turned on, pebbles flew up in the air, floated, and fell back to the ground. Before them, a vast expanse of road lay ready for travel. On the horizon, the great ring split the sky, a carpet beckoning them further into unknown territory.

CHAPTER 12

MENDECK

Yuan Shimes sat at the front of the hovercraft, tapping his arm and smiling a pleasant smile as air brushed past. Behind him, metal railings separated the driver's area from the seating area. Zain sat closest to Yuan, on the man's left-hand side, across from Isaac.

Yuan stood up to say something in incomprehensible Emporian to the driver before sitting back down to share words with Zain. "Mendeck is approaching soon. Do you see ze Red Cloud?"

Off in the distance, the cloud loomed. It had been two days already on the airroads to Mendeck. Zain nodded but kept quiet. He did not want to speak because speaking usually became awkward as it had the previous two days. It was about halfway through their second day on the trip when Yuan had first asked them how their voyage fared. That, in itself, had created a rather awkwardness and had abandoned any normal mannerisms he would have hoped to find. The day before had simply been questions about him and his party, as if polling them for some occult reason.

Yuan had said, "How fared za vaters?"

Zain had feigned not to hear the whisper of Yuan, but that had not stopped Isaac from responding.

"The goddess Anemie blew us straight enough. It only took a month. No storms."

"I'm glad you've had such fair conditions. I vould hate to see ze ship and yourselves in shambles already."

"Already?" Zain had said the word without thinking and bit his lip afterwards.

"I only mean zat if your troupe came sea-stressed zan talk might be minimal. Za sea can play on emotions and minds greatly, somezing ve should not like to see." Yuan smiled and followed Zain's gaze towards a lake due south. "You have a fighter's taste in you, Sir Zain. I see vhat you look at."

In the distance, a lake lay as a lush doormat to a huge building with tall cylindrical towers. Flags stitched with a design of a dagger protruding southward from a purple and white circle waved their welcome in the distance. Although he couldn't distinguish the letters on the flag, he didn't need them to recognize the symbol: Gracie's Academy.

Gabrielle... He let his intrigue die. "Well, I have studied at Gazo's all my life. It's hard not to stare at our sister school when it looms off in the distance."

"I hear you even vere selected to partake in Guardian Eska's recent Trials."

"I was."

"I'm sorry zey did not fare better."

"They fared fine."

"Zat is not as I heard."

Zain wanted to correct him, but what was the point? He hadn't accepted the apprenticeship because of Zakk, and now he searched for his father. *Once my family is safe, Zakk, I'll find you. I know I will.*

"But, zey fared equally poor for Empora as vell, I should add. Ve vill come to conduct an interview wiz Ms. Ravwey soon enough, zough. Lord Zigarda and her vill have much to talk about."

"I doubt she would want to speak to him." Zain crossed his arms.

"Vell, not now. But ve vill send her an invitation soon. It is only *decent* as zey vould say over at Gracie's." Yuan let out a slight giggle. "She is still getting over her loss at ze Trials, but Lord Zigarda is more zan eager to hear how her experience vent compared to his. Did you know zat he vas a Trials participant?"

Zain had known that. He had heard it at some point while he was on the Core, but he forgot when or where. He had learned many things on the Core, and to think that Gabrielle would actually talk with Victor Zigarda was inane. He didn't want to talk more about the Trials, so he remained silent, nodding here and there to feign engagement.

It seemed Isaac had different plans. "She may not be the new apprentice, but she beat Zain."

"Did she, now?"

Zain raised an eyebrow. *Quick with his words. Why did he butt in?* The Academy died off behind rolling hills.

"She did." Face stoic, Zain went along with Isaac's statement.

"Is it true that the women of Gracie's can walk on water?" Isaac asked Yuan.

Yuan chuckled. "I am not a girl. I vould not know." He adjusted his half-hat after a hard gust. "Ze lake before Gracie's is called *Toetouch*, zough, if zat interests you."

"Is Gracie's Academy inside Mendeck's rule?"

Yuan tilted back his head and let out a belching laugh. "Foolish boy, everyone in Empora is under Mendeck rule. Ever since za capital moved from Rydel."

"I meant within city jurisdiction," Isaac corrected.

Where is he going with this?

"No, just outside, I'm afraid. It lays vizin the old capital's jurisdiction..."

"Rydel?"

"Correct."

Strangely enough, Isaac had shut up afterwards and hadn't spoken the day since the incident, not until red particles began to show in the air.

"Is that toxic?" Issac had pointed to the red mist.

Zain held his breath, waiting for Yuan to answer.

"No. Merely Mendeck's signature atmosphere."

Zain exhaled. "What do you mean?"

"Vell, our factories run day and night, employing zousands. Zeir hard verk provides us our knowledge. And knowledge is power."

Zain furrowed his brows. *Where have I heard that before?*

"So you enslave thousands?" Isaac spoke up again.

"Give jobs is more appropriate, I zink." Yuan turned around and gave directions to the driver, pointing with one hand while holding his half-hat with the other as his robes rippled in the breeze.

Yuan turned around. With one hand still on his half hat and the other at waist, he bowed. "I velcome you to za city of Mendeck."

The transport traveled over the crest of a hill. Below, skyscrapers busted through clouds of red that clotted the city veins like blood. Smokestacks gushed out clouds of red air every few minutes, which would linger until blown away.

To Zain's surprise, the city streets weren't as cloudy as Zain imagined. As they traveled down into the city's center, Zain noticed the light on the front of the transport change from yellow to white to separate the fog. The same white light flickered from the streetlights. At points, Zain wished that he couldn't see as well as he did. Bums littered the street, almost as numerous as the streetlights. Tattered clothes and the spirit at their feet gave them their only solace. Houses were crammed together, barely large enough for decent living.

"I thought you said you made jobs for folks?" Zain asked.

"I did and ve do. I did not say ve pay zough."

"What?" Zain stood up on instinct.

"Ve pay zem in living quarters, food stamps and no taxes. Vhat more can zey need?"

"Money for travel, for family, for entertainment?"

"I trust you did not come here to discuss politics, Zain... If you vould have a seat." Yuan gently waved his hand to Zain's chair.

Zain took his seat. *Ka'Che would never allow this. Is Dad cared for the same way?* He hoped better. Before he came, he assumed better, but now his confidence vacillated before the flagrant poverty. *Pain... Hopelessness... Futility...* Gabrielle's words kept repeating themselves over and over.

Twists and turns led them to the heart of the city, if it even had a heart. Poverty died away with every block until Mendeck seemed like a whole new city entirely. Cloaked in proper Emporian style, men wore dark red shirts that tapered down to a V at their abdomens. Below the last bit of cloth, an ornate silver belt of matched the cuffs of mismatching lengths on the sleeves of the shirt. One cuff sat only a hand's length down from the shoulder, leaving the rest of the arm bare, and the other extended fully down. Most individuals wore half-hats similar to Yuan's, while only a handful, Zain noted, wore eye scanners. *Patrol guards?* Women wore garbs of lighter colors that fully covered their breasts but then snaked around their back to end up dangling from the hip by golden or silver brooches of different design. A slim belt held in place the dark-colored skirts that fell to the knees or upper thighs. In this sector of town, women carried their authority as proudly as the crown-like plaited hair style they fashioned.

Every few streets, guards with snakesuits stood post, making small talk with the wealthy passersby. Zain cringed when one of the rare beggars in this part of the city pulled on one of the guard's legs and the patrol delivered a swift punch that knocked the man to the ground. The guard moved fast. Too fast for normal humans. *What kind of suits are those?*

Zain couldn't tell what time of day it was when they finally arrived. The red fog wouldn't let any of the suns' rays in. Nyrin had been right; Mendeck was indeed a Starless City, and a city drenched in red fog.

Up ahead loomed a circular domed castle, built of solid steel and fortified with a tall barrier nearly twenty feet high. A gate of wired iron topped with barbs ran along top of the walls. The castle had three domes, all rising to heights of at least 150 feet at their peak, and behind the first, in the middle of the other two, a tall tower like an obelisk, rose up past the clouds. Around the barriers of steel surrounding the premises, watchtowers rose to halfway to the heights of domes. *Looks like a prison more than an estate.*

"Zigarda's keep is za most steadfast keep zis side of Myoli. You vill see it on za morrow."

Once all party members disembarked, Yuan led them to a well-maintained building with its name emblazoned on its west façade: *Extravagant*. Its flashy name attracted a collection of insects, but none entered through the revolving doors due to the repellent sprayed from the overhang every minute. No guards accompanied them inside, either. Another guard, posted outside the building, nodded to Yuan but continued staring at the lord's keep afterwards.

Inside, tiled marble sat as the base for a spacious lobby with columns of silver and a polished cherry-wood receptionist desk. A hearth of sandstone blazed merrily, and the fire only increased the scent of red ivy that clung to and climbed the rock. No visitors sat on the leather couches next to the fire. A man behind the polished cherry-wood with a golden-threaded half-hat started speaking Emporian, which only Yuan understood. Hands fisted, Zain stood ready.

After a brief dialogue resulting in the handing out of two dozen room keys, Yuan shared a word with them in the Natural Tongue. "Your rooms are on the sevenz level. Zere vill be two to a room. I vill retrieve you midday tomorrow for your meeting. Understood?"

No one said a word.

"Very vell." Yuan left them, his red robe nearly dragging on the ground.

Seven floors later, they found their rooms. Gerald told each pair to canvass their room for hidden bugs or cameras before talking. After a fruitless search, Zain sat, sword on his lap, staring out the window. The hum of Isaac showering lingered in the background. His eyes couldn't help but diverge to the massive steel keep in front of him. The white lights around the perimeter shredded any trace of red mist. He wished he knew how tomorrow would go. The stars afforded him no signs. He wished he had learned more from Yuan during their ride. But he hadn't. Isaac had, though; that is why Zain requested him as his roommate.

Zain pulled his sword from the sheath resting on his lap. Four jewels sparkled in the room's light, making the sword shine. Zain ran his left hand over the blade, stopping at each jewel like Guardian Eska had done when he first examined it. First, the blue topaz, then the opal, then the garnet, and finally the peridot. *All important swords need a name.* He had learned that from Eska. *You were my gift.* "And Gift is what you shall be named."

"Zain, your turn."

Upon the interruption, Zain sheathed his sword. Isaac strolled out of the bathroom, a white towel at his waist. His pallid chest held not a single hair.

"Thanks." Zain turned back to the window.

"Stop brooding over tomorrow. It'll go fine. We're envoys. To attack envoys means cause for war. Even Zigarda wouldn't be so dumb."

Zigarda certainly wasn't dumb, Zain knew, but Gabrielle's three words kept rotating in his mind. "But what if it doesn't?"

"Then let the gods take us."

Gods. Ancients. What are any of them, anyway? Zain clicked his tongue and tightened his fists. There were no such beings. Only the sword on his back and the brain in his skull and the determination in his heart. "Take us where?"

"We will run away from here to safe houses."

"Safe houses. Here?" Zain let out a slight laugh. "Where?"

"Do you wonder why I asked about if Gracie's fell within Mendeck boundaries?"

Zain nodded.

"If they are not legally tied to obey jurisdictions in Mendeck, Gracie's may hold a chance of helping us if worse comes to worse. An academy of female fighters that rival your skill? Why, I doubt even Zigarda would be foolish enough to send troops."

Zain's eyes widened.

"Look at the city, Zain; it's a red fog of disaster and confusion. I'm sure citizens wouldn't stop us if we tried to leave the city. They probably despise Zigarda. If Zigarda doesn't give us your father, we'll steal him away."

Although Zain appreciated Issac's plan and confidence, it implied pessimism, something Zain hoped to avoid. "Don't say such things."

"I'm sorry. Listen, Zain, you should have your father back. That's all I'm saying."

Zain nodded but kept looking out the window. A light drizzle pattered the glass. People who still roamed the streets hurried to find shelter before the downpour. The rain's melody would have lulled him to sleep on other nights, but not tonight. For some reason, tonight it reminded him of the night with Zakk. It had rained that night, too; the night they drifted so far apart, like the stars Zain could no longer see. *After I make sure my dad is safe, I'll find you, Zakk. I promise. I'll make things better between us.*

CHAPTER 13

THE LORD'S WORDS

I t rang once.

Zain fidgeted in Gerald's room before an electronic circular device shaped like a mirror. The device functioned similar to the telecommunicator on Zain's wrist.

It rang again.

Zain tapped his feet. *Why isn't it connecting? Did they forget our check-in?* Gerald offered a rolling chair, but Zain decided to stand and look over Gerald's shoulder. Buttons ran down the side of the device, a red one, a black one, and a white one.

A third ring.

The word *connecting* flashed on and off the glass. Lord Vangle answered. He wore a crown on top of his head made of crude steel; the points shining with bright rubies. "Gerald, ... Zain. I'm glad to see you."

"And us you," Gerald said. "We have the meeting with Lord Zigarda today at midday."

Abraham took a double glance at something in the room. Zain couldn't tell where, based on what he saw. "Then it is soon for you."

"Yeah," Zain said.

"Yes, it is," Gerald added with a slight accent on correction.

"I look forward to news on progress after. May the Twelve be with you. Zain, I will tell your mother."

Zain nodded.

"Yes, sir." Gerald ended the connection.

"Let's go." Zain moved towards the exit.

Gerald caught his arm. "Zain, are you ready?"

Zain searched his eyes. "Yes. Let's go."

"No. Truly, are you ready?" Gerald searched his eyes as well. "I saw how you led before we got off the ship. I want you to do the same now."

"I will." Zain shrugged his shoulders and stepped back.

"Then, let's leave."

Zain followed him out and down to the lobby. Isaac took the elevator down with them, dressed in a soldier's gear of dark red. Grim plates, striped in thin wire, coated the armor.

"How many guards does it take to hold a hotel?" Isaac asked.

"I saw some patrolling the keep...," Zain added.

"Those too... but guards around the hotel. I counted twenty of them while I took a walk this morning. So did Quint. Not all of them wore the snakeskin armor, though. Some dressed as citizens."

"How do you know they're not?" Gerald asked.

"Quiet Quint quietly knocked into one and felt a knife sheath hidden in the sleeves of their coats."

So Quint was good at pick-pocketing. Zain thought it interesting each soldier had his own ability. He wondered if his uncle had sent them as such. Everyone seemed to think they were walking into a spider's web. Zain's side ached at their pessimism.

When Gerald walked into the lobby, sixteen guards stood to attention. Only two were missing from their troupe. Immediately Zain knew who as well: Hector and Sheamus. His time with them thus far had been indelible. And not in a good way.

The lobby doors slid open. Yuan entered on the heels of two snakeskinned guards. To his left was another man, slightly shorter and wearing a black robe, with lines of crystals webbed through the fabric. A black spider on a red background, stitched on the upper left of the robe, stood as the sigil of Zigarda's household.

"That's Zigarda's advisor, Edwyn Lyze," Gerald whispered.

Zain knew the face. When at tournaments around Gladonus, figures of note from every house showed. Zain thought mostly to recruit men soon to graduate. Since the last time Zain saw him, Edwyn had gained weight, and his rotund belly had now fallen victim to gravity. Curly hair did an ill justice to the man as well. Three more guards followed after. The front two stepped aside and the leftmost one heralded, "The Lord Zigarda's receiver and advisor."

Zain chuckled a little at the formality. *He only is missing his horn.*

The two stepped forward, as did Zain and Gerald. Hands were shaken and pleasantries exchanged.

"Is everyone ready here?" Yuan asked, his voice barely above a whisper.

"We have two missing still," Gerald responded. "You come a little before noon."

The doors behind the group of Emporians opened and the missing party members entered.

"As have you." Edwyn looked at the late arrivals.

"Ah, za missing pieces are connected. Shall ve?" Yuan smirked.

Gerald glared at both men who entered and turned back to the receiver. "Of course."

The small garrison of twenty men walked behind Zigarda's men in pockets of five. Gerald quietly chastised the latecomers.

"Why were you both late?"

"We weren't, they were early." Hector snorted and folded his arms.

"Yah, how is ten minutes early *late*?" asked Sheamus.

"And I said fifteen before. You know these Emporians as much as I do. They're always first."

"Someone should have said earlier?" Hector spat.

They walked past a small group of Emporian guards at the gate and hushed, resuming conversation once safely past the gates and out of earshot of Zigarda's men.

"Any earlier and it would cause duress. What were you doing?"

"Surveying." Hector crossed his chest.

"The scouters went out at early dawn."

"Yah, we were *late* for that," Hector said. "Sheamus and I decided to go ourselves."

"And?" Gerald asked.

"I'm sure you've heard from the other scouters."

"I haven't," Zain said.

"Yes, Zain hasn't. And I would like to hear it from you."

"Six towers, ten guards along each wall and two to three guards in each tower's compartment." Sheamus continued walking after he stopped to speak.

"Sentinels on the ground?"

"At least two at every tower," added Hector. "Seems to me you don't trust us."

"I'm sorry... you're right..."

Hector snorted. "That all, then?"

"Yes."

When finished, both joined a pocket ahead of them next to Quiet Quint and Giant Garie.

"Why all the questions?" Zain asked.

"To make sure they were where they said they were."

They continued to walk up a small, grassless hill. "So you don't trust them?"

"It's not that. Being a leader means holding people accountable for their actions. If they said they were scouting, I need to make sure that was the reason. And other times it means being accountable for your own actions. Remember that, Zain." Gerald slapped Zain on the shoulder and then proceeded up a red carpet with the others.

Two guards nodded as each pocket passed through the egg-shaped door into the vast chamber beyond. Inside, the ceiling stood at least one hundred feet tall, only half as tall as the skyscraper that Zain had seen from outside. Steel columns spaced out every fifteen feet supported a loft made of glass that would allow onlookers to gaze at them from above. Two winding staircases, placed at either side, allowed onlookers access to the glass loft. Now, however, the loft was empty.

Men and women stood in the main hall speaking amongst each other with glasses of wine in their hands, dressed in flowing silk riches. Guards gathered along each column. A flicker of movement ran against the leftmost column. Zain squinted but couldn't find the source. It had vanished.

At the end of the columns, the red carpet followed up twenty steps to a platform, level with the height of the glass loft. On this platform, the throne sat in all its steel infamy. At the far ends of the room were silver egg-shaped doors. An older man with little hair in a dark lab suit stood idly by like a guard. At the foot of the staircase to the throne stood guards in black snakesuits. The guards wore faces of stone and dark skin of Zain's color. Lord Zigarda sat alone, cloaked in an obsidian-colored robe, hood shadowing his face and exposing only faded and weary lips. A claret-red silk stitch outlined a large spider, noting his sigil, and adorning it were garnets of the same color.

By the time Yuan climbed the stairs, Zain and Gerald had made it to the front of their group. He whispered words with Zigarda before retreating down the steps to stand near Edwyn at the foot of the throne.

Edwyn cleared his throat and bellowed, "Lord Victor Zigarda, ze fourz in power of house Zigarda."

Zigarda drew strength from his cane and managed a weak hobble and wave to silence the clapping that arose from the onlookers already in the hall. Then he sat back down.

"Announce your names, please," Edwyn said.

"Fool, I know who comes to see me." Zigarda waved his hand. "Gerald Starshine, the Star Slinger, your battle prowess on the Frozen Pass and exploits near the Shrouded Gulf do not befit you. I pictured you to be... taller." Lord Zigarda spoke with an Emporian accent, but not thick enough to distort communication, unlike his receiver and advisor. It was obvious he had been raised to overcome the accent that bespoke many in this nation.

"In battle, with stars as my audience, I rise over many. Surely your troops know that."

Zain had heard about the time Zigarda tried to send Lokigh troops across the Frozen Pass to take Pelopon by surprise, but scouts saw them before they got halfway. The skirmish never had resulted in war, though.

"There are no stars here, sir..." Zigarda's raspy voice cut any respect that once may have lingered. "And Zain Berrese, Vangle's own nephew. I see the resemblance of your father."

Zain knew he had the same jaw and eyes as his dad; people had told him that before. Hearing it from Zigarda, though, made it queer. "Where is he?" Zain shouted.

"He is around," Zigarda answered.

"Let me see him."

"You shall, you shall. Now, before we get to introductions and family re-unions, Lord Abraham made me make sure to address some concerns of yours."

Zain cocked an eyebrow. "Go on..."

"Speak." Gerald straightened his shoulders.

"Lord Abraham claims you believe I hired a thief to steal from you and your family."

"My father's documents, yes." Zain held his ground.

"Tell me why I would need your father's documents, when I have your father?"

That's the reasoning Uncle used. "Well—"

Lord Zigarda stood and descended the steps with support from his cane. "Tell me Zain, do you see the man who stole your documents. Look... look..."

Zain looked around, making furtive glances at his own troops as well. All the men stood behind them in pockets of four. Hector and his friends were immediately behind, and to the right Broadened Barry's group and Giant Garie's group to the left. Nimble Nyrin and Interested Isaac and Quiet Quint were all in a group outside. To Zain's right, Gerald kept focused on Zigarda.

"No, I do not. But the man who stole could change shapes..."

Yuan let out a bellow of a laugh and brushed the hair on his right behind his ear. Soon others followed him in his laughter. "A skinchanger? They haven't been seen for centuries. Since the Conquest."

"My mom wouldn't lie."

"Well, your mother is delusional," Zigarda said, halfway down the steps.

"Excuse my bluntness, my lord, but it does not matter who is delusional and who is not. We only came to make sure his father is alright and to bring him back with us," Gerald said.

"Yes, and I said he will meet him... as my captive."

"Captive?" Gerald repositioned himself.

All around the area, the guards withdrew their weapons. By instinct Zain reached behind for Gift, but Gerald halted him. Zain captured Gerald's glance; it was a moment's stare, yes, but it tried to show safety and caution.

Gerald returned his attention to Zigarda. "We are envoys. We mean you no harm. Lord Vangle simply wishes you to let us retrieve Laron."

Zain followed Gerald's gaze behind him and noticed each man had a hand on his hilt. Each man waited for the signal.

"And I *simply* cannot allow that. I still need him." Zigarda pulled the hood back from his head, revealing a burned face. "And your father is quite stubborn. That is why you'll make the perfect incentive, Zain." Zigarda's lips curled in a way Zain didn't think possible.

"You can't have the boy. He comes back with us." Gerald held onto his morning star.

"*That* is where you are wrong." Zigarda nodded to the soldiers by the pillars and they pulled back their arms.

"You're to betray us?" Gerald stepped forward.

"Betray?" Zigarda laughed. "Betray implies that I was on your side..."

It happened fast. Droplets of blood splashed against Zain's right cheek. He turned to his right to see a sword impale Gerald through the chest, where the green armor allowed for arm movement. Hector was the thruster. Gerald turned around and as he fell to the floor, his morning star swung and hit Hector in the jaw, sending him sideways.

The Star Slinger was on his back, grasping for his missing heart—a fallen star granting a lord's wish of death. Sheamus took Hector's spot, slid over Gerald and slit the throat open. Zain began unsheathing his sword, but halfway through, an arm rustled around his neck. Steel flickered before his eyes and sat below his chin, within a heart's beat. A hot voice whispered in his ears. A voice he had heard so many times before.

"Surprised to see me?"

It was Zakk's.

CHAPTER 14

TO LEAD

Gerald lay on the floor, drowning in a pool of red, his morning star next to him.

The murder caused Zain's party to draw their weapons.

"Hector, how could you?"

"You traitor! All of you."

"Call us what you want, but the fact of the matter is that we be living today." Hector spat and picked up the sword that had fallen from his grasp. Sheamus went to go stand by his comrade.

No. This can't be happening. Zakk's blade tickled his chin. Zain shook his head and bucked, trying to throw Zakk off of him, but to no avail. "Zakk, what are you doing here?" Zain asked through gritted teeth.

Clanging metal alerted Zain that he needed to act. He tried one last time to shake Zakk off of him, but he couldn't.

"Stand down, Zain," Zakk breathed. "Don't you see it's impossible?"

The normal men and women he thought he saw earlier were now men and women with furunculous faces and long noses and wispy gray hair. Some held bows and others knives, but they stood back as Zigarda's snakeskin troops encroached on each pocket of Zain's company.

"Tell them to stand down, Zain." Zakk pushed the sword closer to Zain's neck.

Zain's shoulders slumped. "Men, stand down."

"But Gerald's dead." Nyrin pointed to the carcass on the floor, awash in blood.

While he couldn't move his neck, Zain flicked his gaze to Nyrin. "We can't win. Put your weapons down. All of you."

One by one, each of Zain's men lowered their weapons to the floor. Zigarda's men halted their slow advance.

"Zain, it seems that you have come to your senses."

"Why did you kill him?" Zain turned his attention to Zigarda.

"To make an example to the rest of your group."

"What are you going to do with us?" asked Issac.

"Make another example..." Zigarda waved his hand.

The soldiers that had approached each pocket stepped forward and slit the necks of the men before them. Broadened Barry dropped to his knees with a heavy thud. For the first time, Quiet Quint made a noise—a horrible scream as if he had been bottling sound inside him for years.

Zain buckled to his knees. At least he tried to. But a force behind him, Zakk's force, kept him upright. Zain closed his eyes, but even with eyes closed, he couldn't escape the situation.

Grunts. Screams. Moans. Thuds upon thuds crashed on the floor. Blood. And more blood. The tiles became wet. The carpet soaked. The stench of sweat and piss and death took hold of the air soon enough. Through the chaos, steel made its voice heard, wielded by those soldiers who had been inside the first wave of individuals, those who had time to pick up their weapons and mount one last defense. But none of it matter. Bows twanged and arrows sang amidst the cacophony that now reigned.

The sword prickled his neck. He forced open his eyes. Zigarda looked on in amusement. Zain gulped. He needed to take responsibility for his actions, so he knew what he needed to do to stop it. He knew what it took to lead. Gerald had taught him that. So had Gazo's. His situation wasn't impossible. Nothing ever was, according to Gazo's. *I'm possible.* Zain didn't think about the repercussions of his actions; he didn't think at all. For in times like this, there was no time to think, only time to do.

Pressed against the sword, his skin felt tender, the sword sharp. He fell over sideways, applying pressure all the way. Warm blood left his body. His eyes fluttered. There was no pain. Or futility. Or hopelessness. Not anymore. Not with his decision. After all, there were things worse than death. Things much worse. Much, much worse. But those things wouldn't plague him. Not any longer.

CHAPTER 15

THE BLOOD CHAMBERS

"Zigarda! Zain." Zakk bent down over Zain. Blood came in spurts from his neck. *You stupid fool!*

"We can't lose him."

Everything stopped.

Zakk dropped his sword to the ground. Immediately after, he ripped Zain's clothing off and covered the wound while applying pressure. *You stupid fool!* Zakk looked up to Zigarda. "He has a pulse."

"You two there..." Dr. Cere pointed to two large men in red snakesuits. "Take that one to the Blood Chambers. Tell them he needs his blood clotted immediately." Dr. Cere stopped before the one called the Star Slinger, now just a prostrate man in a pool of blood with a morning star by his side. The doctor glanced around the still room. "Take the rest to the Blood Chambers, as well. They can be specimens."

Zakk picked up his sword, Viper, named for the two tips at the blade's top that looked like a snake's tongue. It had now bitten another victim. *Stupid Zain!*

One by one, those still alive marched past, looking at either the Star Slinger or the ones who betrayed them.

A man who barely looked fourteen shouted from the procession. "Hector, you'll pay for this. All of you will. Lord Vangle will hang the three of you."

Hector massaged his bloody face while he stood next to his two friends. "Lord Vangle will be dead within a year's time," Hector shot back. "The dead can't kill the living."

Zakk snarled a lip. *Too much of a loudmouth.* Zakk turned his gaze towards Dr. Cere, who crouched over the Star Slinger's corpse.

"Will Zain live?" Zigarda asked.

"If they get him to the Blood Chambers in time." Dr. Cere seemed uncon-cerned about it. Instead, he busied his time with sticking a needle connected to a tubular hose into the Star Slinger's body. Once he pushed a button, the tube filled with blood and traveled to a large glass container.

"I didn't lure him all the way here for him to not be alive. We need him for his father."

"I understand that, Victor. There is nothing we can do at the moment, except hope he gets taken there in time."

Zigarda coughed and directed his attention to Zakk. "Why did you let him do that?"

"You were killing his troops after they already surrendered. How was I supposed to know he was going to break down and slice his own throat?" Zakk sheathed Viper and raised his other arm.

"I thought you knew him." Dr. Cere stole a glance at Zakk.

"You were killing innocent people. It goes against Gazo's code. Any leader may have broken down if they felt responsible." Zakk folded his arms.

Dr. Cere continued staring at Zakk, but now with a long, tenuous gaze through the bifocals on his face. "Codes are ideal, but they ever hardly play out in reality. You will learn that someday." He turned back to the dead body before him.

Zigarda coughed again. More violently this time. It brought him to his knees. His advisor rushed up the steps to the throne and retrieved a liquid hidden in a compartment on the armrest, and then hurried down to hand it to Zigarda. Zigarda swiped it and greedily sucked a few gulps worth of the brightest blue liquid Zakk had ever seen in his life. In moments, he returned to his normal self, shoving the clear-colored canteen into a pocket in his obsidian robe.

He pulled his hood over his face once more, as if embarrassed by his condition. "None of that matters, either of you." He scanned each of his closest confidants still in the room, ignoring the shapeshifters that still hung about the pillars. "What matters is that Zain changes his father's mind about the jewels. The Meeting of the Twelve is coming. Eska's apprentice will be leaving the Core at some point, and those jewels need to be with him when he attends."

"I have yet to see za correlation."

"You will, Edwyn. You will. Pirini Lilapa is almost upon us." Zigarda coughed. "The Twelve will tremble."

"How are ve to know that za Curse of Pirini Lilapa will affect zem?"

"It affects everyone, fool! No one is safe. And besides, *he* told me it would." Zigarda looked to Yuan and then to Edwyn. "I need to go make a call to Lord Vangle. You two come with me." Zigarda led his receiver and advisor out.

"What about us?" Hector asked.

Dr. Cere answered instead of Zigarda. "Clean yourself up, then report back here. You have communication timetables we need and all of you can call Lord Vangle together after Victor is done. It will be more convincing if there is more than one of you."

For the moment, Hector and his two friends left, leaving Zakk alone with Cere and the shifters. Cere called over one of the skinchangers. Kneeling, he emulated Cere's action, and within minutes of touching the corpse, the skin on the shapeshifter changed. Where it was loose, it tightened. Where there had been boils, puss oozed out in its white cream. The skinchanger smothered his face in the white puss. When he took his hands away, he no longer had the furunculous face given to him by birth, but the Star Slinger's cut jawline and shaved pate. His body had grown and hardened with muscle. Even as he spoke, he sounded like the Star Slinger (for the brief time Zakk had heard the man), with no need to practice the man's natural cadence or intonation. Through and through, the man had become the Star Slinger's doppelganger.

This had been the first time Zakk had seen this particular process, and he assumed it had to do with *how* he changed. The times Zakk had seen, they had drunk the blood of their future-self and the change had been much more immediate.

Dr. Cere rose, a sealed pint container of blood tucked underneath his armpit. Dr. Cere locked eyes with him. "Go to Zain, and while you're there, take this with you and have it properly stored. Report his condition to either Zigarda or myself."

Zakk took the order as an opportunity to leave. He took long strides, trying to clear the stench of death that the use of cleaning products did little to address.

Once outside the room, he advanced towards a section of the hallway with glass walls and three pods on each side. These pods made navigating the massive complexity that was the Web much easier. Inside the pod, a voice prompted him for his destination. Behind the sliding doors was a glass window and behind that, multitudes of tubes waited to carry people off to different destinations within the building at a word's notice. This was Zigarda's Web.

"The Blood Chambers." He spoke quickly, trying not to think about his destination.

"Access key, please."

Zakk swiped his keycard.

Minutes later, he reached a long hallway. Zakk trudged towards the sliding door at its end, every step bringing more goosebumps to his flesh. After pushing a button to signal his presence, he waited while two men with labsuits of black and red entered the area right in front of him and went to separate control panels on opposite sides of the room. The door slid open and Zakk stepped inside. A spray sterilized him; the temperature plummeted, coaxing more and more goosebumps to his arm. The stench of metallic rot controlled his nose. He was just outside the Blood Chambers now. From a closet on the sidewall, Zakk took a labsuit offered by one of the men. Once he put it on, the metallic rot dissipated.

Another set of doors opened, leading to a room with rows upon rows of beds, all hooked up with bags beside them, collecting blood. The survivors from before were unconscious and being tended to by more staff.

"Where is Zain Berrese?"

A man guided him to an unconscious Zain with a now-clotted dark line along his neck.

"What's his status?"

"Stable. We were able to clot his blood before anything serious happened to him."

"Will he be able to talk?"

"Unsure of that for now."

"Where are his things?"

The man looked at the notepad he held. "Follow me."

Zakk followed the man to the side of the room where his dirty clothes, sword, and a golden feather lay. The feather attracted him more than anything else. For some reason, it looked familiar. He picked it up, twirled it, and set it back down. Zakk then reached for the longsword and examined it, noting each of the gemstones.

"Quite the blade there."

Zakk snickered. "He will not be needing this anymore. I'm taking it to the armory."

"What should be done with the other items?"

"Report them to Lord Zigarda. And, while you're at, report his condition, too."

"Will do." The man nodded and left, attending to some other patients.

Zakk didn't have time to play Dr. Cere's or Zigarda's house servant. He had other things more important.

Zakk left the Blood Chambers and went back into the pod that transferred him here. He spent a minute looking at the options. His fingers brushed over *Armory* and *Blood Chambers* before choosing *Furnace*.

"Access key, please."

Zakk produced the black card and waited. While his pod slid throughout the tubes of the Web, he examined Zain's longsword. *His father must have made this for him. How lucky Zain is to have such a caring father. I didn't even know mine. He was killed before I could remember him.* Zakk spat on the ground. He twisted the pommel, hoping to break it, but couldn't. He punched the side of the pod wall. The pod stopped a few moments later.

A blast of heat stopped Zakk from exiting immediately. His skin prickled again due to the sudden change in temperature. In front of him sat a large furnace with multiple compartments. Five men dressed in light cloths walked around the furnace. When one noticed his approach, he left the others. The other four then proceeded to shovel in loads of what appeared to be red sand into the furnaces.

"What ye' want?"

"This, melted." Zakk extended Zain's sword out to him.

The man pulled on the scabbard to expose its metal skin. "Thing's a beaut'. Sure you want to melt it?"

Zakk clenched his fist. "Positive."

"The jewels won't melt like the metal will."

"What makes you say that?" Zakk looked at the sword again.

"They would have already melted when the cast was made. It seems they are intact to me. Probably some sort of heat ward on them."

Perhaps that isn't so bad. "Give me the jewels when you're done."

"Okay."

"How long will it be?"

"No more than half an hour."

"I'll wait here, then."

Zakk walked with the man to the furnace and folded his arms, surveying the man as he brought out a metal tray large enough for a human cadaver. It sloped to the right and on that side of it had a hole drilled out to catch any liquid. The man put the longsword on the tray and put it in front of the furnace bed. Another man, similar in shortness and pudginess, shoveled two scoops of red sand and placed it underneath the furnace bed. He then turned a switch and nodded to the other to put the tray into the furnace.

The longsword slid in.

Zakk watched. His hand slid over his own sword's hilt, protecting it. Since Zain's betrayal, it had been the only thing with him through it all.

Embers danced about the blade.

The metal melted.

Zakk smirked.

CHAPTER 16

DEPARTURE

B risine woke to a red morning and the cry of seagulls. Throwing on a silk robe of brown, threaded in silver and gold, she then walked past the transparent curtain that blocked the veranda. The stone railing overlooked a vacant courtyard not yet filled with the sleepy castle inhabitants. Out over the walls was the great grayness of the Krine Sea. Death hung on the morning. The red told her so. When she was younger and growing up in the castle, a wet nurse told her that a red morning was a dead morning.

A knock rapped against the door.

Who could that be? She turned from her balcony and shuffled to her door. Outside, a maid ten years younger than Brisine with brown locks, a petite jaw, and the beady eyes of a bug raised her arm, ready to knock again.

"Lady Berrese." She put her arm down. "The Lord's Council has assembled. They send for you as well."

Word of my son and husband? "Thank you for the words." Brisine hurried out the door.

To enter the telecommunication chamber, she placed her hand on a scanner, identifying herself. Glass doors slid open, revealing computers and servers lined against the wall, and at the far end, an oval mirror. The mirror held the technology to contact people on different planets and arrange with them a face-to-face conversation. A long glass table, shaped to the likeness of their planet of Myoli, sat in the middle of the chamber. Generals would gather around it to discuss battle tactics when war occurred. No one stood there now; instead, they all gathered around the oval mirror.

Brisine saw see the falcon eye tattoo on the neck of her brother's receiver, Owlan Mansen, and the fine garnet robe of her brother's advisor, Errion Vesk.

Both of her brothers stood in the center, one as general and the other as lord. The sound of her sandals slapping her soles gave her away, and all turned to smile at her before looking back towards the screen.

Still not hearing any sound, she closed the distance. "Why is it blank?"

"They have already gone to the meeting. We wait to hear back from them," Abraham spoke.

"Why wasn't I notified of this!?"

"You were, sister. The conversation was short, and you did not make it here in time."

Her older brother Lukas spoke for everyone then in a deep voice, hard and confident. A hint of jealousy for Abraham lingered there. Not in the words, but in the way he stole a glance at Abraham before turning his attention to Brisine. She had seen his furtive glance, and some nights, even now, she grieved for him. A part of her thought Power shouldn't matter so much. It seemed her none of her sons had Power, after all.

Brisine bit her lip.

Errion moved back from the crowd to Brisine. "Do not worry, Lady Berrese. They were sent as envoys. By the good word of the Ancients, 'no messenger treating shall come to harm; to this the slayer shall be forewarned.' Zigarda wouldn't be foolish enough to kill any of our men. Ancients know only how he has lived so long; he wouldn't want to defile them now."

Brisine tried a smile. It didn't feel right. She rubbed her arms and looked at the floor. A constant beeping stole her attention: Victor Zigarda. Brisine held her breath until the face of an old, marred man with lidless eyes came on the screen.

"To what do we owe the pleasure of your call, Lord Zigarda?" Abraham asked.

"And what do I owe for the pleasure of a crowd?"

Behind Zigarda stood his advisor and receiver. *Neither is my son. Where is he?* She yanked on Abraham's sleeve.

"Where is my nephew?"

"Zain has decided to stay in my company. He and his father are busy catching up. I know you understand."

"Where is Gerald, then? Let us speak with him," Lukas demanded.

"I am not sure where that one has disappeared off to. Probably with the others, preparing for departure."

"Departure?" Errion questioned.

"Why, it makes no sense for all twenty of your soldiers to stay here and take care of Zain. He is under my care. And besides, you might need them."

What care is that? I want my son and my husband, you senile, Emporian fool.

"Now, is there anything else?" The room remained silent. "In that case..."

"Wait!" Zigarda's hand stopped in midair. He brought it back and coughed into it. In the telecommunication room, all looked at her. Brisine gulped. "A skinchanger came to my house to retrieve my husband's locked things."

"Yes, your son was quite adamant about this skinchanger as well... I already told you I had no affair in the stealing of your husband's documents and, for skinchangers, well, I have no need for ancient lore such as that." Zigarda cackled.

"But the man—"

"Shifters have been dead since the Conquest. You are seeing things."

"But have you seen anything?"

"I wouldn't be able to tell if I had. Good day, Lord Vangle, Lady Berrese, the others."

The connection cut. Brisine's heart sank. *Zain is over there. He is getting to see my Laron, not me.*

"I find that whole discussion rather disquieting," Errion said. "What did Zigarda mean when he said, 'you might need them'? Is he planning another attack?"

Brisine hadn't even noticed that subtlety.

For five minutes, everyone pondered the possibility. Then the screen buzzed and *Gerald Starshine* flashed on the screen.

"Connect!"

"It is going as fast as it can, Brisine. You are not the only one who wants to know exactly what's happened," Abraham said.

Gerald stood center on the screen. Behind him were three other men; men that Brisine had recognized as some of the other troops. All stood in front of a metal building. Light red fog hung in the air.

"Gerald, what is happening over there?" Lukas stepped forward.

"Zain met his father. He wants to stay here until they both can go back."

"You can't stay there any longer. Bring them home immediately." Abraham crossed his arms.

"I don't like it any more than you do, my lord. I still don't trust Zigarda. That's why we're outside. I'll be staying here too, along with some of the others. It'll be safer that way. Hector and Sheamus performed well. They really proved themselves here. Both will sail back with a few of the others will sail back a few days from now. Hector will be in charge of contacting you as they return home."

Abraham spared a glance at Lukas, then returned his gaze to the screen. "That's good to hear." Abraham nodded. "Keep me abreast of your situation. Every day I want a report. Hector, do you understand?"

"Aye, my Lord. That may be hard to do. I do not trust the others around this place. I stay for Zain, though."

"I agree with the Star Slinger. I can contact you, but it will just be more of the same. We will be on sea for a month given the winds."

Abraham clicked his tongue. "Fair enough. Report to me if you have something to report, Hector. Gerald, report to me when you can get away."

Gerald nodded, as did Hector and the others with him.

"Why don't you just bring him home?" Brisine asked.

"He's stubborn, my lady. He hasn't seen his father in months; he doesn't want to spend more time without him."

Finally, Brisine let a smile escape her lips. *He is stubborn. I would want the same thing.* "Will you bring him back safely?"

"He will come back. I promise you. Even if I don't, I will make sure he does."

As her brother caught up with Gerald, a peculiarity still gnawed at her. She was sure she hadn't seen things when that man appeared to be Zain. If Zigarda hadn't sent him, who had? Who else was her husband doing work with? Had he not been telling her everything?

"That is all, then. I will contact you when I can get away." Gerald faded away. His eyes were a foggy steel, a shade darker than the dark blue she remembered.

She put a rest to her anxiety and forced herself to think happier thoughts. *At least Gerald's there. As long as the stars shine, they'll be safe. I know it.*

CHAPTER 17

TRAPPED

Z ain woke to a place he didn't recognize. In clothes that weren't his own. And to a voice he didn't come to expect.

"Wh... whe..." Zain gave up. He couldn't speak. A sharp pain stung his throat. He felt the wound over it. Now he knew how his mother must have felt after her attack.

Images flashed before him. Gerald dying. His men being circled. The rivers of blood from the slaughter. The thuds as they collapsed. Zakk's hot breath.

Zain lurched on his side in agony. He cried for his fallen brethren. He had tried commanding. He did. But he had failed. Again.

"Zain, why are you here?"

In his cell to his left, a man with the same smoky, onyx skin as him sat. Bushy eyebrows, and glasses that clung to a fat nose, protected brown, tourmaline eyes. A beard much too long hung from his chin. *Dad?*

Zain jolted to all fours. He looked around the surrounding area, dipped in the red glow of lowlights on the wall. Caged in some sort of holding cell, he looked to his right and saw another man in a similar cell. The man to his right had short black hair and gruff around the sides of his face. A scar traced down his forearm, stopping before large hands like those of a mechanic.

"Zain, why are you here?"

Zain turned back to his father. "See..." Zain swallowed the pain that came with speaking. Zain crawled near the bars and showed his neck.

"What happened?"

Mom, Zain mouthed.

"Brisine is dead!"

Zain shook his head. "Safe..." The word came out, but it caused much irritation to his throat.

He slid his hands around his father's. His were rough hands. Hands of a jeweler. Zain pressed his face awkwardly against the bars and stretched his arms through the gap in between bars, trying to hug his father.

"Who did you come here with?" His father massaged his son's back and kept his son close.

Blood splatter. Heavy thuds. Slaughter. Complete and utter slaughter. Zakk's hot breath.

I failed.

Zain pulled back from his father's grasp and shook his head. He sniffled and took his palm to his eye, damming his tears.

"Who's—"

"Quit your damn talking. A kid gets zrown here for one damn hour and you're already annoying za piss out of me."

Zain turned around to the man, who interrupted him. He gripped the cell and looked at Zain and his father through oddly familiar blue eyes. A rough face did the man ill justice, for, in normal conditions, he would have been somewhat handsome. Down here, in the red glow, Zain only saw him for his hard features.

"You don't talk to my son that way!"

"Son. Humph." The man spat. "At least your child didn't put you in here."

Zain's eyes widened. The eyes. The hair color. It gave him away. He needed to know for sure, so he crawled closer. The man didn't cower.

"Gab... Gab... re... elle." Zain cleared his throat as well as he could.

The man stared back at him. In that stare, Zain knew. Gabrielle held the same look when she evaluated the other contestants during the Trials.

"What is it to you?"

Before Zain could control himself, he leaned over and punched the man in the jaw, knocking him to the jail floor.

Electricity swept through Zain's body. His father shouted. He shook, then collapsed to the floor. Eyelids barely open. Vision blurry. His father writhed on the floor as well. *What?*

"Knock it off over there."

The guard had stood up. Now near a wall, the guard looked in their direction. *Are these shock bars?* Zain still felt the electricity tingle and crawl up his arms. He grunted and clenched his hands together.

"Zain... Zain... Zain. You never cease to surprise me."

Zakk? Zain's pain subsided, overtaken by the appearance of his old friend who stood next to the guard. Was he a friend anymore? Zain didn't know what to call him. Ghost, perhaps?

"That stunt you pulled nearly killed you."

Grunting, Zain got to all fours. He resisted the urge to feel his neck again. That would only bring back images better left forgotten. Instead, he crawled to the front of the cell to get a better look at Zakk. He noticed a slight scar on Zakk's cheek.

"Wa... why..." Zain dragged a finger along his cheek.

Zakk inflated his chest and crossed his arms over. One hand held a brown sack and hung from his left side. With the other hand, he traced the scar. "You come to ask me about this? Nothing else?"

Zain shook his head. "Hurt..." He struggled.

"It's nothing compared to what you did to me."

Zain grabbed the bars, looking into Zakk's eyes. "Wah... why... why—"

Zakk walked forward and crouched to be eye level with Zain. "Why am I here?"

Zain nodded.

Zakk glanced behind him at the other guard. "Barst."

Electricity. Shock. Pain. He released his grip and fell to the ground, twitching and kicking.

"How dare you ask me why I am here? You should know that better than most. After you tried to kill me, I lost everything."

Despite the previous shock, Zain crawled closer to Zakk. He needed him to see his determination.

"I didn't just lose you and your family, I lost Gazo's and my brotherhood there when you let me go. When you let me go..."

It was quick. Too quick from what Zain remembered of Zakk's skill, but before he knew it, Zakk held a knife to his throat. Again. And again, Zain wouldn't cower. What could Zakk do that he hadn't already tried to do himself?

The knife poked Zain's skin just enough to push the flesh down, but not enough to pierce. With sick fixation, Zakk rotated his wrist as if to open a locked door. After minutes, his gaze shot from the steel to Zain's eyes. "When you let me go, Zain, I lost everything I ever had." After an exhale of breath, Zakk pulled back the knife.

"You could have gone back to Brisine."

Zakk turned to Zain's father. "No. You're wrong. Zain took what trust I had. I couldn't go back to the family that raised him. That family was dead to me." Zakk stood. "Barst, open the cellar." Moments later, Zakk entered. He carried a brown sack of some weight in his hand. "I lost something valuable to me that day, Zain. And I want you to know how it feels."

Zain's face sunk in confusion.

Zakk let the sack drop before Zain's kneeled position. A jewel tumbled from the bag and rolled on the ground. Zain's eyes widened. He peeled back the rest of it to see three more jewels. He recognized each cut and color.

Gift. Zain looked at Zakk. His face gave nothing away. "Mel... mel... te..." He couldn't complete the word. The act itself defied comprehension. *My sword.*

Footsteps shuffled.

A creak.

"You're coming with me now." Zakk grabbed his father and forced him to his feet. "It's time to finish that project."

"I won't." Zain's father struggled.

"If you want to keep your son alive, you will. Barst." After relocking Zain's door, the other guard came over to the cell and grabbed Zain's father on the left side. "You're to help me bring this one to Dr. Cere." Once both grabbed him, his father couldn't struggle.

His father looked at him. "Zain, I love you."

"There's no such thing as love." The man behind Zain spat.

Choler controlled Zakk's eyes. "No." Zakk clicked his tongue. "There isn't." He motioned to the other guard, and they dragged their prisoner away.

Zain wanted to call out to his father but his voice was too sore from trying to speak earlier. He reached out his hand but no one ever took it.

A door closed, leaving nothing.

Zain slouched and looked at the jewels by his knees, bloody in the red light. One by one, he felt them in his hand, ignoring everything else. He tried to find his reflection in them but couldn't, almost as if a part of him was lost. He tried to form some sort of meaning in them—in everything that had happened. And as he thought about everything, his mind kept returning to a singular thought:

He shouldn't have said no.

He shouldn't have said no.

He shouldn't have said no.

PART 11: PRINCE HYDRO PAEN

RECAP:

Prince Hydro Paen received an invitation to participate in Guardian Eska's Trials and was sent off in front of not only his family, but all of the other nobles of Acquava. Also, Pearl, a goddess and one of the Twelve, wished to see him off and bless him before he began the Trials. In the beginning, it seemed that everything was going well; he managed to win the first trial and while in the trial, found a mysterious necklace that allowed him to use Power when the natural source wasn't present—Power could be cast whenever. The necklace continually jeered him to put it on, but Hydro remained steadfast in his own ability, not the necklace's, and refused it until the last trial, when he wore it and managed to make it to the top of Vatu Volcano. To his distaste Eirek Mourse, the Commoner, made it there as well, and the Trials were once again tied. After failing to solve a riddle, Hydro lost his chance to become apprentice. Not wanting to stay and witness his enemy gloat, he told his father's advisor, Len, to pick him up immediately. Little did Len know they would not be headed home.

Now, Hydro leads them both deep within the nation of Chaon, trying to track down a man as elusive as the answers he wants to obtain...

CHAPTER 18

MOUNT KLAFF

"**W**here to now, my prince?"

Hydro tsked. Before him lay an expansive plain with grass as tall as his hip. The further downhill he looked, the less the grass grew until eventually nothing but barren rock and earth coated the ground. A small group of people gathered at the center of the depression. Hydro assumed most were tourists looking at the famous Mount Klaff while it basked in moonlight. Even in the grave of night, Hydro chuckled at how such a sight could attract so many tourists.

As thick as ten sequoia trees, Mount Klaff shot straight up, defying a natural mountain form. It also defied traditional mountain color, taking on the bluish appearance of crystal. He heard that on a cloudless day you could see where the mountain spread like a bowl, as if its base held a large globe. What lay past that? Only the man noted for climbing higher than anyone had before or since could answer that question. But Guardian Eska was on the Core right now, a place that Hydro should be, not Eirek Mourse. His skill was lacking. For all Hydro knew, the man couldn't cast Power. And he held no significance with his name. The only thing he deserved was the title Hydro gave him during the Trials, that of the Commoner. He should never have received apprenticeship. Never.

He would have reflected more on his current predicament, but a drop of rain hit his nose. Then another. And another. Soon, a slight drizzle settled in with the warm night. It reminded him of Acquava. But this was Chaon, not Acquava. He couldn't go back there—losing the Trials made sure of that.

"My prince?"

Hydro spun around to see the two golden front teeth of his father's one-eyed advisor, Len Posair. He was a man older than his father and who wore an eye patch over his bad eye. White whiskers grew around his face, but to Len's credit, he kept them short and at a respectable length. Jewels adorned his fingers, representing the number of languages he spoke fluently. "We head for the nearest inn. It'll rain soon enough. Bring the bags."

"Yes, of course."

Hydro did not wait for Len to grab his things. Instead, he left the proximity of their ship and headed towards a small town road marked by a wooden post—*Proschi.*

For a small town, it had a number of shops and inns, but hardly any homes. Hydro wondered about that. With roads ugly and ungroomed, Hydro took care with every step. As he passed by the villagers, he noticed their copper skin and some even had metallic jewelry hanging from some part of their face. He felt out of place here. *Where is Len?*

Hydro looked back and saw the man at the base of the hill entering town. While Len caught up, Hydro went inside a tourist shop full of families rummaging through trinkets. A wine glass shaped like Mount Klaff caught his eye. A clank of footsteps and heart breathing alerted Hydro of Len's presence.

"Len, how much coin did you bring?"

"A little over 100 bonds."

Hydro picked up the glass and looked it over. "Get me this glass."

Len cleared his throat. "The glass, my prince?"

"Yes, it is not every day I am near Mount Klaff. And if we ever go home to Acquava, I would like to give my brother some sort of trinket." He pushed it into Len's hands.

"So, we are going home?"

Hydro shifted his gaze to Len. "Not yet. Not for a while."

"Your parents will start to suspect something after Coronation."

Hydro clenched his fists. *A Coronation that should be mine.* The smile on the Commoner's face came back to him soon enough. Along with the answer to the tie-breaking riddle—*equals.* Hydro spat. *He will never be my equal.*

"Well, then, we better move. Now, get that glass."

Hydro crossed his arms over his chest. Len made a valid point. This trip wouldn't last, Hydro knew that. His parents weren't stupid. Answers were his goal, however, and he would get those one way or another before he left. He tapped his feet.

Oh, how furious mother and father will be when they hear that a commoner, a low-life named Eirek Mourse, bested their Blessed son. A rather large spider crawling on the wooden porch caught his eye. He squashed it.

"Here is your glass, my prince."

Hydro snatched it. Looking at it made him forget his anger. *Aiton may never make it here, or to the top of Mount Klaff, but at least he will have something to cherish.*

"What now, my prince?"

Hydro tsked. "Well, where is an inn? I am tired."

Len surveyed the area. Across the street Len stopped in front of a sign—*Klaff's Keep*. "This should do. I admit it has been years since I have used my Chaonese. I am glad these signs are translated."

Hydro walked through the doors, ignoring his advisor's statement. Instantly a person with narrow, soft shoulders greeted him. Combed and wavy, raven-like hair hung just below his ears. Piercings on the lips and eyebrows did little to draw attention from narrowed eyes or the unusually strong jawline and cheeks given the short stature of his body.

"May I help you?"

What Hydro had assumed was a male was, in fact, a female. The inflection gave it away. Hydro averted her gaze.

"We are looking for rooms," Len said.

"Together? Or separate?"

"Together," Hydro said. "And a large room at that, a suite."

"Three bonds per night, then."

Hydro choked at the price. "Are you—"

Len interrupted him using a tongue Hydro wasn't familiar with. Hydro stood there as the woman and Len talked in Chaon. At the end of it all, Len dug out two golden bonds and laid it on the table in exchange for a key.

"Follow me."

Hydro glared at the wench, but followed Len up the stairs nonetheless. "Three bonds! We are not even near the capital yet. I hope the rooms are of good quality and the food even better."

"This town has to abide by its governing marquis, Xan Zayno of Qotia. Taxes are greater here because most of the money received from tourists visiting Mount Klaff goes to Qotia to fund their adored academy. I spoke their tongue, which is why we received even that small discount."

"Does Father impose those high of taxes on major cities like Symeria or Sepul?"

"If you spent more time listening during council meetings, you would know." Len frowned at him. "Your father charges tax, yes, but not nearly as great. Most of those taxes funded the creation of the waterroads so that all the islands of Acquava can be connected."

Those meetings were exactly the reason why Hydro had needed to win the Trials. He didn't want to return to duty. To normality. He needed more.

Hydro walked outside to the veranda. Gripping the railing, he looked out to Mount Klaff in the distance, basking in the light of the two moons near the ring that encompassed the planet. "Why is it that people flock here?"

Ask yourself that question. What do you find?

"Hope. Answers," Hydro said to the wind and no one else, not wanting to acknowledge the other voice that clawed for his attention from time to time.

Hydro turned back. Inside, Len was setting his bag on the ground near the foot of the bed closest to the window. Once finished, he joined Hydro outside. "Why are we here, my prince? Why not we just return to Acquava?"

Hydro shifted uncomfortably. "I have yet to figure that out myself, Len. Get some sleep. We are going into Qotia tomorrow."

With nothing more than a sigh, Len walked to his section of the room.

For fear of Len seeing the necklace which he had received during the first trial, Hydro kept the same clothes on.

In the moments before he lost himself to exhaustion, he touched the necklace through his shirt, feeling the black dragon scales that comprised it. He traced it down to the three golden triangles that sat on the middle of his chest. It brought back to him the Power Hydro felt during the fourth trial. An unfathomable Power. One that Hydro would learn to control, or lose himself trying.

A girl stands next to the bed. She's young, no older than nine, but her eyes are black and lost. Her white gown compliments the moonlight and gives her an aura, as if she is the one he is meant to find...

"How did you get in here?"

On the other side of the room, Len is asleep. The girl blocks the view, alienating him. She laughs and dashes out of the room to the veranda. Len is no longer present. Outside, the wood from the veranda is cold, but the air is surprisingly warm. The little girl is on the road. How did she get down there? *he wonders.*

"Are you coming?" she calls.

The wood beneath him dissolves into a ground of green and brown. The posts that were there previously expand into large trees. Canopy blocks the stars. The little girl stands in the middle of an alcove. No one else is around. Yet, something is watching. Hydro is sure of it.

The place looks familiar. Cold steel is at his side.

"Are you coming?"

"Where are we going?" Ankle-high grass gets crushed. She moves fast for a child of no more than nine—his brother's age.

"My father. He's lost. Only she knows how to find him."

"Who is she? How can she find him?"

"She has three eyes, that's why. Her third eye sees everything."

He trips. Hard dirt greets him. A root that wasn't there previously is caught around his foot. A hand enters his view. It's hers. He takes it and gets to his feet.

"Who are you?"

The girl smiles. Two of her teeth slide over her lips, sharp as fangs. A split tongue slides out between them. Her black face transforms into that of a black snake. Her body stretches and grows wings and scaly arms. She twirls around Hydro, hissing. Sweat populates his face as he struggles for composure.

Soon enough the snake's eyes glare into his. They are the same soulless eyes that the girl had. The same eyes he had seen in dreams previous. The same eyes as the monster, Beno Begare, who had guarded the necklace. His advice comes back... Beware of the girl with black hair. *The mouth opens and inside was the girl's face. She was sad and crying. And then...*

Hydro opened his eyes and felt his sporadic heartbeat.

Outside, dawn began to crack night's armor. Hydro removed himself from the room. To his left, Mount Klaff's grayish glow looked sleek and alluring. To his right, a road traveled into the major city of Qotia. According to Len's knowledge, an adored academy was located there. Surely someone educated could tell him of his necklace. Even if not, Len held decent knowledge. He could prove a useful beginning.

Hydro slammed his fist against the railing. Every time he had the dream, he woke up feeling a little less like himself. But this dream was different; the girl was trying to tell him something. What was it? He touched the necklace; it felt warm. He tugged at it, trying to dig his nails underneath where the necklace had bitten down on him, but it wouldn't budge. A tear came to his eye. Hydro squashed it.

CHAPTER 19

MOTIVES

Hydro didn't bother going back to sleep. Instead, he took the moments before Len woke to change clothes into a finespun, buttoned-down silk shirt of dark purple with ebony buttons. After changing, Hydro shoved Len to life. He didn't want to waste a drop of day. "We go to Qotia."

Len yawned. "Under what interest?"

"Mine. This town is dead for knowledge. I do not want to rot here with it."

"And how do you suppose we get to Qotia?" Len tore off his covers and stretched.

"That is your task."

"A pleasure," Len drawled.

"Good," Hydro played along. "Get dressed. I will be downstairs. For two bonds a night this place better offer something for breakfast."

Downstairs, Hydro found a lighter-skinned couple with narrow eyes dressed in clothes of ornate designs. One black and one brown squirrel crawled on their shoulders. *Are they bonded? Who would want to bond with such a weak animal?* On their table were plates of strawberries, grapes of purple, green, and even white, and a bowl of soupy grain with a splash of cinnamon. Hydro followed the cinnamon scent to a long table in the almost-empty dining hall.

He filled his plate and sat alone, occasionally glancing from the window to the couple. The female had rosy cheeks the color of apples, with lipstick as red as her fingernails. Hydro couldn't understand what they were saying, although they spoke loudly enough. *Where is Len?*

He ate alone for a few more minutes until Len arrived, donned in a blue robe with purple stripes. He exchanged a few words with the woman who had checked them in and walked over to Hydro.

"What did you talk about?" Hydro examined one of the white grapes before plopping it into his mouth.

"I asked if she knew of a way to get to Qotia. She said I must have the luck of the Twelve with me because the couple is leaving for there today. They came to deliver food to the outpost here."

"You mean to hitch a ride?" Hydro raised an eyebrow.

"Yes, we do not have much of a choice. We do not have a Chaon license for the ship I brought."

"And why is that? I prefer not be seen as a beggar."

"Because *that* ship is your father's, and in Acquava. We are not in Acquava, young prince. Do best to mind your manners; different nations have different customs and rules."

Hydro clicked his tongue and folded his arms. Len turned and caught the couple just as they were leaving. He shook both of their hands and then bowed his right arm and crossed it over the left of his body. He smiled, pointing back in Hydro's direction, before continuing conversation.

Once they left, Len came back. "They have agreed to take us to Qotia."

"What did you say to them?"

"That we are tourists without a license and wish to see the adored academy there."

"And they bought such a story."

"For four silver spell and six copper cures they did."

Hydro laughed and ate more of his porridge. "Why must everyone ask the rich for money?"

"If they knew we were rich, they would have asked for more. They seem like a nice enough couple, though."

"Sure." Hydro stirred his soupy porridge. "When do they leave?"

"An hour. It gives me enough time to eat." Len maneuvered past Hydro and filled his plate with food.

An hour later, Hydro and Len met the couple outside of the inn. Under Len's advice they sat in the empty hull of the two-seater caracraft full of nothing but the scent of snails, slugs and leeches. Hydro feigned contentment. *If these people are to take us to Qotia, then so be it. There I will get my answers.*

Hydro tapped his feet. "So how long of a trip is it?"

"The couple told me that we will arrive in the city by tomorrow morning at the earliest."

"And at the latest?" Hydro crossed his arms.

"Well, midday tomorrow. The couple will probably not want to drive through the night."

Hydro rolled his eyes and looked away.

"Well, can you blame them? Some rest will do you good as well."

Hydro pushed his lips to one side. "Fair enough, I suppose."

"As a safety precaution, I told them our names were Loo," Len pointed to himself, "and Hymin." He pointed to Hydro. "The name Aylán used to call you."

Hydro didn't know much about his grandfather but he remembered that. His father had pronounced it without the *i*, like *Hymn* because he always had told Hydro that he would make a fine song someday. The name brought Hydro back to thinking of Acquava and giving up his quest. Almost.

Wanting to appear dissatisfied, Hydro rolled his eyes. "Touristy enough names and close enough to our own."

"What will we do once we arrive?" Len folded his hands together.

"I will know once I get there." Hydro hoped to push the conversation off further. In truth, he didn't have a plan; he wished something in his dream would direct him, but there was nothing.

"What are you so afraid of back home?"

Father's disappointment. Mother's scorn. My boring life as a prince. All of these things Hydro thought to say but instead said, "I fear nothing. Can a prince not take a trip when he pleases?"

"Yes, he can. It seems to me, though, you are running from your loss."

Hydro curled his upper lip. "What do you know?"

"I know that you would not have contacted me in the grave of night if things would have gone differently."

"Well, they did not go as planned."

"That does not mean you cannot return home."

"Yes, it does. I lost to a commoner."

"And not everyone can win, young prince."

"But a prince I am!" Hydro pointed at himself and stomped his foot. He exhaled. "A prince I am."

"Do you think you brought shame to the family?"

"What do you know about shame?"

"I know that you may feel it right now, but you shouldn't. Your father is a lord, but he is a father first and foremost. He is more concerned with your whereabouts and your safety than some position."

Hydro wanted to open to the man who served his father for more years than Hydro had been alive. To the man who even knew Hydro's grandfather before mindloss changed him. At the peak of his breath, he wanted to tell, but he needed to press on, for all the reasons he held before, even if it merely meant escaping his life as a prince.

Hydro regained composure. "You talked with Father?"

"No. I was merely saying. You realize that in four days, Coronation takes place. Your father will start to wonder where I have taken off to and wonder why you have not returned."

"Where does Father think you have taken off to?"

"To Pers to help with a hurricane that hit recently. I said I would take a transport to Perét and a ship from there to the island. A two-week trip through and through, but your father expects me to check in with him once I reach Marquis Blocter. And he expects you sooner."

"Yes. Which reminds me. Turn off your telecommunicator. I do not wish to be found until I am ready." Hydro glared at Len until he turned off his device. Confusion and frustration buried in Len's countenance.

"That will not make much difference. You still share your father's blood; he can track your presence."

"He can. But over the span of space and across planets the signal is to be weak at best." A moment passed. Silence at its finest. Hydro studied Len. As nonchalantly as he could, given the matter at hand, Hydro said, "Tell me, what do you know of ancient lore and tradition?"

"The subject of ancient lore is rather broad, but if you are talking about Chaon, I could tell you about the Conquest and the shifters or the birth of Mount Klaff."

Boring subjects. Although it intrigued him as to how a mountain such as Klaff was formed; that was a story for another day. He needed information on a different topic. "Tell me what you know of Zas Banegul." Hydro studied Len's lackluster visage. *Is he hiding face?*

"Zas Banegul, eh? That is a name not brought up often. It is said he created a necklace, dipped it in the blood of the black dragon, Desmós, and coated it with a few of its scales."

Yes, and I am wearing it right now. Tell me more, and something I haven't read already.

"He was the right hand to Ancient Bane and Bane's first creation. Dismissed from the Holy Lands of Gladima by Ancient Lyoen. Cause of the Great War. An ill-guided fate, that one."

Yes, I know all of that too. Something exciting, perhaps? "Where do you figure he is now?" Hydro looked away, seeming disinterested.

"What makes you think he is still alive?"

"Well, you said he was dismissed before the Great War. He has First Blood if he was born on Gladima. I do not see how he cannot be."

"Well, some stories say he died of grief, same as his wife. Others report that his encounter with Desmós sapped him of his mind. If he is alive, he probably has a serious case of mindloss, much more than your grandfather's."

"Why was his wife sad? At his dismissal or what he became? At the war?"

"At Ancient Lyoen for sealing her daughter and her soul in the necklace he created." Len paused a moment to readjust his posture and then continued. "But other stories say he lies somewhere on Chaon, and others say he dwells in the mountains near Mount Volan, and yet others say on one of the floating isles in Mistral."

Silence passed slowly. *Is she the girl I was warned about? The one who appears in my dreams?*

"Tell me, what has taken your interest in Zas Banegul?" Len thrummed the thin goatee, exposing two of his rings—one of topaz and one of ruby.

"Luvan Katore had us run through the Zas Labyrinth as the first of the four trials. I managed to win that one. That is why I ask."

"I hear ill things about that labyrinth."

"I suppose that is why it was chosen as a trial."

"I suppose you are right there." Len crossed his legs.

Hydro bit his lip, deciding how to phrase the next question. Finding no way to ask subtly, he asked, "How would I find him?"

Len chortled, long and deep. "You have better luck at sighting the Four Creatures of Legend than finding him."

"Is that amusing?"

"Rather. Is that why we are here, to find Zas Banegul? Tell me true, what do you hope to gain from a meeting with him?"

Hydro couldn't tell true. But he needed to tell something. Len's behavior annoyed him, but he still had information Hydro needed. "Gains that are my own. You will do as I say."

"Dear boy, we are not in Acquava anymore. You have told us to turn off our telecommunicators. It is clear you will not tell your father anything here. Until I know what business you have with Zas Banegul, I will not follow into this folly."

Damn him to Abaddon. Acquava's seas drown him, too. Red with fury, Hydro knew what he needed to do. He stood and unbuttoned his purple shirt, keeping his eyes on Len all the while. "I did not come out of the labyrinth with only a win." Hydro spread open the lapels of his shirt, exposing Len to the obsidian, dragon-scaled necklace underneath. Tightly pressed to the center of his chest was the necklace's pendant, three inverted golden pyramids.

"Is that..." Len never finished his thought.

"It is."

"I thought it was lost."

"It is found again, and I need to learn how to control it." Hydro left out the dreams. Len would have just responded with the old proverb anyway... *Once a dream, queer it may seem. Twice the same, consider it strange. Dream it three, a premonition it be. Dream it four, and you are dreaming no more.*

"Well, it is said that those of First Blood all have a common bond with each other, just as you and your father have a common bond. It is in their blood to be able to sense one another, but they can also block one another. They also share a bond with Gladima. When someone of First Blood dies, everyone with similar blood feels it and the stronger the bloodline, the more reaction it causes."

"So, to find him I will need to find someone with First Blood?"

"Yes, the Twelve would know."

Hydro ran through the list of the Twelve in his mind. He needed to remember which god or goddess made Chaon their home. His schooling at Finesse in Acquava had required him to learn many things—one of those things being the Twelve. After a little while, Hydro asked, "So, if we find Saeluste, we can find Zas?"

"Yes, most likely she would know. In fact, the adored at Qotia may be able to point us in her direction."

Hydro sat up straight. "It seems the Twelve wish us luck."

Hydro followed Len's logic. As a goddess from the Heavol tribe, she most closely associated with Ancient Lyoen, who was the founder of the adored. Qotia boasted one of the best adored academies in the system. As the goddess for mental health and intelligence, he was positive that men and women studying various potions on vitality, counting the elements, or simply acquiring their chains would know. Why places like these existed to find solutions to ailments like mindloss. Surely, they would know where she dwelled.

Len put up his finger. "While normally this would be good, I am unsure how likely it is to see her."

"What do you mean? I am a prince; she will treat with me."

While massaging his forehead, Len shook his head. "Like I mentioned before, my prince, we are not in Acquava any longer. Saeluste is not as inclined to treat with you as Pearl may be. But, that is not the issue I worry about."

Hydro harrumphed. "Then, what is it?"

"The Meeting of the Twelve fast approaches. I am unsure when the Twelve begin traveling to Mount Volan to meet with Guardian Eska and now this new apprentice of his."

A meeting I should be at. Hydro slumped in his seat. He needed to change the subject. "Is there anyone else who would know?"

"Well, rumors speak of offspring of those with First Blood. Well, Ancient Blood and First Blood to be precise. None more famous than the idea that the children of the Ancients, Galan and Naydeia, birthed a family. I do not know how you would go about finding either of them, however." Len folded an arm and cupped his chin. "That is why it's better if we abandon such a quest."

We can't. "We will press on. For the sake of Acquava."

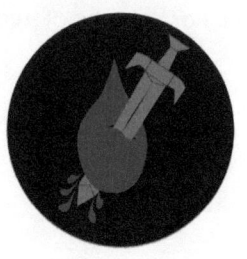

CHAPTER 20

TEACHINGS

"Where is he?"

"You expect me to know?"

"Coronation is tomorrow. He is expected to be there beside Aiton and us. How could he lose?"

"Something I wish to know as well. Mourse is no name of royalty."

Aiton could hear his parents bicker in the hallway. He had left his door slightly ajar after granted a short break by Professor Haruko. The noise beat the silence that usually roamed the halls. Aiton missed the thump of his brother's soles and the tune of his voice.

"Perhaps he is waiting for us there?"

"And if he is not?" his mother asked.

"Let us pray he is..."

The bickering from his parents faded into nothingness, and once again, maps and nations and provinces replaced the brief reprieve. Professor Haruko sat on the other side of the desk. Old and doggish, his face drooped around faint white whiskers. Eyes gray as granite fixated on him, giving no sign of acknowledging the dispute that just occurred.

Professor Haruko pointed to one of the four maps on the table with his meter-long ruler. "What nations make up Agrost, Aiton?"

"Cresica... Epoch..." Aiton paused. He knew the last nation, but learning this wasn't what he wanted. "Where is Hydro?" Aiton dropped his pen and put his hands underneath his thighs. His feet still didn't touch the ground when he sat in grownup chairs.

"Not here. Back to your studies," Professor Haruko insisted.

"Why do my parents fight?"

"They are worried about their son's education. Now, the last one?"

"I don't want to learn. I want my brother. I want Mother and Father to stop fighting."

"*Do not* want to learn," Haruko corrected.

Aiton looked away. *No one ever understands me.* An irritation underneath Aiton's chin caused him to look back.

Professor Haruko held the ruler underneath Aiton's chin. "Hydro is not here right now. But your studies are. Let us continue, okay?"

"But I do not want to. I still hear them even now."

The voices weren't nearly as loud, but Aiton could still hear. The fighting frightened him. *Why can't we just be whole again?* Aiton crossed his arms and leaned back into his chair.

"You have remarkable hearing for one so young. I hear nothing. Perhaps it is my age..." Professor Haruko laid his ruler down and stood. He turned his back towards Aiton and stared out a window overlooking the hedged labyrinth.

Aiton stared at the maps blankly. For the past few days his parent's bickering caused too much distraction for his studies. If they were trying to keep Hydro's absence hidden, they were doing an awful job.

"I know it is hard." Professor Haruko turned around and stared at Aiton. "Should we conclude our session for the day?"

Aiton gazed from his maps to his teacher's eyes. "Why do people fight?"

"People fight because they are confused."

"Confused?"

"Of what they want." Haruko took a breath and reclaimed his seat in front of Aiton. "Some fight for power. Some for love. And some for pride and honor."

"Why are Mother and Father fighting?"

"For love..."

"Love should go away."

"You do not mean that." Aiton was forced to keep his professor's gaze, chin held up by the ruler once again. "If love went away, only pain would take its place."

"At least there wouldn't be fighting."

"No, there *would not* be fighting. There would be chaos..."

A silence settled. Aiton pushed the ruler away from his chin and returned his gaze to the maps. He tried to decode his professor's words. Something lingered in his voice, some sort of knowing only gained from age. Aiton wished he wasn't so young. He wished to be old and powerful and clever like his brother and father.

"Aiton..."

"Yes?"

"Are you ill? You look pale."

"No..." Aiton looked up to Professor Haruko again. "Will everything be fine?"

"If we pray hard enough, I believe so."

He had shortened his prayers of late. Aiton found himself too tired every night and would fall asleep while reciting them. Maybe that's why things weren't fine. Maybe if he prayed, his parents would stop fighting. Maybe Hydro would come home.

"Are you certain?" Aiton asked.

"You ask too many questions. Let me ask some and continue with our studies. What is the last nation on Agrost?"

Aiton sighed. "Mistral."

"Who are the current marquises that your family rules over and their sigils?"

"Roy Tityle, Marquis of Katarh, his sigil is the frozen flower, Blue Kaffir. Marqiss Puwl, Marquis of Rhemu, his sigil is a seahorse trotting over the sea. Hekter Sigurd, Marquis of Roil, his sigil depicts a ship sailing into a setting sun—"

"Or is it a rising sun?"

Aiton stared at his professor, dumbfounded. He had never really evaluated the picture. To him it was always a setting sun. As Aiton contemplated an answer, the professor said, "No one knows for certain. But it shows that images, even names, have more than one meaning. Remember that, Aiton, not everything is as it appears... Now continue."

Aiton shook his head, trying to remember where he was. "Alyn Bloctor, Marquis of the Summer Isles, his sigil is a dolphin leaping over an island. Cadell Periwinkle, Marquis of the Hart Isles, his sigil is the coral reef of East Hart Isle. Lastly is Seth Axyl, Marquis of Talyn, his sigil shows the eyes of the leviathan, Thalassa."

"Very good, Aiton. There was no hesitation."

"Thank you, Professor Haruko."

Aiton could speak the words well enough, and remember them better, but words were water. His brother taught him that. His brother also tried teaching him Power. But Aiton still couldn't cast.

As Aiton listened to Professor Haruko ramble on about their planet's history, Aiton kept a steady gaze of his hand that he held underneath the steel table. He looked up every once in a while to nod his head and feign attention. In truth, he kept his true focus on his hand, muttering words of Power under his breath. Those were the only words that mattered. His brother taught him that as well.

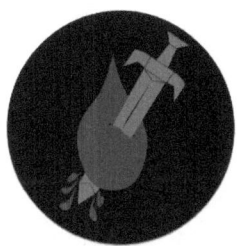

CHAPTER 21

QOTIA

Two days had passed since the squirrel couple left them out in front of a less-than-acceptable inn for a major city such as Qotia. To Hydro's surprise, Qotia was a rather modernized city like his city of Alar on Acquava, similar in population and size. Millions of people roamed its endless and winding streets paved with cement in some places, cobblestone in others, where sections of the old city stood. With its buildings upon buildings of stone and wood, small shacks of buildings and great towers with clay-red roofs.

Like Alar, this city was a shipping port. Alongside the seaside promenade, he had seen a large dock home to seagulls, tourists, but mostly wooden vessels that caught shrimp, herring, crabs, and clams. The most iconic structure, though, was a large circular structure that sat atop of a bridge further down the promenade. Upon seeing it from afar, he had asked Len of its significance, to which Len told him that it symbolized Qotia being a city with a well-respected adored academy.

The academy is where he stood now, pushed to by the gusts of wind coming through the large metallic ring near the bridge and promenade. However much the wind tried to remind him of home with the unusual scent of salt that it brought with it, it couldn't, because it wasn't as fresh. To Hydro, even the sky couldn't compare to Alar for it wasn't as blue; instead, a cloudy gray coated it a little lighter than the color of their sea.

In front of him, the academy, a three-story pagoda, stood inside fencing made of a myriad of different color stones. A copper sign attached to the gate read, "In the remembrance of Ancient Lyoen, for those pursuing the knowledge of understanding." Trimmed hedges in the shape of obelisks served as guides for visitors as they progressed the brick-red walkway to copper doors at the base of the white-walled three-story pagoda that stood upon a pedestal made of granite slabs and bricks.

Hydro paced outside the building where Elias Ward, the adored in his father's charge, had studied during his younger years. *What advice would Elias give me before talking to the adored?* Days ago, while Hydro continued to rest, Len arranged a meeting for him under the false pretenses of him being Hydro's patron and that he had an unnatural gift with adored arts. Hymin and Loo would continue to be their names. Today was his day of testing.

Len stood behind him in silk garb with ornate designs and beads organic to the area in hopes to disguise his birthplace while still maintaining a sense of wealth. Hydro followed suit by wearing a new outfit adorned in the brown and green colors of Chaon.

An hour after daybreak, an older gentleman easily approaching his ninetieth year exited the copper doors and walked towards the gate. Halfway to the gates, he stopped and tilted his head to the sky, covering his eyes with a frail hand that clattered with bracelets of so many colors and sizes Hydro couldn't begin to count. After a minute, he turned his head down to the red bricks and continued toward the gate.

In a croaking voice the man said, "Hymin Proveise?"

Hydro nodded.

"And you are his patron, Loo Navado?"

"Yes, that is I."

"Come in. We are anxious to see the skills of one so young. It is a joy to us that people do not forget the Old Ways, especially when technology threatens to overturn our universe." The man's voice flared as hot as the suns above.

Hydro thought the man senile. Although technology was rapidly advancing, it could never heal like the adored or cast Power like the Blessed. Not yet, anyway. It merely modernized archaic practices.

"The suns are to converge soon," the old man said as he walked back.

"And what a sight it will be," responded Len.

"A sight no one should see. It is evil. I can only imagine what tragedy will befall us next."

"You believe in the Curse of Pirini Lilapa?" Hydro crossed his arms over his chest and gave passing glances to the hedge obelisks in the front garden.

The man abruptly stopped and turned around with one finger in the air. "I believe *only* in things that are real. You will not find me praying to the Twelve, or caring about their meeting in two months, or utilizing Power; Lyoen is our creator, savior, and mentor." The man turned back around and continued, passing a copper statue of Ancient Lyoen in the center of the walkway. "Hopefully, the suns hold off on merging until *after* that Meeting."

"And what will happen then?" Hydro asked.

"Only the Ancients know, but it can't be good. Never is. I will be in the Academy, praying." The man hobbled up the stairs to the entrance. "Come inside." With a groan, he held open the door, and Hydro and Len entered.

Inside, tiles of different colors—similar to the perimeter—bounced light from the ornate chandeliers that hung above. Attached to the lobby's walls, various doors, some open and some closed, all showed Hydro what one could expect to gain here: Knowledge. And boredom, most likely. From the open rooms, he saw some studiers and some snoozers. Most were older—Len's age—but some were only a few years older than Hydro.

"Do you know what the tiles represent?" The old man looked back, a glimmer in his blue eyes.

"The elements," Hydro said.

"Correct. All one-hundred-and-fifty-five of them. Among these, there is one brick, much unlike the rest. Can you guess what it is?"

"Is it air?"

The older fellow laughed. Once he did, Len followed. "No, no. This is not some trick question or riddle."

Good. I hate riddles. Hydro clenched his fists.

"Although, the Blessed would be jealous if we did ever acquire the ability to manipulate wind and air."

"Is it—"

"It is rare. Extremely. That much I will say."

"A tile made of ard?"

"That is certainly rare. But, no. This item is much rarer."

Hydro followed the man to the back of the first floor, where a staircase coiled around the circumference to the second floor.

What is the point of this question?

Hydro climbed the stairs at a slow gait, waiting for the man in front to place both feet on each step before continuing. The silver railing caught his eye. He had yet to see gold. "Is it gold?"

The old man stopped and put a hand on his knees. "Gold is here. We prefer not to deal with such an item of vanity, though. We... keep it here to remind us that it is indeed an element. Good answers, Hymin, but I will just tell you. It is ether."

"My father—" Hydro cut himself short.

The man reached the top of the steps and turned to him with a gleam in his eyes and a smirk on his face. "Go on."

"My father... always wanted a weapon made of ether."

The man chortled. "That is every warrior's dream. And a dream it will remain. Unless you become Guardian, or track down a Smith. If any even remain. You should flush those ideas from your mind, boy. You are here learning to heal and create, not to fight and destroy. A student's task is to find the brick before completing their first year at the academy. A simple task, yet amusing all the same." The man stopped at a set of copper doors. "In you may go." He pushed open the door. When Len tried to follow, he said, "You and I must remain outside. This is his test alone."

Hydro glanced at Len and nodded. Len smiled briskly and stepped back from the door.

Inside, five desks were stationed around the perimeter of a lowered dais. Flames of orange, blue, red, yellow and even white lit the lanterns that stood between each desk. Two suns, five planets, and countless copper stars were painted on the dome of the room.

The adored in front of Hydro ranged from tall to short, skinny to plump, from bald to copious amounts of facial hair hanging past even desk level. They dressed themselves in the colors of the fires closest to them. They all had one thing in common, though—knowledge. On their wrists were bracelets of colors Hydro had never seen before. At least Elias never wore them.

There was no time for pleasantries.

"How many elements are there in the galaxy?"

Too many. Hydro thought back. He had learned about it before when he studied at Finesse. At one point, he was even forced to know all of them by name. But that was too long ago. The old man that had led them through the building mentioned a number. As he opened his mouth, he shut it again, deciding that he wanted to show a wittier side. A side that would get him noticed, and perhaps the information he needed.

"One-hundred-and-sixty." Hydro knew it wasn't the answer they were looking for. He studied their faces. None lifted even a wrinkle.

"One-hundred-and-sixty? Perhaps you have found some we haven't studied yet," said a man with a long face and an even longer beard.

The others chuckled.

Hydro let a sly laugh escape as well, playing along. "The word *elements* is a rather loose term. There are tangible elements like ones of metal and rock, and intangible, controllable ones through Power. The adored study one-hundred-and-fifty-five and the Blessed, four," said Hydro.

"Well, then it seems like you forget how to add," retorted the same man.

"The subject of wind and air throws that number in disarray. Neither profession can control it. It is intangible, yet present. Uncontrollable, yet utilized for its energy."

Hydro heard snickers amongst the five present. Exactly what he wanted. Hydro continued to stare at the middle dark-skinned gentleman, older than the rest of them, with glasses on a short, large nose. A copper necklace dangled from a skinny and frail neck.

The middle man nodded with each lean towards the other gentlemen. "Hymin, correct?"

"Yes, and your name?"

"Adish. Let us keep to Alconysm instead of Gladonity as a whole, shall we?"

Hydro nodded.

"What element cheats rigidity?"

"Zircha."

"What element cheats gravity?"

"Anitron."

"What element cheats weariness?"

"Ard."

"What element cheats death?"

The questions had come in succession from left to right, the middle man keeping his voice silent. A larger man with two chins and drooping cheeks asked the last question. Bushy eyebrows furrowed as he focused on Hydro.

Is this a trick? Surely there is one; Victor Zigarda couldn't have lived so long without it. He couldn't think of an actual mineral, so he chose another clever answer. "First Blood."

Adish chortled. All whispered afterwards, occasionally looking in his direction. The whispers continued for minutes. Hydro stood still as stone. The Guardian of the Core saw him worthy; why shouldn't they?

"Quite the sense of humor you have, Hymin. A trait nearly forgotten in those as aged as us. Tell me, are there any questions you may have for us?"

Hydro didn't respond for a breath. He thought about how to phrase his question. "I must be truthful. I did not come here to join your adored academy. I came here for answers. I am searching for someone, and I know not where to start."

"I did not expect as much, Hymin. Even though you wear the colors of Chaon, your lack of a Chaon accent betrays you. Who is it you seek?"

"The goddess Saeluste herself..." Hydro looked at each of them. They did not huddle, just merely gazed back at him with piqued interest.

"And what business do you have with Saeluste, if I may ask?" Adish folded his frail hands together.

"You may ask, but it is business of my own. I only ask you for your help in tracking her."

The intrigue in the man's eyes died. "I believe the answer you seek is not so easy. Like many of the Twelve, Saeluste has many homes. However, I have heard about a soothsayer that lives outside of Qotia walls. She may be able to help."

A soothsayer? Their art is false. "How do I go about finding this soothsayer?"

"Many of the slavers travel through the jungle boundaries to get to the capital, Kuyan. It is possible they might know how to find her."

"Adored, thank you." Hydro turned to leave after a short bow.

"Hymin is not your true name either, is it?"

Hydro paused and cussed. "No. It is not."

"And I sense an Onkh accent, but it is not one of a Garian. Are you from Sereya or Acquava, then?" Adish moved the glasses on his nose.

Hydro thought about lying, but decided against it. These elders had been nice enough to point him in the direction that would eventually lead to him solving the mystery of the necklace. "Acquava, Adored Adish."

"You are a long way from home... I pray you find what you are looking for. You will find many queer things lurk on Chaon."

"That is a matter of perception. Acquava hosts queer animals as well; they just live under water and yours roam the lands."

Adish laughed. "You have a way with words. A clever fellow. If you ever wish to study the adored arts, truly study the art, do not be afraid to find an institution on Onkh."

"I will. Thank you. All of you." Hydro bowed and took his leave.

Outside, Len chatted with the man who had led them in. Upon noticing Hydro, the old man asked, "Hymin, you return. Did the adored accept you?"

"I was not their best fit," Hydro lied.

Len gave him a curious look, but said nothing.

"I am sorry to hear that. Study and train more. Your passion shows."

"Thank you."

They were led out, and after they walked fifty paces from the perimeter Len asked, "I take it things did not go as planned?"

"To a sort."

"By what do you mean?"

"They knew I was not Chaon born, but they gave me answers, regardless."

"And how are we supposed to find her?" Len scratched his arm as they traveled the clay and dirt paths throughout the city.

"The slavers' market."

"Who is there?"

"Our guide."

Although he didn't know the location of the market, he figured that in a city such as Qotia, it would be located in the squalid section of town. That section turned out to be on the eastern side of Qotia, away from the port. The rather rancid stench from fleas and rats and dirty humans made Hydro want to find his guide faster.

By only asking a few questions, Hydro managed to find the slavers' auction site. Some slavers wore snakeskin armor, while some wore only their skin and a loincloth to cover their essential parts. Hydro noticed a few wealthy individuals here—although a normal person wouldn't be able to tell from their clothing, for they were clothed in robes and had their heads covered by hoods. To Hydro, the rings on their fingers, the style of their shoes, and the propriety of their voice gave their status away. *Is slaving illegal in Chaon?* He knew Acquava didn't allow it, but to Hydro, slave or servant, the terms were synonymous; one was merely treated better.

A large man with multiple tattoos caught Hydro's attention as he showed off a hoard of slaves. He talked in broken Natural Tongue, which pleased Hydro. After his presentation, Hydro approached the man.

"What is your name, slaver?"

The slaver surveyed them carefully before saying, "Nivarre. How many do you want?"

"I am not interested in your slaves. I merely want guidance," Hydro said.

"I sell slaves, not tours. Be lost." Nivarre focused his attention on another man, who requested a certain number of slaves to inspect further.

"I will make it worth your while..."

"And what makes you think that?"

"My name is Prince Hydro Paen, son to Lord Hydro Paen of Acquava. This is my advisor, Len." Hydro ignored Len's jab.

"You are a long way from home, Little Prince."

"And I wish to travel even farther. I hear rumors of a soothsayer outside this city."

Nivarre chuckled. He turned and muttered something to the other man in Chaonese and took the man's coin and cut five slaves loose of their shackles with the large scimitar attached to his hip. The man left with five thicker-stock slaves.

"And how be it you come across that?" Nivarre strummed his double chin. The tattoo of a sun flaring on the man's face showed his exoticness.

"Sources. Do you know who I speak of?"

"I do. But the jungle is not where I am headed."

"Where are you headed?"

"South, to Proschi to sell to tourists. Then I make my way to Faywynne and Valor."

"When will you be back?"

The slaver didn't answer for a little while. Before answering, he smirked. "Months. I have slaves to sell."

Hydro looked around the large man. "How many are left?"

The large man turned around and counted. "Thirty-five by my count. I wouldn't need to travel south if you purchased the rest of the slaves from me."

Hydro tsked. *A filthy cur and greedmonger.* "How do I know you are telling us the truth?"

Nivarre hopped down from the platform. Nearly triple Hydro's size, the man was a wrecking ball. "Even slavers have codes."

Hydro didn't let his intimidation show. "How much for all of them and your guidance to this soothsayer?"

"One hundred golden bonds."

Len coughed at the price. "You are not serious. Hydro, he is taking you for a fool."

Hydro knew that. He did not need Len to tell him the obvious. The slaver named a price; now it was time to negotiate. "Fifty bonds for all of them and your guidance."

"Ninety, Little Prince."

"Not for that lot. They are a scrawny bunch; The man before me took your five most-abled. Why, they have been chained so long they probably cannot even walk..."

"Eighty, then."

"Seventy-five. And you will provide them with weapons."

"Eighty-five if I must provide them with weapons."

"You will take seventy-five or let another slaver become rich. Perhaps a slaver that does not need to travel south." Hydro did not blink or lose eye contact. He knew the fundamentals to a good barter—confidence.

"Seventy-five it is." Nivarre extended his hand.

Hydro took it and clamped down as hard as he could. Although he doubted that his squeeze affected the large hands of the slaver, he needed to show a certain inexorable ferocity so that the man wouldn't think to cross him.

Nivarre opened his other hand. "The money."

"You get none until you show up tomorrow at dawn's crack."

Nivarre's large lips turned sour. He snorted and spit. "You drive a tough bargain."

"I only want to ensure you will not cower on us." Hydro aimed to insult his pride.

"Nivarre doesn't cower. I will see you tomorrow near the skirts of the flea market. We must head east. Good day, Little Prince, One-Eye." Nivarre turned around and pushed all his slaves back into a wooden cart.

"Seventy-five bonds, my prince? That is a fool's price."

"One hundred is a fool's price. Seventy-five is steep, but the man knows who we seek. We cannot afford a month's time, Len."

"How do you know for certain?"

"I am a good judge of character. I know when a person is lying. He was not."

"Your father taught you well then." Len put a hand on Hydro's shoulder. "You've had your gallivant, you've shown your wit. Guardian Eska may not have chosen you for apprenticeship, but you will make a fine lord on Acquava. Why don't we just leave?"

Hydro brushed off the hand and ignored the words. "We leave tomorrow. Now it is time to acquire the rest of our supplies." Hydro walked the way he came, prepared to spend even more money to don the both of them in proper gear. The money spent didn't bother him. He was about to find answers to his questions soon enough—an answer worth more golden bonds than he could count.

CHAPTER 22

FOR THE PAEN NAME

By the time dawn breathed, Hydro stood ready in the flea market located on the eastern side of Qotia. A faint wind carried, flowing through the gaps in Hydro's rhinoskin armor. It brought with it the scent of the sea from the west. It beckoned him to leave Qotia. This city wasn't meant for him. Adventure. Freedom. That is all Hydro ever wanted.

Footsteps in the otherwise barren market caught his ear. A few beggars stirred at the noise as well. Through a street came a man of Hydro's height but stocky, with a large girth and arms as thick as thighs. Branded with different circular tattoos, his brown skin was the only armor. A loincloth covered just enough of the man's privates. Behind him strode thirty-five men—each one of them the property of Acquava.

"One-Eye and Little Prince, you had no heart change."

You are not in Acquava anymore. He could hear Len's advice in his head. "For seventy-five golden bonds I was worried you would have one."

"You dress heavy."

"And you lighter than I had hoped for. Especially my slaves."

"You paid for bodies and weapons, not armor. That's what I provided."

Hydro glared. *Filthy cur. Father's blade could slice you in two in one stroke.*

"Chaons only need courage and weapons," Nivarre said.

"Yes." Hydro clicked his tongue. "Well, we Acquavans are more refined."

Nivarre snorted. "Payment?"

Hydro nodded towards Len, who then tossed a satchel in the large man's direction. The slaver caught it and juggled it in his thick hands.

"It's only half."

"You will receive the other half when we get there," Len said.

FOR THE PAEN NAME   III

Hydro smiled at Len's comment. *Show the slaver his place.*

The slaver belted out a laugh powerful enough to jiggle his unclothed stomach. "And how do you suppose we get there?"

"That is up to you. That is why we paid you," said Hydro.

"You paid me to be your guide, Little Prince. And guide you I will once we reach Slaver's Jungle, but if we plan on going there by foot, it will cost us another two weeks."

"You insubordinate lying cur—" Hydro reached for his hilt. Halfway through unsheathing his sword, Len wrapped his arms around him.

"My prince. My prince. Please." He turned Hydro around and whispered in his ear. "We do not know if these slaves truly belong to us yet. While you may be a good fighter, the sheer quantity of them will ruin you. Let me try and work out a deal, okay?" Len pulled back, his hands firmly on Hydro's shoulders.

Hydro looked from his advisor's eye to the slaver who had his arm over his belly, hand on a hilt of his own sword. "Okay," Hydro muttered.

Len turned around and cleared his throat. Then Hydro noticed something strange happen. Besides his advisor's shift in language to Chaonese, he noticed Len bow and point towards Hydro, which shifted Nivarre's gaze as well. After showing that token of subservience, he continued nodding and putting his hands behind his back, almost as if he were the passive one in the conversation. Occasionally, he pointed with his hands and slipped into Natural Tongue, but most of it was in Chaonese. Nivarre glanced at Hydro once or twice, but for the most part kept his eyes on Len and pointed to spots around the area. When all was said and done, Len gave another five golden bonds to Nivarre and then rejoined Hydro's side. After putting the newly acquired coins in the small purse at his hip, Nivarre disappeared down an alleyway in the nearby flea market. The other slaves stayed still.

"You bowed to him?" Hydro contorted his lips.

"I offered him an apology for your effrontery, which he accepted. With these people, Hydro, you must do things differently. Do not attack their character so publicly, for that is what they live by."

"How do you know that?"

"Darien and I both know about customs and treating with other nations. It is why your father hired us."

Hydro shifted his weight to one leg and crossed his arms. "So, what will happen?"

"Nivarre is going to go get us transport that we can use to arrive at a small outpost near Slaver's Jungle. We will stop there two nights from now and make preparations to enter the jungle two dawns from now."

"Fine."

"Remember, my prince, you are the one who forgot to look at the map. Nivarre gave us his word he would lead us there. He never said how. A good ruler, like your father, always knows the specifics of any deal he makes, for not doing so could be catastrophic."

"Yes, yes, yes." Hydro had heard it all before whilst he sat in meetings with his father's council before the Trials. He didn't need to hear it again. "Where is this slaver?"

A humming reverberated from behind and a large hoverbus entered their premises. Well, it would have been a hoverbus, but the top had been retracted to allow for the open air.

"We are to ride in—"

"Yes, we are. Sometimes getting the answers you seek means going places you don't like. Accept that."

The hoverbus stopped ten feet from their location and powered off, landing with a small thud on the ground. Nivarre stepped off the bus.

"The driver will take us to the edge of the jungle. Let's go, dawn is becoming noon."

Len pushed Hydro onto the bus, keeping his hand on Hydro's back the whole time to remind him of his presence. The slaves packed themselves into the remaining plastic seats in the back. Nivarre sat up front next to them and the driver. After everyone boarded, the vehicle jumped to life due to the anitron that powered it. Then they traveled east, Qotia vanishing behind them.

Hydro closed his eyes, wanting to sit in silence. Len had other plans for him. "Have you thought about a plan once you are in Saeluste's presence?"

Hydro kept his eyes closed. "I will tell her my name and position."

"Like I mentioned before, Saeluste is not Pearl. Your title means little to her here. What else can you think of?"

"Well, I'll make her answer me." Hydro opened his eyes and looked at Len. "Pray tell. How?"

"I have my ways." Hydro moved his hand to his hilt.

Len followed his movement and then laughed. "You cannot kill a god. Don't be foolish. Even not as renowned a fighter as some of the other Twelve, Saeluste is still far more capable than you."

Hydro's eyes flared. "Then I will show her the necklace. That will get her talking."

"And if that fails?"

"Leave me be. I will think of it on the way."

"No, I will not leave you be. Like I've told you before, this quest is folly."

"*Fear not what blade can slice or what magic can touch* were the words of my father and his father and his father's father. There is nothing folly about this quest while we have skill and competence. Are you an Acquavan or not?"

"Yes, I am. Your father pays me for advice; I just do not understand why you cannot take it as well. You may have skill, my prince, but not the competence required here."

Hydro furrowed his brows. Nivarre still looked ahead, oblivious to their quarrel. He returned his gaze to Len. "What do you mean? Why go through this trouble of helping me find my answer if we are just to turn back now?"

"To show you how truly lost you are, my prince. Without me, you would have never secured a ride to Qotia. Without me, you would have never secured a meeting with the adored. Without me, you would have never secured this transport. Without me, you—"

"Would have peace and quiet." Hydro cut in. "I will hear no more of this nonsense. If you are worried about your lack of skill, do not be. I have enough skill for both of us. We have thirty-five slaves at our disposal and a guide."

"I..." Len sighed. "Well then, I might as well consider my life forfeit."

"If you do not continue, you might as well consider your life forfeit, Len. That is all I have to say." Hydro closed his eyes and tilted his head back.

"What do you mean?"

Opening them once more, he looked at Len long and hard, then said, "What do you think?" Len looked away. He did as well, trying his best to return to a comfortable position while the hoverbus traveled closer to its destination.

Two dawns later, they woke at the outpost. Time was crucial, but not as crucial as it had been before. Nivarre had never mentioned a designated time for leaving, although before noon had been implied. The position allowed them time for an easy breakfast of porridge, toast, and a variety of fruits left for them on tables in the inn. Nivarre or the slaves were nowhere to be seen, however.

After breakfast and upon Hydro's request, Len helped Hydro into his rhinoskin armor brought with from the Trials; otherwise, the advisor had been eerily quiet towards Hydro, offering only memorized courtesies like *please* and *thank you* when Hydro helped Len into his own, boiled leather with a coating of chainmail and a steel cap. After, Hydro offered a short tutorial of how to wield a sword and the basic strikes and slashes one could do for protection. To that, Len feigned interest, but Hydro found it better to not stretch their taut relationship any further, so he didn't comment on his observation. Instead, he merely suggested their departure.

Stepping outside, a road of dirt strewn with pebbles guided them to the brim of the jungle. As they approached larger trees, roots grew out of the ground and became hazards to avoid. At the jungle's mouth, Nivarre sat on a large stump, whittling a set of heavy branches with his scimitar. His slaves were in an open field in front of the slaver, ten paces from his position in five rows of seven, whittling away heavy branches as well. All of them seemed fit enough for a stroll in the jungle, but physique didn't equal skill.

"Little Prince." Nivarre didn't look up from his branch. "I thought you may have started to have second thoughts. You come so late."

"You never specified a time."

"I thought you would have woken at dawn with how bad it seemed you wanted answers."

"Yes, well, some things are more important. Len and I were discussing strategy."

The slaver shifted his eyes between them for a moment and then laughed. "Keep moving until you must rest. Keep your weapon drawn at all times. And keep one eye open when you sleep, that is the only strategy needed in these jungles."

"When we sleep? How long of a voyage is this?"

Nivarre stopped whittling to answer Len. "From here, perhaps two to three days, depending on the pace we keep."

"What are those staves to be used for?" Len asked.

"So we don't get lost. Finding the prophetess is only half the journey, One-Eye." The slaver chuckled.

"You mean we are to travel to there by foot?" Hydro looked around. "Is there not some sort of device we can use?"

"Little Prince, you have thirty-five slaves with you, the money to buy devices for all of them and you and One-Eye, why I doubt even you have enough bonds for that. And, the jungle is thick with trees and foliage. Foot is the safest route." Nivarre continued chiseling his wooden staves.

Len grabbed Hydro's shoulder. "Hydro, again I implore you to cut your losses and return to Acquava now. Three days in a jungle is a long time; what if something goes awry? We do not know for certain she will even be able to help."

Nivarre responded faster than Hydro. "There are two things for certain, Little Prince and One-Eye. You will not return from this journey yourself, not if you listen to what she has to say. Second, the advice she gives *is* certain, has been and always will be. What is uncertain is whether you believe her." The large man hadn't looked up; he still chiseled away at his pikes, showing the strength of his arms and the skill of his labor.

"Tell me, how did you come to meet this lady? What is her name?" Hydro asked.

"I call her Three-Eyes. The tribe she lives in is where I am from. She came to the village one day, twelve years ago." Nivarre continued whittling all the while. When he reached the last of the sticks beside his feet, he looked up to the sky. "It is high noon. We should begin."

Hydro looked at the man's pile of staves. "Are you ready?"

Nivarre cleaned another of his pikes, stripping the copious amounts of bark and rough edges from its side. "I was only waiting on yours, Little Prince." The man stood up and sheathed his scimitar. He grabbed a pile of shaved branches and divvied them to Hydro and Len both, keeping some for himself. "When I say *plant* one of you needs to." After, he turned to the slaves and shouted something foreign, causing them to shield their weapons and carry their sticks.

Hydro straightened his chest and tightened his face. Len wore no smile, only nervousness as apparent as the eye-patch on his face. Behind, the platoon of thirty-five slaves held neither fear nor delight. Simply stoic—ready to do Hydro's bidding. For one last moment Hydro glanced at Freyr; Lugh trailed behind it. Then he lowered his gaze through the thick canopy and bulging boughs of the trees that stood before him—the jungle that he would conquer.

Hydro stepped upon the stump the slaver had vacated and unsheathed his sword. He watched it reflect Freyr's rays and then proceeded to point it towards the jungle. "Onward, for the Paen name."

Behind him, Hydro imagined cheers and war cries howling at his courage as if he were a hero.

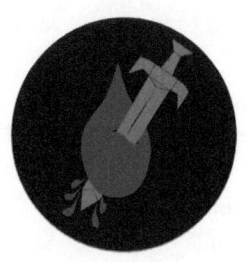

CHAPTER 23

THE BROWN SEA

T he thick canopy lessened the heat considerably. It locked in a certain moistness within the jungle atmosphere, allowing them to make better distance.

Hydro had run out of sticks to plant, and Len held his last few. The large man still carried plenty, though.

"Plant!" Nivarre commanded.

Len lurched over and heaved the spike down with all his might. "It has been days, my prince. And nothing."

Hydro was about to respond, but the large man interrupted. "One-Eye, I told you the difficulty of this journey; you are here now because your little prince wants answers. And he will find them once we arrive."

The man's hearing perplexed Hydro. He wondered if growing up in the jungle had trained his ears for sound like Hydro had been trained for prowess by tongue and sword within the castle grounds.

"Plant."

"How much farther do you believe it will be?"

"It will not be more than half a day once we reach the Brown Sea."

"And... how far... is that?" Len asked through puffs of exhaustion. "I have yet... to see any... river flowing... through here."

"This sea is made from no river, that is why it's called the Brown Sea, One-Eye." He stopped and turned to look at Len and Hydro. "I believe we will see the Brown Sea today, so we are no more than a day's voyage."

Hydro glanced back at the procession of slaves following him. It seemed as though the number had shrunk, but Hydro knew that wasn't true, as there had been no danger yet. Monkeys had traveled with them for a while, swinging from bough to bough, until they eventually stopped. And one time a few tigers had been spotted off in the distance, through the foliage by one of the slaves, but they had never approached further, probably due to the number of their group. Although, when they had stopped to notice the tigers, Hydro could have sworn one of them looked at him intently, as if truly seeing him, before retreating. The stare pimpled Hydro's skin, but another hour's trek through the jungle had caused Hydro to forget about it.

Fifty paces ahead, Hydro noticed an alcove. *Good a spot to rest.* "Len, we can stop—" He tumbled to the ground. He didn't appreciate dirt's kiss. It was gritty. He looked back. An overgrown root. He spat out the aftertaste. Len's hand offered help.

"Are you okay, my prince?"

"Yes." Hydro took his advisor's hand and pulled himself upward.

Over Len's shoulder, past Nivarre, in the alcove he noticed something white. Usually white. Hydro shook his head and squinted. The white turned out to be the dress of a black girl standing in the middle. *She hadn't been there a moment ago.* Hydro pushed past Len and Nivarre, ignoring any words they might have said. He darted towards her. She stood there, looking northeast, back turned, black braids falling just past her tiny shoulders. *Could it be?*

Beware of the girl with black hair... Hydro stopped a few paces from her. Her shoulders heaved. She wept. Only Hydro heard her. Enthralled, he reached out to her. Under his weight, a twig snapped. She glanced back at Hydro with lost black eyes.

"What is your name?"

Anne. The girl smiled.

The smile slid into a sour frown. Her teeth changed into fangs. Hydro was yanked back and pushed to the ground. The air was cut. Hydro blinked and cussed as he landed on strewn branches. In between his legs rolled a serpent's head, its tongue still licking the air in the aftermath of death. Nivarre stood above him, wielding a sword wet with blood.

No. It can't be. Nivarre shouted incomprehensible words and slashed open a snake that tried to strike him from his side. All around larger serpents, thick as humans, wound their way around the trees.

Len pulled up Hydro from under his armpits. "Hydro! Are you alright? What were you doing?"

"We should never have come. We need to leave."

"The snakes are out, Little Prince. There is no returning now. We press onward." The slaver cut another snake across the belly.

Terror clung to Len's face. Through the cacophony of his slaves' shrieks and the slithers and hisses of the snakes, Nivarre shouted them onward. Despite the realization of his mistake, Hydro knew he couldn't turn back now. Now he needed to be strong. For himself. For Len. For family. Some part of him needed to believe everything would be alright.

"These are no snakes." Len held onto his steel with a crude grip.

"You are right, One-Eye. These are much too large for snakes. These are basilisks. Don't look into their—"

It was too late. A basilisk slithered out from behind a tree branch and dropped right in front of them. Hydro couldn't help but stare into red, vicious eyes. It coiled back its head and refocused on Hydro. *It's going to strike.* Hydro crouched, pulled his sword, and came clean across the neck as the snake lurched forward. Then he saw Len. Not moving. A statue of flesh, still as granite.

"Len!" Hydro touched his advisor's lifeless body.

"Little Prince, we must leave." The slaver squinted, keeping his eyes mostly shut. He yelled something incomprehensible to the slaves still alive and pulled Hydro.

"I cannot leave him." Hydro reached for his advisor's petrified body.

"He's dead, Little Prince. Rejoice that you are alive. We need to get to the village. There we are safe." Nivarre laid a hand on Hydro's shoulder.

"This is all my fault..."

"Swallow your sorrow. Now we run."

More serpents gathered on their location. Len's one eye was wide open. His face, a grim line, forever hiding his teeth of gold. *Len, I'm sorry.* He couldn't say the words.

"Little Prince!"

Nivarre yanked Hydro from his melancholy. Hydro tried keeping up with the man thrice his size. Behind him, he heard footsteps and crackling branches. Soon, even those dissipated. Although tempted to look back, Hydro kept his gaze ahead. Nivarre jumped over overgrown roots and fallen branches and sliced his way through the thick foliage.

At another alcove, after another ten minutes of solid running, they stopped for a moment's rest. Two slaves had kept up with them, both now coated in red blood and brown dirt.

Hydro sat on a large, toppled tree. *Len. He's gone. I should have listened. You needed more. You have more.*

Hydro gulped as the female voice penetrated his thoughts. It was strange. The whole exchange was strange. How could a necklace speak to him? Why did it chill him, yet soothe him at the same time? Like something bad done under good intentions.

"What else will I get?" Hydro spoke aloud, wondering if the necklace would respond.

It didn't.

Perhaps he didn't need any more at this point. He had a name now. Anne. He wondered if the three-eyed prophetess would know of her.

"Nothing else. That's enough rest." The large man took a fallen branch and snapped it in two on his thick leg, breaking Hydro's concentration. He shoved the sharp end into the ground.

The slaver, covered in blood and sweat, unfazed.

Does he know what just happened? Does he care?

Nivarre furrowed his bushy brows. "How are you still alive, Little Prince? I saw you glance directly into its eyes."

"I... I... do not know... truly I do not..." *Is Pearl's blessing still with me?* He thought back to the time before the Trials, when his father took him to see the goddess Pearl. She had told Hydro she had blessed him, but throughout the Trials, nothing had seemed different. But why would one of the Twelve lie to him? It was in her interest to have Hydro succeed, and he disappointed her. And his father...

Pearl's blessing has never been with you.

Hydro's heart singed. He clutched his chest and bent over.

"Are you alright, Little Prince?"

Hydro inhaled and exhaled multiple times. He straightened his posture and looked around. "Did you see the little girl?" Hydro meant to think it, to ask the necklace, but instead he had said it aloud, and Nivarre answered.

"Little girl?"

"Back there, before the snakes." Hydro stood and pointed backwards.

"You talked with no one. A snake came from behind the stump and that is when I pulled you back."

"You mean to tell me there was no girl?"

"Little Prince, there was no girl!"

Am I succumbing to mindloss like Grandfather? Hydro surveyed the area, trying to find her. Trying to prove to himself and to Nivarre that he wasn't losing his mind. The two slaves still alive spoke something in broken Chaonese to the large slaver, who answered in the same tongue. Hydro searched and scanned, but found nothing. Then something moved. It jumped on the bare shoulder of the taller slave. It was small, like a squirrel with bat ears and slanted eyes and as brown as the little wooden spear in its hand.

Hydro backed up. The slave tilted his neck towards the irritation. Hydro collided with Nivarre's large belly. He searched for words he couldn't find and pointed to the taller slave. It was too late. The little creature took the spear and shoved its little point into the slave's neck. The slave screamed in a foreign language. The slaver pushed past him and with deft precision sliced the little creature in two. More of the creatures came in herds.

The slaver muttered something foreign to both of the slaves, who nodded. "We run. Now." Nivarre turned around and darted off due east.

Hydro followed, not sure what else to do. The surroundings swallowed him. Sea or land, animals like these weren't on Acquava. He darted through foliage as swiftly as the large man in front of him. When a scream occurred, Hydro resisted the temptation to look behind. For minutes, he ran and ran to the sound of his stomping feet while straining his ears to keep track of the little patters behind him as well. His castle training helped him here, but even he wondered what training formed the endurance of the man in front of him.

Hydro paused when the man stopped in front of a large sea of sand. Thick trees blocked out most of Freyr's rays, but it still shone through, sparkling on the sand. He and the slaver were alone.

"What... were those things? What happened to the others?"

"They weren't fast enough, Little Prince. And those things, those things are marenches. They dip their spears in frog poison."

"Is it lethal?"

"It's poison, Little Prince. The village is past the Brown Sea." Nivarre pointed towards the other side.

"Let us go, then." Hydro walked forward but was pulled back.

"You can't just walk across." The man pointed at a leaf falling through the air. Once the leaf landed, the sand swallowed it.

"What kind of sand is this?"

"Devils-sand." The man tilted his head. "The marenches still chase us. Follow me. Jump."

The sandy sea, in itself, was an enigma to Hydro. Five parts of it were barren, not accepting any weight on top of it but its own granules. The other parts, however, held twigs and leaves and other pieces of foliage. *How is that—*

"Look for the drowned pillars, Little Prince." The slaver jumped towards the sea of sand. He stood, turned back, and waved his arm.

Hydro squinted and saw marble columns barely poking above the sand. If the slaver hadn't said anything, he wouldn't have noticed.

A pain erupted in his neck, and Hydro stumbled forward, almost toppling into the sand. He reached his hand around his neck and pulled out the irritation—a tiny spear. The tiny creatures had caught up to them.

"Little Prince!"

Hydro was hit again. *I don't have time for this.* Ignoring the wounds and pain, Hydro leapt. Rough marble greeted him. His hand touched the sand. He yanked it back, fearing the same fate as the leaf. Once he regained posture, he jumped to the next pillar, and to the next and so on. All the while, spears hurled through the air, sticking to Hydro's triceps and legs—it was a good day to wear armor.

When no more spears flew through the air, Hydro looked back and saw no more marenches. *I've survived. They're gone.* On land, Nivarre bent over and plucked the spears out of his skin. Hydro crouched, determining the distance. *Did he jump all that way?* It was far. Farther than the other ones. A quick scan before revealed no other pillars.

Hydro inhaled and inched as far back as possible. With a little room now, he bounded ahead. Just before he leaped, something hit the back of his head, pushing him forward, off-kilter. He soared. And landed. On the sand. Eight paces away. *What in Abaddon?*

He looked back and noticed the marenches had returned with a contraption resembling a slingshot that they now loaded with medium-sized rocks. Shielding his face with his elbows, he yelled. "Help!" His feet sunk. The heavy sand ate his ankles. As the pelt of stones continued, Hydro trudged through the sand, ignoring his pain as best he could.

Sand filled his shoes. Now it was up to his calves. Each step became more arduous than the last, each beat of his heart harder, and each breath heavier. The sand was sucking him down to an unknown fate. He staggered forward now, almost there, making sure to keep his body upright.

At the cusp of the sandy sea, he was up to his waist in devils-sand. "Help!"

"Give me your arms."

Hydro flailed. The spears that had sunk into his arms still hadn't been removed.

Rough and large hands grabbed his forearms. His weight shifted. His eyes fluttered. His head pounded. Rough ground. He felt rough ground. His hands groped aimlessly, trying to find anything to latch onto. His midsection seemed to want to rip apart. His eyes burned and blurred. His neck itched. His shoulders burned from keeping his arms erect.

Exhaustion overtook him.

CHAPTER 24

PURPOSE

Freyr and Lugh shone on the stone court. Korth stood in front of Aiton, wooden sword in hand, wearing the seachrome armor Aiton had seen on the trainer so many times before. Aiton wore leather padding and a leather cap strapped underneath the chin, just covering the ears.

"Young prince, you did well today. Remember to keep your footing as fluid as water. Remember, warriors still standing do not stand still."

Aiton admitted to not moving as much as he should. *If only I were like my brother. If only he were here.* His brother's absence at Coronation worried Aiton, and although he enjoyed sparring, he couldn't help but become distracted by his family's fracture.

"I will do better next time."

"I hope so. I do not like bruising one so young."

"Are you done with the young prince, Korth?"

Aiton stepped two paces to the right and saw Professor Haruko walking forward from the shadows of East Tower. The professor wore a purple cloak with the Paen sigil in royal blue on the upper left.

"I am," Korth said.

"Do you mind bringing the basin of water, then?"

"I will be back shortly."

Korth left. Aiton liked Korth and his accent. It was melodic and warm and inviting. Because of it, Aiton was more willing to obey. It beat the croak of Elias any day. Aiton twirled the wooden sword in the air, disappointed that the sword didn't gleam in the light. His mother didn't allow him to swing steel swords yet.

"How was your weapon's training today, young prince?" Professor Haruko asked.

"I did well."

"Hopefully you are not too tired for Power training."

"Of course not!" Aiton rolled up the cuffs of his long-sleeve silk shirt in anticipation for the session. *Maybe today is the day.*

"Such an eager child. Perhaps that is why you are my favorite young prince."

"I am the only young prince here, Professor Haruko."

"Aye, that is also why you are my favorite."

The old man laughed, and Aiton smiled. He relished days he trained his body and his tongue instead of his mind. For the past couple days, since coming back from the Core, he spent more time with this type of training, at his parents' request.

A few minutes later, Korth brought over a basin of water. If Aiton were to rule Acquava, he would need control of its most abundant element. A true Acquavan could do it. That's why his brother was so good at it, as was his father. Aiton hoped to have it twirl around his hands today like the way Hydro controlled it before he left.

Aiton walked over to the basin and peered into the water, seeing his reflection, also seeing the man he wished to become, someone who could slosh the water, who could control it and bid it to do his will—a man like his brother or father.

"Aiton, do you recall the true word for water?"

"*Vesi.*" Aiton never took his gaze off the water.

"Good. Now look at me." Professor Haruko pulled up the cuffs of his sleeves and placed a hand in the air. "*Vesi.*"

Soon, the water stirred into waves, and the waves formed a controlled miniature hurricane that grew in height until it circled the professor's hand. "When you control an element, Aiton, never let your mind lose grasp of that control. This is the most difficult thing to learn, for it requires you to think separately yet similarly at the same time.

"Think of using Power as you would think about the process of befriending someone. You must first know that person's name and trust that that person will do you no harm, and only when you come to that realization will you be able to call them friend. And once finally friends, there is no telling what you can do together. Why you could make it twirl in your hand... or rise like a geyser... or, perhaps form a mirror in front of you."

Water followed each of Professor Haruko's suggestions. At the end, his reflection rippled in the oval water-mirror before him. Aiton bounced on his toes. His heartbeat quickened. The water flowed back into the basin. *This is it.* Aiton raised his right hand and let his mind ease into thinking about water. First, he started with the sky, as blue as water, then he thought about oceans, then seas, then lakes, then the basin. The more he qualified his search, the more he tightened his mind. *Water, I am your friend. Come to me.*

"*Vesi.*"

Aiton reached with his fingertips, trying to grab the intangible water. Not even a ripple. He focused harder. And harder. A gust slapped his cheek, and the water rippled. He strained his face and neck as he thought about controlling water. *I am an Acquavan. You will do as I say!* For minutes he reached. And reached. To no avail.

Shoulder getting sore, he let his arm fall, declaring defeat. "I am Denied..." Aiton looked down to the stone court. *The wind can make water move, but I cannot... I'm a failure.*

Large hands gripped his shoulders from behind. "Do not be sad, Aiton. You are still young."

"Korth speaks the truth. There are many examples of young princes that do not cast their first until they enter their teenage years."

"But I did everything you told me to do. And it still would not move." Aiton sneered at the basin.

"Aiton..." Professor Haruko put two fingers underneath Aiton's chin and raised it. "Do you know why it is that some people cast later than others, and some people cannot cast at all?"

"No." Aiton shook his head, reaffirming his answer.

"In our faith, it is the Twelve that brought the secret words of Power to our ears. They showed the good lords and ladies everything they could do with it, and thus made it our charge, your father's charge, to carry on that Power.

"Now, as bloodlines grow fainter, so does the ability to cast Power, and that is why some family reigns end after so long of a time."

"It will end with me, then?" Aiton looked down.

Professor Haruko yet again brought up his chin. "No. Some take longer to cast than others because the Twelve are waiting to see them mature. The strength that they will be given will be much greater than the others. What color is fire?"

"Red," Aiton said, then added, "and orange."

"Ah, yes, but it can also be white and blue. Watch me, Aiton. *Palo.*"

From Professor Haruko's hand, a blue flame glowed and wrapped around his wrist.

"Hydro's is orange."

"Yes, it is. I said my first spell when I turned fifteen. And when I cast fire, I cast a blue one. Do you know which color of fire is the hottest?"

"Red," Aiton said.

"It the most common, that is certain, but the hottest is blue. Very few individuals cast a blue flame. Most, like your brother and your father, cast an orange or a red flame. That is typically because they develop their Power in the usual manner. Thinking they are prodigies, some cast much too early and have the ill luck of having a white flame, which is hardly as hot as it should be." Professor Haruko let the flame die and put his hand on Aiton's shoulder. "What I am saying, young prince, is do not be anxious to cast. You may, someday, and your spells will be stronger and fiercer than the other's." Professor Haruko smiled. "Good things come to good people."

Aiton smiled and briefly forgot about his failure.

"Now, go get cleaned up for lunch."

"Okay."

On his way back to the mansion that sat inside the fortified walls of the castle, Korth traveled with him.

"Do you think I will be able to cast, Korth?"

"You have your father's and your brother's blood in you. Of course."

"But, what if I cannot?"

"Then you still will do great things. Power does not equal greatness, young prince."

Yes, it does. Hydro said so. That's why he went to become Guardian until that other man robbed him of his title. "But, I will not be prince anymore."

"And many a people have done great things without being royalty. Edwyrd Eska became Guardian."

"He could use Power, though."

Korth held open a door leading inside the mansion. "Then, how about Damascus Steelshine?"

"Who is he?" Aiton stepped inside.

"A warrior who invented the traditional strongsword in model after the eleven fabled Ether Weapons."

"And can you name another?"

"Gazo Sabore."

"Is he who Gazo's Academy is named after?"

"Yes. He led Pelop Swander to victory against Empor Rydel. He used nothing but a sword and—"

"Sir Korth!"

Past Korth, Aiton saw Rafael, his father's oldest servant. White hair, ending in a braid, hung past the man's slumped shoulders. The doggish face reminded Aiton of Professor Haruko.

Korth turned away from Aiton and straightened himself. "What is it, Rafael?"

"Your presence is requested in the lord's chambers."

"I will be there in a little while after I finish—"

"They insisted that you come immediately."

Korth's shoulders sunk. The guard turned around and crouched to Aiton's level again, looking him in the eye. "It seems I must go." Korth put his hardened hands on Aiton's shoulders. "Know this, though, young prince; a fight does not need to be with a weapon. A fight is your goal, what you want to accomplish. And I will be there to help you accomplish any goal you set your mind to." Korth brushed a hand through Aiton's hair, stood up, and followed Rafael down the hallway.

Aiton slumped his shoulders. *What could Mother and Father want? Perhaps they saw my failure today on the stone court.* Aiton sighed. Fighting didn't come to him like it did for his brother or father. He couldn't cast Power. He found himself looking at his hands and wondering, *Is there anything I can do? What is my purpose?*

CHAPTER 25

THE THREE-EYED PROPHETESS

Hydro woke to alien sights. Above him, tarp stretched out forming a tent held together at various spots by large wooden posts. He put a hand to his forehead, trying to stop the dizziness. His arms, bandaged at multiple locations now were crusted with some sort of herb. *Pearl's waters, where am I?*

A noise somewhere in the tent caused Hydro to stay awake. Foreign voices alarmed him. "Len..." Hydro called out to a man who could never answer.

Hydro coughed. A tall man walked into the tent. The right side of his face displayed jewelry from a gauge for his earlobe a few centimeters wide to a piercing above the eyebrow.

"Where is Nivarre?"

The man blankly stared at him with vacant, dirty brown eyes. A hand grabbed the tall man's shoulder and he stepped aside.

"Little Prince, I thought you were gone to us."

"How long have I been asleep?"

"Two days now."

Hydro noticed the same herb-crust material bandaging Nivarre's wounds. "What is this?" Hydro flexed to show the bandage.

"It's succubus paste, acquired from the nectar of the succubus flower. It sucks venom from your body. That is why you're alive—why we're alive."

Has Pearl's blessing left me?

You never had her blessing. Since you wore me, mine has never left.

But what blessing are you?

A true one. A powerful one. You would be dead without me.

How?

Do you think it luck you survived a basilisk's glare?

Hydro patted his chest, feeling only his armor. He resisted the temptation to pull his collar forward.

An uncertainty chilled Hydro. He thought of the prophetess and if she'd be able to tell him more about this blessing. The necklace burned at his chest, but he wouldn't take it off. Before going to Zas Banegul, he would need to take more precautions.

"Where is she?"

"Here. But first, other payment." Nivarre held out a large hand.

"I do not have it."

"Where is it?"

"Le... Len has it... back..." Hydro hung his head.

"That is... Most unfortunate."

Steel being drawn alerted him. "What are you doing? Where is she? Where am I?" His hand went to his side; he didn't have his sword.

"No payment, no meeting, Little Prince."

"I will give you the money when we return."

Nivarre curled his lips. "No money—"

"Nivarre, a prince's word is good enough."

Alongside the slaver stood a woman with streaks of faint blue in her hair where the gray hadn't settled. She looked old, near her sixties, but she had hardly any wrinkles. The only thing that gave away her age was her hair. She wore a gown made of copper coloring, spotted with silver stars. On her left hand was a band—one half silver, the other copper.

"Prince Hydro Paen, what takes you away from Acquava?" She gazed upon him with blue eyes with a hint of slight purple. Entrancing eyes, if Hydro had ever seen any.

"How do you know my name?"

"You bear your father's countenance."

"Then how do you know my father?"

"I am not from around here."

Hydro could tell that; her skin was a different complexion, and she didn't have any of the piercings or tattoos that seemed alien to Hydro. "Where are you from, then?"

"Many places, but no place at all now."

She speaks like a prophetess, saying many things but nothing at all. Hydro bit his lip and pivoted his gaze between the two. "What do you mean by that?"

"That is unimportant. Nivarre says you are here for me."

"I am."

"You lose those dear to you, just to find me—a lady whom you have never met, led here by someone you have never known. That is quite unusual."

"I have an unusual situation."

She turned towards Nivarre. "You may leave us."

The large man grunted. "Bye, Little Prince. Bye, Three-Eyes."

She let out a little laugh.

"Why does he call you Three-Eyes? I see no third eye."

She laughed again. "You will see. Follow me to my tent."

It took effort, but Hydro managed to get up after failing the first time due to stomach pain. He staggered to the tent's exit. Outside of the tent were various other tents, no more than twenty, but no less than ten. In the middle of the small village was a large, rectangular fire pit the length of fifteen paces. Carved wooden statues sat outside each tent, but there were no plaques to signify the meaning of the statues.

Hydro limped through the village. Gaze after gaze lingered upon him as he tried to keep the lady's cadence. They all had copper skin, like Eska's Conseleigh, Ethen. Unlike him, however, they were less modest about their jewelry. Women wore snakeskin hides around their chest and buttocks and a central nose ring, like a bull, and two lip rings, one on each side. Most had as black of hair as he, but others a fainter brown. Men wore gauges in their ears and most had pierced eyebrows. *If Len were with me, he would be able to explain the villagers' mode of dress and decoration.*

"We are here."

In front of him, a curtain of beads hung as the door to a small tent with a wooden star carved outside. Hydro pushed aside the beaded curtain and entered. Inside was a bed, a shelf of feather-bound literature, and another shelf of vials.

The woman sat on a stool at a high table that came to Hydro's abdomen. A purple silk cloth with silver stars covered the table and stretched the length of its legs. She removed a silver cloth, revealing an orb, slightly smaller than those during the second trial. "Sit."

"You are a starseer then? I saw the star outside."

"I look at stars, Prince Hydro, the same way you look at swords—with interest, but that is not all I do. The only two stars that concern me now are Freyr and Lugh, and their convergence."

"You do not believe in such a thing, surely?"

"The Curse of Pirini Lilapa *is* real. You will find out soon enough."

What does she mean by that? Hydro found his gaze returning to the orb. It was a cloudy gray with sparkles of amethyst. *Is that?* Hydro put a finger to his chin and hunched forward. He glanced from the orb to the woman's eyes and noticed the same shade of amethyst lingered there as well. *Could she be...*

"Is something interesting?"

Hydro straightened his posture and his mien. In an attempt to act nonchalant, he ignored her question. "So this is your third eye? What can it tell you?"

"It tells many things, young prince."

"Did you know I was searching for you?"

"I did not."

"You are no prophetess then. Otherwise you would have predicted my arrival."

"I was not searching for you. Seeing is a precise art. I have never met you. Why would I see if you were coming to find me out of the millions that roam the galaxy?"

"Even if seeing is a precise art, as you say, everyone knows no one can tell the future."

"Why do you say that?"

"Because that makes it seem like we are not in control of our fate."

"Are we?"

The lady stared at him with such intensity it kept Hydro silent. He looked away and to the orb. He blinked and reached out to touch it. When the lady spoke again, he pulled back his fingers.

"You have the look of a man who wants to test what I know, but is afraid of what he will find. It was the same look your father had."

Father? "I... I..." Hydro looked deep into her purple eyes. There was something there; Hydro knew it. Untold stories and ludicrous hypotheses began inundating his mind. "I need to go. I feel queasy."

"Rest well, Hydro Paen."

Hydro turned, stopping at her voice.

"It takes a man of great strength to face uncertainty, but sometimes it takes even more to find out what certainty really is."

"And did you tell my father what certainty really was for him?"

"No; he never wanted to know."

Hydro let the words sink in. Maybe it was the coolness in her voice or the way she spoke, but she enthralled him. As did her orb. But he wasn't ready. Not yet. In truth, he may never be ready. Somewhere along the way in the jungle, he lost himself. He couldn't pinpoint where. Perhaps with Anne or Len, or at the Brown Sea, but his usual bravado had died.

He left her, letting the beaded strings jingle in a dying breeze.

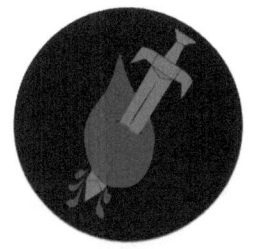

CHAPTER 26

CAPTIVE

A nother two days passed since his first encounter with the three-eyed prophetess. Each day, he became less lethargic. He had been given his sword back the day before. But even with lethargy leaving him, he still sat and brooded, not wanting to touch his blade. Whenever the thought of talking to her came to mind, his skin prickled. His imagination took control and constantly he found himself searching for the advisor not there. The one person who could help him make sense of the insensible. He thought about how she knew his father, or why his father never wanted to know what she had to say.

Those red eyes... Hydro lay on the table he called his bed, starting at the ceiling. *How am I alive?*

Slathering on his arm drew his attention to a man by his side. Hydro didn't say anything. From a thick bowl made of an empty coconut, he dribbled gritty paste up and down Hydro's wounds. The lacerations were getting smaller. Hydro fingered the scabs. *If only my doubt would decrease like these wounds.*

"Have you had your fortune told by this three-eyed prophetess?" Hydro asked the man.

The man looked at him and continued applying the paste.

"Do you know anyone who has?"

He responded in a language Hydro couldn't understand.

"He doesn't know what you're saying."

Nivarre entered the tent. The slaver said something in Chaonese to the lanky man, and he put down the coconut bowl and left.

"Tell me true, Nivarre, does this lady know everything?"

"She knows many things, but no, not everything. What she doesn't know, her third eye does."

"Has she told your fortune?"

"I have never asked. I have seen strangers come to her, but they always leave different than when they arrived."

"How do you know that?"

"Do you think you are the first one that's been taken here, Little Prince?"

"Did my father come here then?"

"I do not know your father."

Hydro felt stupid for asking the question. "How is it that she came to this place?"

The woman entered, wearing a shawl of copper threads and a gown of sleek silver. "Why do you not ask me yourself?"

Hydro gulped. "Well..."

"Prince Paen, I came here years ago. I've lived and loved and have given life, but hubris and humanity take from me what they take from everyone." She paused and looked at Hydro with a solemn demeanor. "Life... I live here because I cannot return home, not yet. I cannot see the loves of my life, not yet. But there will come a day that I will, whether here or there."

"Why?"

"We must all make tough decisions. The Ancients know I have made some. Sometimes they turn out to be sacrifices. And sometimes those sacrifices are for their own good."

"But why here? Why do you stay here?"

"The place fits me. It guards me. And secludes me." She spoke to Nivarre in Chaonese. The large man grunted and stood, hand on his hilt.

"What are you doing?"

"Your being here intrigues me. I think it is time for you and I to have our talk. If you are not going to come to me, I will make your decision for you."

Hydro winced as Nivarre grabbed him by the elbow and followed her out of the tent. The villagers watched as he was taken to her tent. His mind raced; and his heartbeat quickened. He wanted to fight, but he couldn't break the goliath's grip. Also, the confidence in her art and the knowing in her voice enraptured him. More so than he had ever been with anyone. If she were to make his decision for him, it would be easier than making the decision himself.

Nivarre sat Hydro down on the stool in front of the orb. He kept his arms folded across his chest as the woman sat down in front of Hydro. "You may leave us, Nivarre."

The man left, and Hydro looked from her to the orb and back. The amethyst lines swirled in clouds of gray, flashing and fleeting. Her eyes darted to and fro, watching the orb. She looked at Hydro. "Nivarre tells me interesting things about you, Hydro Paen."

"Such as?" Hydro pinched his knee to control his shiver.

"How you managed to look a basilisk in the eye without dying." The woman steepled her hands and raised an eyebrow. "You should be dead right now."

"But I am not."

"No, you are not. That allures me. The only explanation is you are meant to bond with a basilisk. But, that lends itself to another peculiarity." She tucked strands of blue hair behind her ears.

"What peculiarity?"

"Are you familiar with the process of Blood Bonding?"

Hydro nodded. It was a process that allowed people who shared a drop of blood with another to keep track of each other. They could sense one another because they had a little part of the other flowing through them. This worked indefinitely for those of actual relations, but anyone could bond blood together, they would just need to constantly refresh that connection every month to replace the cells that died within the body.

"I cannot trace you."

"You do not have my blood."

"I do. It was taken from you yesterday as your wounds were being bandaged."

Hydro's mouth stood agape. He felt his skin. *How dare she!* After his shock faded, curiosity still lingered. *Why can't she trace me, though? She should be able to.*

"You interest me. Why is it that you are here?"

It is now or never. Hydro studied her eyes, which studied his in turn. "I am here to find Zas Banegul."

She leaned forward, hands folded across the table. "And what type of purpose do you have with Zas?"

"Purpose that is my own."

"What makes you think that I can help you find him?"

"Because you interest me as well." Hydro regained his confidence. "If I did not know any better, I would say this orb is actually one of the eleven Ether Weapons." When she narrowed her vision upon his words, he continued. "The amethyst lines swirling in gray give it away. If you truly knew my father, you would know my family has the Ether Weapon, Purge. I know what they look like. It makes me believe you have First Blood."

"Perceptive." She put her hands in front of the orb, as if to shield and protect it. "However, your logic doesn't make any sense. Your father has no First Blood. What would make you so certain that I possess some?"

"My father is a lord to one of the longest ruling dynasties on Onkh, and he is a capable warrior like his father before him and his father's father. It is only fate that a weapon of such renown would come into my family's possession at some point. You, here, in the middle of nowhere, possessing a weapon that has no true eq—" Hydro paused. He didn't want to say the word. Not that word. "That has no true rival. That is intriguing, especially when you don't seem fit to be a fighter."

"Looks can be deceiving." She gave a quick smirk. "But, perhaps I just am a collector of ancient artifacts; do you not see the ancient lore on my shelves?"

Hydro glanced behind her, taking a quick moment to scan the shelves. He redirected his attention towards her. "The books only make my hypothesis stronger."

"And what hypothesis is that?" She furrowed her brows and folded her hands together on the table once more.

Hydro crossed his arms over his chest. "You are the goddess Saeluste herself."

The woman didn't laugh. She merely surveyed Hydro with even greater curiosity. "What makes you assume such a thing?"

"My family treats with Pearl, the goddess of water; we believe in the New-Way. Because of that, I know each god or goddess lays claim to a different part of the gestalt that is the Twelve. If I am not mistaken, Saeluste's claim is mental health, wisdom, and intelligence. That is why you are a starseer. That is why you possess ancient lore on your shelves. That is how you have such knowing laced in every word of your voice. And, that is also why you possess an Ether Weapon."

She smirked. "Perceptive, young prince. You have quite the imagination."

"So, I am correct?"

She snickered. "No."

"What do you mean?" Hydro leaned forward. "What is your name, then? Your real name."

"We did not come here to discuss my name; we came here to discuss yours, young prince. Do you intend to judge me by my name?"

"A name tells a lot of things."

"It does. More than you are aware, I am sure. And something your father never wished to know. Unfortunately, you are not privy to my name. Only a handful are, do not feel slighted."

The handful that are the Twelve. She is lying to me. Hydro curled his lips, crossed his arms, and studied her. For the first time, however, he couldn't decipher lies from truth. *I suppose everyone has their secrets.* "Very well." He relaxed again and glanced at the orb. "What can you tell by a name?"

"Well, some are given for greatness. Others merely fit for fate. And yet, some, some are simply sung for sorrow. The Zas you seek, his name was sung for sorrow."

"Which am I?" Hydro spoke his thoughts without meaning to do so.

"So you wish to test my knowledge? You are already braver than your father."

Hydro straightened his posture and stared into her deep purple eyes. "I wish to find answers to my questions."

She held his gaze. "And I, mine. Perhaps we will find our answers together." She held her arms up in the air and then slowly lowered them, placing her long fingers on the orb. She rubbed continually, looking inside. "You carry the burden of your sister's death. The sorrow of your family's pride. And you feel greatly for a Len Posair."

"He was my father's advisor. He... he... died while in the jungle."

Her fingertips massaged the orb, and her eyes glowed. "You competed in Guardian Eska's Trials, but since losing, you feel lost. You feel bound to uphold your family's duties now, and that is why you run. But, why do you run to Zas?" Her head disappeared behind the orb.

Her knowledge prickled Hydro's entirety. She knew everything. *How, how is this possible? She must be the goddess.*

"You... you..." She looked up from her orb. "This is the first time I cannot see. What do you carry on you? Why do you seek Zas?" Her voice rose now. She seemed distraught.

Hydro's heart quickened. *Should I show her?* Cautiously, Hydro slid off his armor. Then, button by button, he uncloaked himself. As he did so, her eyes became wider and wider.

"Where did you find that?"

"The Zas Labyrinth."

She peered into her orb once again. Her hands massaged it. "This was during the Trials?"

Hydro nodded.

She paused and bit her lower lip. "Given for greatness... his name was given for..." Her thoughts trailed off.

"Whose name?"

Her eyes glowed a purple Hydro had never seen. She ignored his question and asked her own. "Have you seen her yet?"

"Who? Anne?"

"You know her name... Then it is too late..." Without so much as a moment's notice, she yanked the orb from the table (it was now actually a longstaff). Grabbing it by the orb, she jabbed the tipped butt of the staff towards Hydro.

Out of reaction, he tilted to the right, avoiding the jab. However, he wasn't as fortunate when the weapon was brought down from his left shoulder diagonally, slicing skin open with ease, but missing the necklace. Hydro pushed himself away and rolled backwards, taking his stool with him. The lady yelled in Chaonese. Past the beads, Hydro saw Nivarre turn and run towards the tent. Once inside, Nivarre's smile turned sour, and he withdrew his sword. Hydro bashed the stool into his legs and crawled out of the way of an impending sword slice. *What in Abaddon's name?* The villagers eyed him. They inched toward him.

Nivarre swung again. Hydro said, "*Maa.*" A clod of earth shielded him.

Hydro stood and walked backwards, cautious of everyone. His hand found the hilt of his sword. Wind blew. Beads rattled. The three-eyed prophetess stepped out of her tent.

"Why did you do that?!" Hydro clutched his chest, trying to lessen the blood oozing out.

"Because you have a name sung for sorrow, and that is all you will ever bring so long as you wear that." The woman examined the staff in her hand. "That necklace started the Great War. Now you, Hydro Aylán Paen, will start another. I cannot allow that to happen. Seize him!"

A tug on his hand pulled his attention. Anne stood next to him. *Use me. Escape!*

Without a second thought Hydro said, "*Maa!*" All around him a tower of earth went up. Before it went up in front of the woman, Hydro noticed a look of disbelief on her face. Like she saw something. It was split and quick, but it was present. He didn't have time to analyze it, for he felt Anne tug him in the other direction. He ran with her, keeping with her agile little legs. He never loosened the spell, but ten steps later, he looked back and saw the towers of earth gone, the woman with them, but the villagers sprinting after him.

All the while, he was pulled along by Anne. He jumped when she jumped and slid when she slid. But when he found the brown sand ahead of him, she disappeared. He snapped back, shocked at her abandonment.

The chants and shouts of villagers alerted him that they still followed. He scanned the area. *Where is it? Where is it? Found it.* Hydro took five steps back and then leaped. And leaped again, more graceful this time with his footing.

When he reached the other side he said, "*Vesi.*" Water blocked the sanded area and his pursuers halted on the other side.

Hydro stumbled and tripped over his legs until the sand faded behind him. Shoulders heaved. Heart pounded. Lungs competed against one another for air.

It's not over yet. You need to run and leave.

Anne sat on a fallen tree branch. She slid herself off and ran through the forest. Either she had disappeared again or she was too quick for him, for he ended up following the trail of death instead of her. It took him to the stakes, and as he counted the bodies that he passed, he couldn't help but think that his name really was sung for sorrow. *All of these men died by me.* Finally, he saw Len. Still frozen. Still stoic as stone. Still frightened.

Hydro's legs gave out. And he crawled and sat with his back to Len's legs. His hand brushed against something. He looked down and saw the stem glass of Mount Klaff. After picking it up, he twirled it in front of him. *Is there really a wish at the top of you?*

Silence.

Then footsteps.

I never asked to cause the Great War.

Hydro removed the glass from his view and saw Anne behind it. "But you did."

Anne stepped closer. *No, it was Bane's ideals that caused the Great War. Do not believe what she says. She merely resents the fact that—*

"Hydro!"

Hydro looked behind him and saw Korth as well as four other acqua guards behind him.

"Hydro, what are you doing here?"

"Little Prince..."

Hydro turned. Nivarre and some of the villagers stood in front of him, weapons drawn. Hydro crawled backwards into Korth's company. The three-eyed prophetess wasn't there.

"Hydro, who are these people?"

"They are trying to kill me."

"Your little prince will cause great suffering. He needs to die."

"You will need to kill us, then." Korth drew his weapon, as did the other acqua guards.

Nivarre surveyed each guard individually. He clicked his tongue and resheathed his scimitar. "Don't think I didn't warn you." Nivarre turned with the other tribe members and ran back into the jungle.

"Hydro, who was that man?"

"No one. He was no one." Hydro glanced at Len's frozen body. No one had noticed him yet, and it would be better if they didn't. Not yet. He would take questions later. "I am sick of this jungle. Let us leave."

Hydro pushed himself up, keeping the wineglass in his hand. Turning, he followed the stakes back to the skirts of the jungle, never stopping to wonder about his purpose.

CHAPTER 27

RETURNING HOME

Hydro spoke to no one. Words escaped him. Adrenaline had also left him, leaving him with an ache in his legs and a pain across his chest. His hand brushed against the necklace, warm to the touch. Then he felt the warmth of blood. *How did she possess an Ether Weapon, anyway? She must have been Saeluste!*

"Elias is in the ship with healing salves, Prince Hydro."

"Elias is here?"

"He did not feel comfortable trekking through the jungle, and he would have only slowed us down. Fortunately for you, he stayed behind."

Hydro leaned against a tree. It had been two days with Korth and the other acqua guards, and during those days, all had asked questions at to Hydro's latest predicament. He had answered as briefly as he could, not wanting to expand upon how he had gotten to where he was, the wound on his chest, or about Len's death, other than that it was at the hands (or eyes rather) of a basilisk. And he certainly didn't care to answer why he didn't return home after the Trials. However, his apathetic answers only brought about scrutiny, further interrogation, and chastisement from his guards, ostracizing Hydro during the voyage home. He only spoke to them when needed.

"He can save his medicine." Hydro spat and then pushed himself off the tree and continued forward towards the next stake.

When he reached the next stake, he stopped to catch his breath. Yunva's long face, thin mustache, and dull-brown eyes came alongside him soon enough.

"Why are you so reluctant towards our help, Prince Hydro?" Yunva's hand squeezed Hydro's shoulder. "We are only trying to help and you brush us off."

Hydro brushed off the older guard's grip. "Because I do not require such a thing."

"I beg to differ," Yunva retorted. "That man clearly wanted you dead. Why?"

"Because he is crazy." Hydro stalked through what remained of the forest, not caring to wait for any of them.

"And sometimes the weirdest truths are the craziest ones," Yunva called out.

"Yunva..." Korth said.

What does she know? Just because she has an Ether Weapon, or is one of the Twelve, she thinks she has Power. Pearl claimed to have Power, but I never saw it during the Trials. Otherwise, I would be apprentice right now. Saeluste thinks she can see my destiny. We make our own destiny. I am not hopeless. I can do things by myself. Alone, Hydro leaned against another tree and sucked in air. A tear came to his eye. It ran down his cheek, but he caught it before it fell. *Len knew nothing. She knows nothing. They know nothing.*

No one understands you, Hydro Paen. I do, though.

"Anne? What do you mean?"

No one understood me, either. They never understood my ability.

"What ability is that?"

To have the Power to do anything. Her eyes glowed black. *The same ability you now possess.*

Hydro shuddered. His heart singed. He buckled, but held on to the tree. The next thing he knew, Korth was underneath him, helping him stand.

"You certainly do need that medicine, Prince Hydro. We are almost at the brim of the jungle. Come on."

Hydro walked with Korth the first couple of paces, looking around. "Anne..." Hydro didn't mean to say her name aloud, but he did.

"And what?" Korth stopped and looked at him.

His heartbeat raced as fast as his mind wandered. "And... how did you manage to find me here, anyway?"

"You should know that every ship is registered with a tracking number," Korth said.

"That does not explain how you managed to get to Qotia and find me on that path, nonetheless."

"Questions, Hydro. We asked questions. And Elias studied in Qotia. He knew folks there and the stakes in the ground made it rather obvious."

"I take it Mother sent you?" Hydro pushed his bodyweight off Korth and continued walking without support.

Korth kept Hydro's pace. "Lord and lady sent us, young prince."

"Why?"

"They miss their son. You may not want to talk with us, but they will certainly expect you to talk to them. If you don't, they will not be pleased."

"My parents will not be pleased by many things. They never have been." He finally exited the jungle, seeing the shark-shaped ship come into view, fins opened downward, ready for boarding.

Just before Hydro climbed the steps, Korth grabbed his shoulder. "Any parent holds expectations for their child. Do not think, though, that those expectations get in the way of love."

I do not think that, I know it, is what Hydro might have said. Instead, he simply boarded the ship, not caring to answer his trainer.

In the lounge, he crossed his chest and hid his wound as best he could, sitting across from Elias. He surveyed Hydro thoroughly when he had boarded and then directed his attention as the other acqua guards entered. After the ship took off, he pushed himself up on his cane and sat alongside Hydro.

"You will need to unfold your arms."

"I do not need your help, Elias."

"You do not *want* my help, Prince Hydro. But you do need it. Your mother sent me here to bring you back, and you will come back to her and your father alive."

I am sure my mother sent you to take care of me. Hydro kept his right arm over his necklace and surveyed Elias as he applied the salve to his wound. Upon the application of alcohol, Hydro bit his lip.

Elias dabbed a cool solution onto his chest to alleviate the burn. "Why did you not return home after the Trials?"

This again? He did not want to go into another round of interrogation, so he said, "Are you my father now?"

"No. Merely curious. Your father is quite upset."

"He will be even more so once we tell him of Len's death." Hydro stared at Elias.

The old adored held his mouth open in surprise, paralyzed by the news. "Len is dead?"

Hydro nodded.

"I... Well, that is most unfortunate news." Elias continued dabbing Hydro's chest. "This is quite the mark. It will scar, you know. How did you acquire it?"

"I tripped."

Elias bowed head and furrowed his brows. "Unlikely. Try again."

"A tiger scratched me."

"That is better, but I do not believe it's the truth."

"Why?"

"Because there is only one line. Now, when are you going to start opening up to us?"

"Do not be bothering, Elias. He not be behaving like a prince, anyway," Cassius scolded.

And your dialect is broken, Garian scum.

Elias finished his task and returned to the bench across the room. "My contacts at the adored academy told me you tried to find a soothsayer. Did you find her?"

She was more than a soothsayer. Korth crossed his chest, focusing on Hydro, who fidgeted underneath top trainer's gaze. Underneath all of their gazes. He nodded.

"And what did she tell you?"

"Nothing."

"Well, it seems as though your trip was very pointless then." Elias hummed afterwards. "I hope she was worth it, because right now we are all growing tired of tirelessly trying to help someone who is too tired to care."

Elias stared directly at him, with a look in those deep blue eyes he had never seen come across the old man's face. Disappointment weighted his gaze, and agony kept him under that deep blue current, as if he drowned from Hydro's half-heartedness.

Hydro gulped and crossed his arms. *I should have never gone to the adored academy...* But then he thought about it—if they hadn't had come when they did, he would have died. Surely he would have. He watched the band around the planet and the two moons—they were so large, so spectacular, but foreign. As of late, everything seemed foreign to Hydro. He didn't know if returning home would help. The only thing he knew was that he was returning home.

"Entering Onkh in one minute. Turbulence is expected. Strap in."

The sound came from the lounge speakers. Shortly after, his home planet came onto the screen that hung above one of the couches. Clouds covered much of everything, besides a stretch of land that Hydro knew as the nation of Gar. The ice nation of Sereya was present as well, located at the northern pole. But his nation still had yet to come into view.

As they descended lower, past the clouds, Hydro's stomach tightened. He no longer felt pain, but something else. Something he couldn't quite describe. Whether in fear of reprimand or the fact that he would need to face his family's hurt pride, he didn't know. For so long he had understood perfectly his role in life, but now he wasn't so sure. *Is my name truly sung for sorrow?*

To combat the foreign feeling, Hydro spun the stemmed wineglass in his hand. *At least there is Aiton.* Hydro closed his eyes, meditating on what would come next. He gulped when slight shock waves finally told him that they had arrived.

It was nearly sunset when they landed—Lugh had taken its absence and Freyr began to hiding behind the horizon. Hydro walked out first amongst them. Not by choice, however.

The castle walls seem larger than I remember. It had been two months since Hydro had stepped foot on Acquava. And even though it wasn't long, he knew a lot had changed, and much more still would. He made it 100 paces before seeing his father, mother, and the receiver for the family, Darien Dornell, standing in front of the castle gates. None made any effort to walk towards him.

With a polite shove from Korth behind him, Hydro walked towards them, a man forced to walk the plank. His father's cape billowed in the breeze, as well as his mother's gown. The draft made it colder here than he remembered. During his walk, he stared straight ahead towards the family in waiting, arms locked by his sides. When within shouting distance, his father called out to Korth.

"Thank you for retrieving Hydro."

"Of course, my lord."

"Elias, thank you, as well, for keeping Hydro in line," Hydro's mother said.

"It was by no design of mine, Lady Paen."

"Is that so..."

Hydro didn't cower under his mother's gaze. He looked at the three of them in turn. Darien was there because of formalities. His father was there as he should be and his mother, well, Hydro assumed his mother was there to see him scolded. But he wasn't concerned about her. The only one who concerned him was his father, for he shared his name, his pride, and his respect.

"Where is Len?"

Only silence answered.

Voice raised, his father asked again. "Where is Len?"

"Not with us, my lord."

"What do you mean?" Hydro's mother asked.

When silence stood its ground again, Hydro finally spoke. "He is dead."

Every eye gazed upon him now. Death held so much weight to it. So much finality. His father, mother, and Darien held their voices. The others around Hydro fidgeted with their hands. Hydro kept his hands tight to his hips, but he never looked down. He would face the reprimand before he would cower.

Unlike the prophetess, the three in front of him—the men around him—held no special powers foreign to him. They weren't the Twelve. He could face this challenge.

"Darien, take everyone back inside. Atesia and I need a moment alone with our son."

"Of course, my lord." Darien strapped his sea-leather gloves before turning on his heels and retreating.

Hydro felt alone. He always had.

His father fisted his hands and then relaxed them. "How did he die?"

Hydro remembered the eyes of fire that should've killed him. He saw Len die before his eyes. The body turning to nothing more than a statue. The look of horror. The—

"Hydro, your father asked you a question."

Hydro shook his head free from the flashback. "I wish not speak of it."

"What you wish is not what you will. Len was a trusted aide and gave good council. Now I will have to find a new advisor. Do you know how difficult that is? Especially now when we have one son that abandons us and the other who has yet to cast?"

Aiton still hasn't cast his first? It worried Hydro, but Aiton was still young.

"Now, how did Len die?"

"A basilisk."

"How in Abaddon did you manage to come across one of those?" His mother asked.

There was more than one. Images of the large serpents slithering to their position in the alcove replayed in Hydro's mind. The head rolling between his legs. The red eyes. Those fiery red eyes. Len dying. Hydro bit his lower lip. He wouldn't crack. Not here.

"You will answer me!"

Hydro opened his eyes to his mother, grabbing his chin. He sucked in air. Cold hands and even colder forest green eyes had him locked. Speechless. *She doesn't know. Neither of them knows.*

"Hydro!"

Hydro shifted his eyes to his father. "I have nothing else to say." Hydro talked, though his mother still grasped his jaw.

She let go and smacked him across the face. Her rings made it sting even more. "You deal with him, Hydro. It is clear he does not want to speak." She tucked the hand between her elbow and waist and left.

Leaned over, Hydro spit. He stood straight, only to falter under his father's gaze. They stared at each other for a long while, not saying anything until Hydro no longer felt the sun.

"Why did you not have your name read?"

Hydro's father shook his head. "What do you mean?"

"The starseer. You saw Saeluste, did you not?"

His father surveyed him. He was about to open his mouth, but decided to shut it when a breeze long and hard swept through the open field. Confusion contorted his countenance into a furrowing of brows that had placated his interminable stare.

Hydro didn't need his father to respond. His face told him everything. Everything except why.

His father put a hand over his mouth and coughed. "Your brother has been waiting to see you. He is in his room. Speak nothing more of starseers; they are in a past, forgotten." His father left.

Hydro stayed stationary, musing about his father's past alleged adventure. He watched the guards travel the battlements of the castle, occasionally glancing at him from their perch above. A gust of strong, salty wind helped to push him past the castle barbican.

In the house, no one spoke to him. Their eyes and silence made him feel like an outcast. He walked faster, hoping to get to the one person who cared about him—Aiton. He took the stairs two steps at a time. *I am almost there.* Hydro held the cup in his right hand and let his left hand slide on the marble railing as he made his way down the hall. Aiton's door was kept slightly ajar, like usual. Hydro stood in front of it, but didn't knock right away. The closest he got was a raised arm and his fist two inches away from the wood. Hydro inhaled. *This is silly. Surely Aiton is the same. Surely he is.*

Hydro exhaled and knocked. He pushed the door open with his left hand and peeked in to see Aiton watching the stars from behind a desk located by the window. "Aiton."

His brother turned around. "Hydro!" Aiton leaped off the chair and ran over to hug Hydro across the waist. "You are home. You really are."

"Yes. I really am." Hydro smiled for the first time in weeks. He crouched down, hugged his brother, and lifted him up. "I am glad to see you." Hydro set Aiton down and brushed a hand through his coarse brown hair.

Aiton stepped back. "What is that?" He pointed towards the cup in Hydro's hand.

"A gift for you from Chaon." Hydro handed it to his brother.

"What is it?"

"That, Aiton, is Mount Klaff."

Aiton rotated it in his hands. After a little while he said, "You saw Mount Klaff?"

"Yes, I did. It is larger than I imagined."

"I am going to climb it someday. Truly I am."

Hydro bounced on the sole of his feet. "And I believe you will, too. You are a Paen, after all." Hydro came close for another hug, but Aiton backed away.

Aiton frowned. He fidgeted with the cup in his hand. "Why did you not come back?"

Heaviness entered his body with the question. His heart shrank. His stomach clenched. His chest tightened. In his search for truth, Hydro had perhaps let down the most important family member of all. Hydro dropped his head and closed his eyes, wishing to avoid Aiton's presence. When he knew he couldn't, he swallowed his disappointment and sighed.

"Every man has things he must do. My absence was one of those."

"Mother and Father were fighting here all the time over you."

I never thought my disappearance would affect Aiton. Disappointment pricked Hydro's heart. "Well, I am here now, and things are going to be different, okay?" Hydro rubbed Aiton's shoulders until his brother looked at him.

Aiton nodded and offered a weak smile. His shoulders slumped. After a moment or two, he looked up at Hydro. "Tell me more about Mount Klaff. Please? What is it really like?"

"It extends above the clouds..." Hydro reached his arm towards the ceiling while still crouching. "The base is as thick as our home..." Hydro kneeled and stretched his arms out in an invisible hug. "And it is as blue as the water flowing from the fountain in the labyrinth."

"One day I will climb the whole mountain."

Hydro smiled at his brother's ambition. "And what are you going to wish for at the summit?"

"Power. You told me that is all that matters. I want to be as strong as Guardian Eska."

"Guardian Eska is certainly powerful." *And a fool for choosing the Commoner. I should be his apprentice.* "Did you talk with Eska about your goal while you were on the Core?"

"No. Mother and Father would not allow me to speak with him. Only they were allowed to talk."

Figures. They always need to be in control.

"What would you wish for?"

"Power is important." *That is why I left. To learn how to control it.*

"But you already have that. You're already so powerful."

Hydro grinned. "And you will be just as powerful someday." He brushed Aiton's hair again. "I would wish for respect..." Hydro's voice trailed off into thoughts. *If I had respect, then maybe love and Power would follow.*

"You have my respect." Aiton tugged on Hydro's torn shirt. "What's that?"

Wide-eyed, Hydro pulled away from him. "Nothing. It's nothing." Hydro readjusted his shirt and then took his brother's hands in his own. Trying to redirect the conversation, Hydro said, "And you have my Power, Aitey, whenever you need it." He swooped down and picked his brother up into one long hug.

In the hallway, he noticed his mother by the threshold, staring at both of them. Her eyes said everything, her lips didn't. She crossed her arms and walked away as if she had never even been there.

Hydro squeezed his brother more tightly, making up for his months of absence. It was then that Hydro remembered the little things, and how that was all that mattered.

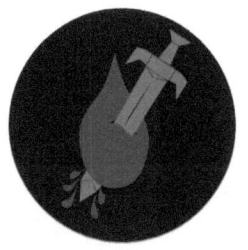

CHAPTER 28

SILENCE

"**N**ext!"

Hydro's father boomed. Cassius and Kent of the acqua guards led the woman and her son out of the Council Chambers, where Hydro, his father, Darien, and Elias sat. Korth stood at the base of the dais, in between those who spoke and the lord who listened. One seat was empty, right next to his father's. It would be for a while.

The two guards brought in a man with a torn-up and dirty red shirt, wearing pants with the knee area more worn than the other parts of his attire. When he took the patched hat off his head to make introductions, he ran rough fingers through wispy hair.

"Your name?" Darien asked.

The man put a fist to his mouth and cleared his throat. "Aylán Haier."

"Aylán, a good name. That was my father's name." Hydro's father smiled and looked at Hydro, who returned a weak one in comparison. "What can I do for you, Aylán?"

"Well, my lord, I am a farmer in Fjord."

"You have traveled a long ways then."

"Yes, I have. Three weeks with only my horses." The man nodded. "I have come to ask a favor of you."

Hydro's father leaned forward in his chair. "And what may that favor be?"

"The farmers of Fjord are experiencing a horrible growing season..."

His father's smile flattened. He still maintained his engagement though, something Hydro hadn't been able to keep for the past two-and-a-half weeks while he sat at the meetings designed to get him back into the arms of duty. Duty, a cold and unrelenting enemy. Hydro would kill her if he could. For now, he tapped his feet and stared blankly at the man who wove a story that many others before him had woven.

After a long while, long enough to where his father's other council members began turning their heads, his father raised his hand to silence the man. "Aylán, your tale is not unlike many others I've heard."

Aylán tilted his chin up to look at Hydro's father directly.

"And just like the many others before you, I must implore you to do whatever means necessary to grow your crops. I have already lowered the tariffs for the season to a reasonable level."

"My lord, if I may, that is not enough. The suns don't allow us to grow enough." The man pointed upwards.

"You do not grow enough because you do not work enough," Darien said.

"The suns' heat is why we don't work as much, and we don't produce enough money to hire hands to work while we rest."

"What would you have me do, Aylán?"

"I do not know, my lord. That is your decision." Aylán bowed.

"Well, I can tell you what we cannot do. The only other nation that surpasses us in agriculture is Cresica, but the suns affect their growth as well. I have tried to talk with Lady Clayse about leveraging embargoes, but her nation supplies food for much of Gladonus, and simply put, there is not enough generosity to go around. You must find a way to utilize our abundance of fresh water in order to best the heat."

"There are small areas of fresh water in Fjord, but we are near a peninsula—"

Hydro's father waved his hand. "Yes, I know of your town." He turned to his left. "Darien, you were born there. What are the irrigation systems like?"

"To speak truly, there are but a few. It is a rather small town in the Acquis province, but definitely the most beautiful."

"Hmm..." Hydro's father strummed his chin. "I will send another irrigation system from Symeria."

"The delivery will take weeks."

"Yes, long enough for you to get back to Fjord and announce its arrival. I am sorry; there is nothing more I can do."

Hydro could tell the man wanted to say more, but he didn't. Instead, he merely nodded and said, "Thank you, my lord."

Cassius and Kent led the man out, and while outside the chamber, talk resumed.

"That must be the one-hundredth complaint I have heard this week having something to do with these damn suns." Hydro's father shook his fist to the ceiling.

"The Curse of Pirini Lilapa may be on us already, judging from all the complaints we've heard," Darien said.

Elias dabbed his head with a handkerchief. "Does Guardian Eska offer any aid or words of wisdom?"

"Aye, I have not asked for any. Surely he is busy training his apprentice for the Meeting of the Twelve fast approaching. I do not want to appear incompetent in handling my own matters."

His father kept his eyes on Elias for a time until he shifted his gaze towards Hydro. He looked at the ground. The shingling of seashells on the acqua guard's armor didn't draw him back to attention, nor the clack and flop of the soles of those walking. Nothing could. But her.

From his peripheral vision, Hydro saw Anne beside the wall near Cassius. The acqua guard led the next person in, but she remained there, standing and smiling.

Hydro looked around, wondering if the others noticed her. The young man spoke, and his father and his father's council listened. Cassius acknowledged Hydro but returned to stoic normality soon after, mimicking Korth and Kent.

Anne walked past Cassius and Kent and down the long chamberway. She stopped where it bent to the exit and looked at Hydro. She waved for him to follow.

Does no one see her?

Hydro took another glance around. The man still spewed his story. When his gaze fell back upon the end of the chamber, Anne had vanished. *Where did she go?* Without thinking, Hydro stood and walked in the direction she had gone, paying no heed to any looks or voices that may have called out to him.

He found her again outside, in the courtyard. She smiled at him and walked away into the labyrinth of hedges. Hydro followed her and soon found himself in the middle, looking upon the statue of a dolphin in memory of the first Paen ruler of Acquava—Lyonell Paen—and his bonded animal.

She stood there too, looking towards the statue, facing away from him. *This is where she is buried, isn't it?*

"Where who is buried?" Hydro feigned. He didn't want to hear the answer he knew was true. His wish went unheard.

Your sister. Anne turned to him. *Anya. What a pretty name.*

Hydro recalled his sister being put in a casket and pushed into the base of the fountain. A large cobalt tile, unlike the others, noted her spot. There was no name though; nothing. No one else would have known if they hadn't been there to watch the process.

"Mother insisted it. She said that Anya was the greatest thing our family ever had, and it was lost, just like Lyonell was lost to Acquava. My father never spoke... Throughout all of my mother's diatribe, my father never spoke..." Hydro hung his head. He clenched his fists.

I can sense the sorrow in your voice, Hydro Paen.

Hydro tore his gaze from the dolphin to look at her. She had black eyes. Sickly black eyes. "What do you know of sorrow?"

I know the sorrow a broken bond can bring. She looked back at the statue. *It is the greatest pain anyone can ever face.*

"What do you want?"

I want to go home, Hydro Paen. It's been too long since we've been together. Much—

"Hydro!"

Hydro's body jerked. Korth, Cassius, and Kent all enclosed him, hands on their hilt, eyes upon him. Hydro looked to his left. Anne had vanished.

His lips pursed in thought. "How long have you been here?"

"We just arrived. A servant said she saw you entering the labyrinth. Why did you leave? Who were you talking to? Is someone else here?" Korth gestured for the other guards with him to search the area.

"I am alone."

The others stopped searching.

"But you were talking. To someone it seemed. When we arrived." Korth furrowed his nonexistent eyebrows.

Hydro exchanged glances with all three. "Well, I became with bored with the silence." Hydro cleared his throat. It wasn't too far from the truth.

"Yes, well, your boredom be the lord's excitement. We be to escort you to your father's chambers," Cassius said.

Ever since finding out Cassius had failed to become one of Gar's elites, the man left a sour impression on Hydro. By being an acqua guard now, Cassius made his father's guards look less than extraordinary.

"What does he want?" Hydro folded his arms.

"He and your mother want to talk to you. Will you come with us?" Korth extended a hand.

Hydro eyed it cautiously. "I suppose I have no choice."

"No, you do not," Cassius said.

Hydro shoved past the three guards and into the labyrinth's depths once more. Past the labyrinth, he ascended three flights of steps to his parents' chambers, located on the floor above his own.

When he entered, his father and mother were in discussion. She crossed her arms and looked away from him. His father nodded to the guards apathetically. "Cassius, Kent, you may leave. Korth, please stay in here with my son."

Korth nodded. "Yes, my lord."

The others left, leaving the four of them.

"Why did you walk off today during the middle of a hearing?"

"I was bored." Hydro crossed his arms, imitating his mother.

"Hydro, I know these meetings are tedious and dry, but it will be your duty someday to listen to the people."

There it was again. The word. Hydro kept silent.

"Hydro, your father is trying to speak to you. Why are you not saying anything?"

Hydro shuffled his glance to his mother. "I am listening. Someday I will need to do that."

A slap. He massaged his face. It was his father's slap.

"That mouth of yours has gotten you in trouble."

"It seems when I do not speak you want me to and when I speak you slap me. I am unsure how speaking gets me anywhere."

Hydro's father raised his arm to slap him again.

Korth stepped forward.

His father put his arm down and glared at Korth. "What are you doing?"

"My apologies, I shouldn't have. Do you not think it better to discuss what needs to be discussed?"

Hydro's mother regained composure and closed her slack mouth. "Yes, I suppose it is better."

"Sorry, my lady. I will beat him up for you on the training court if you wish it. It may be better there than here." Korth nodded.

"You are more than able to beat him up on your travels. Do not ruin his face, though."

"Travels?" Hydro hadn't meant to speak. Korth's actions still shocked him.

"Ah, so you can speak?" Hydro's mother walked alongside the bed to stand beside her husband.

Hydro looked towards his father.

"Hydro, your mother had a thought..."

Hydro tensed his neck.

"You are only a few years shy of twenty-five. If something should happen to me, we need to make sure our reign continues." Hydro's father clasped a hand on Hydro's shoulder.

Hydro didn't say anything. Shock paralyzed him. *Courting... Now?*

"Korth will be traveling with you to the various houses, and you will spend a month's time in each of their care until you find someone suitable to bring back here."

Hydro looked from his mother to his father to Korth. Still, Hydro didn't speak. All of this was new. Too new.

"When do we start?" Korth asked.

Hydro's mother narrowed her focus on Hydro. She smirked. "Immediately. By the end of next week. I have already told Marquis Axyel of Talyn. It will give them enough time to prepare for your stay. Is that understood?"

"So soon?" Hydro's lips betrayed him once again.

"I thought you liked traveling? You made it rather apparent when you did not return home after the Trials."

"Atesia..." Hydro's father glared at his wife long enough for her to shift her posture. When she did, he turned his gaze to his son. "Hydro, your mother suggested this to me upon your arrival home. After seeing such a disinterest in the meetings here, and the life here, I cannot agree more with her."

Hydro didn't answer. He no longer had a choice to disobey. His father now thrust him into the world he was bred for.

"I will take good care of him, my lord and lady."

"We know you will," Hydro's father said.

"I will have an outline of the schedule by the time you leave," Hydro's mother said.

Hydro didn't say anything to any of them. A silence controlled him. And like his father, he never argued.

CHAPTER 29

THE LITTLE THINGS

E ach of the next two days after the meeting with his parents, Hydro revisited different parts of the castle and the surrounding area. A man sentenced to walk the plank, Hydro looked out to the seas, to where his next adventure would take him, and the usually lush and rejuvenating waves now seemed rather lugubrious and rigid. The brine on the wind no longer caressed him as it should have, rather, it clawed him. Castle walls, once filled with joy and exultation, were now rather constricting and silencing. And the luster that he had once seen in his zircha sword now lacked. His home, his surroundings, his life had become foreign yet again.

Shoulders slouched, he now stood in the center of the stone court, trying desperately to hear the noise of a past he should know, but he could hear no rhythmic beats of his sole slapping the ground, nor the wind rushing past his ears, nor the steel clanging and chiming in ballads of songs. All he heard was Korth, but even his accent didn't sound the same.

"We should get some training in before we leave for Talyn. You will want to impress the southern island ladies, will you not? That is where your mother hails from."

Hydro looked back at Korth. *No, she doesn't. That's a lie.* He was surprised that he didn't know the truth, living and being around the castle all day, but Hydro guessed it wouldn't be a very good secret if everyone knew. In truth, his mother came from the small town of Crake in the Roil province, but to convince everyone she had royal blood, and thus save face from marrying a commoner, his father and his father's confidants had made up the elaborate scheme that she hailed from Talyn and was related to Marquis Axyel. The marquis was old and on his last wit, so the lie stuck.

Not caring to correct Korth, he answered, "You have training with Aiton."

"In an hour's time. More than enough time for you and me."

"I have lost my passion for fighting..." Since returning home, his sword had stayed in his room. The few times he had picked it up, it felt as useless to him as dirt to a beggar.

"You have lost your passion for speaking, as well, your parents tell me."

"And it seems my parents have lost their passion for me. You heard them. They are sending me away." Hydro spared a brief glance at Korth and then moved his gaze towards the sky. The suns were overhead, and they looked magnificent, so close together. Their paths wouldn't eclipse yet, though.

"They are your parents; they care, and they want you to come into the man you are capable of being."

If they cared, they would be here right now, talking to me instead of you.

"Do not think they do not love you, Prince Hydro. Some just have queer ways of showing their affection."

"Surely you do not show your affection to your wife and kids by ignoring them or sending them away for a year or more to spend time with lesser houses." Hydro walked away.

"Prince Hydro—"

"I am going to the labyrinth to clear my mind. Have fun training Aiton." Hydro called out while he was walking away.

Unlike the first of Eska's Trials, there were no beasts with skin of dripping tar in this labyrinth. At its center there was no demon who warned him of a little child but never told him why he should be afraid. And inside the lone tomb here there was no necklace that made him hallucinate or acted as a warrant for his death.

Last time he was here, he was so close to learning. So close. Hydro sat on one of the four golden benches that circled the water fountain. *If only I knew what to do...*

I can show you.

Hydro removed the hand that had been covering his eyes in contemplation. Anne sat on the edge of the fountain. "What can you show me?"

What you need to do. All the things you need to know.

"How were you able to—"

The necklace allows me to know your thoughts. It allows me to show myself to you.

"Why do you show yourself here and not anywhere else?"

I show myself where strong bonds are present.

"Why?"

Because I once had the strongest bond... a bond I wish to have again. But, I cannot see him again. Not yet. Together we can help one another.

Hydro shook his head. "I do not need your help." Hydro cringed as the girl approached him.

Without my help you would have never been able to defeat Beno Begare in the Zas Labyrinth. Without my help, you would have never been able to complete any of the Trials. Without my help, would have died along with your advisor. She stepped closer with every statement. *You very much need my help, Hydro Aylán Paen.* By the end of her talk, she stood directly in front of him. She put a hand on his forehead. Cold surged through his body. Sweat drenched his hair. *What is happening to me?* Hydro yelled and collapsed, seeing no more.

When he awoke, he did so to his mother's personal maid, Salina, crouching over him. Red hair fell in front of her face, parting enough to show her eyes, which were the color of new leaves.

"Are you alright, Prince Hydro?"

Hydro looked around; he had fallen off the bench to the cobblestone ground. The water fountain towered over him, keeping him in its shadow. His head felt clear and his body not as cold. "I am fine."

"I will go get Lady Paen then and tell her what has happened." She turned to leave.

"No!" Hydro grabbed her hand. "You will not say anything to my mother." He stared her in the eyes.

"But you are ill. Surely she wants to know." She sat on her knees.

"I am fine. The suns' heat bested me." Hydro felt his forehead.

"Your good mother and father have been searching for you all day."

No, they haven't. You have been searching for them. "You spend more time with my mother than any of the others; do you really believe she is good? Tell me true, Salina."

She looked at him with frightened eyes that quivered like the string after an arrow has been released. "Yes, she is most wonderful."

You lie, but I do not blame you. Living lies is easier, and you will live much longer because of it. "What is it that my mother and father want?"

"They would not say. But supper is near."

I've been out that long, have I? "Right." Hydro stood and combed his tunic for wrinkles.

Her complexion and deportment, and the fact that she was only slightly older than Hydro, would have made her attractive, but her name and position bore no greatness. If names truly did hold a wealth of Power, Salina would never be the one to hold any of it. She had reached the height of her potential, unless some baron, lord or marquis decided to wed her. *What if I married her, Father? Would you approve of my same misstep or meet me with derision? Would Mother?* The preposterousness of the idea caused Hydro to let out a slight giggle.

"My prince?" Salina clasped her hands together.

"It is nothing. Thank you for waking me, Salina." Hydro left and maneuvered his way through the labyrinth to the dining hall.

Unlike the day he departed for the Trials, there were no other families of Power dining with them. It was only his family and Darien that dined. Although Hydro wished Darien hadn't been eating with them, for he brought tension into the room, making dinner longer than necessary.

"Any word on who will become Len's replacement?" Darien asked.

"No. The matter perplexes me; I am still not sure how to announce his passing."

"Rumors spread as quickly as rivers; it will not be long before Acquava knows."

"This I know, Darien. This need not have happened..." Hydro's father cut his sentence short, giving Hydro a long gaze before returning to the squid and seahorse on his plate.

"I hear that you want to speak with me?" Hydro's gaze lingered back and forth between his mother and father.

"You have found your voice, have you?" His mother twirled her fork in seaweed and put it in her mouth.

"Enough, yes."

"Good," his father said. "Korth told us that you have lost your passion to fight. Did the Trials do this to you?"

"He does not have the fire in him, Hydro. *He never has.*"

His eyes flared. He stood up and walked towards the exit of the dining hall. He heard two things on his way out, the first being, "You start your training again with Korth tomorrow," said by his father, and the second, a feeble attempt by his mother to call him back into the room.

Outside, he saw a flash of black hair. It disappeared into a hallway. He followed the sound of soles clacking on the tile. As soon as he got to the corner, he saw the white blouse and dark-skinned figure of Anne dart around another corner. *What is she doing here?* Despite his warnings about her, she enthralled him like the knowing in the soothsayer's voice.

At the staircase, Hydro saw her tiny figure already on the second level. Two at a time, Hydro took the steps and paused before the hallway. Anne stood at the third of three doors on the right. It had been a door that had been shut for nine years—ever since Anya died.

Hydro walked forward. Anne smiled devilishly at him and then walked through the threshold as if there were no wooden door blocking her. *She can't go in there. That's Anya's room.*

Outside the door, Hydro stopped in contemplation of whether he should open it. He had forgotten how it looked. *Are the walls the same coral coloring?* Hydro gripped the knob. His hand shook. He felt ice enter his fingers. *Get over your past.* Hydro shook his head free of qualms and entered the room.

The room was dark. The shades had been pulled down. A bed made neatly lay on the right side; dust crawled over it from nonuse. On the left side was a full-length mirror decorated with a seashell border. Dressers, a desk, and a closet took up the remaining space.

Hydro couldn't find Anne anywhere. *Where is...* Hydro found himself moving towards the dresser. The tips of his fingers dragged across the hardgrain wood, collecting dust. He picked up a photo of his sister locked inside a seashell frame. Brown hair fell past her shoulders. Hydro fingered her smile. *Anya...* Again, coldness crawled into his hands. He dropped the picture to the desk and leaned over. He exhaled heavily. *Anya...*

A flicker to his left caught his attention. Anne climbed onto the bed, taking a spot near the window, and looked outwards.

"What are you looking at?"

The suns. They are beautiful, are they not?

Hydro ignored her. "What did you do to me back by the water fountain?"

Tap into your Power, like you have mine. Like the suns meeting, we will too. And when that happens, you will be a stronger man, in both body and mind.

"Why did that monster in the labyrinth tell me to be weary of you? Why did the soothsayer—"

They do not understand. Beno Begare was given Power he couldn't handle; it drove him mad. And the soothsayer is jealous of my master.

"Who?"

I can't say...

"Anne, tell me." The girl faded slowly as the suns' light diminished. "Anne!" Hydro moved forward and swiped his hands through her. "Anne—"

"What are you doing in here?"

Hydro spun around to his mother's voice. "I... I..." He couldn't produce anything.

She stormed in and slapped him. "How dare you try to say her name! Why would you come in here? You are the last person she would want in her room." She slapped him again.

Hydro could only flinch, wince, and grimace. The slaps escalated into fists that pummeled his arm. Soon the fists found his chest, and his soreness from the dagger, not yet completely healed. Hydro fell. She yelled and cursed him with any god or goddess she could name. Her screaming and sobbing brought tears to Hydro's eyes.

"I hope Abaddon takes you, and casts you in its fires for what you did today. I wish I never gave birth to you." Her heels clacked out of the room.

Hydro thought he heard her say something else as she left, but he couldn't focus. Tears slid down his cheeks, and he had not enough strength to catch them. To the floor they fell, a curse on their own. *A mother is not supposed to say something like that.* Hydro shivered and shook and sobbed. He cried more than he ever had, not caring enough about life to catch any of the tears. He heard a small patter of footsteps, but he still lost himself to his thoughts. *It wasn't her name. I would never speak Anya's name... never.*

A soft hand came to his cheek. It was a boy's hand, and it felt warm. "You must not let these fall, brother."

The comment only induced more tears. Now, he wasn't even a Paen. He was worthless.

Aiton kneeled next to him. "Do not cry. Please stay strong, for me."

Hydro looked at his brother, the same green eyes as his mother's stared back at him. But these were kinder. A tear slid down his brother's cheek, and Hydro reached out to catch it with his index finger. *I will not let your tear touch, brother. I will stay strong. For you.* Hydro sniffled and straightened his posture. "I am sorry, Aiton."

"Why was Mother so mad?"

"Please. Not now. Not here. I will tell you someday, Aitey. But not now," Hydro sobbed.

"Is it about my sister?"

Hydro nodded his head. He knew Aiton never knew his sister, being born a year after she died. Aiton never knew that Hydro's ineptness to cast Power caused his sister's death. He never told Aiton because he didn't want to appear weak in his brother's eyes. Aiton was the one person who had never held a grudge against him.

"Will I ever get to know more about her? Mother never says anything, and Father only says little."

"Someday you will." Hydro forced a smile.

"Do you promise?"

"Yes, Aiton, I do."

Aiton crawled forward and hugged Hydro. "I love you, big brother."

"I love you too, Aitey. I love you too." Hydro rubbed his brother's head.

They sat there together, leaning against a post of the desk and the wooden chair next to it. In the time Hydro was awake, no one else had bothered to come check on him. His eyes grew tired when he heard Aiton snoring on him. Succumbing to exhaustion, he closed his eyes. Hours passed where Hydro held Aiton in his arms, being strong for the brother who was strong for him.

CHAPTER 30

PALO

Hydro awoke during the night to a backache caused from leaning against the wooden leg of his sister's desk. Aiton had since sprawled himself on the floor, but both were still in Anya's room. Hydro had expected nothing to stir, but footsteps pounded the tile, audible because most others in the castle were asleep. It drew closer. And closer. At night, fires lit the staircase at each level so guards on watch duty and servants on night cleaning shifts could see more easily.

When Anne appeared at the threshold to Anya's room, she brought with her no shadow. Still, her footsteps echoed as she entered the room. He glanced down to Aiton, who still slept. Cautiously, Hydro slid his hand over him.

"Are you real or a shade?" Hydro asked as she approached.

Both. Real to you and a ghost to most others.

"What is your purpose?"

To show you truth, Hydro Paen. To show you why you need me.

"What truth is that? What need do I have for a shade?"

Do you see how your brother loves you? Anne approached.

Hydro looked towards Aiton. He was still sleeping, not stirring even the slightest.

How many times has your mother declared her love for you? How many times has she hugged you?

"I know my mother hates me."

Family should love you no matter what. Has your father ever declared his love?

"He has expressed it, yes."

Concern is what he expresses. He loves what you symbolize, not who you are. To him, you are only an heir. A tool.

"Prove your words or be gone." Hydro waved his hand, trying to ward her off.

As soon as he gets his son back, he is ready to ship him off again. Is that not evidence enough?

Hydro sat and contemplated.

Her voice spoke again. *Has he ever said he loves you?*

Hydro ran through every conversation with his father before and after the Trials. *"You will do it as your duty." "Duty to marry."* He couldn't recall the word *love* ever being used. *Does Father only see me as a tool?*

You are starting to realize. If you stay here, you will lose your freedom. You are meant for so much more. Anne approached further.

"What *am* I meant for?"

Anne walked closer. She was within arm's reach. *I will show you.* She reached out and touched her hand to his forehead.

Hydro saw a desolate landscape. A land he had never seen before. It was empty, torn asunder by something. A war, perhaps? Something great had happened there, though, Hydro could see that. Then, all of a sudden, animals prowled the land freely and without charge. They looked up towards the sky, noticing a large shadow move on the floor. A sinewy, serpentine shadow that snaked its way across the war-stricken land. As the shadow passed through the land, it began to heal itself. Recover. Rejuvenate. The desolation became lush with vegetation. The surreal change prickled his skin. His breathing intensified, until at one point, a figure descended from upon the clouds. An angel drenched in fire, with eyes as orange as suns.

His heart singed. The vision stopped.

"What was that?"

The past. The present. And the future, Hydro Paen. The future I will have.

Hydro gulped. "What do you want?"

Anne smirked. *I told you. To go home.*

"How do we get there?"

Anne touched his face and dragged her hand downwards. She stopped at the necklace. *They say home is where the heart is. So I only want what is closest to your heart.*

A pain surged through Hydro, greater than he had ever known. It was as if his heart erupted like the volcano of Vatu. A fire gushed through him, deep and fierce and hot. He squirmed and flailed and crawled out of the room the best he could. He fought the pain and the urge to yell at the top of his lungs. Past the threshold of his sister's room, Hydro found the marble railing of the second floor. He clenched his fist and hit the marble flooring multiple times, resisting the urge to scream. He looked back; Aiton still slept.

Within minutes, a guard on patrol duty found him. By then the pain had ceased and had left Hydro short of breath. To his surprise, he felt invigorated, like after a sparring session.

"Prince Paen? I heard commotion. Are you alright?"

Hydro rubbed his head. *What is this feeling?* Power surged through him; he felt incredible, like he could do anything—climb Mount Klaff if he wanted to, vanquish the monster Deimos like Eska once had, or even defeat Guardian Eska himself.

While he lay on the floor, he fluttered his eyelids, taking in quick glances at the face of the freckled man with ginger eyebrows who hovered over him. A steel half-helm fitted his head, and his cheeks were rather portly. The man stared in shock at Hydro.

"My... my... my... prince... your... your eyes..."

"What about them?" Hydro stirred and roused himself to stand.

"They're black."

"You are foolish. Do not lie."

"As black as night, my prince."

Ask for his sword so you may see his lies. She stood beside him, smiling. Her presence didn't bother him. She felt necessary to him now.

"Give me your weapon. I wish to see this."

The warrior cautiously looked to his scabbard and withdrew his sword. He shook with some unbeknownst fright. "He... here... my prince."

The leather grip felt odd to Hydro, but not every soldier carried zircha steel. He held the steel up to his face, using the fire present to cast his reflection. Hazel. All he saw was hazel.

"You mis-see."

"Black, my prince. They are black."

Kill him. He lies. A liar deserves death.

Hydro looked towards Anne. She stared back, unblinking.

"Do you see now, my prince?"

Hydro examined his eyes again. They were hazel. What did this man see? Hydro looked down at Anne.

Do it. She thrust forward with her arm.

"No. You must learn not to lie."

Without warning, Hydro thrust upwards, sliding the sword through the man's chin and up past his brain. It happened so fast, not even a scream escaped. Only a large clatter of steel plating echoed through the halls as the man collapsed. Dead.

He walked down the hallway, stopping outside his room. The door, slightly ajar, called to him. He pushed it open and entered one last time. On his desk lay the zircha blade that had gone so far untouched since his return home.

If indifference is what your parents show you, show them no love in return.

Guided by a feeling he couldn't explain, he picked it up. Tonight he would show it love and warmth. For a moment. He left the other sword in his room and left.

He took the stairs one at a time. His parents' chamber was on the third floor, directly where the stairs ended, to the right of the veranda that overlooked some of the estate. At any time, day or night, his parents' chamber was guarded by no less than two guards—one of them an acqua guard and another guard with at least five years of experience. At the top of the stairs, the two stood still as statues.

"Prince Hydro, what be the matter?" Cassius asked.

"I need to speak with my parents."

"They be sleeping. Speak with them in the morning."

"I do not care. There is an intruder in the halls. I woke up and saw a body lying dead on the second floor."

"You are certain?" the other man asked. Hydro recalled his name was Shamus, a stocky man who preferred an axe to Cassius's mace.

"Yes."

"Where?"

"The second floor." Hydro pointed downstairs.

Shamus took a few steps forward. Once past Hydro, Hydro turned, took the man by the head, and slit his throat, tumbling the man to the ground in a fountain of red. Out of instinct, Hydro turned around and held up his blade, meeting Cassius's mace. Hydro held out his left hand and said, *"Palo."* Fire from the torches nearby flew towards Cassius and slid in between the gaps of his armor, burning the guard alive through the seachrome suit. *Garian scum.* Hydro plunged his sword through the neck of Cassius, and instantly the man screamed no more.

Their squalls during death would fall on powerless ears. For the most part, anyway. His father was sure to hear. His proximity to the bodies that writhed on the ground would ensure that he heard. He scoured their figure for their knives, took both, then looked at the double doors in front of him.

His father was just beyond the door. Since he shared blood with his father, he could feel his father's location. Although the commotion would definitely have aroused him enough to draw his sword, Hydro doubted he wore any armor; Hydro didn't either, for that matter. That would make things a bit fairer.

His zircha steel couldn't hold weight to his father's weapon, but it could constantly change, meaning it would never truly break unless if the vertebrae of the weapon was severed or the information center stored in the weapon's handle was damaged. Hydro knew that he could impact his father's sword naturally, but not the other way around. To best avoid harm to himself, he would constantly need to switch his weapon to make his father miss, for any lucky stroke may cause the vertebrae to sever.

Without thinking too long, he kicked in the door and immediately held the sword to his face. The sword broke, but Hydro reformed it upon a thought to a shield. He brought it upwards, meetings his father's blade. When he pulled the shield away from his face, his father realized who it was that he faced and backed away. His mother sat up in bed, bed sheets covering her nakedness.

"Hydro, what are you doing here? What is happening outside? Why can I not sense you anymore?"

Hydro did not know the answers to his father's last question, but he responded to the first two. "Death. You want to ship me away to continue your reign; I am here to claim my inheritance." Hydro pointed at his father's blade.

Lunging forward, Hydro's steel collided another few rounds with his father's blade, maneuvering the chamber space as efficiently as if it were the stone courtyard. Each step in Hydro's offensive meant a change in his weaponry.

His father ducked one of Hydro's slices and kicked his son in the stomach, sending him back a little. "Hydro, stop this nonsense. We are family."

"Family loves you. No matter what. And that Commoner does not love anything!" Hydro pointed his sword past his father to his mother.

Almost faster than a reflex, Hydro threw one of the knives towards his father. He batted it down, but the movement supplied Hydro with a diversion to breach his father's defenses.

Hydro punched his father's stomach at the same time saying, "*Voima.*" Hydro siphoned his own energy to multiply his strength, sending his father flying into the bathroom area.

His mother screamed. Hydro jumped on top of her. He had never seen her so terrified.

Show her what she has shown you. Anne stood at the side of the bed, watching his mother flail and kick. Still, she remained a shade to them.

Hydro held firm and lurched over her fists to stop the flailing. "You squirm too much, Mother. Let me solve that." Hydro took her right hand and forced it against the black walnut bedpost. Taking the other knife, he plunged it through her hand, pinning her there.

She screamed and sobbed. "Why are you doing this? I am sorry. Truly I am."

"Lying will not make you live longer."

Hydro saw her eyes shift to the right. *Father...* Hydro jumped off the bed to the side and put his sword up to deflect the slice. His father's hair was ravaged, and his eyes glowed.

He wishes to test your Power. Let him. Show him your new strength. Say, Palo.

Anne's voice called to him. And he obeyed. "*Palo.*"

Fire formed around Hydro's hands as it formed around his father's. They shot it at one another. The feeling as he combated his father was invigorating. His father was strong. He was a lord, after all. Normally, Hydro would not have been able to stand to his father's might, but the necklace gave him strength—Ancient... lost... strength.

The fires burned nothing, but they intensified, rising like a flower blossom. *Push now.* Hydro dug deeper into his soul, reached forward with his fingertips, and flicked his hand. The movement flung his father into the hallway, his body and steel clattering on the marble. Hydro waved his hand and commanded the fire to block the entrance to the third floor. A great and marvelous fire raged outside of where his father struggled to regain himself.

Hydro turned back to his mother, who tried desperately to yank the dagger from the bedpost.

"You monster. What evil has taken you?"

"Only truth has taken me." Hydro towered over his mother and collapsed on top of her. "Tell me true, Mother, have you ever loved me?"

She sobbed. Desperately, she tried to yank the dagger from the bedpost. Hydro only pushed it in further, watching the blood trickle down her frail wrist, like the tears that slid down her cheek.

Hydro took her under the jaw. "It is your turn to answer me!"

"Once, I did. Yes, yes, Pearl's waters, I did. I still do!" She cried and screamed.

"You lie. Since Anya you have never loved me."

She sobbed and shook her head.

"Now all you love is Aiton."

"Your brother is different," she sobbed. "Please, Hydro. I do love you. I love you like... Aaahh." She squirmed as Hydro pushed the knife into her palm.

"You say that I never have had the fire in me." Hydro set down his sword. He leaned in closer. "Let me show you the fire I have." Hydro clenched her chin. She squirmed even more. Her breaths hit his face like hot gusts of wind. Her eyes widened. Hydro brought his other hand to her face.

"Please, Hydro. Forgive me. I have sinned, yes, yes, I have. I have not acted like a mother. Please... please..."

Hydro pulled deep within himself from a place forged by his mother's malice and mistreatment. As he pulled from within, his heart rate quickened. From mind to heart he felt Power surge into his arm and then into his palm. Pressing his right hand on top of his mother's face, he saw her green eyes. She gave the look of a woman who knew she was about to die. *Where is your taunt now, Mother? Let me show you my fire.*

"*Palo,*" Hydro said and released a flame long and bright and harsh.

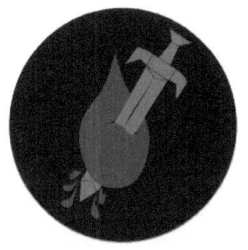

CHAPTER 31

INHERITANCE

A s his mother's body writhed in the bath of flames, Hydro sat on top of it, bathing himself in the melody of her misfortune. He inhaled deeply. *Justice.*

Anne took hold of his right hand. *It feels good, doesn't it? To have what you deserve?*

The screaming stopped. The smell of burned flesh and death would have bitten Hydro's nose normally, but not tonight. Tonight, it felt necessary. *It does.*

"You killed her."

Hydro shot a glance to his left. His father.

"You actually killed her." His father dropped to his knees. The tip of his sword dug into the floor. Through the smoke that lingered, he looked at Hydro. "What demon possesses you?"

Hydro crawled from the bed, clawing away the smoke as he made his way around to face his father, still kneeling. "No demon possesses me, only the truth."

"What truth is that?" His father looked up.

With the hand that held his zircha sword, he pointed towards his mother. His other hand still held onto Anne's. "You do not love me. Not like you loved her."

"The love a man and his wife have is so much different from the love a father bears for his son. I could never love you equally."

With a swift flick of his wrist, Hydro let his blade fall underneath his father's chin. Heat fell upon them both, still blazing from the wall Hydro had created to isolate them from the others. Through the cackle of flames, however, Hydro heard footsteps approaching, and he now even had the strange ability to look through the fire and see the silhouettes of those trying to ward the heat and see the aftermath.

"It pains me to see so much of myself in you, Son."

"What do you mean?" He lifted his father's chin upwards.

"Your desperation."

"I am not desperate."

"But you are... Yes, yes, you are... I once took an adventure. With your mother." From looking into Hydro's eyes, he nodded towards the charred corpse of his wife. "To Talyn Island. In the name of love. Your mother enthralled me back in my youth, but your father would not let me marry her. I, too, did not think he loved me, but I used the tools at my disposal to convince him."

"What do you mean?"

"I know of whom you mentioned. The starseer."

"Why didn't you want to know?"

"Why would I bother to know? Words are water. Atesia and I didn't need our heads and our decision rattled by some soothsayer's words. Is that what plagues you now? Did she do this to you?"

"No." Hydro shook his head as if to convince even himself of his words. "How do you know her? How did you meet?"

"I happened across her and her husband, an adored with an exhaustive understanding of potions. Although the woman proved pointless, her husband gave a potion to let me fabricate a story about Atesia to Marquis Axyel. And, he gave me another one, to make sure my father would be convinced as well... That is how your mother came to be my wife. I, too, committed sins against my family."

"Then you should understand!" Hydro yelled. He removed the tip from underneath his father's chin. "You should understand." Hydro repeated himself, quieter this time. Lost. He sheathed his sword.

His father stood, sword and scabbard in hand.

As he was about to walk past the threshold of the bedroom, his father extended his arm, Purge an extension to himself, blocking Hydro's exit. "And you should understand why I cannot let you leave here."

"You mean to keep me here?"

"You must face the crime you committed. Words are water, but actions are ice. You should know that." His father looked at him with a stern, stark look. Hydro had seen it multiple times before. It was the mien of a man that needed to cast reprimand.

Anne squeezed Hydro's hand. He turned his attention from his father to Anne on his left. *He means to kill you. You cannot let him do that.*

I would kill my own father?

You must survive. She squeezed his hand once more. Tighter this time.

Hydro's hand shifted to the hilt of his blade.

"Son, do not make me do this." Hydro's father tightened his grip.

Hydro looked at his father. Truly, for the first time, seeing him as the fires blazed upon their faces. He didn't retract his arm; he stood there, a lord pinned to uphold his duty. He sniffled. Wetness clung to his face. He sniffled again, trying to retract the fresh tears sliding down his cheek. Hydro took his hand and brought it to his father's face, stopping the tears before they hit the floor.

"I am sorry, Father."

First, Hydro ducked, making sure to clear Purge. On his way up, he had uncovered his own blade and pushed it backwards towards his father, focusing on changing it to a lance. A soft squish, a momentary resistance. Hydro pulled back, wet red now dotting the floor.

Hydro's father took his hand and wiped it against his thigh. He brought that hand to his mouth. He walked past the threshold of the bedroom, stepping across the two bodies of his guards, giving them each only a momentary glance. "This is the path you have chosen?"

"I see no other way, Father." Hydro held his lance ready.

"Then I am sorry, too, Son..." He threw down his scabbard to the tiled floor behind him, letting the clinging cover the sound of his lips.

From beneath Hydro's feet, the floor shook. It opened up. Hydro jumped forward to avoid falling through the hole his father had created. He met his father's blade in midair with his lance. The lance fell apart, the Ether Weapon cutting through it as if it were nothing. Hydro focused and changed the weapon to an axe, redistributing the liquid steel. Hydro sidestepped his father's downward slice, and using the arm of the axe, swiped the Ether Weapon out of the way. Following through his movement, he spun towards his father and sliced open his arm near the shoulder. Blood slid down.

His father grimaced, losing control of his spell. The floor returned to normal.

Hydro jumped backwards, nearly avoiding his father's weapon, but the tip caught his shirt below where the necklace hugged to his chest. Blood trickled down him as well.

Hydro Paen, you must take greater care. That was too close.

Hydro didn't need some shade to tell him that.

They circled each other, ignoring any discomfort.

Overtop of the fire, people yelled through the flames. Korth ordered for guards and maids alike, any of the watchers, to gather buckets of water. They were going to try to eradicate his spell. Hydro would need to leave soon if he wanted to escape. One on one, Ether Weapon versus liquid steel was as fair as a fight as he would receive; if more people were brought into the fray, especially acqua guards, Hydro would have trouble.

When Hydro began to run forward, his father did as well. They charged at each other from one end of the floor to the other. His father laid various traps of earth for him, but Hydro sidestepped them all. He, too, could have cast earth to try to slow his father, but that would have meant a weakening of his mind and his fire wall, something he could not afford to do. He needed every bit of cognizance for this fight.

An odd cadence of steel clashing, missing, breaking, and reshaping trumpeted past the clacking of soles and the heavy breaths each of them took.

You must get the weapon out of his hands. It is yours.

A sharp glance to his left to where Anne lurked in the shadows momentarily blinded him. A pain came to his arm. Hydro yelled and crumpled to the floor, losing his weapon. A large gash now bled out from his left shoulder. *Pearl's waters!* His eyes flittered between his father and his weapon and Anne.

His father swung at him again. Hydro rolled out of the way, diving towards his sword, making sure to apply pressure to his other shoulder. During his roll, he grabbed the blade. Turning around, he batted away his father's first strike, but had no time to prepare for the counterattack. Instead, he merely held up his blade to protect his body.

The Ether Weapon cut through it. Shards flew everywhere. The vertebrae had been severed.

Hydro's eyes bulged. Now only a makeshift dagger remained in his hand. *Sword.* Nothing. *Axe.* Nothing. *Shield.* Nothing. His father advanced on him. Realizing he was now without a weapon, Hydro flung himself backwards towards the corpses of the sentinels. He grabbed the closest weapon he could find—Cassius's mace.

He stood, jumped back, and examined his options. A makeshift dagger that had been his zircha weapon in his left hand, and a short-reach mace in his right hand, against his father's long-reach Ether Weapon. To his left, he heard chants and shouts from Korth to take position. *They must have returned with the water buckets.* Hydro would have to end this quickly. Taking one last glance at his weapons and then at his father, he devised a plan.

Hydro sprinted forward. *"Maa."* For a brief second he let him momentarily lose control of the fire spell, and focused on making binds for his father's feet. When the tiles started shifting under him, his father jumped forward. Hydro slid, crossing over his weapons, hoping his father would attempt to strike him upon seeing his defensive position. It worked.

His father brought down his Ether Weapon vertically.

"Maa." Hydro focused again on earth, letting his grip on the fire spell falter.

"... One."

Hydro heard the soldiers count across the fire, but still he focused ahead.

His father, expecting the spell to ensnare his feet, misjudged. Instead, the pillar of earth rose in front of Hydro, underneath his father's arm, catching it like a brace. The sudden shift in momentum caused his father's arm to buckle and stop. Still sliding, he spread out his legs to stop directly in front of the pillar of earth. With the makeshift dagger, he slashed at his father's wrist, cutting it open, and flung the mace towards his father, hitting him square in the chest. The two-pronged attack was enough to cause his father to let go of the weapon and drop to his knees. Hydro caught Purge.

"Two..." Korth yelled this time.

Hydro released the earth spell. Now it was only him and his father.

"Three!"

In a simultaneous moment of subconsciousness and surrealism, the heat upon his face died while his arm moved the blade forward to the kneeling man. Easily, it went through. He had no time to examine his father's face, for in the next moment he heard a voice that brought him back from the brink of instinct. To a place he wished he hadn't needed to be dragged to. To reality.

"Brother!"

"Aiton..."

Instantly, the boy was carried away by Korth. Hydro looked back at his father. Horror clung there, and a fleetingness brought about by battle. His eyes flittered.

"My... son..." He fell backwards from his knees.

Not wanting to look at the crowd, Hydro grabbed the scabbard that lay close to his father on the floor and then dashed to the veranda window. Acting only upon the instinct of survival, he jumped, never to look back.

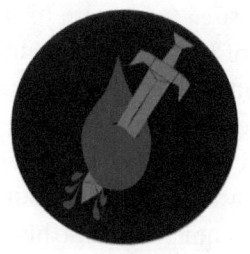

CHAPTER 32

COMMOTION

Footsteps were the first thing Aiton heard, followed by yells and shouts and screams—horrible screams like someone was burning alive. He smelled smoke and tasted it too. *Are we under attack?* Aiton got to all fours and looked around the room. *Where is Hydro? Did he go to fight off the intruders?*

Aiton rubbed his eyes and stretched his back. Slowly, he crept out of the room, and upon turning the corner, he went back into the room. *He's dead. Someone is actually dead.* Aiton peeked around the corner again. Guards rushed up the stairs. Aiton couldn't focus on them, though; a man lay dead near him! Blood spilled from his neck. Aiton nearly gagged. He had seen blood before, and had even seen people die for injustices they committed against his father, but there was something different about this death—it was one of *their* guards.

Although he didn't know who he was, he felt sorry for the man. Did the killer know he and his brother lay sleeping in the other room? Did the guard try to defend them? Did the guard know? Aiton slipped past the body, towards the noise of shouts and screams and clanging steel from the third floor. Every so often, the floor would shake, as if Power bit into the foundation of the third floor. *Is Father in trouble? Where is Hydro?*

When he passed his brother's room, he noticed the door open. He looked inside and saw a bloody sword. Aiton jumped back. *Brother!* He looked around for Hydro but couldn't find him. *Was he taken?*

From outside, guards continued rushing up and down the stairs. He left the room, shaking a little with every step, and watched, for a moment, the hustle and bustle of the scene. None noticed him.

Fire roared on the third floor, calling to him. Aiton obliged, dragged to it like a fly to a light. Men stood there, not moving at all, oblivious to his presence and most likely the presence of those around them. Fire had ensnared their attentions, kindling their other senses. It gushed outwards at the ceiling, greedy to devour more, not satiated by its current meal, half of the third floor staircase. *Who is doing this?*

Shouts rang above the cry of steel. *Hydro,* they called. *Do they call for my brother or my father? Or both? Is an attacker so powerful that it takes both my father and brother to kill him? Is it Deimos?* Aiton had no clue what Deimos looked like, but even Guardian Eska himself needed help to control the beast. Had someone freed the monster from its chains in Chaon? Had the beast followed Hydro here to Acquava?

Aiton squeezed through the tight crowd that lined the stairs. His heart beat faster with each step he took. *Please Father, please brother, slay the demon. Keep Mother safe.*

As Aiton ascended, the steel song became louder. At the top, Aiton pushed his way through. No one seemed to notice him. Their eyes were fixated on the battle ahead. Through the flames, Aiton barely saw anything. Silhouettes danced, raising steel to shadowed steel. The fire warmed Aiton's face, but in doing so, caused him to squint whenever he tried to look through the fire. At the front of the flames stood Korth, armed with his sword. The smell of rancid death lurked from behind the flames.

"Why aren't the water basins here yet? We need a source for Power if we are to combat this flame. It is too strong for our own."

"Here. Here they are, Sir Korth."

Two men brought forth water basins and placed them near the top of the stairwell. No one had noticed him yet. Korth shouted directions, and other acqua guards formed the front lines and directed the people behind them. Aiton did not know if it was his size that caused him to go unnoticed or the importance of what lay behind the fiery curtain. Steel sang, chorused by footsteps and heavy soles. Tired soles.

"On my count, we use the water to douse the flames. Everyone, draw from its source. One..."

Aiton tried focusing on the water as well. He wanted to help if he could. He needed to be strong for his family. Someone powerful was fighting either his brother or his father behind the flames. Aiton needed to find out who. Aiton reached through his fingertips and focused.

"Two..."

He drew his attention towards the basin closest to him, two soldiers down to his right. Aiton looked ahead again. The battling had almost seemed to cease.

One figure was on his knees, collapsing to the ground with a sure thud. The other figure strode over to him.

"Three."

Aiton focused and water rose from the buckets, whether by his will or the will of the ones around him, he did not know. It surged forth and covered the flames, which refused to die. For minutes, it seemed the fire stayed strong, but slowly it began to weaken, like all Elemental Power would when combated against the nemesis of their hierarchy.

When the flames died, Aiton wished he wasn't in front. Aiton wished he didn't see what he saw. His tongue moved and voice spoke before his mouth could shut itself. "Brother!"

At the very moment he spoke, Hydro drove a sword through the man kneeling on the ground—his father. Hydro turned to him with eyes as black as night, as dark as his hair—soulless.

"Aiton..."

He thought he heard his brother call him, but his father looked at him as well, with horror in his eyes. Korth dashed in front of Aiton and picked him up. Aiton still saw over the burly trainer's shoulders to his father now lying on the ground, blood pooling around his body. His brother had vanished from the third floor.

"Lord Paen has fallen. Fetch Elias, immediately," someone in the crowd said.

The acqua guards had chased Hydro out to the veranda. *Did they make the jump with him? Will they catch my brother? Was it really him?*

"I heard fighting. Was that really..." Aiton couldn't fathom the possibility, but he needed to ask. "Was that really... Hydro?"

Korth didn't respond; he hustled past the lines of guards, carrying Aiton to the second level. Aiton hugged Korth tightly, not wanting to believe what his eyes saw. *Brother, was it really you?* He cried, letting Korth's shoulders catch all his tears. As Korth set him down by his room, he heard someone from up above shout loudly and fiercely.

"The lord lives. The lord still lives. We need Elias immediately."

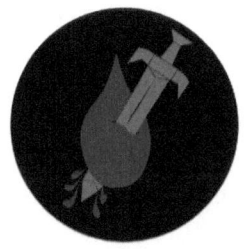

CHAPTER 33

A FATHER'S WORDS

Aiton looked at his father. He stirred slightly in his sleep. His chest and torso were bandaged, as were his jaw and cheek and arms. Multiple sword strokes had found him. Aiton couldn't fathom how his father carried on through all of this. It was a testament of his strength, a strength Aiton hoped wouldn't falter. *Please live. Pearl's good name and the Twelve let you live.*

The apothecary was located near West Tower inside the castle walls. A room of modest size, it boasted twelve resting stations for wounded soldiers and enough walking space for Elias and the other younger adored to tend to the needs of those that had fallen in battle.

Aiton shivered a little as a cool, midnight draft wafted in from outside. Upon noticing this, Korth stood up and closed the window. Elias reappeared from a workroom in the back with a wet rag and placed it over Aiton's father's forehead. The caretaker showed no clues as to his father's status.

Elias finished checking the multiple wounds on the lord's arms and body. "Korth... Darien... Haruko... may I have a word with you?"

"I need to stay by Aiton's side." Korth patted Aiton's shoulders.

Elias nodded. "Very well. Darien. Haruko."

Aiton fidgeted with his fingers as Elias and Darien and the professor disappeared into the back room. Korth kept a padded sea-leather glove on his shoulder. Aiton was glad for Korth's devotion, but Hydro wouldn't want to hurt him. Would he? Then again, Aiton never thought he would hurt his father. Images flashed back through his mind of the blood splattering on Hydro's face. *Those eyes. Those black eyes. Hydro...*

In front of him, his father lay motionless. Outside, the wind howled against the castle walls. *Even the wind doesn't like this...* Aiton made his way to the window and looked up at the night sky, trying to find Asiqu—the North Star. His brother used to tell him that everyone had a star, and that if they found theirs, they could make a wish. On a night such as this, when all the stars seemed to shine, Aiton hoped for a miracle to find his, but would he wish for his father's recovery or to have Hydro back again, to the way he had been before any of this? Aiton felt a tear slide down his cheek and quickly caught it with his finger. *I need to be strong. For family. Hydro would be...* The thought of his brother only made him cry more. Soon he couldn't catch the tears with a single finger, so he used the sleeve of his blue tunic.

Why did any of this have to happen? If I could have cast Power, then I could have eased mother's tension. If I could have cast Power, then my brother would be proud of me; he wouldn't have done this. If I could have cast... Aiton looked down to his hands and slammmed his tiny fists into the stone, breaking the skin on his knuckles. "Aarrghh," Aiton yelled.

"Easy, young prince. It will be okay," Korth said.

"Aiton..."

Aiton spun around. "Father!"

The door at the back room opened, and Elias and Darien and the professor strolled out. Darien exchanged a private word with Korth and then joined Elias and Professor Haruko near Aiton's position. Elias rested a hand on Aiton's shoulder. "Aiton, your father is trying to rest."

"Elias..."

"My lord! You mustn't speak. You need to conserve your strength."

"You know... well enough... that I do not have the strength... to recover..."

"Do not say such things, my lord," Elias said.

Aiton's confusion gave way to a glare. *Is that what the exchange was? Is that why they wanted to speak with Korth?* Aiton hated being insignificant and young. If he were older, if he could cast Power, or be as confident as his brother, no one would ever ignore him. *He is my father and your lord. I should have a right to know his condition...* Aiton hated Elias and Darien in that moment. *Would Korth have told me?* He looked upon the man who had been such a significant part of this castle. *Yes, he would have. I know he would have.*

"Elias. Haruko. Who else is here with me?"

"I, my lord," said Korth.

"I, as well, my lord," said Darien.

"And Aiton..."

"I am here, Father." Aiton brushed up against Korth's figure and took one of his father's hands into his own. Aiton cried a little and wiped it away with his free hand.

"Darien... I entrust... you to find a proper advisor... for my son... You are the sole... seneschal... to this family..."

"I will begin arrangements immediately, my lord." Darien bowed.

"Korth... Find Hydro..."

"The other acqua guards and a thousand troops are searching now, my lord."

"Find him, though... An evil possesses him... This I know."

"We will track him. He cannot go far," Korth said. He clenched his fists and put his knuckles together.

"You will be Aiton's sworn shield... Protect him... no matter what... Through him our name... our name..." He coughed. "... continues."

"All guards who are not searching for Hydro are on alert here at the castle. The young prince will be protected. No harm will come to him, my lord." Korth pounded his chest. "I will make sure of that."

Korth stood strong and proud. He didn't fear. Aiton wished he could be like Korth; he carried so many dominant qualities, so many qualities that reminded Aiton of his father... and his brother. *I will be as strong and proud as the family name...*

"Elias... Haruko..."

"Yes, my lord," both answered in unison.

"Study tomes... study... Find a cure for..." His father coughed again. "... for Hydro... He is taken by something... by a Power I know not of... but his eyes were black... black as night..."

Aiton's skin prickled as he recalled the eyes again.

"I will look in the spell books for something," said Professor Haruko.

"And I will look for medicines, my lord."

"I pray you both find something...," he drawled. "Leave me with my son now."

"My lord, I cannot do that. If Hydro comes back—"

"Hydro is not coming back, Korth. Leave now. All of you."

Aiton watched the four of them give each other a quick glance and nod. Before departing, each one stole a glance at Aiton and put a hand on his shoulder. After each touch, Aiton felt more alone, and he wept; there was no end to his river of tears. He was an Acquavan after all—made of sea and water. The tears didn't stay there for long; Aiton removed them with his sleeve. While glancing at his father, he needed to remind himself to breathe.

His father's eyes fluttered. "Aiton..."

Aiton whimpered. "Yes, Father..."

"Before your brother... left for the Trials... he wanted me... to do one thing for you... Do you know... what that..." His father coughed and covered his mouth. When he removed his hand, Aiton saw blood. "... What that was?"

Aiton shook his head, too nervous to speak.

"He wanted you... to retain your youth... to not grow old... to duty..." His father stretched out his hand.

Upon seeing the red on his father's wrist, Aiton took it and cried. He didn't bother drying his cheeks, but his father grimaced and reached over with the other hand—the one he coughed into—and caught the tears. Mixed with Aiton's own tears, the blood from his father's hand marked Aiton's face. It stuck there.

"I... I have done this... as best as I could... but... the world is changing... and now... now I cannot be so naïve..."

Aiton's heart quickened, but he remained silent. The proper words never seemed to form.

"You... Aiton... you need to become... the man our family... needs you to become..." His father smiled. "... Not tomorrow... or the next day... but today... Right now..."

"I will. I will." Aiton sobbed. Eyes too full of tears, Aiton couldn't look at his father. "But, you will not die, not yet. I need you..."

"Aiton..." He smiled once more. "... My time has come... I never thought... never thought... it would be by my own son... How cruel fate is..." More like a whoop this time, his cough forced him to cover his mouth with both hands. When he pulled back, he put his hands to his chest as if the cough had agitated something in his body.

When the episode finished, Aiton retook his father's hand, not caring about the mess of blood. "Hydro is good. I know he is. I will fix him. Whatever is wrong with him, I will fix," Aiton pleaded.

"I pray you do, son... I pray you do..." He smiled, leaned his head back, and closed his eyes once more.

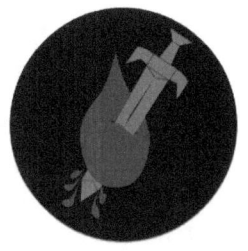

CHAPTER 34

FREEDOM

T he salty sea was close now; Hydro could smell it on the air as he drove the hovercraft west. His father's sword, Purge, sat in its scabbard in the seat next to him. Also in the seat next to him was Anne.

Bloodied hands gripped the steering wheel of the hovercraft. Blood coated his tunic and face. Most of it was the blood of others, soldiers who had the unfortunate task of trying to stop him as he left the castle. His father's Ether Weapon cut through them all like tender meat.

The hovercraft swerved.

Stay on track.

His fingers trembled. "What have I done?"

Only what was right. Family should love you no matter what.

"Aiton..."

Aiton is the only one who has ever truly bonded with you.

"What will he think of me?"

Anne never answered.

"Where are we going?"

To freedom. A coolness accompanied her voice, matching the wind that flowed past them now.

"Freedom from what?" Hydro looked at Anne.

She looked at him. *Duty, Hydro Aylán Paen. Duty.*

At the gorge of the Viper's Tongue, Anne directed him southbound. Hydro knew where they were going, then, to a town called Perét. Normally the drive would have taken a day and a half in a hovercraft, but Hydro hadn't stopped since he left the castle, and so he came upon the city the day after, in the grave of night, yet again. He wasted no time walking. Instead, he drove straight to the docks at the western part of the village.

Drive over the water.

"It is not possible with this type of hovercraft."

We need to get across the water.

"How far are we going?" Hydro raised his brows.

Far away.

The pickings for an appropriate ship were slim, but Hydro didn't care; he would pick one. But before that, he would need medicine. The wounds his father gave stung and were deep. If he were to combat the breeze against him, he would need to replenish his energy and close up his wounds. To solve this problem, Hydro found a medicinal shop near the eastern outskirts of the city and kicked in the door. There was no light, but for some reason, it didn't affect him.

How is this possible?

You have my eyes now, Hydro Paen. We are bonded.

Hydro stole one vial of ard leaves and enough healing salves to fill his arms. On his way back to the ship, he noticed a guard roaming the streets lit only by sporadic firelight, perpendicular to his location. Hydro paid him no more attention and found a small skiff. If the winds were to pick up, this would be difficult to control, but it was the only ship small enough for him to operate by himself. And it would also be the only ship likely to go unnoticed by the scouting party surely on his trail. He laid his plunder in the skiff.

You will need your father's blade to cut the ties.

Even if he didn't need his father's blade to cut the ropes off the skiff, he would still take it along for protection. Only ten other Ether Weapons existed. He leaned over the side of the hovercraft and grabbed the scabbard.

"You there. Halt."

Hydro spared a glance at the guard and then walked away.

If he follows you, you will need to kill him.

Hydro kept walking, trying to ignore both of them. The leather hilt felt foreign to his hand, and the steel was much heavier than his zircha sword, almost to the point of requiring two hands to hold it.

"I said halt."

Hydro quickened his pace but didn't run. Anne kept up with him. Suddenly, a tower of earth sprung up from before the docks, then two more on either side of him. Hydro looked at her and she at him. The nod she gave him said more than words could. Hydro paused and exhaled. He stretched his sword wrist. Hydro turned around.

"Who are you, sir?"

"Prince Paen. Please let down these walls."

"Where is your sigil? Or your ring, if you are the prince?"

Hydro glanced down at his garb. The shirt he donned did not have any sigil on it, and his necklace he had left at Eska's estate before departing with Len. "I misplaced them."

The man walked closer, hand on his sword. He wore brigandine armor with a steel cap. "That is convenient." When the man talked, his lips did little to cover his gums, or the parted upper teeth and crooked lower teeth. "I saw you stealing from the store. A prince wouldn't do that. Lower your weapon, and I will leave you with only a charge for breaking the door."

"Go. Pretend you never saw me."

"I have a duty to my people and my city."

You will grow to hate duty. "And you will live to serve another day if you let me leave."

The man walked closer. "I cannot do that."

Hydro noticed movement from behind the man.

More are coming. He attracts eyes.

Without too long of pause, Hydro lunged forward and slid the sword right through the man's abdomen. With his other hand, he covered the man's mouth. "*Vesi.*"

The man gargled and flailed. Water slid from his eyes and out of the orifices of his ears. A mixture of mucus, blood, and water flushed out of his nose. Soon, his will wore out, and he collapsed, and with him, the pillars of dirt that had been blocking Hydro's path.

When within range, Hydro cut the ropes of the skiff and hopped aboard. To gain momentum, Hydro used water's Power to push him from the coast. By the time others had arrived at the man's dead body, the pier was too distant to see clearly. Hydro turned around. The expanse of water lay in front of him. Nothing to shelter him, Hydro remained open and vulnerable to the gusts that found their way to his wounds. He swabbed his open cuts with the stolen salves and tore pieces of his leggings and shirt to bandage them. To conserve energy, he let Power die and rowed.

After a league of rowing, Hydro took an ard leaf to replenish his strength. By a little after dawn, Hydro found himself, with Anne's instruction, on the island where the lords of Acquava were buried. His eyes were as tired as his body, but he refused to rest. There was still much to accomplish. His supply of ard leaves had grown thin during his voyage, but two remained. At Anne's heeding, he cleaned off the blade's blood with seawater and used an extra piece of legging he had torn off to dry it. Also upon Anne's advice, he cast a spell of earth to gut the boat with a small spire.

Hydro left the remains of his boat upon a sandy shore and walked uphill to the mouth of a cave. Shivers crawled on Hydro's skin as he dragged his feet across the checkboard tiles of blue and white. "Why did you lead me here?"

What is this place called, Hydro Paen?

"The Hall of Lords."

It should be called the Hall of Duty. What you see is that. And only that.

"They are dead. They no longer have any duty." Past the statues now, Hydro descended to the Watery Path until he came to an invisible wall that held the water in place. Inside the transparent hallway, sharks roamed to and fro, their red eyes searching for anyone unworthy.

Are you sure?

"Of course I—"

You see now, yes?

"The sharks." Hydro fixated on the sharks before him.

When you die a lord, you become a shark and roam these waters. You know this, Hydro Paen.

Hydro didn't answer. He looked ahead, caught in thoughts. *Is my father one of these sharks yet?*

What lies at the end of the path?

"Pearl."

And who do these sharks protect?

"Pearl."

So whom have the previous lords fallen to? Who established their duty? Your duty?

Hydro clenched his fists. "Pearl."

To free them from their burden, who must you defeat? Anne's black eyes pierced him.

"Pearl," Hydro spat and walked forward.

Wait! Anne tugged on his tunic.

Hydro looked down at her.

Before you cross, take the rest of those leaves.

"The ard leaves."

If that is what they are called. You will need your energy.

"You don't know about these?"

My blood allowed me more endurance than you human beings.

Hydro furrowed his brows at her comment. It seemed off. Strange. But he assumed she was merely referencing her First Blood.

He followed her advice. His senses were numb to the gritty, ashy taste that plagued his taste buds. An overwhelming feeling of relief flooded Hydro. He felt as invigorated as when she came to him in his sister's room.

Hydro rolled and relaxed his shoulders. He took a deep breath in. When his eyes opened, they did so with new found determination and purpose. His grip tightened on his sword—he would need it to combat the sharks if they were to attack. As soon as he crossed the threshold, two giant great whites circled him, eyeing him with eyes as red as blood.

You have a bond with them, Hydro. They will not harm you.

The words soothed him. For the first time Hydro took in the sights. Underneath him lay sandy beaches that extended as far as the expanse of blue did. Various sharks, from great whites to hammerheads to thresher sharks, swam these parts. In turn, they all examined Hydro's worth, but none of them attacked. *Do they think I am my father with this blade?*

When he made it past the Watery Path and above the granite steps, Hydro saw the familiar whitewashed walls and cobalt columns holding up the circular alcove. Closed clams opened slowly at his arrival, and mermen and mermaids soon showed themselves. Their daffodil-colored eyes scanned him thoroughly as he walked further into the room. Above, at the top of the mound of circular steps, sat Pearl, her scaly arms folded on the side of the fountain. Her dark-blue eyes focused on Hydro. Seaweed hair clung to her face and extended down to her shoulders.

"You do not belong here, Hydro Paen."

"I am heir to my father's throne. To see you is my right."

"A right you have forfeited yourself since committing patricide. I see all in this room. You are being hunted, Hydro Paen." Pearl sat up straight, showing the scales that covered her body, dissipating near her lean midriff. Bare, light skin lay underneath her shirt of clams and shells. They rattled slightly as she raised her arm upwards and pointed to the ceiling.

Hydro followed her finger to the watery ceiling. Troops searched in forests. Others flew on hovercrafts. And others yet questioned civilians in town. All of them searched for him. Hydro knew that.

Anne brushed against his side, pulling his attention from the ceiling. *Do not worry, Hydro Paen, they will never find you. Tell her it doesn't matter.*

"It doesn't matter if they search; they will never find me."

"It is only right they find you for what you have done. I will make sure justice is upheld."

Anne spoke again to him. *She has no authority. She can provide no justice. Tell her.*

"And what right do you have? What justice can you maintain?"

"I am a goddess. One of the Twelve. How dare you disrespect me, the one who has given you a blessing to help you succeed."

Her blessing was a weak one. Mine is stronger than hers. Mine will allow you to win.

Hydro kept his eyes focused on Pearl, hearing Anne's voice but not acknowledging it. He spat on the tiled floor. "Your blessing did not allow me to win."

Pearl slithered closer, the clams covering her chest clattering as she descended each step of her throne. "Perhaps you were not capable of winning."

"You wanted me to lose so you could continue to control me like you have my family."

"You are being led astray. What has taken hold of you?" Pearl swung her arms up, and as she pulled them down the mermaids and mermen strummed their instruments.

Crisp and fluid music filled the air. Hydro tried moving but couldn't. *The music is keeping me locked.* The music intensified. It burned Hydro's ears, but he could not move his hands to cover them. Pearl came ever closer and put both hands on his chest. Dragging her nails deep into his skin, she tore apart his shirt. Her eyes locked upon the necklace of dragon scales locked into his skin and the golden pyramids that hung as its pendant. Startled, she slid back a pace, looking at him now with eyes of ire.

"Now I see. You must die for the sake of Acquava." Just as the music was to crescendo, it stopped. Pearl looked around in confusion. "Play. I command it."

Anne stood in front of the mermen and mermaids with her hands up. She glanced back at him. *My bond with these creatures is stronger than hers. Tell her what you know is true.*

Hydro smirked. "You will not control my family any longer. Acquava will not listen to your command any longer. And you will not *be* any longer." Hydro pointed his sword towards Pearl.

"I command more than you could ever hope to." Pearl's eyes glowed. "I gave you the blessing for foreign liquids not to harm you, for I am generous. I let you cast a mightier water spell, for I am your goddess, one of the Twelve. And I command the sea because *I am* Acquava!" With each statement, water inundated the room. First, it trickled around Hydro's feet, climbing up from the steps behind; then from the sides of the wall, it covered the circular cove in a blanket of mist; and finally, it came from above, a waterfall like jagged teeth, hungry to devour the unjust and nonbeliever.

"You are no true Acquavan. But I am. The sea and water and all of their properties are mine to command. *Vesi.*" Hydro reached for the Power of the water as well. He found Pearl's influence there and together they battled for control of the water.

Pearl swung her left arm forward and the mist took the shape of a harpoon and shot towards Hydro. He pushed back on her influence. The water from above and to the left halted, not knowing which owner to obey. From behind, the water in the fountain rose and carried Pearl to Hydro's position. Although Hydro did his best to avoid her, she slid like a shark through water and swiped at Hydro with her nails, clawing him multiple times. Rips and tears and blood soon spotted Hydro, but he knew not to let his focus slip from controlling the water around him.

If you do not fight back, she will overpower you.

Anne's voice caused Hydro to lose control momentarily. The watery harpoon shot towards him. Hydro ducked. Not controlling himself, his fist hit the water, now up to his shins, and splashed over his face, blinding him. Pain sliced across his back. With a firm grasp on his sword, Hydro jerked backward and swung. He missed. He wiped his eyes clear. Movement, to his left. Hydro ducked, avoiding Pearl, dragging his blade along her tail in a counterstrike that had no success.

In a pattern of pivots, he tried locating her. Pearl was fast, much faster than he was. The cobalt columns hid her long enough so that she could sneak up on him with an attack. Some resulted in a successful dodge, most, however, resulted in pain and fatigue and mars on his skin that would eventually scar. If he lived. Dizziness controlled him now; too many things were happening at once. *Where is—* He scanned.

Anne walked back and forth in front of the row of clams. In front of each one, she swung her hands downwards, repeating the motion while saying something to them. Strums of harps and blows of flutes echoed throughout the cavern alcove.

"Anne?"

Water fell closer to him from above.

Keep your focus. Do not worry about me.

Hydro returned focus to the water above. It was halfway to the floor now. The water Pearl slid on became stagnant. The goddess herself appeared to have slowed in speed, making it possible for Hydro to avoid and parry, but whenever he sliced, his attacks would slip off of her scaled arms or tail. *Why is this sword not slicing her whole?*

She wards her scales. Find skin and slice.

The music intensified. Hydro's concentration broke. Water came closer. Refocusing, Hydro stopped the falling water. The water from behind now swamped his knees. He could move, but slowly. Pearl couldn't, though. Not now. Not with the music.

The battle for water intensified. *She knows she can't move.*

Hydro reached within himself and pushed the water that swallowed his feet aside. Small step by small step he trudged through the water, making a little path for his feet to follow.

Closer. You must get closer, Hydro Paen.

Hydro grimaced. His fingers twitched. His muscles twerked in spasms, rippling across his body, as he fought back Pearl's influence. Step-by-step he fought her, two great wills clashing, a storm threatening to capsize a ship. The music played in the background, louder than it ever had. It held Pearl in place, but it forced Hydro to concentrate even harder.

"Your blade has no effect on me. I am of First Blood."

Slice off her head.

Hydro grabbed her seaweed hair and yanked her chin upward. Her eyes glowed even brighter now, and Hydro felt a final surge of energy engulf him. His mind lost control of the water. With his loss of focus, it rose to cover his whole body, it deluged upon him, trying to push him away. He held his breath and held on to her hair. It crushed and rose at the same time, like jaws devouring him. He wouldn't let go. Not now.

You must do it now.

His arm struggled through the waves of water slowing it down. Hydro gargled, allowing water to enter his mouth, drowning him, but also giving him the boost of momentum he needed. The slice was anything but clean; the water slowed him to the point where it felt he was cutting a stump with a dull blade. As he pulled the head off, the water from above razed Hydro to his knees, and the water from below slunk away behind him. He did not let go of her seaweed hair, nor his blade. Through a sick series of ventilations, Hydro lurched forward and puked, mostly water, to the tiled floor. Pearl's final charge had failed.

Hydro cried out in pain. He pushed himself back and looked at the head still in his grasp. Blood dripped from the neck. His eyes rolled backwards and he collapsed on the floor, losing grip of both his sword and the seaweed hair. The sword clattered on the ground, but the head plopped and rolled, to where Hydro did not know or care. *They are not gods. None of them. True deities can't be killed.*

The revelation made Hydro wonder if anything about the Twelve was true. Had he been praying to the wrong deities his whole life? Whom should he owe his thanks towards, Anne? Was she a locked deity? Did he need to free her?

Exasperated, Hydro lay there, looking at the ceiling. It was a watery dome. He knew it could show any location on Acquava and transport one there, for he had experienced it when his father had taken him here before the Trials began. At that time, the gateway transported him to the pick-up location for the Trials. It showed no particular location now. His eyes weakened and closed.

When he woke again, not knowing how much time had passed. Dozens of mermen and mermaids stared down at him.

"You killed her," said a merman.

"Thank you," said a mermaid.

"Why did you help?" Hydro asked.

"We were told to," both responded at the same time.

Hydro looked for Anne but couldn't find her.

"You wish to leave Acquava?" asked a mermaid.

Hydro nodded. He needed to get to a spaceport, but not Acquava's—he would be captured there surely. "Will you help me?"

"Anything for our freer," a merman said. Scales came up to just below his abdomen; he had thick orange hair on his chest but a small goatee. "Where would you like to go?"

"Sereya, the Arctic Port in Iberene. Can I go there?"

"Very well, anywhere for Prince Hydro Paen. Goddess Slayer. Freer of Chains."

Hydro closed his eyes as chords strummed. Slowly, the music intensified.

The sea sways us
The sea guides us
The sea steers us
The sea! The sea! The sea!

The sea listens to us
The sea demands from us
The sea allows us
To see! To see! To see!

At the song's conclusion, Hydro opened his eyes. The watery dome rippled, eventually stilling on a portrait of ice and snow and a large metal facility. Snow obscured any fine details about the facility.

Something slid towards him. A familiar, scarred face came into view; it was the same mermaid from before the Trials. Pearl had clawed her to make her sing. Even with the scar marring her beauty, his groin still tightened upon seeing her.

The mermaid leaned in and kissed him on the lips. It was short and sweet and salty. "You have our gratitude, Hydro Paen. Songs will be sung of you. We leave now, but behind the throne is the doorway. Take it when you are ready to leave Acquava behind."

Hydro said nothing as she and her other kindred slid away. How long he continued to lie there, he couldn't say, but he kept his eyes focused on the flurry of snow that shone from the watery dome. Whenever he saw winter and ice, he couldn't help think of death. Maybe it was Anya's accident that caused him to think like that, or maybe it was because nothing grew in the gelid snow, but as Hydro lay there, he was mesmerized by it, falling and falling and falling, so white and so pure.

PART III: EIREK MOURSE

RECAP:

Eirek Mourse was also accepted into Guardian Eska's Trials and immediately felt out of place because the others had been groomed for battle. He made an unlikely friend in Cadmar Briggs, a Garian who despised Prince Hydro Paen almost as much as the Prince despised Eirek. With the help of Zain Berrese and Prince Cain Evber, Eirek won the second trial. However, when Zain Berrese turned down his offer for apprenticeship, it fell between Eirek and Prince Paen. Solving the riddle that was used as a tiebreaker, Eirek became Guardian Eska's new apprentice. After a tense Coronation, Eirek was accepted as Guardian Eska's apprentice with votes from seven of the twelve Families in power—the minimum amount required. After, Eirek met the Sages and learned that he would be training with them in the days leading to the Meeting of the Twelve. At the end of the novel, Cronos, the only Sage who speaks, helped Eirek cast his first spell of Power.

Now, Eirek finds himself in the midst of training with the Sages, trying to master his newly found Power and impress those who remain unimpressed...

CHAPTER 35

THE TWO SUNS

A fter casting Power for the first time, Eirek had the most restless night he had ever experienced. The wind howled like the days of his Trials. He thought he heard movement during the night, but it was probably just servants.

And when he started his training, Eirek would have never imagined that there was actually green on a planet he had only known to be sandy and dirty throughout the month and a half duration of the Trials. Sure enough, though, green lay past the row of mountains Eirek had constantly wondered upon during the Trials. When the Sages took him there the day after Coronation to begin his training, they referred to it as the Valley of Power.

The rivers that cut through the mountains' spine tapered off into the mouths of small ponds. Throughout the valley that stretched miles wide lay four temples of different colors: red, gold, blue, and brown. Each was as large as Eska's estate and had four columns that held a slanted roof. An emblem, carved on each temple's gable, signified each temple's affinity.

"These temples, boy, are where you will learn to use Power," Cronos had said.

Eirek had remembered being in too much shock to still care about being called *boy*.

"There are fifteen years for the training of an apprentice. Do you know why that is?"

Eirek shook his head.

"Because as Guardian of the Core, you will need to know Power, all forms of it. You will need to be able to empathize with every nation. And you will need to learn how to fight like the Ancients themselves."

Eirek looked at Cronos, who spoke for the other mute Sages. Even though Eirek had never heard them speak, they kept their eyes fixated on him all the same, and throughout his training, he learned to ignore them the best he could.

"You will dedicate one year of your training to Elemental Power, another year to Telekinetic Power, and then half a year to knowing the rules and regulations of Bonded Power. Those are the first three tiers of Power. After you have learned enough to protect yourself if you should be attacked, to communicate privately if needed, and to bond if somehow you manage to find the animal that would have you as its partner, then each year of your next twelve will be spent in different nations. You will learn their ways and their customs and build rapport with their royalty and citizens alike. Finally, after all of it, you will return to the Core to study the Guardian's Power, a fourth tier that no one else has the privilege of experiencing, culminating with a ceremony known as the Passing."

Hearing the information from Cronos instead of Guardian Eska felt weird to Eirek, but he didn't question the training process.

"The suns are coming together." Cronos pointed to the sky, and Eirek followed his bony finger. "That means we practice water. When it is cold, we will practice warmth. When our training becomes dry, we will electrify it, and when you grow to hate electricity we will bury it and move on to the next part of your training, understood?"

Eirek nodded.

And that was that.

Afterwards, he had toured the water temple and found the innards of the temple refreshing when compared to the heat outside. Water slid down cerulean walls, filling Eirek's ears with the sound of flowing water. Sapphire vines crawled upon the cobalt columns that supported the structure.

Once the tour of the temple was complete, Cronos had let him train inside the temple for one week, and then slowly he progressed further away from the temple each week after that. Now, four weeks into training, he stood yards away from any shade the temple provided. After this session, just like every other, he would need to check into the apothecary, if not to regain his energy, then to get treated for sunburns.

The suns were close now. In about a month the blue would pass on top of the red and create an eclipse known as Pirini Lilapa. That's what his uncle, Angal, had mentioned when they were at the Clayses' mansion before the Trials began.

"Now make a dome."

Eirek let the spell die. "How?"

"Power comes to those who have the ability and confidence. Use this confidence and control it. Power was created to be controlled and will obey its master. Once you control it, think of the form you want it to take, and it will shape to your will."

Eirek focused. He pulled from the rivers, still barely visible. He ignored the palpitation of his heart, caused by the grueling suns overhead, and he cast aside any uncertainty that had, at one time, crippled him. *Obey me.* "*Vesi.*"

"Expand the dome."

Eirek pushed its circumference further. Shoulders grew heavy. Eyelids drooped. Fingers twitched.

"Now dome us."

Eirek tried pushing further but was stopped.

"No, not in your dome. Give us a separate one."

Eirek focused. He did. Until he collapsed onto his knees. The water slid away from him and he found himself on the ground with the wrath of the suns' gaze. And the Sages'.

"Your skills are still simple, at best. When you are able to control multiple sources of the same spell, we will transfer to the next spell. You are tired now. We are finished for the day, boy."

You make me run to the Gamrol Cliffs and back before the suns shine every morning. It's no wonder my skills are still only simple. He wanted to say that, but he didn't have enough energy. He never did. Eirek couldn't stand. He had a hard enough time tilting his neck to see the Sages board a hovercraft. Cronos drove off, giving him a slight glance as he drove by. Eirek let his head hit the ground. He would make it back to Eska's estate, eventually. Eventually.

CHAPTER 36

SECOND RATE

G uardian of the Core Edwyrd Eska assumed it was another hot day, for the suns were overhead and there wasn't a cloud in the sky to blot them out. If there was heat, though, he didn't notice. Growing up on the planet of Pyre for twenty years of his life had made him hardened to the troubles most others faced when heat was involved. Tundra was weaker. He could tell by her loss of enthusiasm at dinner conversations and her raspy voice, not like the soothing he had come to admire from her. She had never experienced Pirini Lilapa before, and the suns weren't even at their strongest yet. He wondered if she would survive.

Eska tightened his grip on the railing and peered off into the distance. *Eirek should be visible by now.* Fifteen minutes before, he had seen the hovercraft the Sages rode come out of the valley. Once a week they paid him a visit to discuss in detail how training went. That would be today, and he hoped they brought good news. So far, all of it had been rather disheartening.

He scanned for his apprentice. The Twelve's Power gave him better vision than most, but only just enough to reach the outskirts of the dunes. *Come on, Eirek, where are you?*

Minutes later the door behind him closed, but still he didn't turn his head.

Silence accompanied the five men in the room for a while longer.

When Eska finally spotted Eirek on the run home, he turned around and asked, "How did training fare today?"

"It didn't. The boy can cast a water spell simple enough, but he still struggled to make two pools of the same spell."

"How is that possible? He is gifted in Power. I saw it when he cast for me after Coronation. His flame was blue, almost purple. I have never seen a fire quite like it. Surely, that means something?"

"Yes. Surely, it does. But—"

"What does it mean?"

Cronos cleared his throat. "*But* what it means, I cannot yet be sure. Certainly there is raw Power within him. Learning to channel that energy, though, is a different task entirely. Since that moment, there hasn't been another. It makes me wonder if we weren't both just seeing things. Perhaps the lighting was off that night."

His shoulders slumped. He bit his lower lip. "How can we correct that?"

"A new apprentice would be a start."

"I'm being serious." Eska turned back to the desert view.

Cronos joined him on the veranda. Old face, hooked beak, and sagged wrinkles bespoke his age. "I *am* being serious."

Eska waved off Cronos's suggestion. "Well, there is no one else."

"There was Zain."

"Yes, and he denied my request. Plus, you've tested him before at Gazo's for Power. He doesn't have it."

"There are always surprises. But, no, I do not believe he does." Cronos put his fingers in between the spikes on the top of his cloudy gray staff with amethyst lines and leaned forward. The coloring gave away that it was one of the eleven Ether Weapons. The top of the staff looked like a C, and in the center of the C was a metal eye. "He wouldn't have been able to complete this part of the training. It makes me curious why you had even considered him." Cronos raised an eyebrow.

"Perhaps... When I picked Zain, though, I could tell there was determination in him. And fortitude. Given the shot, he would have trained harder than even myself."

"Yes, well, he would have needed to if he didn't have Power."

I could have used my wish to grant him that ability is what Eska might have said, but he didn't want to draw attention to the fact he had found his star. Only he knew that. Instead, he said, "Then training would have been altered to accommodate him. And, besides, he could still use the reimaje in time." Eska resisted the temptation to adjust the black bandanna on his head, the source of his Power. Many who met him for the first time expected him to wear a crown, but he was no king, or lord; he was merely Guardian and as Guardian he needed more Power than a crown could give him. The reimaje blocked his thoughts from outsiders and stored every thought and vision any Guardian ever had. And there were other abilities, but those could only activate when he dared to remove it.

"Yes, in time. But, you know as well as I do that to master a tier of Power such as that, one should know the other types... One does not simply climb the tallest mountain first, they climb hills to begin... That is why Prince Paen would have been an excellent choice."

"A solid choice indeed. Courageous. Competent. Confident." Eska nodded. He took one last look at Eirek and turned to Cronos. "But not kind. The same training that made him strong made him hubristic. He could have used a lesson in humility before arriving. Then he would have been the one running back to the estate most likely."

"That is what training could have done for him."

"Cronos, enough..." Eska sighed. "Eirek is my apprentice, no one else. What can be done?"

"He will grow into his own in time, I am sure."

"The Trials have never given us an inadequate apprentice," Eska said.

"There have been only three. He is the fourth. But, yes, you are correct, it may just take more time with this one."

Eska tapped the balustrade, watching as Eirek trudged through the dunes. "Continue to work with him."

"Of course, Guardian Eska."

"You and the others can leave. Send up my conseleigh."

In the intermission between, Eska ruminated on the options he had before him. The thoughts of others in Eirek's place had only crossed his mind during the Trials. Now, Eirek was the apprentice, and nothing could be done but to train him to be the best he could be. His conseleigh would help with that.

Even before they were at the door, he felt their presence. Per requirement of being conseleigh, they were bonded with him through blood, and because of it, he could track their presence if he wanted to.

The door opened.

Eska turned around before all of them entered. He did not want them to catch him in his musings. His gold and crimson cape billowed behind him from the sharp movement and glided on the air as he paced to his throne. He sat down and waited for them to gather around him. When Riagan entered, he narrowed his focus. *So he returns.*

Directly after Coronation, he had sent Riagan Inferno to the nation of Therus on Pyre to investigate Zakk Shiren's appearance on Vatu Volcano. It was true that Tundra had an idea of how it was possible, but he did not want to see her go, not unless she absolutely needed to. He hoped Riagan brought good news, but so far any news he had been given was second rate to what he wanted.

"Riagan, what news of Pyre? Any lead on Zakk Shiren's apparition?"

Riagan glanced from the three other conseleigh to Eska. "No. I spent weeks with Lord Requart going through travel logs at their spaceport, and he was never accounted for as a passenger."

"How about stays near the site of the volcano?"

"There are no tracking methods for those who paid in bonds or spells or cures. And it would be impossible to track down the coins used for fingerprint analysis, for they have most likely switched hands in that time."

Dammit. Eska clenched a fist. He didn't like having loose ends. "Ethen, contact Gazo's Academy and trace records for the—"

"It will not matter, Edwyrd. Zakk Shiren appeared out of thin air on that volcano. I am positive that while checking in, he was also invisible on the ship."

"Then heat sensors still would have detected his body heat," Luvan said.

"Unless, of course, he used a device to keep his body cool," Riagan said. "Tourists who flock to Pyre always bring those devices with them. It would be unlikely he would be detected through that."

"We need to focus on the ship then..."

"There is no clear image of the ship on the monitor. The trackers were not in a position to catch the ship. They only caught Zakk Shiren walking on screen and then off," Riagan said.

Tundra crossed her arms and stared him down. "Edwyrd, let me go."

Eska knew she wanted to go to Sereya. She thought that there was a possible lead there, but she never said more. "We will table the discussion for now." He didn't want to let her go. Not yet. "Where do we stand on matters regarding Pirini Lilapa? Any signs of the Curse yet?"

"No reports of anything on Agrost, Guardian Eska." Luvan straightened his shoulders and placed his hands behind his back.

"Nor Onkh, Edwyrd," said Tundra.

"Nor Myoli." Ethen folded his arms over his chest of an army green long-sleeved shirt.

"The animals seem to be getting more aggressive on Pyre."

All heads turned to Riagan, the newest of Eska's conseleigh, only four years as his aide.

"There have been a few reports now of wyverns and dragons going outside of their typical boundaries. Their fights caused trouble before, but now, well, now there are more of them."

"What towns have been affected?"

"Brandell and Ardell, minor cities in Therus under the supervision of Marquis Carmine of Burnet. Their proximity to the Nova borderline does not help matters. Carmine took the complaints of his people to Lord Requart, but even the lord doesn't know if it's the Curse or merely the hotter weather that is causing them to act strangely.

"I surveyed the towns while I was there, and the damage does seem to be devastating. So far thirty deaths, five each week. I am not sure what Marquis

Carmine can do, nor what Lord Requart can do since the enactments to stop animal violence passed earlier in your term."

All animals have a right to live. There wasn't any detected malice in Riagan's statement, only truth. Eska hoped it wasn't his bond with a dragon that made him think that no harm should come to animals. He never thought it was. Just what was fair and equal. But now it seemed that perhaps it was too soon of an act by a Guardian who hadn't even seen his first twenty-five years in the position.

Tundra turned her head towards Eska. "The suns are still a month or so from converging. Surely it couldn't be the Curse?"

Eska eased a little in his chair. "No. With each day the suns grow in ferocity, but if the Curse of Pirini Lilapa happens, it will be something to affect Gladonus as a whole, not just one planet."

"How about reports of nations' reception towards Eirek and Coronation? The lords and ladies should have publicized it by now."

"They have on Onkh, Edwyrd."

"And?"

"Neither reception nor remorse. Many, if not all, do not know who he is yet."

"Same on Myoli as well, Guardian Eska. He is a name floating without a body."

Guardian Eska strummed the stubble on his chin. "And what of Agrost and Pyre?"

"Nothing," Riagan said.

"Nothing."

Eska raised an eyebrow at Luvan's response. "Even on Cresica?"

"There is cheer that the next Guardian of the Core will be from Cresica, but no one knows the name *Eirek Mourse*. Very few in his hometown even know of him."

What does that say of my candidate choice? Eska fought the temptation to bite his lower lip and furrow his brow. However compelling his will was, it wasn't strong enough.

"Strength comes in forms as various as the flowers on Chaon, Guardian Eska." Ethen said, almost as if to reassure Eska.

Eska managed a grin and nodded toward Ethen. He knew his third-eldest conseleigh couldn't have read his thoughts, but all were adept in reading faces. "I suppose you are right. Time may be against us, however."

"What do you mean? There are fifteen years in the training program."

"Aye, but only a month until Pirini Lilapa and its Curse, Riagan." Eska noticed the confused countenance of his youngest conseleigh. "What would happen to the boy if this Curse gets the best of me? What if it is worse than Deimos?"

Silence. All conseleigh looked at one another.

"You must not say things like that, Edwyrd."

Eska looked at Tundra for a moment longer than he meant to. "Yes, I suppose you are right." He looked at the others. "You are free to go. Make sure you obtain biweekly reports from your nations about the activity. The sooner we can notice disruptive activity that may be the Curse, the more likely we can stop it before it grows into such a threat to overtake Gladonus, understood?"

They all said their agreement and turned to leave. "Tundra, would you mind staying a moment longer?"

Tundra brushed a strand of faded blue hair behind her ear. "Of course, Edwyrd."

Before the doors closed, Eska noticed Luvan give a glance of curiosity. Regardless, he stepped out, and he and his eldest conseleigh were alone. Again.

"Thank you for your support. I sometimes ramble in my thoughts."

"I live to support you, and your thoughts are more than rambles. The issues you raised were serious."

"Very." Eska let his eyes fall over Tundra, not in a manner of lust—this wasn't the time for it. This time it was in a manner of trust and loyalty. "Do you really believe there are answers in Sereya concerning Zakk Shiren's apparition?"

"I do."

"But you will not tell me what?"

Tundra glared at him. "I do not want to misspeak."

She is being stubborn. Eska changed topics, "Tell me true then, do you believe Eirek will make a fine apprentice?"

"He completed the Trials, did he not?"

"You didn't answer the question."

"Yes, I believe he will. Like Ethen says, there are many types of strengths. He just needs to find his."

"Will you help him find it?"

Tundra stared at him without speaking for a few minutes. The blue eyes that usually chilled him were dull due to the suns. "Why not Luvan? He chose Eirek for the Trials."

To this day I do not know why that was the case, either. "He was only a politician in the senate before coming here."

"And I was only Lady of Sereya. Why not the others?"

"Because they are not as qualified to handle the situation. Eirek is rougher than I imagined; Cronos tells me he still needs more help..."

"A woman's touch?" Tundra smirked and raised an eyebrow.

"Yes, some sort of refinement."

"Then I suppose I am the most qualified." Tundra bit her lip. "I will assist you in refining Apprentice Mourse if you allow me to leave for Sereya soon after I catch him up to speed."

She is bargaining with me now? Well played. "Tundra, you know—"

"Edwyrd, I will be fine. You will be fine. At the first sight of trouble from the Curse I will come help you. Wherever you are."

"What if you arrive too late?"

Tundra closed the distance between herself and Eska and put her hands over his. "I have never seen you like this before. You reveal too much." She lowered her head and kissed his gloved hand. "I will come back to you, Edwyrd. You will not have to face whatever Curse happens alone. But you should not have to face anomalies either. Whoever sent Zakk Shiren up that volcano to taunt Zain, said something to him to change his mind in becoming your apprentice. Whoever is behind this wants to tamper with your Guardianship, but I will not let them affect you receiving a good apprentice. I will work with Apprentice Mourse, but you must let me go."

After a short sign of concession, Eska's lips gave way to a smile. "Make arrangements for your departure, then. But only after assisting Eirek."

"Very well." Tundra put a hand on his cheek. "I will warn you, though, he will not be smooth like snow when I finish with him."

"What will he be?" Eska longed into her eyes.

"Hard and solid, like ice." Her eyes glowed and her lips pursed.

"That is what I was hoping you would say."

He leaned forward and kissed her. It was short, but tender. He looked into her eyes and thought for the first time since Cronos brought him news of Eirek's incompetence that everything would be alright. Everything would be alright. And in that moment, it was.

CHAPTER 37

FREE TIME

Dear Angal,

I can cast Power! You always told me not to doubt myself, and it looks like you were right. I haven't been able to write you sooner because I have been so tired after training every day. It's four weeks into my training as apprentice and, although it's still difficult, my body has at least gotten used to it being difficult.

I don't know when I get to see you next, or Jahn or Sheryin or Jerald, but these men who are training me say that part of my training is spending a year in each nation. I hope that day comes soon. Perhaps I could stay with you in Syf? I may have to anyways if part of the training is getting to know the royalty better there, but I'm not su

A knock came to his door.

Who's that? Eirek set down his pen on top of the letter and rose to answer the door. Outside, the left wing butler, Dominic, stood waiting for him.

"Apprentice Mourse, you are to report to Guardian Eska immediately."

Eirek looked back at the letter.

"You will have time to finish your letter later."

Eirek gasped, shocked at how observant the servant was. He supposed it was a requirement for anyone in Eska's hire. Trying to hide the annoyance in his voice, Eirek asked, "What does he want to see me about?"

"I merely deliver words, Apprentice Mourse, nothing more. If you will follow me."

Eirek sighed. He closed the door behind him and followed the butler into the lobby. With routine precision, Eirek stepped on the middle platform and waited for Dominic to hit a button located somewhere on the railing of the marble steps that wound up to the second floor.

The third floor greeted him soon enough with twelve portraits hung around the circular entranceway. Above him, a chandelier hung from a canvas of the creators of Gladonus, Ancient Lyoen and Ancient Bane. They stood far apart from one another, one body's length, swords in the ground and holding a regal pose.

A click drew his attention from the cupola. A metal plank extended from the bottom of the platform to connect to the otherwise inaccessible third floor. Eirek walked across and down a short hallway that led to Guardian Eska's chambers.

Inside Eska's chambers, Eirek saw the familiar terrain of the main compartment, which boasted a veranda that looked off into the dunes and mountains northward, and a golden throne with plush cushions. In the far left corner of the compartment, a desk and monitor sat unused. On the walls of the main compartment hung four paintings of various places Eirek wished he could visit sometime during his training.

"Eirek."

"Guardian Eska." Eirek tilted his head slightly, hands locked together in front of him. "What did you request me for?"

"Another gift came for you today."

Eirek raised an eyebrow. In the month and a half after the Trials concluded he had started receiving gifts from every family in power regardless of whether they voted for him or not. Eska had told him that it was tradition. So far, Eirek had received a chess set from Daven Evber of Epoch, a complete and updated wardrobe from the Clayses marked with his unique crest—that of a sword with a pommel that looked like a planet with two rings around it—(in the celadon and brown of house Clayse, of course), a zircha sword from Farah Scule of Lurid, zircha armor from Rhagoh Requart of Therus, mythril chainmail from Garrett Omyon of Nova, a hovercraft from Liliana Voux of Mistral, and exotic wildflower cologne from Zalos Kapache of Chaon.

"From whom?"

"This one comes from Lord Abraham Vangle of Ka'Che." Eska handed a small box to Eirek.

He opened it and looked inside. "A watch?"

"A telecommunicator. Much more than a watch. It can also let you communicate with people from anywhere in Gladonus, assuming you have their telecom number."

Eirek looked it in awe. He had no technology like this in Creim. But his uncle did. Performing his tales of lore for the wealthy of Agrost had earned his uncle many valuable trinkets.

"I programmed my telecom number in it already."

"Thank you."

"You should not be thanking me, you should thank Lord Vangle. Sending a thank you may be a good first step in establishing rapport with him."

Eirek gulped. He hadn't sent out any thank yous yet. In truth, he hadn't even thought of it. The letter he was writing to Angal had been his first letter of anything since training began.

"Yes, of course." Eirek smiled weakly and put the watch back in its box. "Is that all, my Guardian?"

"No."

Eirek tensed his neck. "What else is there?"

"It concerns your training."

Eirek moved his hands behind his back, fumbling with the box. "What about my training?"

"The Sages tell me that you are not doing well. They provide me a progress report every week, and every week it has been dismal."

Eirek grew hot in the cheeks.

"Four weeks into training and you have yet to cast two of the same spell."

"My Guardian, I am not making excuses, but it is because they tire me out before I begin training."

"They are increasing your endurance. You will come into situations where you are not at your full strength and still need to cast spells."

"Yes, my Guardian." Eirek nodded.

"What happens if you enter a battle with more than one opponent against you; how will you compete with them?"

Eirek had no answer, because he knew what answer Eska expected. And it was an answer that his ability would not let him say yet.

"What happens when Pirini Lilapa plagues the land and you are not properly prepared?"

Eirek held his breath.

"What happens when you assume my role as Guardian?" Eska's eyes bore into him.

Eirek held the glance for as long as he could before looking down. He gulped. He began to say something, then paused, considering its worth. "My Guardian, why do I not train with you first? Surely it would advance my skills faster than training with the Sages."

"Eirek, do you know of Mount Klaff?"

"Yes."

"If you were to climb it, how would you climb it?"

"I have never seen it before, my Guardian. All I know is that it is quite big."

"It is the tallest mountain in Gladonus. That is all you need to know. Now, how would you climb it?"

Eirek couldn't think of a response.

"Would you climb it right away, or would you practice first?"

"I would practice first..."

"How would you practice?"

Eirek saw intention and purpose on Eska's face. He was clearly trying to tell Eirek something. "I would..." Eirek paused to think. "I would learn about how to do it first?"

"And how would you do that?"

"By studying other mountains?"

"Exactly, to climb the tallest mountain, you must first master the smaller mountains. Training with me, Eirek, would only leave you confused and restless. The reason why you train with the Sages first is so that you can build your basic skills. They are the sole beings in the system who test people for Power; they are trained to find it and bring it out in people. That is why you train with them first. Why, after a month, a progression of your ability is yet to be seen perplexes me."

"Yes, my Guardian." Shoulders slumped, he looked to the floor.

Eska let silence dominate the room for a few moments before speaking again. "Dominic tells me that you were writing a letter."

How? Eirek tried his best to remove the shock from his face before looking up from the floor. "Yes, to my uncle."

"And what are you saying to your uncle? Anything about your training?"

"Only that it is hard. And, well, Cronos mentioned that I am to spend one year with each nation at some point."

"Yes, you will. But you need to master the first three tiers of Power first before you can begin. I want you capable of protecting yourself before you are on your own."

Eirek listened to Eska's words, not responding.

"You miss him, yes?"

Eirek nodded.

"Think of spending a year in Cresica a reward you have to earn. Perhaps that will help your training. That is what I did to further my own training when I was in the spot you are standing now."

Eska smiled. Although it was faint, Eirek could tell it was there. "Yes, my Guardian. Is there anything else?"

"No. You may go."

Eirek turned on his heel to leave.

At the threshold of the door, Eska called to him, "Eirek, do not make me regret my decision in making you apprentice."

His hand on the door, he turned around. "Did I not impress you at Coronation?"

"Yes, Eirek, you did." Eska paused. "*At* Coronation."

Eirek thought about the statement. He pushed open the door. "Goodbye, Guardian Eska."

He let the door close behind him, not waiting for a response. Returning to his room, he threw the box with the telecommunicator on his bed and slumped himself in the wooden chair he was in before. He let the anxiousness that he felt while walking through the estate loose in one massive exhale. The letter still sat on the table, although now no pen sat on it. *Perhaps Dominic read it and reported to Eska.*

Eirek snatched it and reviewed it. With a dissatisfied grunt, he crumpled it up and threw it away. He didn't have time for such foolish things.

CHAPTER 38

EARLY MORNING

"**G**et up."

Eirek hadn't even heard his door open. The lack of light in his room equaled the lack of light outside. "What time is it?"

"Time to get up. Move."

"Conseleigh Iycel?" Eirek blinked a few times, his vision still adjusting.

"Yes." Tundra muttered something Eirek couldn't comprehend through his grogginess.

Water fell on Eirek. "What the..." Eirek jumped out of bed, soaked in his clothes that were too large for him. Since receiving new clothes that fit him, he wore the old ones his sponsors, the Clayses of Cresica, gave him as his robes for sleep. "Why did you do that?"

"So that you would get up. Follow me." She turned on her heel and walked to the threshold of the door.

Eirek shook his arms, flinging water to the floor. *What just happened?* He began to take off his shirt, saying, "Let me put some new—"

"Keep the clothes that you have on. Follow me."

Eirek huffed and let the shirt fall back to his body with a tiny splat. He put shoes on, instantly regretting not drying his feet before doing so.

With a squishy step, he followed her outside and around the estate to a circular court that displayed Eska's sigil of an outstretched dragon breathing fire in crimson colored bricks. Golden bricks circled the court at the base of golden benches. Four pillars, erected to resemble swords, lit the grounds and the water that flowed from a path near the estate.

"You will practice with me until your clothes become dry again."

"What are we practicing? I have training with the Sages at noon. I need to eat and run before I get taken out to the valley."

"Then I suggest we not waste any more time. *Vesi.*" Tundra twirled her right hand.

Water gathered from the stream nearby and formed a pool ten feet above him. It dropped. Eirek hopped to the left, avoiding some of it, but not all. His right side took a hit from the water. And it was cold. Much colder now that he was outside in the open air before dawn.

"I..." Before Eirek could finish, another pool formed overhead and dropped, this time completely soaking him.

Eirek wiped the water from his eyes. She had stopped for the moment, her arms folded across her chest. *Did Eska put her up to this? Do the conseleigh see me as a failure too?*

"Either move quicker, or combat me using water, Apprentice Mourse."

"I..." Eirek slumped his shoulders. He sighed. "How?"

Tundra smiled. She let her arms down and walked over to him, her crystal heels clacking on the stone floor. "Use your imagination." Tundra put her finger to his head.

Eirek didn't realize his jaw was open until Tundra continued.

"Do not seem so surprised. You are intelligent, Apprentice Mourse. You succeeded in my trial, after all, and solved my riddle. Use your brain to conjure the solution to the problem at hand. This exercise is nothing different, only wetter." She laughed a little.

"But how can you and I use water at the same time?"

"Many times a battle with Power will involve using the same spell, Apprentice Mourse. The element chooses to obey who is more deserving of it."

A silence lingered before Eirek asked, "How does it know?"

"Because it senses your emotion and your want and your drive. It's in your intonation."

"It has nothing to do with how strong you are?"

Tundra chuckled. "It does. But the strength you are thinking of is physical, and the elements do not care about that type of strength. The elements obey only those who are emotionally and mentally mature and strong enough to handle them. Now are you ready to begin again?"

Eirek gulped. "I think so."

"Good." Tundra turned and walked back a few paces.

Before she stood still, a pool of water came from the stream and doused Eirek.

"I thought you were ready."

"I..." Eirek shook himself like a dog, trying to fling off as much water as possible. "I was waiting on you..."

"I do not need to see you to cast a spell." Tundra narrowed her eyes on Eirek. "Now, again. Match me. *Vesi.*"

Water formed above him. He turned to the stream and focused on water. "*Vesi.*" He uppercut the air and formed a circle of water above him. Pitter patter of rain drops fell from above, and he noticed water trickling down the sides of his makeshift water umbrella. *I did it.*

The scene above him engrossed him until a splash of water hit him in the face. *What the...* Water fell and soaked him.

"Never gloat in your ability, and never lose focus of your spell." Tundra walked in a circle around Eirek. "Still, a good beginning. You even managed to make an umbrella. Again. *Vesi.*"

Eirek scanned his immediate area, found the pool, and countered. "*Vesi.*"

Singular instances like this continued for another hour. With each time, the previous spell dissipated more quickly and the next spell appeared sooner. Finally, at one point, they came in such succession that there was no intermission between the spells. When Eirek saw a door of water come from the left, he waved his right hand toward it and said, "*Vesi.*" A screen blocked it.

The moment paused.

Eirek looked in disbelief. Above him, water shielded him and in front of him, it screened him against another blow. After a few moments to himself, he noticed Tundra was not behind the watery screen, nor was she anywhere in front of him. Eirek turned around to a splash of water. He shook off the spells he had under his control before getting the water out of his eyes.

Tundra smirked. "Congratulations, Apprentice Mourse, you remembered to not lose focus on your spell."

"I..."

"Yes, you cast two spells at the same time."

"How did I do that?"

"You used your mind and reacted to the situation." Tundra pointed to her own faded blue curls.

Eirek clenched his hands into fists. *I did it. I really did it.* He grinned.

"Do not gloat in your ability, Apprentice Mourse. It is nowhere near where it should be after winning the Trials. Even my late husband's nephew could do such a thing by the age of ten."

Eirek shook his head and put a hand through his hair, feeling the wetness. As the suns began to shine, he could tell he was drying more rapidly. "Where should I be?"

"Edwyrd can cast ten of the same spell at any given time. One for each finger." Tundra twirled her fingers, then crossed her arms again. "It would do well to be there."

"But he is Guardian."

"Yes, and that is where you will end up, is it not?" Tundra cocked her head.

"Yes, it is, but..."

"But what is Guardian from an apprentice?" Tundra closed in on Eirek.

"Uhmm..." Eirek couldn't think of an answer.

"It is merely fifteen years, a day, and a ceremony, in the best case."

"And in the worst?" Eirek gulped.

"An unexpected death." Tundra examined him with her blue eyes. After a few moments, she spoke again. "Get some breakfast, Apprentice Mourse. We are finished here. The suns are awake." She stepped past Eirek, withdrawing from the court, not waiting for his company.

The great red sun, Freyr, was now fully above the horizon. Lugh, its blue, smaller counterpart, was behind it, slowly gaining. In less than a month they would rise and fall together for a week. Known as Pirini Lilapa, it was supposed to be beautiful. But a Curse came along with its beauty. And in remembering that, he realized why everyone seemed on edge at the estate and hated himself for not being as competent as the other contestants surely would have been. *Is this Eska's call for help? Does he know what is about to befall Gladonus?* Eirek clenched his fist and put an arm above his eyes as a visor. The suns entranced him, and if it weren't for their luster and the fact that he would lose his vision if he stared at them too long, he doubted he would look away.

But he did. He needed to run to the cliffs, change clothes and eat before entering the Valley of Power with the Sages. Another day of training was ahead of him. And now that he knew what was at stake, he needed to be ready. For himself. For Eska. And for Gladonus.

CHAPTER 39

MANY A GIFT

"Eirek, I hear from Cronos that you managed to control two separate levels of a similar spell the day before yesterday?" Guardian Eska stated.

It had been three days since his early morning training with Tundra. Eirek poked the salmon on his plate. Another part of his training was his diet—lean meats, vegetables and fruit. He noticed his physique slimming and becoming more defined due to the switch, but it was difficult to give up red meats. Coming from Cresica, that was a majority of the meat offered there.

Eirek looked from the Sages to Guardian Eska and his conseleigh. "Yes. It was difficult. But, I finally got it."

"He did very well," Cronos acknowledged. "Too well." Cronos arched his eyebrows.

Eirek gulped. "Why?"

"For a boy who has never used Power before in his life, who cast his first spell at nineteen years and who has thus far been incompetent in his training, there is no way you mastered our training yet."

"I helped train him," said Tundra.

"You did what?" Cronos looked from Tundra, to Eirek, to Eska. "You overstep your place."

"Everyone needs to start getting better somewhere. Perhaps he is just talented, Cronos. He did pass the Trials. He secured the votes of the families in power. And he is Edwyrd's apprentice, after all." Tundra dabbed her light blue lips and smirked at Eirek. "What does it matter how he gets there as long as the boy gets there?"

"I don't believe in those ideals. It is the journey that matters. Not planned or done properly and he'll end up like Bane."

"An Ancient? Well, that wouldn't be so bad?" Tundra laughed.

"No, Lady Iycel. Dead. And, for some of you, that may be bad." Cronos eyed everybody before returning to his soup.

"Please explain."

"Bane had an ideal that everyone was meant to cast Power. And the completion of that ideal began the Great War, but only because the journey was flawed. Done in a better way and all of this," Cronos said as he motioned with his arms to the whole room, "could have been avoided. And the Ancients may still be here."

"I would like to see you provide another example."

"Enough. Both of you. Cronos, do not be mad at Tundra. I asked her to help train Eirek. You mentioned there may be Power inside Eirek, and I wanted to mine it out of him faster. While I agree with you that a particular road must be traveled in training, Pirini Lilapa is nearly upon us. The more Eirek knows, the better." Eska examined the room.

"Onto another topic, perhaps? Have you had the chance to try on your gift from Astor Grime?"

"What did Lord Grime give you?" Tundra tucked a strand of faded blue hair behind her ear and turned her attention to Eirek.

"A mammoth-hide cloak and gloves and mammoth fur boots."

"A warm welcoming gift for the apprentice," Cronos commented.

"There is no use for it now..." Eirek sighed. "But it is nice that they fit."

"When you spend a year in Sereya, you will see a need for it. Even if you think you can cast fire as if you were Fueoco himself, you will still need protection from the bitter winds," Tundra said.

Her blue eyes dulled with every passing day. They still chilled Eirek, but not to the extent they did while he competed in the Trials. On the contrary, Eirek had noticed that the amber of Cronos's eye brightened with every day. Cronos's other eye, the blue eye, remained unfazed.

"It's nice. I suppose I never thought of that." Eirek looked at his plate. He hadn't touched his asparagus yet nor the cup of chicken broth.

"So that makes Gar, Empora and Acquava the sole nations who have yet to gift you?" Eska asked.

"Yes."

"They will come. Some nations just require a little more time in finding an appropriate gift," Luvan said.

"It's true. When I sent gifts out to people from Therus during my time as lord, I made sure I sent a gift truly unique that nobody could copy."

Eirek hadn't considered how hard it was to pick out the perfect gift. Something that couldn't be replicated. Something that was him and yet elegant enough to be considered worthy as an apprentice's gift.

Even the idea of a gift was foreign to him. While living on Cresica, he barely received any gifts from the Mourses. The gift, if anything, was a surprise visit from his uncle, which ended up with lots of talk. Some of it good, some of it bad, and almost all of it about his abandonment when he was seven years old into the arms of Sheryin and Jerald Mourse.

"Have you tried training with your new zircha steel?" Ethen asked.

Eirek shook his head. "I haven't had time," Eirek lied, well, partially. It's true that he hadn't had time to train with it for the most part, but, in truth, he hadn't picked it up because he had no idea how to use it and was too embarrassed to ask. With Eska already questioning his worth, he figured the less incompetent he appeared, the better.

"What of yesterday? We gave you a day off," Cronos said.

He would take note of that. Eirek looked around; Guardian Eska surveyed him. *What does Eska think? Is he searching for something in me?*

Eirek slumped his shoulders. "You're right. I should have used that day to practice. Perhaps I can add a sparring session every other day with you, Conseleigh Rorum, to help me familiarize myself with the zircha steel."

"I would be delighted to teach you." Ethen leaned over his plate and grinned at Eirek.

Cronos still eyed him suspiciously.

Eska's gaze moved from Eirek to the doors that led to the dining room from the hallway.

Just then the doors opened, and Colin came to the head of the table and leaned in close to Eska. Tundra, who was closest to Eska, leaned in towards both of them as well. Eirek heard bits and pieces of the whittled whispers, but not enough to make sense of anything.

Colin straightened his posture.

"You are certain?" Guardian Eska asked.

"Yes. It is very urgent."

"Dinner is dismissed. Everyone, follow me to our telecommunication chamber—Acquava is on standby."

CHAPTER 40

PAEN'S PAIN

E ska set his golden linen on the table. Colin had already retreated. When he stood up, the others followed. Eirek walked between Luvan and Ethen down the silver-painted hallways that led from the dining room. He did not know where they were going, and he spoke nothing as he walked.

Instead of taking the path to the lobby, Eska turned right and stood beside a glass pedestal, his ungloved hand hovering right above it. "Eirek, come here." Eirek moved to stand by the glass pedestal. "Only I and select others are allowed to access this place. It is called the telecommunication chamber. It can connect us with any telecommunicator device in any nation on any planet. This is how I communicate with lords, senators, marquises, General Satorus, and the like. Do not reveal what you are about to see, understood?"

"Yes, my Guardian."

Eska placed his hand on the pedestal. A humming noise rose and fell in accordance to a bright white and red light underneath Eska's hand. After a few seconds a voice from speakers located right above the doors said, "Welcome, Guardian Eska."

The glass doors slid apart. He stepped forward, and Eirek followed.

Inside was a large chamber that dipped below the mansion. Twelve monitors, as large as most dining tables, were attached to the walls at the far end of the room in a circular section that was lower than the rest of the room. A series of four control panels stood in the center of the chamber, with smaller computers lining the base of the wall. A small screen on a table on the upper deck showed an image. Eirek couldn't quite make it out, for Eska and Colin blocked his view as he walked closer.

"Colin, put Acquava on all twelve screens."

"Yes, my Guardian."

A boy with coarse brown hair and green eyes, who was no older than ten, appeared on the large monitors at the end of the room. Eirek stood by Eska, near a railing that overlooked the lower deck. A look of bafflement betrayed Eska's face. One Eirek hadn't seen since Zain refused apprenticeship. He regained composure so quickly, Eirek wondered if he had seen his confusion at all.

"Are we connected?" The boy with brown hair looked somewhere off screen.

Is that Hydro's brother?

"We are." A man in his fifties with a thick mustache and similar brown hair sat down beside the boy to his right. He had an alluring accent, one that the boy didn't have and probably the only distinct difference between the two besides age and facial hair.

Another man, who had sea-blue eyes and wore a variety of rings on his fingers, sat to the boy's left. His jaw was lean, but he still had plenty of hair on his head despite the fact that wrinkles bespoke his pressures and duty. "Guardian Eska, I am Darien Dornell, receiver to the late Lord Hydro Paen. I am sure you remember Aiton and—"

"Did you say *late*?" Guardian Eska's voice rose with the question.

Heavy gazes fell to either Eska or the screens in the front of the room. The boy in the middle bit his lower lip, but the other two looked back with endearing realism.

"Yes, I did. Lord Paen passed away just a few hours ago in bed."

"How? So, Hydro rules now, then?"

"It... it is not quite as simple as that. This is something I would like to talk to you about more in person. There have been..." Darien paused for a brief moment. "There have been instances that I do not believe appropriate for a virtual chat. If you could come to the funeral, there will be time to talk before and after."

Silence.

Eirek couldn't see Eska's face, for he was hunched down on the railing, shoulders blocking any view of his head. When Eska straightened his posture, he asked, "When will the funeral be?"

"It will be in four days' time. We are in the process of contacting all other families of Power and telling them the news, as well."

"We will make arrangements to be there, then." Eska nodded.

The boy sobbed at the end, but still managed to say his farewells before the connection cut.

Eska strummed the stubble on his chin with his ungloved hand. Eska eyed him with curiosity. Or was it worry? Most times Eirek had trouble distinguishing Eska's countenance.

Eska shifted his gaze to the conseleigh and the Sages. "We plan to leave for Acquava two days from now."

"The Meeting of the Twelve is only weeks from now, Guardian Eska," Cronos pointed out.

"Yes, this comes at a most unfortunate time. It does not make sense to go to Onkh, then back to the Core, then to Onkh again." Eska pivoted his vision once more. "Your training will be postponed for the moment, Eirek. Luvan, Ethen, Cronos, you will make sure you pack well enough for the journey to Gar and Mount Volan after the funeral." Eska clasped his hand on Eirek's shoulder. "Make sure you pack for your travels as well. This meeting will be an important one." Eska scanned his conseleigh then, letting his eyes rest on Tundra. "Tundra, you will ready your things for your trip as well."

"Are you not going to accompany Eirek to the Meeting of the Twelve?" Luvan asked.

"If it were any other year, yes. But I will need to focus in order to have a chance in stopping the Curse of Pirini Lilapa before it escalates any further than it must. That is why I'm sending two conseleigh and Cronos with him. Understood?"

Luvan fidgeted his gaze. "Yes, my Guardian."

"Good."

"What about me, my Guardian?" Riagan asked, pulling Eska from his gaze.

"You stay here. There must be someone present on the Core at all times."

"Yes, my Guardian."

"You are all dismissed now." Eirek turned to leave, but Eska held him firmly. "Not you, Eirek."

The others left, looking back on the pair before doing so.

Eirek gulped. *What's this about?*

When the glass doors slid shut, Eska asked, "During the Trials, did anything happen that stood out to you about Hydro?"

"I do not understand your question."

"The Paens took me aside on the day of your Coronation and asked me where Hydro went. Lord Paen couldn't track his own son. Do you know why that is odd?"

Eirek shook his head.

"Because those of the same blood are bonded to one another. You can track them at any time, the only exception being those of First Blood who can cloak their trace at their whim."

Eirek searched the ceiling for answers. He had never heard of the process before.

"The ceiling will not provide you answers. Did he mention to you where he planned on going?"

Eirek came back to meet Eska's gaze. He put his hands behind his back, fidgeting with his fingers. "No, he never spoke to me, really. Unless if it was a taunt."

"Was there anything unusual you saw during the Trials that may lead us in some direction?"

"I... I saw him hurry to his room with a book one time. Before... before the second trial. I found it odd because he didn't taunt me even though he looked right at me."

"What book was he carrying?"

"I don't know."

Eska studied him for a long minute. "Very well. Spend the next days packing your things and studying Acquavan culture. You will be spending the next week in their territory."

"Yes, my Guardian."

"You may leave."

Eirek waited a second for Eska, but it was clear Eska was going to stay in the room. On Eirek's way out, near the door, Eska called out to him. "Yes?" Eirek stopped.

Eska didn't turn around. "What is knowledge to you?"

For once, Eirek was glad Eska didn't look at him. "I... I don't understand the question, Guardian Eska."

"Do you think knowledge is an asset like Power that should be hoarded and used? Or, do you think it's a feeling that you get, like your intuition? Or, do you think it's more akin to understanding, like when you know a person or surroundings intimately?" Eska folded his left arm across his chest, fingers tapping his right arm.

"I think it's the last one, my Guardian."

"Interesting... Why not the other two?"

What is he looking for? Eirek tapped his fingers on the side of his pants leg until he found an answer. "Knowledge shouldn't be something hoarded and kept from others. And sometimes, well, sometimes your intuition can be wrong." The end of the fourth trial came back to him; how he sat in the ship as it took off, not willing to risk his life to save the others.

Eska grinned. Small and subtle, but a grin nonetheless. "You will join me and my conseleigh tomorrow for a ceremony in Blood Bonding. It is time we increase your understanding."

CHAPTER 41

BLOOD BONDING

E irek positioned himself on the middle of the sapphire circle. From some-place on the railing, Dominic pushed a button and gears shifted underneath the platform, and slowly it was raised.

Before he knew it, Ethen greeted him with the habitual strum of his conical beard.

"Apprentice Mourse, you come wit 'aste."

"I need a break from packing." In truth, he would still rather be packing. At least packing wasn't this. Whatever *this* was.

Since Eska's talk with him the day before, he had busied himself to keep his mind off the ceremony and to look competent to any servants who may report back to the Guardian. To him, Eirek feared this ceremony would just be another demonstration of his ineptness.

"It will be a long trip for us both in te next month." Ethen smiled and used the hand that had been stroking his beard to guide Eirek to the double doors.

Eirek tensed at the formality. But, then again, why shouldn't things be formalized? He was training to become Guardian, after all.

In Eska's chamber, the conseleigh and Eska stood around in a half circle with a large silver bowl placed on a pedestal in the middle. Rigid lips and steady eyes gave nothing away. *What is going on?*

"Eirek, join us," Eska said.

Ethen let go of his shoulder and moved to stand beside Luvan to the left of Eska. Eirek inched forward, stopping at the edge of the circle in between Ethen and Riagan. His eyes went from all six of them to the large silver bowl in the middle.

"Eirek, what do you know of bonding?"

Eirek gulped. *He asked me yesterday about knowledge, and now this? I should just quit now.* Struggling to find an adequate answer, he said, "My uncle told me stories about being able to bond with animals. That every person has an animal that can be bonded, just like every person has a star that can be found; it is just a matter of finding it."

"You mean like my bonding with Vesel?"

Eirek nodded his head.

"Very good. The bond I have with my dragon is one type of bonding, but as I mentioned to you yesterday, there is another type of bonding. It is called Blood Bonding. Do you know the implications of it?"

Eirek shook his head.

"I said yesterday that it was strange that Hydro is unable to be traced because he shares the same blood as his late father. The very same blood that his brother, Aiton, shares with him as well. Even though the father is dead, Aiton should still be able to trace his brother due to this bond. This bond, Eirek, is how I communicate with my conseleigh, through telepathy, and it is also how I can track their whereabouts when they are not by my side."

"Are there limits?"

"Limits?" Eska raised an eyebrow. "The only stipulation is blood. The more of it you share with an individual, the easier it will be to communicate with them. Power is a boon as well, but not necessary."

"But we do not share blood."

"That is what this ceremony will solve. My conseleigh and I do this every month in order to keep our bond as strong as possible. Because we share no family ties, we do not have a consistent flow of akin blood in our body. As the body produces more blood, the connection established becomes weaker until it is non-existent."

"So there are no limits on distance?"

"It is harder the farther away from one another, yes, but it is even harder based on the frequency of your encounters with the individual. Because of this, it leads to why it is so pertinent you are brought here today.

"The next month will be a test for all of us. If we are to survive Pirini Lilapa and whatever Curse it brings with it, we all need to be connected with one another."

Is the Curse of Pirini Lilapa really that dangerous?

"It is time you bond your blood with mine and my conseleigh, so that we can keep track of you and you, us, if you should ever find yourself lost without us by your side." Eska held out his gloved hand. "Luvan."

From a notch on his belt Luvan drew a knife, tossed the blade in the air with unsurpassed fluidity and caught it by the hilt, handing it to Eska afterwards.

"Thank you." Eska stretched out his arm and opened his ungloved hand. He drew the knife across his palm to create a streak of blood. Not a single pang of grimace left Eska's face. He extended the blade, hilt first, to Eirek. "It matters not what hand. Once you are done, you can pass it to one of the conseleigh."

Eirek grabbed the hilt of the dagger and let the point touch his flesh. It was sharp and warm, wet with Eska's blood. He bit his lip, clenched the handle more tightly, and poked down. At first, it stung. Then, as he began to drag it across his palm, he did all that he could to not cry out or cower. He was successful in that regard, but by the time the point drew its last bit of blood from his palm, his face was blushed, and his eyes held a faint wetness.

"Take my hand." Eska extended his marred hand, reaching across the silver bowl.

Eirek passed the knife to Ethen and then grabbed Eska's hand.

Eska cupped it with his other hand and said, "May we bleed, may we bond, may we share thoughts and feelings from this moment on."

Eirek felt warm blood smear against his. He expected something to tingle inside of him like the first time he cast Power. But there was none of that. Each conseleigh repeated the process with him, saying the words that Eska said. And each time, he expected something. But he felt nothing. *Perhaps it takes a little time.*

When Riagan put the knife in the silver bowl, Eska spoke. "It only works if you want it to work, Eirek. Concentrate on one of us and feel that presence in your mind."

Eirek closed his eyes and thought about Ethen.

"Formulate a vision of that person now."

Eirek created a mental image of him. A feeling crept through him, and he could feel Ethen's presence. Like a pulse, it beat, reassuring Eirek of his presence.

"Now try conversing with him. Speak with him through your mind."

Ethen.

Nothing.

"Focus on the pulsing you should be feeling. Reach out to it. It should amplify slightly."

Nothing. Sweat ran down his forearm. He hoped his head wasn't sweating also, but it felt cool. Tundra furrowed her brows. Luvan frowned.

Hoping to ignore the stares of his failure, he closed his eyes. "I can't do it."

Eska cleared his throat. "Perhaps it'll come in time." A hint of disappointment lingered.

Ethen leaned into Eirek's ear and whispered, "It's okay, Eirek, not everyone succeeds t'eir first time."

"Eirek, go pack your things. You may want to include the telecommunicator Lord Vangle gave you, so that we can stay connected."

Eirek blushed. "Yes, Guardian Eska."

He left without saying another word, and as fast as his feet would carry him. While passing through the threshold to Eska's room, he looked back and noticed Tundra talking to Eska. Eska turned his gaze towards Eirek and gave a look of curiosity. But then the door closed.

He boarded the platform. As the third floor disappeared from view, he tried finding the pulses of Eska and the other conseleigh. But he found none.

He didn't go back to his room right away. Instead, he went outside and sat on the steps of the porch. *Why can't I sense them? Why can't I communicate with them?* Thinking about another blotched attempt to impress Eska brought a tear to his eye. Even though he had everything anyone could ever want, Eirek still had nothing.

Scanning the stars for his planet of Agrost passed the time. Angal, his only blood relative, was on there, in Syf. He focused on his uncle's face, focused on the time they spent together, the few times a year they did. Regardless of the time they spent, he knew Angal had a way with words. And, even if he couldn't see him until later in his training, he needed to speak to him. He needed advice. So, he called out in his mind, *Angal... Angal...*

But no response ever came.

CHAPTER 42

TIME TO LEAVE

E irek spent the entire next day taking care of a few essentials. First, he packed the most formal clothes he had to look presentable at the funeral, and after that, the Meeting of the Twelve. Next, he had Colin teach him how to use his telecommunicator. Although embarrassed to go to the old man for help, Eirek figured it was better than going to the conseleigh or Eska. It took only a few hours, but by the end of it, Eirek had the personal numbers for each of the conseleigh, knew the basics of receiving a call by pressing the crown and sending a call by scrolling through the database and pressing a button on the side of the device. Finally, Eska had recommended to travel with a weapon, just in case things went awry at some point in the travels, so Eirek decided to stick with his original sword, not caring to utilize the one he received from Farah Scule. He had received his first sword from his uncle before the Trials even began, and unlike most other swords Eirek had seen, this one had a cloudy gray coloring with amethyst vines. On advice from Ethen, he packed his gift of mythril chainmail as well.

By the time supper came around, he was exhausted. So, to avoid speaking to the others, he ate all of what was on his plate, taking his time to chew slowly in hopes of lasting the whole meal.

As Eirek chewed on his side of salad, Eska asked, "Are you packed, Eirek?"

Eirek nodded. Taking his time to swallow, he put a fist up to his mouth. "I believe so. Food will be provided for us, yes?"

"Yes, food and transportation will be arranged. Do not worry about that, simply clothes and trinkets you may need." Eska smiled and ate a piece of his turkey breast.

"Have you been studying your families of Power on Onkh?" Tundra sipped her wine.

"I... No, I haven't. I haven't had time."

"That is a shame. Most likely all of Acquava will be there at the funeral."

"Why haven't you studied yet?" Eska folded his hands together.

Eirek tensed his neck. "Like I said, I haven't had the time," Eirek admitted.

"I see." Eska cleared his throat and returned to his food.

Was it so bad of him for wanting to rest if he did get a moment to himself? Seeing Eska's lackluster eyes, Eirek said, "I will try to get some studying done tonight."

"No need. There isn't any more time. I take it you do not know the Acquavan tradition for crying?" Eska raised his eyebrow while cutting.

"Why would I..." Eirek stopped himself. He realized he was about to say something stupid. *Of course people will be crying at a funeral.* "No, Guardian Eska, I do not."

Guardian Eska looked at Tundra and nodded.

"Do you remember from Coronation the sigil of the Paen household?"

"A tear drop pierced by a sword."

"Correct, Apprentice Mourse. Those of the Paen household are told to not let their tears hit the floor. Many here might be sobbing, but many will also be catching their tears in respect for the family. I suggest you do the same if the instance occurs."

Eirek cut a piece of turkey meat. While chewing on it, he thought about the custom. It intrigued him. "Why do they do it?"

"Not let their tears hit the floor?"

Eirek nodded.

"It goes back to the old Acquavan tradition of dragging a casket of a dead lord on the sea. The body's soul is supposed to seep into the water and then manifest itself into one of the many sharks. Because eyes are commonly referred to as gateways to your soul, they believe that the water or tears that come from them contain a part of their soul. If it touches the ground, instead of the water, there is a chance they will never be returned to the sea upon death. They will never return to their birthplace."

Eirek dug into his meat once more, buying time to digest the information.

The action begged a response from Cronos. "The boy will make a mockery of you."

"He may, Cronos." Eska eyed the old man. "But so may anyone. If he does, Eirek has a whole year with Acquava to make amends. It is more the Meeting of the Twelve I am concerned with. Eirek, are you prepared for that?"

No. Not at all. I don't even know what it is. This time, Eirek tore off a piece of his croissant and plopped it in his mouth.

Again, Cronos spoke at the silence. "Silence. Again. It seems the only thing this boy knows how to do is eat slowly. He will make a mockery of you on Mount Volan if he can even manage the Sacred Passage. Why, he probably doesn't know each of the Twelve nor the attributes they are assigned to."

Eirek swallowed his bread. *Actually, that is something I know. The Mourses taught me that.* Eirek cleared his throat and said, "There is Fueoco, the god of heat and fire, his opposite being Pearl, the goddess of sea and oceans. There is Orekus, the god of the underworld, his opposite being Anemie, the goddess of the heavens and sky. Luenar is the god of moons and night. Myethos is his opposite, the god of the suns and day. Tomahawke is the god of war and death and suffering, and his opposite is Lucine, the goddess of birth and peace. There is Theothe, the god of physical health and beauty, whereas Saeluste compliments him by promoting mental health and wisdom and intelligence. Crestal controls the cold winds and winter seasons, and then there is Trema, the goddess of the lands." Eirek raised a finger with each god or goddess named so that he made sure to cover all twelve.

Eska chuckled. "Well, it seems as if someone knows his Twelve."

Cronos glared at him.

I bet you feel stupid now, old man.

"Yes, it seems the boy does... I am sure he hardly knows his Ancient lore, though. Does he know what tribes each of the Twelve derive from, hmm? Can he list them off into Heavol or Evolic?"

Eirek's inflated posture slunk once again. He didn't understand it very much, no. In fact, the obscurity between the Twelve and the Ancients had bugged him ever since Lord Omyon's question at Coronation.

"Excuse me..." Eirek paused; he hoped the next part wouldn't come off as ignorant. "But... but if I'm going to be truly ready for this Meeting, I suppose I would like to know who the Twelve truly are? Why is there a rift between the Twelve and the Ancients? What—"

"Easy, Eirek, easy," Eska said. "That is certainly a dense topic."

"Yes... yes it is," Cronos said. "I don't think the boy is ready."

"Well, if the Meeting of the Twelve was not so soon, perhaps there would be more time, but as it stands now, Cronos, there is not time. No, Eirek hasn't demonstrated a willingness to learn, but his knowledge for understanding is there. I know that." Eska smiled at Eirek, then turned to Cronos. "At the very least, if we inform him, it will be one less thing that may possibly go wrong on the trip." Eska turned back to Eirek. "Finish your supper. I will tell you a little of what you will need to know."

Cronos coughed and glared at him. "I suppose you're right."

Why does he hate me so much? Eirek didn't wallow in the thought; he finished the rest of his food as quickly as he could without diminishing decency.

A half an hour later Eirek found himself with the conseleigh and Cronos on the third floor, right outside of Eska's chambers.

"Look at the portraits, Eirek. What do you recognize?" Eska asked.

Twelve portraits hung around the circular wall, all spaced out evenly. Eirek obliged Eska's request and traveled to the closest portrait. He had never bothered taking a look at them before. *Pearl.* Eirek walked to his right and saw another. *Orekus.* And then he traveled around the floor and saw the rest of the gods. *They look no different than I do.*

"These are the Twelve." Eirek looked towards Eska, who stood in the center of his conseleigh and Cronos to his left.

"Yes, they are. This is how the Twelve used to look, when the Ancients ruled over Gladima in the times before the Great War."

Eirek shook his head. "Used to look like? What... what do they look like now?"

"All of their forms are different, taking on characteristics of where they call home, or what they claim to be the deity of," Cronos said.

"What... what do you—"

"For example, Pearl now looks like a mermaid more than anything else because she lives on Acquava and has claimed the sea as her home."

Eirek couldn't fathom that. *How... how does anyone change like that?* "So, they will not look like this at the Meeting?"

"No." Cronos shook his head.

"Why?"

"It goes back to the process of bonding. Because they come from the planet of origin, Gladima, their life form reflects the planet's life. The planet is dying and decaying and deformed," Cronos answered.

"But, you have First Blood; why aren't you deformed?"

Cronos chuckled. "I am old. That is my suffering. And I still believe in the Ancients, not the Twelve. My faith keeps me from the crueler effects."

"Let me expand on that idea for you, Eirek," Eska said. "But before I begin, do you know what the Great War is?"

Eirek nodded. "Ancient Bane and Ancient Lyoen fought one another."

"Yes, you are mostly correct. It is much more than that though. It wasn't just them, but their clans as well—the Evolics and the Heavols—and..." Eska paused. "*Others* too." He quickly continued. "After the Great War was finished, Gladima was no more..." Eska placed his hands behind his back. "After this war, Eirek, the Ancients were no more, but there were survivors."

"The Twelve?"

"Yes. Them and others, too, like Cronos and the other Sages with him. It was the surviving warriors, however, who titled themselves as the Twelve. The Core, what we are standing on now, blankets the planet of Gladima underneath. It is mountains and lakes and dirt that got ripped from the very ground itself as the Ancients battled.

"These Twelve thought that since the Ancients were no longer, they would provide the order still needed to be brought to Gladonus, and so they declared themselves the new rulers. No one could determine which tribe would rule over the Core, though, so that is how my position came to be. They decided to split up the other planets into separate provinces, where each would rule. Throughout the ages, especially earlier on when chaos triumphed after the Great War, they used the Power granted to them through having First Blood to mystify the civilians. They would take normal blades to their skin and not draw blood, they would cast powerful spells unlike anything seen, and some would use their Ether Weapons to cut through unthinkable items like mountains or other metals. The lords and ladies heard of these feats and were mystified themselves. When royalty knew the Twelve were of First Blood, the lords and ladies no longer had claim to any throne. But, the Twelve didn't want any thrones; they just wanted to be declared gods. And so they were..."

"So, they are just regular people?"

"No, they are not regular," Cronos said. "They have First Blood in their veins and are strong in battle and in mind and ability, on top of their natural longevity."

"But, they are mortal?"

"Yes. Only the Ancients are immortal, but to kill one of the Twelve is committing heresy in the eyes of the nations and their people. When they claimed themselves as deities, people believed them and toted their names as gods, not knowing they were, in fact, committing apostasy by idolizing them. I suppose in that time, though, who could blame them? The people saw the Twelve. They saw their unnatural abilities given to them by the Power of their First Blood, like their inability to be killed except with one of the eleven Ether Weapons. They saw the way the Twelve would take normal weapons to their skin and remain unscathed. They saw how they cast Power greater than any king or lord. And quickly, they turned away from the idea of Ancients, whom they had never seen because they weren't privileged enough to live on Gladima."

"Do the Twelve acknowledge the Ancients?"

"They acknowledge their predecessors, but Power and rule have deceived their minds now, so they believe the Ancients are no more," Cronos said. "And because of their ignorance, they have grown deformed."

"Do they know that is the reason why?"

"Yes. It will most likely be what they will be talking about at the meeting. They talk about reversing the effects every year," Guardian Eska explained. "But, that's enough for tonight, Eirek. Get some sleep now. The next days will be tiring."

Reluctantly, Eirek nodded. Old lore fascinated him. It was probably the reason why Angal could so easily make up for all the wrong he did. Although his uncle was constantly gone, he knew how to tell a story, and the stories he told almost always contained Ancient lore.

"Cronos, thank you for your help in explaining. You may leave with Eirek now. Conseleigh, stay. I need to have a word with you all in private."

Eirek's chest tightened. *I need to ride down the lift by myself with him?*

Cronos waved his hand and stepped onto the circular lift. Eirek looked from Eska to the conseleigh to Cronos and then stepped onto the platform, not wanting to appear timid or childish. Cronos eyed him with his amber and blue eyes and tapped the platform with his staff. It descended. Slowly, the third level went out of view.

It was then Cronos asked, "What do you believe in, boy?"

"I..."

"The Twelve or the Ancients, boy? Who?"

"Both." Eirek gulped.

"Foolish! The Twelve are nothing."

"My uncle believes in only the Ancients."

"Your uncle is a wise man. What is his name?"

"Angal," Eirek gulped.

Cronos studied him. "Why do you not believe his way, then?"

"I never saw him, really. He abandoned me at seven when we moved from Epoch. Now he weaves tales of lore and history at the palace in Syf. But... but when I did see him, he would tell me things about the Ancients. Wonderful stories. But since I spent more time with the Mourses, who believe in the Twelve, I see both ways."

They passed the second level.

"Is that so?" Cronos chuckled. "Your answer is similar to most. People do not believe in what they cannot see."

"I am sure not many people have seen the Twelve."

"Aye, but they have seen lords and ladies who claim to have seen them."

"But there are people like you who have seen the Ancients. Why don't people believe you?"

"Oh, some do. Older folk usually. Wisdom ripens with age. Your uncle, is he old?"

Eirek nodded.

"How old?" Cronos raised his eyebrows and leaned on his staff.

Eirek's mouth dropped open. "I... I don't know if he's ever said, actually."

"Well, if he believes, perhaps he's as old as I am." Cronos laughed.

Eirek chuckled at the impossibility.

"It is hard to trust in something with complete faith. Do you agree?"

Eirek nodded. The platform touched the ground level.

"Good. Faith is important here. Not everything that you see is true. Sometimes to be blind is to see."

Cronos stepped off the platform and walked up the spiral staircase, leaving Eirek to muse over his words.

CHAPTER 43

HOWN

Silver bands hung low to the Core, lower than normal, and reflected the glow and warmth Freyr distributed. The rays spotlighted a golden ship streaked with crimson, much smaller than the tank-of-a-ship Eska had used to retrieve them for the Trials. After listening to Eska give brief instruction to Riagan of what to do while remaining on the Core, Eirek boarded the ship and sat in a compartment with Luvan, Ethen and Cronos—Tundra and Eska were in the front of the ship operating the controls.

After takeoff, they entered the single wormhole that led from and to the Central Core. To get to the other planets, like Onkh, the ship would need to travel in different wormholes. The common analogy used to describe the system was the human body, in which many veins and arteries led to and from the heart of the system, the Central Core.

Not even a minute after they exited the wormhole, a ship came into view. It was comparable in size to Eska's ship, but painted red instead of gold. Eight jet thrusters, four on each side, extended from its large body, making it looking like a spider.

Then another ship came, this one from Hown, the asteroid that floated right outside of the wormhole. That ship was similar to the tank-of-a-ship Eska used to retrieve them prior to the Trials' commencement. Although he had never seen Hown before, or the militia stationed there, Eirek knew of their reputation. The best fighters and trackers in the system were stationed there, ready to do Eska's bidding at a moment's notice. However, he didn't know how often Hown forces were actually utilized, but perhaps in the weeks leading to Pirini Lilapa they would be called if it truly did bring insurmountable chaos, as everyone claimed to say.

On a monitor above the sliding door in the lounge area, a man appeared. He had a long scar on the right side of his face and another slight one on the left side of his forehead. If he had hair, Eirek couldn't tell because of the golden helm he wore. Dark gray eyes and a lean, strong jaw credited the man with a ferocity that could have gone unmatched.

"Guardian Eska, an Emporian vehicle requests transmission and a moment of your time." The voice boomed.

"What do they want?"

"I do not know, my Guardian. The man wouldn't say."

"Put them through but stay on our feed."

"Of course, my Guardian."

Is that General Satorus? Eirek had only ever heard the name, but had never seen the man. It may be Eirek, but he couldn't picture anyone else fitting the picture of the man in charge of Eska's militia.

A man with a half-hat and black hair parted to the right came on the screen. He wore an eye scanner over half of his face. He wore rings around his fingers and a black cloak studded with garnets. "My name is Yuan Shimes, receiver to Lord Victor Zigarda of Empora. I came here to deliver za young apprentice's gift."

So, Empora has finally decided to send me something?

"We are just leaving for Acquava, Yuan. I am sorry. The gift will have to wait."

"Aye, but it cannot wait. Za young apprentice vill not be back on za Core for at least three veek's time. Zis gift has already been most overdue."

"How do you know this?"

"Lord Zigarda is... vell, I suppose I should say, vas good friends wiz Lord Paen. Za family notified us of his passing. And, I believe from zere, Eirek is to attend za Meeting of za Twelve?"

How does he know all of that?

"He is." Eska's eyes flashed to the left of the screen. "Hmm... very well. General Satorus..."

"Yes, Guardian Eska?"

"We land on Hown. Make proper arrangements."

"Aye, my Guardian, follow me."

The large ship turned away, and the spider ship followed it, with Eska's ship closely behind.

Eirek raised the question, "How do they know I will be attending the Meeting?"

Ethen answered, "It is common knowledge tat someone from the Core attends te Meeting. Typically it is Eska, but since he has an apprentice now, I am sure many lords and ladies assume you will go."

Eirek crossed his arms. *I wonder what Empora has for me.* The asteroid came into view on the monitor as they started their descent. Cracks and gorges and an uneven surface showed all too well. Within a big bluff of rock sat a white building with many windows. On the ground, Eirek saw tanks upon tanks, the kind used to retrieve the contestants. What looked like long-barrel cannons stuck up from the ground, and down below humans moved back and forth, all without protective gear.

"How are they able to breathe? Why don't they wear protective suits?"

"At the core of the asteroid, there are two large generators, each the size of those tanks you see on the ground. Each one sends out a signal—one coats the atmosphere two hundred feet above with an invisible bubble that also pumps oxygen into the asteroid's atmosphere, and the other sends out an electromagnetic wave, coating the asteroid with a thick UV shield that helps protect those stationed here from Freyr and Lugh," Luvan answered.

The ship landed. The door to the cockpit slid open, and Guardian Eska and Tundra emerged. "Let us have a look at what treat Lord Zigarda bestowed you with," Eska said.

The density of the rock and uneven terrain made it hard to keep a steady gait. But luckily, Eirek didn't need to walk far. They were greeted by Yuan Shimes and two others behind him who wore red snakeskin jumpsuits. In his left hand, the receiver carried a large metallic briefcase.

"Guardian Eska, it is an honor." Yuan bowed.

Guardian Eska nodded, but said nothing.

Yuan then directed his gaze at Eirek. "And you must be za apprentice."

"I am." Eirek nodded further compliance.

"Zese are for you, zen." Yuan smiled and laid the metallic briefcase down on its side and encouraged Eirek to open it.

Eirek stepped forward and kneeled at the same time. He unlatched the sides and opened it. A bug that resembled a mosquito flew up at him, but he swatted it away. He shivered. *Bugs... Especially mosquitos... here?*

Eirek didn't reward the insect any more of his attention, for inside the twelve jewels on display stole the rest of it. Half of them he couldn't recognize. But he could recall some. The amethyst got his attention first, then his eyes slowly recognized the beryl, emerald, sapphire, topaz, and diamond jewels laying in the briefcase as well.

"They're beautiful." Eirek twirled a jewel in his hand and looked to Yuan. "What do they do?"

Yuan coughed. "I beg your pardon?" He raised an eyebrow.

"Do they do anything special or are they just jewels?"

Yuan gave an awkward laugh. "Unless you vant zem to do somezing special, zey are simply jewels."

Eirek slouched his shoulders. His watch was actually a telecommunicator. His sword and shield could morph into other things. He could wear most of the other items he had received in some fashion; but what was he supposed to do with twelve jewels? *Am I supposed to merely fondle them or look at them? Am I to sell them?* Surely Guardian of the Core doesn't need any wealth. It was then he recognized how empty of a gift the jewels were.

With the utmost reluctance Eirek managed, "Thank you."

"Take it wiz you to your travels in Acquava. I pray za ceremony goes well. It is an awful shame to hear vat happened. Zigarda vill not be present; he has become very busy in Mendeck since za news."

"Thank you, Yuan, for the gift," Guardian Eska said.

Yuan reentered his ship, and in time, the rest of them embarked on their ship as well. They left the rocky terrain of Hown and continued their travels to Acquava, where a whole new adventure awaited.

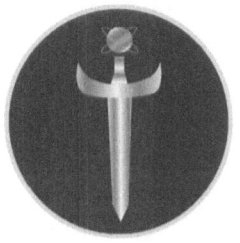

CHAPTER 44

ARRIVING IN ACQUAVA

C oming into Onkh's atmosphere, a series of dark clouds and a slight rainfall didn't do too much to stop Eirek's observation of the planet's scenery. The minority of Acquava was land, and the majority was water in the forms of sea, lakes, rivers, islands, and a northern icecap. Although the docking port for Acquava was located in the northeastern island province of Rhemu, Guardian Eska's ship was able to land anywhere. Because of this, Eska landed close to the castle, on the largest island, on the outskirts of a large forest with a mountain rising from its bowels. Past the forest, large cliffs jutted out from the water. Westward, the island was a large mass of land with lakes and flat plains.

"Put on your raincoats. The castle is still a league from here." Luvan tossed Eirek a golden plastic coat from a cabinet in the back of the ship.

By the time everyone donned a coat, two hovercrafts pulled up beside them, with two men on each. The passengers stepped off of the hovercrafts and greeted them in raincoats of a similar plastic, albeit blue. A tear pierced by a sword let Eirek know that he was in the presence of the Paen family. He recognized both men from three days previous, when they had made contact with Acquava in the telecommunication chamber at the estate. One's name was Darien, Lord Paen's receiver, and the other—a man of a grizzled beard, thick mustache, and stocky body—introduced himself as Korth, head of the acqua guards.

Eirek boarded Korth's ship along with Ethen and Cronos. Eska, Luvan and Tundra traveled with the receiver. The next few hours were spent traveling back to the estate. Cronos continuously looked from Eirek to the scenery around him, tapping his staff on the hovercraft's floor. The other Sages weren't with him. Because of the intermission of Eirek's training, they left the Core to return to their home on Agrost in the depths of the nation Epoch. Ethen sat with his arms folded against his broad chest and every once in a while he stroked his conical beard. Korth was a man of Ethen's stockiness and a few years his senior.

When they arrived at the castle, guards were walking along the castle's battlements in armor of a hue between silver and blue. They wore helms of the same material but no raincoats. The smell of slugs and sea and salt crept into Eirek's nose, and a slight breeze caused him to shiver in the increasing rain. Located inside the large castle, Eirek noticed a mansion, a hedge labyrinth, and a stone court. The drivers dropped them off at the steps leading into the mansion and drove off to a different part of the castle's interior.

Once inside, Eirek pulled back his hood. Servants came up to the group and took their raincoats. A large staircase in front of him led to a second floor, and various hallways led to different parts of the home. The distinct smell of disinfectant ruled the house, wafting back and forth on the tail of the busy servants bustling around the castle interior.

"Follow me," Darien said.

He led them around the steps and through an open door behind them that led to a basement level. Automatic lights flickered on as they descended. At the bottom, a narrow hallway seemed to stretch on for longer than Eirek had thought possible. They didn't travel its whole length. Instead, Darien led them into the second room on the right.

Eirek entered a large room with sapphire tiles and white walls. A monitor hung on the left-most wall and a large table shaped in the likeness of the nation sat in the middle of it. The young boy with shaggy hair already sat on a chair, and an old man with liver spots on his head, who wore a variety of bracelets on his wrist, sat to the left of the young boy, comforting the boy's fidgeting hands with his own. To the right sat another older gentleman with a doggish face. Faint white whiskers and eyes as gray as granite told his age if the wrinkling skin already hadn't. Darien took a spot next to the old man with liver spots and Korth, next to the other older man.

"What is this about? What happened here?" Eska sat down directly across from the receiver.

The four looked at each other. A heavy, long sigh escaped Darien's mouth and after a nod of approval from the others, he began speaking. "The late Lord Hydro Paen was killed. Along with his wife and other lesser people from the castle in a brutal attack a few nights ago."

"How?" Tundra asked.

There was a silence then. Long and cold and severe.

"His son," Darien said.

Eirek couldn't believe what he heard. He shook his head and looked towards the others.

"Who?" Cronos asked.

"Hydro, his son."

"You are certain?" Luvan asked.

"I saw him plunge a sword through his father with my own eyes," Korth said. Eirek's jaw hung slack. *He killed his father? His mother? Why?*

"Why did he do this?"

"That is something we have yet to determine, my Guardian. The late Lord Paen believes Hydro was possessed by something or someone, but neither mine nor Elias's research has proved fruitful thus far," said the man with the doggish face.

"How did he come to this conclusion?"

"His eyes were black." Aiton spoke for the man with the doggish face.

"What did you say?" Eska turned his attention to Aiton, who had been silent until that point.

"Black as night. They were black."

"I do not know of such a thing, Guardian Eska," said the older man. "I—"

"You weren't there, Professor Haruko. My father saw it and I saw it. His eyes were black."

"Korth? Care to shed any light on this?"

"Ignis, I... I am unsure myself. When I noticed Aiton at the scene, my attention was diverted. I didn't get a clear look."

"Well, I have never heard of such a thing while in the academy on Roil." The man locked his fingers together, resting his elbows on the table. "But I am making plans to return and research the situation."

"Yes, as Haruko points out, we have not found a solution yet, but we are searching. For the moment, though, he is gone and we do not know where he is," said Elias.

"How did he manage to escape?" Eska asked.

"He jumped from the veranda and stole a hovercraft. We tried tracking him, we've tried tracing him, but it is impossible." Darien stood and pointed to a point on the table near a large gorge that cut its way through the central province of Acquava labeled Aquis. "The closest we came is locating where he left his hovercraft, in a small town westward of here called Perét. He killed a guard there."

"And from there?" Tundra stood as well, examining the table.

"We know he stole a skiff, but we haven't been able to locate it yet," Darien explained.

"Where do you tink 'e plans on going?" Ethen stroked his beard.

"The ship he took couldn't cross the Summer Ocean to Gar. The waves would crush it. We told Alyn Blocter of the Summer Isles to let us know if Hydro arrives, but so far there has been no word."

"What of the Hall of Lords?" Tundra surveyed the four.

"That is certainly a possibility, but Pearl would be there, Tundra. I do not think he would be foolish enough to test his might against her," Eska said. He redirected his attention to Darien. "Do the other marquises know what Hydro has done?"

"No... We... we are unsure of how to release news such as this." Darien fidgeted with the rings on his fingers.

Silence settled in once again. Eirek looked at Aiton, who had his head down, shoulders heaving up and down. A sniffling gave away that he was trying his best to hold back tears. The other men were hard and stern and stoic.

"I don't think Hydro would do this."

"I didn't think so either, Apprentice Mourse, but I saw it with my own eyes. So did Aiton." Korth straightened his posture and nodded at the young lord.

"No. I mean the Hydro that I knew wouldn't have done this. The man I faced in the Trials was mean to me and rude." Eirek looked to Aiton. "But your brother was overly proud, too. To a fault. It would go against his morals to do this. I... I... well, maybe this is nothing, but I know Hydro left the night I was named Eska's apprentice. Where did he go from there?"

It was then Eirek heard a tale of Hydro's supposed journey to Chaon, and how they tracked him down to a jungle. How a man with a sun tattoo on his face told of Hydro bringing great suffering. How he needed to die. The words, made even more alluring by the accent Korth spoke with, made Eirek wonder if the suffering would be finished now that this tragedy happened, or if it would continue with his disappearance. Eirek had noticed at one point in the story, Luvan fidgeted in his chair and bit down on his finger, as if he was lost in a memory of a time past.

Others in the room fell under the same kind of rumination, for a silence slithered its way inside and wrapped its sinuous body around everyone, suffocating them in deep thought. Except one. Aiton.

"It's the necklace."

It was the second time that the boy spoke. He raised his head from his forearms. His eyes were red and puffy, and his skin was paler now.

"What did you say?" Eska asked.

"A necklace..."

"Necklace? What did it look like?"

"It had black scales and gold. Some of it was gold."

"Black scales, you said?"

Aiton gulped. "I... I think. Some of it was gold. At the bottom. I couldn't see all of it." Aiton said, sniffling. "Hydro didn't want me to see it, I know. He pulled back when I noticed it."

"He... he got it during the first trial. He found it in the labyrinth somewhere," Eirek said. "I didn't know he kept it."

He looked back to his elders. Besides Cronos, all of their eyes were glowing, but their lips remained steady. *They're using telepathy. Are they talking about what I said? I should join.* Eirek felt for the pulses. They were fast and vivacious.

He steadied his thinking, and as he did so, the pulses seemed to slow, like they were allowing for him to latch on. When he locked onto a singular beat, he nearly pulled back as voices yelled back and forth.

"The necklace hadn't been seen for centuries since the Pavos family. How was I supposed to know it would end up where it was stolen from?"

"Did you even check the labyrinth for danger, Luvan?"

"Yes, tar creatures crept its innards, but I saw nothing else."

"You lie. Now your further incompetence—"

"What is this?" Eirek asked.

The conversation stalled. Upon realization that their eyes no longer glowed, Eirek quit as well. *I used telepathy. I actually used...* Eska's glow gave way to a glare. Luvan glared at him as well. All gave him a look in one form or another. Eirek gulped.

Saving him from the stares, the old man with bracelets around his wrists asked, "And what labyrinth was this?"

"The Zas Labyrinth," Cronos muttered.

Cronos knows? How? Do the others? Eirek looked towards the young prince and his elders; they wore blank faces. Perhaps Cronos knew because he lived in Epoch, for it was clear that the reputation of the Zas Labyrinth meant nothing to the Acquavans. But Eirek lived just a nation away, in Cresica; he had never heard of this labyrinth before the Trials. What was the big deal? But it must have been a matter of serious concern for the conseleigh and Eska to all use telepathy.

"Will... will Hydro be alright?" Aiton scanned over them all. One at a time. His eyes were green like emeralds, polished with worry and concern.

Eirek opened his mouth, about to speak, but Eska and Cronos spoke at the same time, stopping him. "No... I'm afraid he won't."

CHAPTER 45

THE FUNERAL

It was midafternoon. Despite the tall castle walls, a cold wind had managed to sneak into the castle's compound and carried with it a cool breeze of eastward waters. It would have been frigid if not for the suns directly overhead.

Eirek sat in the front row of cobalt chairs in between Tundra and Ethen. Cronos was to Ethen's left, and Luvan was to Tundra's right. Ever since the day before, there had been some inexhaustible tension between the conseleigh and Eska. Luvan had stayed more silent than usual, and Eska observed him with more diligence. The Guardian sat atop a circular stone dais with Aiton and the group of people Eirek had met the day before, minus Korth. By the westward wall stood a wooden bethel, doors closed. A blue carpet extended from its entrance to the large pool of water that sat in front of it, to the right of the circular stone dais. In front of the pool were two large columns of chairs set up with a large aisle between them, where a rolled-out black carpet led down to the pool of water.

Guards in their armor the color of silver and sea watched from behind the parapets. Behind him, Eirek thought more than a thousand people had come to either sit or stand to see the funeral's progression. As Eirek craned his neck and his back he saw that the men wore black suits with sapphire handkerchiefs sticking out from their breast pockets, and the women wore black dresses with sapphire frilling and, depending on their rank, Eirek assumed, sapphire jewels crusted on. *This man was loved.*

"I hear Lord Paen was stabbed to death."

"I hear Lord Paen was burned alive."

"No, that was his wife. While she was flailing on fire, she stabbed him."

"Why was she—"

Tundra turned around. "Deyna, do not speak ill of the dead. Your mother would be ashamed."

Eirek turned around to see a woman in her early forties bat her eyelids and purse her blue lips. She slid her hand into the hand next to her, which belonged to a stocky man with gray eyes and coarse hair. A stubble had grown along his cut jawline. Next to each of them were seven children of varying ages. On her breast sat a coral reef.

"Sorry, Conseleigh Iycel. My lips will cease."

"They best; the ceremony is starting."

Eirek turned back around and focused on the dais ahead. Darien stood up and put his arms in the air, quieting the ruckus. He gave a short but powerful speech that collected many a hurrah from the families there.

When Eirek heard a rustle behind him, and he noticed people standing, Eirek rose in accordance. Like the others, he clapped along.

"I will now let Aiton speak." Darien placed his palm on the cobalt pedestal, and it shrank to Aiton's height.

Aiton looked at Elias before standing and walking towards the pedestal. Aiton gripped it with one hand while he coughed into the other to clear his throat.

"My... my father was a great man..." Aiton paused and took a deep breath. He wiped his eye and then continued. "He was a man who knew how to join us together through not only words but his actions as well. Although I am only nine now, I have heard of his feats from those around me..."

Aiton nodded and pointed to somewhere in the back. Eirek turned around. From the end of the columns of chairs two horses emerged, led by reins held by Korth. Unlike horses that Eirek had seen on Cresica, these horses were dark blue with light blue manes. Just above the hooves, on the heels, were retractable fins like a fish's back. Eirek redirected his attention to Aiton.

"... And when hurricanes ravaged the isles of Summer and Hart, my father sent aid in the form of soldiers, bonds and food. It was with my father's and my grandfather's doing that the boundaries between Sereya and the northern province of Katarh are now established. My father continued the support by building the oceanic bridges to connect our islands together, improving commerce and communications."

Aiton spoke slowly to keep pace with the progression of the horses, which dragged cobalt caskets behind them. A band of onyx wrapped around each casket, along with gold lettering.

The horses kept moving forward towards the pool in front of them. Without hesitation, they stepped into the pool and disappeared under the water, leaving the caskets to float atop the pool's surface. Eirek shook his head. *Did that just happen?*

Aiton looked to the floating caskets, then stopped. The microphone on the pedestal caught his sniffling, but Eirek was close enough to see he fought the acknowledgement of his parents' death. The old man with a liver-spotted pate stood and walked towards Aiton. He whispered something to the boy and rubbed his shoulders.

"Will he be alright?"

"I do not think so." Tundra crossed her arms. "An event like this may traumatize him."

Eirek opened his mouth to say something but decided not to. The ceremony stopped as Aiton and Elias talked.

Taking this lull in activity as an opening, Eirek leaned over towards Tundra and pointed towards the caskets and the small pond. "How is that possible?"

"Those were seahorses. They can travel on land or water. Simply majestic, aren't they?" Tundra smiled at Eirek.

"Yes, they are. I have never seen them before."

"You have not seen many things, Apprentice Mourse."

"No... I haven't..."

"From what I saw yesterday, I believe that you will see many things in time."

"What do you—"

"Sshh." Tundra put a finger to her lips. "We are at a ceremony, Apprentice Mourse, you forget."

"Although I am not my father, I will make sure that I do my best to live up to his legacy. I will live up to the expectations of all of you, and do my best to not fail you... I... I ask now that if you choose to, come forward and pay your respects to my father and mother and share any offerings you may have... Thank you."

Aiton stepped backwards into the arms of Darien, who led the young prince around the pool, stationing him to the left of the casket. At this time, two individuals came from the sides of the columns and ushered people, row by row, up to the caskets. When Eirek went up along with the conseleigh and Cronos, he saw that one casket lay half open, exposing Lord Hydro Paen from his chest to his face. Eirek saw once again how similar Hydro looked to his father—the shaggy hair, the jawline, and the build. Aiton, on the other hand, must have taken more after his mother. That casket was kept closed; however, the wife's disfigurement hidden from the world. The lord looked at peace, but Eirek wondered if he truly could be, knowing he was killed by his own son.

When it was time to say his condolences, Eirek shook the hands of all four individuals he had seen the day previous and said, "I'm sorry for your loss." He felt shallow for offering such a short sentiment, but what else could he say?

Tundra said more, but he didn't stay around to hear it. He was sitting in his chair again by the time she finished.

As the others came to pay their condolences, he noticed many of them throwing light blue flowers into the pool around the caskets. "What flowers are those?" he asked Tundra when she returned to her seat.

"They are blue kaffirs. They are only found in the northern polar cap of Acquava. They heal burns and are quite rare."

Eirek kept quiet, then, in contemplation as he watched the rest of the others pay their respects.

When the procession of condolences ended, Darien took Aiton by the hand and led him back up to the dais and Guardian Eska. After guiding Aiton in his chair, Darien whispered something to Guardian Eska, and Eska nodded and stood up. Eska straightened his black shirt and walked to the pedestal, placing his hand on the glass to raise it to more of his height.

"As you have sat through this ceremony, there is probably a thought that has danced throughout your mind. Perhaps two. That first thought is how Lord Hydro Paen and his wife became deceased. To that matter, from my understanding as I have talked with the people behind me, it is still under investigation but will be solved once Lord Paen's son, Hydro Paen, is found. Which brings me to that second thought you have probably wondered: Where is Prince Hydro Paen? Why is it Aiton here giving the speech? To this matter, I do not know. On the night in question, Prince Paen seems to have escaped the castle and has avoided scouting forces thus far. I implore everyone to let the Paen family know if anyone has information on where young Prince Paen is, or where he might be. It is crucial we find him, for he may play a vital role in helping us determine what tragic event happened here. I will be letting the lords and ladies of other nations know that he needs to be found, as well. I thank you for your cooperation."

Eska stepped back from the pedestal, allowing Darien to take his place.

"Thank you for coming. We will keep you informed on any new developments that occur." Darien turned around and huddled with those on the dais.

Eirek remained seated. Others stood around him. He watched Eska chatting with others. *I will need to make addresses like that someday. I will need to be as confident as he is when talking with people he hardly knows.* He then looked to the conseleigh around him. All of them remained mute, Luvan with a more musing face than typical.

He shifted his focus to the caskets that rested on the bed of blue kaffirs. If Eirek hadn't known there was water underneath, he wouldn't have been able to tell. It had seemed like every single person had left some sort of flower, but the distinct, chilling ice-blue of the Katarh flower overpowered the others.

What happened to you, Hydro? The question bothered him enough to bring a tear to his eye. Eirek stopped it with his gloved hand, not letting it touch the ground. Even though he didn't know much about Acquavan culture, he had been told enough to stop it in respect for the family that had seemingly just lost it all.

CHAPTER 46

THE SUMMER ISLES

E ska had left hours after the ceremony. Eirek, the conseleigh, Cronos and those who had traveled with Marquis Alyn Blocter left after supper. That sat fine with Eirek; the mansion had an eeriness to it now that he knew what all had happened. Also, because Pirini Lilapa was a little over two weeks away, darkness hardly had sway over the day. So, even leaving after supper, they still managed to make it to the western port of Perét on God's Bay by nightfall of the next day.

Three hovercrafts had carried them from the capital of Alar to Perét, so Eirek spent a few hours with Cronos and Ethen. Also, with them were three black-skinned guards, all in suits of clams strung together with tight fishing line. On their backs were large turtle shells and their hands were coated in a gray material that smelled of the sea. The other hovercraft carried Luvan and Tundra and two other guards. The last one consisted of Marquis Alyn Blocter's family.

After a morning meal the day after, the group continued to travel past Pearl's Isle. This time Eirek arranged it so that he boarded the ship with the marquis—a man of dark skin, a beard that certainly covered another chin. Shorter than Eirek, this trait made the marquis very rotund and robust. His wife was a pudgier woman and her one-piece dress of gray helped little to conceal that fact. A brown scarf added to her pleasant demeanor.

"Apprentice Mourse, is it? Glad you joined us."

Eirek nodded and sat across from Marquis Blocter in the enclosed hovercraft. "This is my first time traveling across the sea."

Water splashed up onto the windshield but was quickly wiped away. Unlike traveling on land, this hovercraft had a glass dome around it to prevent water from leaking onto the ship.

"Is it, now? I hear you are from Cresica?"

"Yes. A small town of Creim."

"Hmm... I see..."

"So, what was Hydro's father like?"

"He was a good lord. Fair and honest. He wasn't afraid of much and has done many things to help out the Summer Isles."

"How long have you been marquis for?"

"Nearly twenty years now. I attended the late lord's wedding, his induction into lordship, and have been to various council meetings conducted by Lord Paen. Throughout the time, I saw him flourish as our lord and saw his son grow into adulthood." Marquis Blocter furrowed his brows and rubbed his thick arms. "Where is Hydro? Why should we, of all the lords, be on the lookout for him?"

"Tracking on him was lost at Perét. But, we know he took a boat, which is why you were notified." Eirek didn't know how much he should say about the situation.

"Was his son involved in the murder? I heard people talking at the ceremony." *Imagination does flow like the current. I can only imagine what will happen when they learn the truth.* "I cannot say. I wasn't here."

"But surely the family must have told you something!"

Eirek looked away and clutched his hands. "I cannot discuss those things."

"It matters not; your answer tells me what I need to know."

Eirek's face hardened. Surely people would start to put the pieces together? What could he do? He wasn't exactly sure what his position or authority was as apprentice. If anything, he wanted to wait until the conseleigh were with him to release information, but he was alone now.

In the remaining hours back, not much talking occurred. Some idle chatter about the sickness of the sea when Eirek started feeling queasy. The marquis told him about an old sailor's trick to get rid of the feeling, so he moved to the middle of the seacraft and focused solely on the horizon. Eirek was surprised at how well it worked.

Around three leagues from the Summer Isles, dolphins jumped and guided them as fast as they could to the islands. Although they couldn't keep pace with the seacraft, it was a spectacle to Eirek, nonetheless. When midday arrived and the suns became too hot overhead, Marquis Blocter tapped the man driving the hovercraft on the shoulder and muttered something to him. Shortly after, holes appeared in the glass, allowing the passage of air.

When they finally arrived at the sandy beaches and piers, the scent of brine and seaweed engulfed Eirek. The air here was fresh and untainted. Not like he experienced tainted air on Cresica, but this air was different; this was ocean air, not land air. The constant breeze kept him cool.

Eirek followed Marquis Blocter and his wife up man-made steps to a town with dirt-paved roads, short grass and palm trees. Islanders, mostly of black skin, walked to and fro in loose clothes of exotic and warm colors. All, however, wore Marquis Blocter's sigil—a dolphin leaping up over the islands.

Eirek wandered along with the marquis, glancing back every so often to see the conseleigh and Cronos following behind, observing the scenery and him on occasion. *Are they evaluating me?*

"This is where you will stay." Marquis Blocter pointed to a white house that boasted an impeccable impression. It reminded Eirek a little of the Clayses' mansion, for parts of it were uncovered, preferring to bathe in night or day.

When Marquis Blocter took them inside, Eirek was even more impressed. Past the living room with hand-scraped hardwood floors, a marble lanai provided an unobstructed view of the ocean beyond. Light sconces in the shape of dolphins clung to the wall and traveled up to the second floor. Above, a cypress ceiling with slits of glass let the suns see them at any time. There was a room for each person and a kitchen, fully prepped with meat from different ocean creatures and fruits from some of the trees native to the island.

"Thank you for your hospitality, Alyn." Tundra strode forward after the tour of their compound was complete.

"Of course, Conseleigh Iycel. Supper will be served in a few hours, and tomorrow you leave at midday for Gar. If you are hungry, your kitchen is fully prepped. I will leave now to put together a crew for you and a ship capable of making the voyage across the Summer Ocean."

"It is much appreciated." Tundra smiled.

Eirek copied her smile and shook Marquis Blocter's hand, thanking him as well.

Then the others left to go to their rooms, but Tundra pulled him aside to the lanai. "You did well in creating relations today, Apprentice Mourse."

Eirek beamed. "Thank you..." Eirek looked at the beach and those playing on it. Further down, piers stretched out to where the water changed from a light blue to a dark blue. There, at the pier's end, were a variety of wooden huts made from the branches of palm trees, a community living on the sea. A slew of jutting rocks prohibited people from swimming too far into the deep and open water, but also served as a rather perilous walkway from one community to the next. While tapping his fingers on the marble railing, he glanced back at Tundra. "Marquis Blocter asked if Hydro was involved in the death of Lord Paen."

"And what did you tell him?" Tundra raised a thin eyebrow. The scar on her face stretched in accordance with her inquisitive look.

"I... I said I couldn't say..." After a moment of silence, he continued. "What should I have said?"

"As Guardian, Apprentice Mourse, you will hear your conseleigh's advice, yes, but each action and decision is yours and yours alone to make. Although you're new to your role as apprentice, it is important you start formulating your own thoughts rather than waiting on ours. Sometimes there will be instances where you do not have time to think, only to do, and that is where you must be strong and confident."

So I failed. Eirek sighed. "Thank you, Conseleigh Iycel."

"It is simply my duty. I promised Edwyrd I would help you."

Eirek cocked his head. "Is that why you woke me so early?"

"It is." She leaned forward and put her arms on the railing.

"Eska is disappointed in me, isn't he?"

"He is."

Eirek hung his head as Tundra continued to talk.

"But he is loyal in his choices, to a fault." Tundra let out a slight chuckle. "Well, almost. He will not forsake your apprenticeship; he is merely preoccupied because of Pirini Lilapa."

"I am sorry I can't fight."

"You can, Apprentice Mourse. I have seen it in you."

Eirek thought about that for a moment. "Is that what you meant at the funeral? I thought Eska was mad at me."

"Edwyrd is not mad at you, he is..." Tundra glanced behind him, then turned back to Eirek and with a hushed breath said, "Mad at the situation Conseleigh Katore put him in. And, of course, tense about Pirini Lilapa. Luvan's mistake of forgetting to check for the necklace in the labyrinth was a simple one, an honest one, even, but it may have repercussions we have yet to fathom."

"Is... is Hydro really that dangerous now with the necklace? What can it do?"

"I do not know what it does, but if Edwyrd and Cronos fear its Power then surely it must be something to take note of." A sea breeze lifted strands of faded blue hair to fall upon the scar of her face. Tundra quickly tucked them back into place. "If anything, Edwyrd is glad that you communicated telepathically while discussing the situation on Acquava. After the Blood Bonding ceremony, Edwyrd became despondent by your incompetence. Your intrusion, I feel, may have had a positive effect on him because now he knows you need not rely solely on that telecommunicator on your wrist."

Tundra's words bit. To hide his face, Eirek looked down at the device. He hadn't used it yet. There was no need to when he traveled with the people for whom he had telecom numbers. "I... I thought he would accept me after the Trials. I thought they were meant to test us."

"And they did test you. All six of you that made it to the Central Core. But you did not win the Trials, Apprentice Mourse; Zain Berrese won." She stared off into the sea. "Other factors prohibited him from accepting, however." Her voice became rigid in that instant.

"I'm sorry I am not Zain."

"You do not have to be. What you need to be is you. Every person has a unique strength; the Trials made sure of that. What Edwyrd needs from you is to define that strength, advance it, so you can aid in the fight that is about to occur." She looked back towards Eirek. "When you are on Gar, I want you to observe Lady Aprah. Watch her mannerisms. She is someone worthy of emulation."

"Lady Aprah. Why?"

"Because she has the same strength her parents had. A strength to lead a tired and beaten nation to revolt and succeed. A strength of vision to see new possibilities for the future. The strength of a leader. And although you may never be as charismatic as her, you may discover other strengths about yourself while you travel on this journey."

What is my strength? Eirek looked down at his hands, as if expecting an answer. The sloshing waves brought him back to attention. Everyone on the beach looked happy. If something evil was to occur soon, the people playing on the beach didn't know it.

"How does he know it will happen?"

"Because the Curse of Pirini Lilapa is finite and absolute. The only unknown is where."

"You say it like you've experienced one before."

"In a manner of fashion, yes, I have. And the sooner you realize its threat, the sooner you will become the man Edwyrd, no, Gladonus, needs you to become." She turned to walk away.

Eirek called out to her, stopping her. "And what is that?"

Tundra let out a slight chuckle. "Is it not obvious?" She turned to face him, her light blue eyes no longer chilling him. They were too dull. "The Guardian of the Core."

The next day, after the morning meal of ham and fruit, Marquis Blocter ordered provisions to be stocked on the ship. The trip to Gar would take a week, depending on wind conditions. Eirek insisted on helping, but the marquis was even more insistent that his men perform such duties. Regardless, the ship got stocked shortly before midday.

Eirek's eyes fluttered when he saw the ship with three giant sails, one flying the crest of the Paens and the other two smaller ones flying the sigil of the Summer Isles. The crew, built of thirteen men and two women, were toned and tan and ready to work. They appeared competent, more so than Eirek; this was only his second time ever at sea.

At the bridge to the deck of the ship, Alyn Blocter looked on with a keen interest at the final preparations for the voyage. After a few shouts to people in the distance, a voice finally called, "All aboard."

Ethen and Luvan boarded the ship first and then Eirek. Then Cronos and finally Tundra. She said her thanks to Marquis Blocter, and he exchanged his, but then he said something Eirek was not expecting.

"I was talking to your apprentice yesterday and he would not say much about Hydro's situation."

"It is his choice not to disclose that information," Tundra replied.

"Which is why I am asking the elders now. If Hydro shows on our isles, should I be scared?"

Tundra looked back at Eirek. She was about to speak when Cronos, who had hobbled over to the conversation, spoke for her. "You should be terrified." The old man pushed Eirek onto the ship to avoid any further talk.

CHAPTER 47

CONTEMPLATION

What are you going to be this time? Eska stared in contemplation at the suns overhead. He tapped his fingers on the side of his veranda railing. Closing his eyes, he felt the space around him. Wind brushed against his cheek. Warmth slid over his face. And his necklace tingled on his throat. *My fate begins with this...* Eska recalled his conversation with Zeph from the night after Coronation. And as he ruminated, he couldn't stop fingering the necklace hiding underneath his shirt of darknether.

He thought back to when Deimos scoured Gladonus. How the wind called to him. It begged him to come to that cave in Gamrol Cliffs, and from there, sucked him through a portal to her. To Zeph. Wife to Ancient Bane. He wanted to see her again, but she only visited him on her whim. He would go there again when she called. She was a woman best kept secret.

What do I do?

A roar.

Eska scanned the silver skyline for Vesel. The silver-scaled dragon glided towards him and landed on top of the estate with a thud that Eska had grown quite accustomed to. The mythril-silver underbelly pulsed as silver flames spewed from its mouth into the air. Dark-red eyes, with a hint of orange, pierced Eska. It seemed that the suns were making him stronger. In turn, that would only increase Eska's strength, as he was the one bonded to him, but Eska knew that accounted for little. He doubted that they would be together during Pirini Lilapa. It was too dangerous. For both of them. If one of them were to die, the other would surely fall as well, in time. That's how being bonded worked. Gift or a curse, it was hard to say.

Using his necklace's ability to control wind, he levitated himself up to the roof so he could stand side by side with his friend. Eska scratched the muzzle and patted the dragon's nose with his gloved hand, staring into Vesel's eyes. The same deep red he had taken for his cape. Every time he saw them, he thought of his sister watching over him. Bonded with the creature that killed his sister—how fitting. But that's all his life ever was—fit for fate, as some said. *Alicia...*

Vesel roared and pointed his nose towards the suns.

"Yes, I know, my friend, Pirini Lilapa is coming," Eska said.

Vesel snorted.

Due to a request Eska had made long ago, during their first years together, Vesel remained mostly silent, only communicating in roars and flaps. Eska wanted it that way. Eska did not want to hear his dragon's voice because every time he did, it tore his sister's memory away from him, little by little. He wanted to remember her in Vesel's eyes, and the way he moved freely in the open air, and the way he was powerful with each gust of his wings and each breath of fire. When he spoke, however, that façade vanished into the thick, male voice he knew not to be hers.

Vesel folded his wings and lowered his back.

"You want me to get on?"

Vesel nodded.

Eska climbed onto his dragon. He breathed in the excitement of riding again. Then they were off.

Vesel climbed high into the sky, past the lowest of the clouds. Flames of silver stretched the length of the clouds when Vesel stopped at his zenith. The suns shined brightly in their jealousy of such beauty. His dragon then flew southward, using the bottom of his talons to touch the top of the clouds as if he were a frog jumping off lily pads on the pond.

The clouds cleared and an open expanse of southern mountains and lakes appeared below. Vesel dived downwards towards a group of mountains located by Crimson Lake. When he saw a golden pyramid hidden between the mountains, he knew where Vesel was taking him—the Guardian's Crypt.

Eska leaned forward. "Thank you, good friend."

Minutes later, they landed near the golden pyramid. Only his top aides knew of this place. But none of them knew the secrets inside. Out of the many responsibilities the Guardian of the Core held, protecting this place, and what it represented, was his greatest task.

Carved out at its base, a hallway large enough for Eska and his dragon led both to a golden door barred by two armored statues, each with the wings and beak of an eagle; they each held a long lance in their hands, the top of which was shaped like an ankh. Their stony eyes leered at him and then towards the dragon behind him. If someone who was not Guardian approached, they would animate themselves and guard the door to their death. Because Vesel was bonded with Eska, he was a part of Eska and, thus, able to go anywhere and everywhere the Guardian was allowed.

On the door of the palace was a handprint with a triangle design in the middle. He undid his glove of darknether, pulling it off one finger at a time. When fully exposed, a bright light shined from his palm—the Guardian's light. The light came from the mark on his palm that resembled a pyramid. Inside the pyramid, the letter *G* was carved in rigid lines to make three separate, but equal, pyramids. He placed his hand on the imprint and the door opened, exposing him and Vesel to the wonders and space inside.

In front of him, raised on a platform much higher than the floor, ivory columns stemmed from golden plinths that supported a massive roof. It was comparable to the temples of Chaon and Mistral, but smaller and extended horizontally rather than vertically. He walked the golden steps to the shrine leveled off in three separate sections. In a slight depression, in the area on each side of the shrine, stood a sole pedestal. They held a purported purpose, but would never be fully utilized until the day his position ceased to exist.

Stone protectors in the form of different animals watched his every move, ready to guard the crypt if need be. At the first level, sphinxes with golden bodies and deep onyx claws and adorned with sapphire headdresses kneeled before each visitor. Black bulls of cabochon with ruby eyes stood guard on the second level. Golden lions, standing as tall as he, guarded the third level. Their manes collared their necks, and apricot eyes stared intently at him. Vesel soared off to another part of the pyramid, preferring the open space to the confines of the temple crypt that Eska ascended.

Once he reached the marble flooring, he neared two tombs cased in diamond. The cuts in the shiny stone did not affect his view of the embalmed and preserved Guardians before him. Neither of them had bonded with an animal; but he had. It made him wonder if Vesel would receive such crystalline treatment at his Passing. Behind the statues, on thrones of fire, sat golden replicas of Jorey Raule and Matthau Crevon when each had been Guardian. And behind them, a slab of earth that contained a mystery that Eska would never see. Neither held a weapon—the weapon of the Guardian, Adonis, was a longsword, one of the eleven Ether Weapons, handed down with each generation. Although statues, they retained a part of the deceased Guardians' souls, only springing to life if another Guardian entered.

Guardian Raule's statue on the left opened its golden mouth. "Guardian Eska, what troubles you so?"

The fire throne had never felt hot to Eska. Growing up on Nova and being bonded with Vesel, fire and flames never affected him. "The Curse occurs again. Soon. Pirini Lilapa is almost upon Gladonus now."

"Why have you come here?" Guardian Crevon's voice resonated more deeply than Guardian Raule's.

"To... seek advice."

"I do not know how much advice we can give, Edwyrd. Pirini Lilapa is constant, but random." Guardian Crevon looked towards Raule.

"So you say, but I am not so certain."

"I echo Matthau's sentiment, Edwyrd. The only pattern is death and chaos." Eska hung his head.

"What makes you believe otherwise?" Guardian Crevon tapped his fingers on the throne of fire.

Should I mention Zeph? Guardian Eska looked into each of their eyes for a moment before answering. "What if it is the Other?"

Their heads tilted towards him. *That got their attention.*

"And what makes you think this?"

"When Deimos came into the world, it could do things that only Ancients ever could. I could not destroy it, either, no matter how many times I plunged Adonis through the beast. The Twelve were also ineffective in stopping the beast. All we could manage was to seal him in his chained confinement deep within the nation of Chaon."

"There were only ever three Ancients, Edwyrd, not four."

"Yes, but the Other created animals. Who's to say there wasn't strength to create Deimos in his image; to make it immortal?"

"Or some form of it, like the Twelve. I doubt the beast you faced was immortal. But what of the other events then? How has the Other affected them?"

"All the citizens of Gladonus think there has only ever been Ancients Bane and Lyoen. Why is there no record of the Other?"

"Because Bane cast a spell before he vanished from Gladima that made saying his true name impossible. A name brings with it Power, Edwyrd."

A name brings with it many things, as Zeph would say: fate, sorrow, greatness, but never Power. At least, she didn't believe so. "Even if his name wouldn't be able to be spoken, would it not still be documented in books and texts?"

The two Guardians looked at one another, then back to Eska.

"Yes, but most texts were destroyed during the first Pirini Lilapa where..." Guardian Raule paused for a moment. "You believe the Other did that? It would make sense... but why would he want such a thing...." Guardian Raule cusped his chin. "The second Pirini Lilapa dealt with the Conquest. That is an issue unrelated, an issue I had to straighten to allow those bonded with animals to be free from prosecution for fear that their animals would turn rampant like some did."

Eska looked upwards and noticed Vesel in flight around the pyramid. "Like I said before, the Other created animals. Perhaps he has some sort of sway over them still, like he can control those not human."

Guardian Crevon raised a golden hand. "Even if Pirini Lilapa is related to the Other, what is his end game?"

"My theory is he snuffed his name from the face of history during the first Pirini Lilapa so that he could hunt the offspring of the Ancients freely. And perhaps every Pirini Lilapa since, when he is at his fullest might, it is his chance to hunt them once again. They are the only ones with the Power and blood to stop him."

"You speak about Galan and Naydeia?"

Eska nodded and added, "And whatever offspring they may have conceived since."

"Do you have proof of this continued lineage?"

"I..." Eska paused, thinking if he should spew his thoughts. After a moment of contemplation he said, "I believe there was such an individual on the battlefield with the Twelve and I during the battle with Deimos."

Guardian Raule leaned forward, flames almost licking Eska's countenance now. "Is that so? What makes you believe that?"

"When we fought against Deimos, another man had joined in the fray, a man I had never seen before, yet who was not one of the Twelve."

"What would make you suspicious that he is an offspring of Galan or Naydeia?"

"Any man brave, or stupid enough, to be involved in that battle must think highly of himself. The kind of hubris given to you knowing you come from the Ancient bloodline. And he had possessed an Ether Weapon."

"Where is the man now?"

"He died on the battlefield. I remember that clearly..." Eska's voice fell with the remembrance of the incident. "He had taken it upon himself to battle Deimos greater than the rest of us. His axe could actually harm the beast. Multiple times I heard it yell, but only when *he* attacked it. Whether by accident or intent, Luenar made an assault on Deimos, killing this man in the process. The man's axe was then taken by Tomahawke. Tomahawke struck Deimos with it multiple times, but without similar effect. It was after this we realized we needed to band together and seal him."

"You spin an interesting story, Guardian Eska. What you mention makes sense, for I, too, heard the rumors of this bloodline when I was Guardian," said Guardian Crevon.

"When I was made the first Guardian of the Core, the Twelve told me of this rumor as well. But, even if we know his endgame, how can we help the people who do not want to be found? It is obvious they live in recluse for this reason, and their Ancient blood allows them to cut communication with anyone, even each other."

Eska sighed. "I do not have an answer for that."

"And neither do I," Guardian Raule said. "You make good points, Edwyrd, but until we find either Galan or Naydeia, we cannot stop the Curse from occurring."

Eska cupped his hands behind his back and turned around. He eyed the three pairs of animals that guarded the steps up to the crypt. "So, it will still happen."

"I am afraid so." Guardian Raule paused, and then continued, "But, you knew this already, didn't you, Edwyrd? Come now, what is the larger concern here?"

"Death." Eska turned back to face them. "If I cannot stop the Curse of Pirini Lilapa, I am afraid of..." Eska paused. "What if I cannot stop it?"

"Others will take the charge then. Perhaps your newly elected apprentice?"

Eska looked to the ground and tapped his foot.

"You are afraid he is not strong enough..." Guardian Raule tapped his fingers on the throne of flames. "That is what all of this is about, isn't it? Wanting to stop Pirini Lilapa so that it does not fall onto the shoulders of your apprentice... Interesting." The golden Guardian looked to the other statue and turned back to face Eska. "Did the Trials not do their job?"

"They did," Eska said, then added, "in a fashion."

"Explain."

Eska sighed. "My original selection denied my request. And, this new one, he is..." Eska paused, thinking of a way to word it, and decided upon, "*less* than I had hoped for."

"How so? What are his strengths, his weaknesses?" Guardian Crevon leaned forward.

"He cannot wield a sword. He is weak with Power. He does not know how to articulate his thoughts. He—"

"Surely there must be a positive?"

Eska nodded. "Yes, Guardian Crevon. The boy has a yearning for knowledge. He wants to learn. I believe he is intelligent."

"The boy sounds like me," said Guardian Raule.

Eska smiled, but continued to fidget with his fingers.

"It seems to me," Guardian Raule continued, "he has the most important quality. The one that cannot be taught."

Eska bit his lip.

"It is okay to be nervous, Edwyrd. It is okay to be brash and to be blunt..."

Eska remained silent among the diatribes of his predecessors.

"... but, it is not okay to be unsupportive. The Trials have always done their job in selecting the most qualified candidate. They chose me for my intellect to handle the Conquest and implement laws and bring order to a disordered Gladonus."

"And they chose me for my ability to heal and my knowledge of the adored arts when the Plague killed off millions of Gladonians. Why did they choose you?"

Eska bit his lip in contemplation. Vesel flew across the upper area of the large pyramid. "They chose me for my strength to combat Deimos."

Guardian Raule smiled. "And perhaps they have chosen this man for a reason you have yet to figure out. But you will, in time."

Eska furrowed his brows. He turned his eyes upward. "Vesel!" The dragon soared down to him and flapped its wings to slow its decent as it got close to the crypt. It continued flapping its wings to hover right outside of the place Eska stood, for the columns were too close together to allow his dragon entry. "Vesel, we are leaving now." He turned back to Guardians Jorey Raule and Matthau Crevon. "Thank you, my Guardians."

"I hope you found the answers you were looking for," Guardian Crevon said.

Eska nodded. "I did."

Turning on his heel, he walked down the steps once again, meeting his dragon at the bottom. Although he didn't have any idea of what Pirini Lilapa was going to cause, the words of his mentors encouraged him to see past the physical ineptness of his apprentice. Perhaps the Curse of Pirini Lilapa wouldn't take physical strength, like it had for Deimos. He couldn't say for sure. What he was sure about was that in a few weeks, it would occur, and Eska would have to respond.

CHAPTER 48

GAR

The voyage took a week. Nothing eventful happened. Perhaps once they saw a whale jump out from under the water, but that was all. Otherwise, it had been a starless voyage for the most part, as the suns drew even closer together. A week and a half now and they would converge. For how long, Eirek didn't know. Luvan and Ethen were on edge. Tundra, although strong, was weaker. Eirek could see it in her eyes. He, too, felt sluggish, but he thought it was the heat, not any curse. The only one who appeared stronger, surprisingly, was Cronos. The man was still slow, but his amber eye glowed brighter every day, showing to Eirek a vivacity he had never seen before.

When land was finally spotted, a hurrah of joy ran amongst the crew. The port town called Eastbarrow awaited them, and there Lady Aprah's receiver, Gøti Lanam, introduced himself. He was a man with fewer rings on his fingers than most receivers Eirek had seen. He wore a pin of a clock, the receiver's badge, on a brown robe that surely covered up a frail body underneath, for it looked even larger on him than Lord Clayse's clothes did on Eirek during the Trials. He had a gaping jaw that never seemed to close and muddy brown eyes. The man's ears drooped just like the loose skin on his face.

"How was the voyage?" Gøti asked. He scratched a beak of a nose and then put the hand back to his cane.

"Long," Luvan said.

"We still have two days before we get to Visis. We will stop for the night at Pebbleton and arrive before supper the following day." Gøti looked at Tundra and said, "There is your craft, as you requested. Lady Aprah is sad you will not be dining with her tomorrow night, Conseleigh Iycel. You will be staying with us until Pebbleton, however?"

Tundra shook her head. "I wish I could, Gøti, but pressing matters draw me north to Sereya. You have informed Marquis Bernal of my arrival?"

"That is a shame then." Gøti's voice quivered. "Yes, Rowan knows. Everything is arranged. There is a navigator in your craft to get you to Nore."

"Many thanks." She faced the rest of the group. "Have a safe passage in your travels."

"You as well, Tundra," Luvan said.

Ethen extended his hand. "Stay strong, Tundra."

"Once I get to my homeland again I should be fine, Ethen. Thanks."

"Your presence will be missed," Cronos said.

"Bye, Conseleigh Iycel," Eirek said.

"Farewell." She grabbed Eirek by the shoulders. "Remember what I told you on the isles, Apprentice Mourse."

Eirek nodded.

She smiled and relinquished her grip.

Afterwards the two hovercrafts went their separate paths—Tundra went north and the larger craft occupied by the rest of them went northwest.

Eirek looked out into the nothingness. Dirt and earth stretched out for miles, it seemed, with very few inhabitants. "So, this is Gar?" Eirek muttered to himself.

"Have you ever been to Gar, Apprentice Mourse?"

Eirek swung his head. "My friend told me it was different... not... *this*."

Gøti laughed. "This is only part of it, Apprentice Mourse. Wait until we get to the city."

"What is the city like?"

"You'll see."

The day after their stay in Pebbleton, they arrived three hours past their lunch in a suburb of Visis called Banad. They had left the small town of rock dwellings, where there had been more houses than businesses, to gangling mountains of steel and concrete and glass. As Visis came into view, Eirek couldn't decipher when Gar had stopped hosting a landscape most modest and ordinary to boasting one ostentatious and futuristic.

Gøti turned around. "Apprentice Mourse, conseleigh, Cronos, welcome to Visis." He beamed.

Upon the multitude of mountainous skyscrapers that was Visis large screens displayed various images that rotated every thirty seconds. Men donned shirts of plated metal. Women dressed in varying colors, but all wore bracelets around their wrists. Some were skinny and others corpulent. Hovercrafts flew on two levels, what appeared to be lower-tier models on the lower level and fancier ones utilizing the airroads above. Robots and droids followed some individuals on the streets made of chrome. Other people hovered in pods large enough for their bodies, instead of walking like some of the population. Yet others hovered by the soles of their feet, which propelled them off the ground.

Eirek's eyes widened as much as his jaw dropped. *How is there such a change from dirt and earth and mountains to a bustling metropolis?* Multiple times Eirek caught himself blinking too many times or shaking his head at the lights and sights.

"Impressed, Apprentice Mourse?"

"I... My friend is from Gar, but, but I never thought it would be this. He only ever mentioned mountains."

"Perhaps he is more of a southern Garian, then. What is his name?"

"Cadmar Briggs."

"Corrigan's son. Interesting he would give you that impression. They most certainly live in Visis. Well, his father and he anyway. The mother lives in the south."

Cadmar lives here. Eirek looked around, taking it all in. "Will I get to see him?"

"Our mission is to go to the Meeting of the Twelve, not reconnect with old friends," Cronos said.

Eirek's shoulders slumped.

"Despite that fact, the request would be quite impossible right now, anyway."

"What do you mean?"

"Currently, Mr. Briggs is completing the Passage. He aims to become an elite like his father. He left forty-four days ago." Gøti produced a grandfatherly smile, shifted his attention, and pointed behind Eirek. "Look. We are here."

A steep hill with more brown than green and a surrounding metal gate came into view. The gate remained locked by a piece of metal cut to look like an eye with metal pinchers as eyelashes and a ruby pupil at its center. A keyhole lay in the middle of the pupil and, upon arrival, a guard standing near the gate inserted a key, allowing them entrance to the estate. The pilots dropped them off and then steered the ship around the other side of the city enclosure.

"We go up," Gøti said, and pointed to the metal steps that led up the steep hill.

The old man walked up the metal steps at a surprisingly fast pace. Eirek followed. At the top of the steps (he had lost count after 161), his calves were sore. Two guards at the top stepped onto metal squares located on a small platform raised above the ground.

Click.

The metal steps retracted and sloped to form one long slide. *That's a defense mechanism if I've ever seen one.* Eirek wondered how useful a feature that could be in the capital of Syf.

"Each of you, step onto this." A guard pointed to a different, circular platform that was in the middle, right before a set of double-steel doors.

"What does it do?" Eirek asked.

"Check you for any toxins you may be carrying. We do not want our lady dying from illness."

Surely with all the technology, they aren't afraid of a harmless cold? If I were them, I would be more worried about the weapons we carry. Or are they that confident in the lady's protection? Eirek stepped into the sphere after observation and uncertainty. The wind whirled around his body. Then he felt a cold vapor on his neck, as if the sphere depressurized. A virtual screen appeared in front of him with the word *clear.*

With approval of one of the guards, he walked forward, ready to enter the estate.

CHAPTER 49

A GUARDING GIFT

C rystal flowers hung around the wall of the dining hall like sconces, the bulb of each flower emitting a bluish glow to the room. It sat perhaps twenty comfortably at a rectangular table made of ore. Now there were only eight individuals in the room. Eirek's group of four, Lady Aprah, her advisor—who introduced himself as Jöðurr Eldredge, Gøti, and another large man who Eirek supposed was an important guard.

"How fared your travels?" Lady Aprah asked as they all sat down.

Eirek took a spot between the conseleigh, across from Lady Aprah. The others of Lady Aprah's group looked from Cronos to the conseleigh, but only after they had lost interest in Eirek's inability to answer. The stares intimidated him.

After long enough, Luvan spoke, "Long, but nothing slowed us."

Eirek sighed. He slouched as best as he could but the steal chair kept his posture upright. *Find my strength. Be a Guardian. That is what Eska needs from me.*

"That is good to hear, then." Lady Aprah smiled. "You've been acquainted with Gøti and Jöðurr already, I know, but Horm Dubhalen here is the head of my elites." She gestured to the large man, who merely nodded in acknowledgment. He had arms the size of Eirek's head and probably the only person Eirek knew who could make Cadmar look small. A necklace, the same eye that Lady Aprah took for her sigil, hung over the man's dirt-brown long-sleeved shirt.

"It is a pleasure to meet you. All of you," Eirek said, hoping to correct his passiveness.

"The pleasure is ours. Anything for Guardian Eska. He was implemental in the secession of Gar from Sereya. Something we will never forget. But..." Lady

Aprah grabbed a fork on the table. "Enough of that kind of talk. Let us eat. I am sure you are all hungry."

Eirek tilted his neck to Lady Aprah's dialect. It wasn't as rugged and guttural as Cadmar's had been. There was a slight accent to it, but it was refined and polished, like a smooth gem instead of one freshly mined.

After they had stuffed themselves on goat meat, dirt pudding, and a loaf of bread, the conseleigh and Cronos were shown to their quarters by Gøti. Lady Aprah made it a point, however, of wanting to see Eirek alone in her room. So Eirek followed her up the stairs, Horm by her side, and then down a long hallway with marble flooring. At the end of the hallway were two guards who, upon seeing Lady Aprah approach, raised their shields and banged axes against them three times. Eirek's ears rang, and he tucked his shoulders to his ears. *I would never be able to get used to that.*

"Stand down," she commanded, unaffected by the custom.

The soldiers lowered their shields.

"I, too, will stand watch, Lady Aprah."

"Nonsense, Horm. Spend time with Abigayl and your sons. Lectum and Haus here have it covered well enough."

"Very well, my lady. Thank you." Horm bowed and left.

Eirek noted that. Tundra had told him he should observe Lady Aprah. Was this why? How did she get such support from everyone? How was she so well loved? Eirek had little time to contemplate the questions, for once inside her room, Lady Aprah directed Eirek to accompany her on the balcony.

The night air was warm and crisp with wind. From the vantage point, Eirek saw the metropolis of Visis and in the distance, hills and mountains. The dichotomy astounded Eirek.

"Pretty, isn't it?"

"Yes." Silence. Somewhere in between looking at the stars and the city lights that tried to mimic them, Eirek asked, "How... how does Gar.... I mean... how did Gar manage to become so advanced in such a short time?"

"The long story is for another day." Lady Aprah smiled wryly. There was an attractive ruggedness about her in her dirt-brown hair, defined jawline, and thick eyebrows. "But, the short version is that we found a way to harvest the minerals in the mountains for energy." Lady Aprah pointed to an orange glow to the northwest. "Do you see that there?"

Eirek nodded.

"That is Roan, a mining community in the northwest. There are dozens of these set up throughout Gar. Just as Cresica is known for its agriculture, and Acquava for its water, Gar is known for its minerals." Lady Aprah touched his forearm. "And we have vision. My parents' vision." She grabbed his shoulder and pointed up to the sky. "Do you see that star there?"

Eirek squinted. Not many were out yet, but he assumed she pointed to the larger one with a reddish glow to it. "I think."

"We call it Eshleeng, our North Star. And, do you see the constellation that the other stars form around it?"

Eirek tried to make out the other stars. "I... I don't know."

"An eye." She turned his shoulders so that he faced her. "This eye." She exposed a tattoo similar to that of her sigil on her forearm. "It has watched over us since my parents led our revolt. It lets us see the difference we're able to make in those people indifferent to make any. It gives us strength and purpose."

"That is good." Eirek heard the echo of his uncle's advice in her words. He knew now the reason why Tundra wanted Eirek to observe her.

"Yes, which leads to my reason for bringing you here. You are to attend the Meeting of the Twelve, I hear, on Mount Volan?"

"Yes, the conseleigh and Cronos will accompany me as well."

"There is strength in numbers, but Volan is a wicked mountain with danger- ous beasts that roam the Sacred Passage. Or, so I've heard. You will need more protection." She walked inside, continuing to speak with him all the while. "I know we have not given you a gift for Coronation yet, but that is why you are in my quarters now." Lady Aprah disappeared from view for a moment.

Eirek went inside to look for her and found her standing at the back of a hallway, mesmerized by something. "Lady Aprah?"

No answer.

Eirek continued down the hallway. Once again, he called out to her.

She turned around this time and smiled. "Come." She bobbed her head, motioning Eirek towards her.

Eirek stood beside Lady Aprah. Two weapons encased in glass stood before him. "What are they?"

Her fingers pressed against the glass case. "They were my mother's weapons. Tanfas they're called. Since she died, they have been here, hoping to not see another day of battle." She lowered her hand, felt in the shaded area around the case, and pulled out a ring box. "Whenever I see them, I always spend so much time looking at them. They were my mother's only legacy." She closed the closet and exhaled. "Anyway, this is for you."

Eirek accepted a tiny box and opened it. Inside was a ring with a metallic crystal on the crown of the ore band. He looked at Lady Aprah, hoping she would give some direction.

"This is an invention we just stumbled upon here. It is a shield. It harvests the energy from the quartz crystal on the crown which..." She grabbed the ring and placed it on her finger. "By putting pressure on the quartz it emits an electromagnetic pulse that collects all the particles in the air to form a lightweight, mobile shield." She pushed the crown and Eirek saw a shield form almost instantaneously. "Go on, touch it."

He reached out to the slightly purple, yet translucent, shield. When his fingers made contact, it felt hard and gritty. "This is the dust from the air?" Eirek pet the shield.

"Yes, it is. Incredible isn't it."

"It repels any weapon?" Even though he didn't need to, Eirek poked his head around the shield to look Lady Aprah in the eyes.

"We assume any weapon besides the fabled Ether Weapons. As we do not have one in our possession, we cannot proceed to test its qualities for that specific encounter. It is more than adequate at stopping the other weapons, though." Lady Aprah touched the crown again to deactivate it. "And it is yours. To protect you while you travel through the Sacred Passage as you make your way to Mount Volan."

"Thank you very much, Lady Aprah." He looked back to the closet. "Why do you keep it in there?"

"Just as tanfas were my mother's legacy, and she was unmatched in her skill with how to use them, this will be my legacy. Many of my citizens will now be much safer once we can get a full-model type on the market. It will revolutionize the way of war." While she spoke, she moved back to the balcony.

Eirek kept with her. On the balcony, he exhaled and then asked. "How do you do it?" Eirek turned to look at her.

"Do what?"

"Become well adored by your followers."

"My parents raised me with the belief of freedom and equal labor. And that ideal spread into a contagion that infects everyone here."

She can't relate. She has parents. I never did.

"But, I've never even seen them. I've only heard stories about them from the people who raised me, Gøti and Jöðurr. But it doesn't mean I can't still know who they are through others. And those others have helped me become who I am today." Lady Aprah paused before continuing. "Gøti tells me I am as passionate as my parents about our people, and that makes me smile. But, I have also learned from them to be wise; it is them who have taught me to lead. You can learn much from your elders."

"That... that is why I asked. Conseleigh Iycel mentioned I should examine you and learn."

"Conseleigh Iycel told you that?"

Eirek nodded.

"It is interesting that she said that." Lady Aprah smirked. "I always figured she was rather resistant to me because of my parents' secession from Sereya."

Eirek could say nothing to the comment.

"It's a shame she went north. I would very much like to discuss that with her now. I suppose, in the same vein, Lady Iycel is someone to learn from, for while she ruled, there was no Gar or even the idea of a new nation, or so I believe." Lady Aprah smiled. "Like I mentioned before, learn from the people who care for you. They know what is best."

Eirek thought back to the Mourses. They had been his only true parents. He had never seen or heard anything about his real parents. The Mourses didn't know them, and Angal never spoke of them.

"I will keep that in mind. Thank you very much, Lady Aprah."

"The pleasure is mine, Apprentice Mourse. I am flattered you would even ask, or that Conseleigh Iycel told you to. But I could see that you had wise elders around you that day when you secured my vote at Coronation. In fact, I was particularly interested in how you answered the last question. The one Lord Daven Evber posed to you about what defines a good leader."

Those who are good at chess lead the best. Eirek blushed as he thought about the saying. "Cadmar told me that saying of Gar's as we played chess one day during the Trials."

"I hear you like to play the game. That it is more than a hobby for you."

"I... I wouldn't say that, but I do love it."

"Come tomorrow; I will have a time arranged for us to play. I, too, am an avid chess player."

"Cadmar told me that. He said you'd give me a dash for my coin."

Lady Aprah smirked. "I know. Before he left for the Passage, he told me the same thing as well about you."

CHAPTER 50

CHESS

It was after lunch. The others were readying for the future travel, while Lady Aprah insisted Eirek play chess with her before he left and had told one of her servants to ready his things for him, so that he could do so. Not moments before, Lady Aprah had gotten up from a white leather chair in front of him to go get a chessboard. An actual chessboard. Not some virtual game where you typed in the actions and watched the pieces move.

Lady Aprah came back holding a wooden board with a small wooden box placed on top. She sat down across from Eirek and crossed her legs, bent forward and put the board on the glass coffee table that separated them, moving the box to the side.

"Do you like it?" Lady Aprah asked.

"What?"

"The board. It was my father's. Jöðurr said that he used to play with the other miners near a town called Hal. That's where he met my mother. She beat him."

The board wasn't polished but made of a hardwood that had seen some time. Lady Aprah reached into the box and set up her field with wooden pieces painted red, laying them on the appropriate red and brown squares that made up the board. Eirek did the same with his brown pieces. The wood felt archaic in his hands. Everything else here was so advanced, but this wasn't. It was merely chess. Some of his colors were chipped and scratched, but Eirek found a rugged beauty in them that came from them being original—the same type of beauty he was sure many found in Lady Aprah.

"This board actually is how I chose the colors of my sigil—the red and the brown." She laughed a little. "I was not even ten when my council gave this to me as a present. It may be silly but it's true."

"How did the silver come to find its way into your sigil?" Eirek finished setting up his board. He kept upright, trying to mimic Lady Aprah's posture.

"Silver has many meanings, Apprentice Mourse. It is the color of ore we mine, of the steel we use, and of the medal that symbolizes that you are second, not first, and therefore have to continually strive to better your nation." She tucked a strand of hair behind her ear, revealing little shovel earrings which matched her loose-fitting silver gown. "Are you ready to begin?"

Eirek nodded.

"I let you take the first move. You are a guest in my house, after all."

Eirek bit his lips and cocked his head slightly. *Is she really that confident?* He eyed the field and then moved a pawn out two spaces. He took his fingers off the head and waited for Lady Aprah to make her move.

She slid her fingers around a knight's neck, looked at Eirek, and then moved her fingers to a pawn and moved the pawn forward. She sat back and bit her lower lip, studying Eirek. Could she see that he was trying to devise a strategy? He always focused on forming a perimeter with his pawns first so that they could protect one another.

"So, tell me true, Apprentice Mourse, is Lord Paen of Acquava dead?"

Eirek nearly fumbled the pawn in his hand. He placed it in position and then looked at her and asked, "How..."

"News like that travels as fast as ships through wormholes." She moved a knight forward without almost any thought. "So, is it?"

Eirek scanned the board. Lady Aprah was playing more aggressively than he had anticipated, already claiming two of his pawns. When he moved a rook forward to capture one of her pawns, he looked at her and nodded. "He and his wife have passed."

"Some say he was taken by one of his own sharks. Others say he forgot to put a shielding spell on himself while sparring. And yet others claim his son killed him. Which of them is it, really?" She moved her bishop diagonally, preventing him from moving the pawn next to his lord.

Where do some of these rumors start? She is bold in asking that. Eirek remembered Tundra's words. What would it matter if Gar knew the truth; surely everyone would know in time. "Hydro Paen killed his father, yes. And his mother. That is what the survivors of Lord Paen's estate told us." Eirek examined the board, trying to find a suitable move. He decided to move the rook to the left, creating pressure on her main force. Also, it would discourage her from moving the bishop she had in place.

"What a tragedy. So, where is Hydro now? Certainly he doesn't rule if he killed his own father."

"He is missing. Aiton rules now, with help from the elders around him." Eirek moved his knight to force a retreat from one of her rooks.

"Not so different than my story, it seems. Except it was a war that took the lives of my parents..." She moved her lady forward, ready to diagonally flank the other side.

She is moving her lady too early. That'll be her downfall. Eirek countered with a simple exchange of rook and lord—a move called castling. It would allow his larger units more mobility now that the board had cleared up a little.

Lady Aprah examined the board more thoroughly this time, not moving as fast as she usually did. To combat the silence, Eirek asked, "I... I remember at Coronation you wore a dress that revealed the tattoos on your back. It is similar to the weapons you showed me yesterday, right?"

Lady Aprah giggled. "You remember such a thing yet forget about your rook?" She moved a knight Eirek had forgotten about to take his rook. Swapping the tokens she said, "Identical. I was inked at eighteen, when I knew my body was done growing and that I had turned into an adult. It reminds me of them, even though I do not remember seeing them."

Eirek's defenses were crumbling to the forward progression Lady Aprah dealt him. He moved his other rook forward to take a pawn that had stayed back to defend the lord. "Check."

Lady Aprah quickly countered by moving the bishop back to take the second rook. "Aiton will find some way to remember his parents if he hasn't done so already. It is the only thing that keeps people like us sane... So does training..."

Am I not sane, then? I have no recollection of my parents, and Angal would never tell me. Is that why the test to be an elite is so difficult? Is it meant to break them?

Eirek moved a bishop into position. "Check. Tell me, why would a lady need to train and fight? Especially when you have the strength of the elites with you?"

Lady Aprah moved another pawn two spaces forward, blocking his check and forcing the retreat of his bishop. "Lords and ladies need to share in the struggles of their soldiers." She moved a knight downward. "Check."

Eirek took the knight with his lady stationed close by. "Do you not think it wise for a lady to fight with words and pen, and her soldiers to fight with steel?"

"Lords rush into battle with their troops all the time; why can a lady not do the same?" Lady Aprah took Eirek's lady with her rook.

She is dangerously close. How could I not see that? Eirek moved a knight forward, putting pressure on her lady.

"If you want to be well-respected, you cannot send your pawns into battle while the lord and lady stay back..." She grabbed her lady and moved it diagonally. "Otherwise... check..."

Eirek sighed and hung his head. *Only one move left.* He moved his lord back one spot.

Lady Aprah quickly moved her rook down. "Otherwise... you'll never win. Checkmate." With her rook, she tipped over Eirek's lord and extended her hand out to him. A sly smile spread across her face.

"You definitely play well. Cadmar was right," Eirek said. "A good game."

"It was. Hopefully, you'll know someday what it's like to earn the respect of those below you, instead of always trying to impress those above you."

There was a certain truth to her words.

"I will strive to do that. Thank you."

"You are welcome. I pray you success at the Meeting."

"Thank you."

"Your things and provisions should be readied by now. To aid you in your travels, two of my elites will escort you there. It will be a two-day journey." Lady Aprah led him to the door. "One of your escorts I believe you already know." She opened the door.

Waiting for him outside was none other than Corrigan Briggs. Helmet off, prominent amber eyes looked down at Eirek. "My son would want me to make sure you be getting to that Passage safe. And that be what I do." The scars on his face crinkled awkwardly as the man formed what could have been a smile. He raised his shield and banged it three times.

He cringed.

Lady Aprah chuckled. "Still not used to our greeting, I see."

"I do not think I can ever get used to it."

"When you live here for a year during your training, you will." She looked at Corrigan. "You and Horm are responsible for getting him there. Do so."

"Of course, my lady." Corrigan shifted his gaze from Lady Aprah to Eirek. "Follow me. There be a hovercraft waiting for us, and you have a mountain to climb."

Corrigan gave Eirek a wry smile. Eirek feigned one in return. He gulped and then followed Cadmar's father, unready and unsure of what was to come when he arrived at the Sacred Passage.

CHAPTER 51

THE SACRED PASSAGE

To say that Eirek was nervous as he walked down the stony path of the Sacred Passage was an understatement. It wasn't so much nerve that he would fail; he couldn't. He needed to impress Cronos to his side and the two conseleigh, Ethen and Luvan, behind him. Cronos saying that all Abaddon was about to break loose when the suns finally did converge is what made Eirek scan the rocky plains to his left and right. It was what made Luvan clutch the handle of a large knife on his belt and why Ethen kept his fingers around the baton at his side. Cronos, however, seemed rather unfazed by the ordeal and rather invigorated despite his own foreboding. Unlike the others, he did not have shortness of breath or sweat that plagued his body. The disparity distracted Eirek. *Perhaps he has learned some secret on how to stay safe during his life here.* He wondered if the others noticed the difference as well.

After hours of walking in the open corridor of stone, the path curved to the right. The walls, which had been growing as they descended, leveled off. Fifteen paces further down the path, the walls encumbering them shot out to the sides, and Eirek and the others stepped out into a vast plain of openness. Boulders dotted the terrain, with multiple paths that cut into the bluffs surrounding them. *How is that possible?*

"It is possible, boy, because this land is sacred." Cronos stepped beside him. His amber eye examined him.

Did he read my thoughts? Can he? "How did you?"

"Your body language... Now let's continue... You lead the way... This is your task and will be your meeting, after all."

Eirek looked back. Ethen and Luvan gave an appreciative nod. Eirek turned back around. Movement along the bluff stopped him. *What was that?* Eirek walked towards the action; his hand dragged on a large boulder next to him. The boulder shifted, stood, stretched, and looked down at him with eyes of dirt. Eirek fell backwards. The earth around him shook. The boulder yawned and then curled back up. The shaking stopped.

Eirek got to his feet. "What... what are those things?"

"That is a stone golem. The creature along the bluff was a centaur. They guard Mount Volan and feed off of people who fail to make it there," Cronos explained.

"Are... are they human... or animals..."

Movement came from his peripherals, but by the time he turned his head, it had already vanished. *What else lives here?*

"They are demigods."

"What are demigods?"

"You know very little, boy. Very little."

"He is not as old as you, Cronos. Explain to him. It is your job at this phase in his training."

Cronos snickered at Luvan. "Aye, I wish he was more competent, is all." Cronos paused, then began again. "Just as the Twelve gave a trait of their Power to Guardian of the Core, they also selected animals, individuals and creatures who were greedy for longevity to become demigods. Some were taken voluntarily, others were simply taken. The Twelve wanted some way to keep themselves safe and rule over the mortals."

"Why haven't I seen any on Cresica?" Eirek noticed a centaur with long jade hair and a lean jaw. She carried a bow around her exposed chest. She pointed downwards, signaling for another centaur (this time a man with orange hair) to examine them.

Eirek stopped. Five others came along the bluff during this time. When Cronos and the others came next to him, the group darted off.

Cronos squeezed Eirek's shoulder. "Demigods exist on every planet, some in different forms. Onkh and Myoli hold the mountains that can lead to Axiumé, to the very heavens themselves. Agrost and Pyre have deep descents that lead to the fiery pits of Abaddon. On Agrost that place is known as the Abyss. Most likely, the demigods live there, right on the cusp of the mortal world and the one beyond."

Uncomfortable, Eirek continued forward, leaving Cronos and the others behind. He walked until he came across a lone tree with blue bark and green leaves.

"The Ancients had a say in each planet's development. They wanted the secret of the Ancients kept hidden and not so easily obtained. That is why they test the worth of everyone who tries to conquer the mountains, or those who try and travel to Abaddon."

"If Eska couldn't climb all the way up Mount Klaff, then how is he seen worthy here?" Eirek asked.

"Because the Meeting of the Twelve takes place only halfway up Mount Volan in a palatial palace of gold and silver and copper. Even Eska's failure of climbing the entirety of Mount Klaff is still seen as worthy here. Enough so that the demigods know to respect his authority. Everyone knows Mount Klaff is much harder to climb..." Cronos said.

"'e makes tis journey every year, Eirek, but now you are te apprentice and it's your turn." Ethen clasped him on his shoulders.

"We are only here to help deliver you there safely," Luvan said.

"So, they will try to hurt me?" Eirek asked.

Eirek took a path that allowed them to all travel side-by-side. The cliffs were high. To the right, tiny rocks tumbled over the cliff. Faint trotting halted. The female centaur with jade hair pointed her bow downwards. She shot an arrow. It passed by Eirek's eyes and stuck into the stone wall next to him. The centaur smirked and galloped away.

"No, they will not physically hurt you, but the demigods may test you," Cronos said. He pointed to the arrow. It held a piece of parchment on it.

Eirek walked over to the arrow and pulled it from the wall. The piece of parchment slid down into his hands. He unraveled it and looked at what it said.

Volan lies ahead, but to travel north you must face the south
You will be fed answers only drizzled in drouth
Like the taste you won't, but that is the price paid
To reach the domain where gods lie and Ancients create

A riddle? Eirek read it aloud to the others. Then he read it to himself a few times. After, he looked Cronos in his amber eye. It was bright. Vivacious. "And what if I fail their test?"

"Well... then, they might."

CHAPTER 52

FACING THE SOUTH

After two days of traveling at a cautious pace, they came to a greener section of the Sacred Passage. Bluffs of mountains still surrounded them, but instead of just seeing cracked, rocky floor underfoot, they now strode over mounds of green and stepped over little rivulets of water. There were more trees now, still of the same blue bark and green leaves that Eirek had first seen in the open expanse. Here, zephyrs blew past the boughs of trees to slap Eirek's face.

"The heat is horrible." With his forearm, Eirek wiped his forehead. "Can I just... *Vesi.*" Water from the rivulets floated towards Eirek.

Cronos watched intently. Then his eyes flicked to the sky.

Veins of purple shot into the blue. A sizzling and crackling cacophony came with it, as if the very sky itself burned like leaves in a fire.

The beads of water en route to Eirek evaporated. Heat clawed at his neck. He turned his attention upwards, as did the others.

"Pirini Lilapa... The time has arrived..." Cronos muttered and staggered off, hobbling on his cane. For someone who had appeared in even better condition leading up to the suns' convergence, the eclipse now left him leaning against a nearby tree, alone.

Eirek moved forward, but Luvan stopped him. "Let him be."

Eirek nodded and redirected his attention to the sky. Lugh had descended upon Freyr, covering all but the outer rim of the larger red sun. The purple aurora swept out from the epicenter of the eclipse, blotting out the blue.

"Rather pugnacious, isn't it?" Luvan folded his arms over his chest.

Ethen nodded and unstrapped his pack. "Let's 'ope the fight only occurs up tere." He pointed. "We should take a break now, anyway... We have been walking for hours. It will give Cronos a chance to recover."

"Agreed." Luvan took off his pack and set it down on an area of patchy grass near them

Eirek stretched his fingers outward, thirsty for the nearby water.

"No need to be drinking tat water anyway, Eirek. Lady Aprah provided us wit provisions."

Eirek stopped. *Ethen is right.* He sat down with the other two and opened a capsule that held a sandwich packed inside. While he munched, he ruminated about everything that had happened so far. From canteens he drank Garian water, which, although cold, had a slight taste of grit and iron.

"You think there is something wrong with that water?"

"Could be," Ethen said. "We 'ave seen men tat are horses and boulders tat are actually creatures. I wouldn't trust tat water. 'abit of Chaon, I suppose. T'ere is no fresh water, so we always 'ave to rely on outside sources."

"Ethen is probably right, Eirek."

"We have been traveling for two days now, how..." Eirek paused. He tilted his head, then pulled out the riddle he had received from the centaurs. "Answers drizzled in drouth...," Eirek muttered. "Maybe we aren't supposed to drink."

Eirek took a swig from his canteen and thought about how fortunate it was for Lady Aprah to supply them with provisions, especially in the wake of Pirini Lilapa. He looked at the purple aurora in the sky once more. It truly was beautiful. Candose, the moon, hung in the sky, a useless ornament. It would remain that way until Pirini Lilapa finished.

"Is the Curse of Pirini Lilapa real?" Eirek asked aloud.

Ethen and Luvan turned their heads to one another. "Get Cronos," Ethen suggested. "He would know. And, it will be good for him to have food."

Eirek turned around. Cronos still slunk against the tree. Eirek crept up behind him. The Sage was muttering nonsense to himself, as if he were in a different place. *This is really having an effect on him.* Blushing and somewhat uncomfortable, Eirek tapped him on the shoulder. He didn't respond, but contained muttering nonsense in a language Eirek couldn't understand. Eirek pushed his shoulders harder. Cronos spun around, open-mouthed. His amber eye almost appeared orange and red with fire, like a comet. His blue eye blazed with the same fire as well. Together, they seemed to have the same ferocity as the suns overhead. Then it ceased. *What was that?*

Cronos cleared his throat. "What do you want?"

"Would you like to eat with us?" Eirek suggested.

Cronos looked from Eirek to the other two. "Very well."

The only time this far, Eirek walked to Cronos's slower gait. "Are you okay?"

"Yes. Why wouldn't I be, boy?"

"I..." Eirek was taken aback by the sage's retort. "I just... It seemed strange over there."

"The talking?" Cronos raised an eyebrow.

Eirek nodded. He wanted to ask about the eyes, but thought it rude.

"It happens every Pirini Lilapa. Pay it no mind." Cronos sat down on the grass, away from the others.

"How many times has it happened?"

"This will be its fifth time." Cronos looked towards the sky.

"How will we know if something bad has happened?"

"You will know..." Cronos opened his own provisions and drank water.

"Will Deimos break free from his bonds?" Ethen asked.

"Doubtful. The Twelve and Eska made those bonds. They won't break unless the worst happens."

"The worst?" Eirek gulped.

"Think about it." Cronos spooned vanilla paste into his mouth.

That is why Eska has been on edge. Eirek clenched his fists. *It all makes sense now. So much rests on him. So much rests on being Guardian. I will help him.*

"You are beginning to realize how important of a man the Guardian of the Core is, aren't you?" Cronos eyed him.

Eirek took a bite of his sandwich. "How does sealing bonds work?"

"Do not talk with your mouth full of food, Apprentice Mourse. You represent Guardian Eska. Here it is fine, there..." Luvan pointed north towards the top of Mount Volan. "The Twelve will be watching you. Intently."

Eirek swallowed his food. "I will be better," he apologized.

Cronos swooshed the paste around his mouth while studying him. After gulping it down, he asked. "Why do you want to know?"

"You mentioned Deimos can't escape. Why is that?" Eirek leaned forward.

"The process of binding and sealing has been around since the Ancients. That necklace that Hydro wears, if it truly is the Zas Necklace, hides within it a girl with black hair."

"Who is she?"

"She is the daughter of Zas, and as punishment for him making that necklace, she is sealed within."

"Why?"

"That necklace was given to a very peculiar man named Beno Begare."

"What was strange about him?" Eirek asked.

Cronos glared at him. "I was getting to that... Beno Begare was the only man born on Gladima who couldn't cast Power. He was the first Denied person with First Blood. After his birth, others on Gladima began not being able to use Power as well. Ancient Bane sought to remedy this problem. Like a pandemic, it caused immediate concern in his eye, so he tasked Zas Banegul to find a solution..."

"The necklace?"

"Aye, the necklace, boy. But, the Power the necklace was made with was not a Power meant to be replicated... It was never meant to be replicated..." Cronos sighed. "So, when Beno Begare put this necklace on he could finally use Power, yes, but it consumed him and led to countless murders. One of those individuals killed was Ancient Lyoen's husband. In retribution, Lyoen sealed Zas's daughter, killed his wife, and banished him. Thus the Great War started." Cronos ate a little more, then continued. "She will be sealed in that necklace forever, for Ancient Lyoen will never die, and since she has disappeared, she cannot reverse the process."

"Husband? Lyoen is a woman?" Eirek shook his head in disbelief.

"She is."

"I... I thought..."

"That because of her actions she must be male? Or to be as powerful as she is, she must be male? A woman has her own strength, boy. Some of the fiercest creatures that roam Gladonus are female."

"Like who?" Eirek's voice shot up.

"The Four Creatures of Legend."

His jaw dropped a little.

"And judging by your expression, you do not know who they are either. You have much to learn, boy. *That* is a story for another day, though." Cronos spooned more of the paste into his mouth and chased it down with water from a canteen.

Eirek sat for a while in silence, then asked, "What do you expect this Pirini Lilapa will bring?" Eirek asked.

"Chaos and death...," Cronos muttered.

Silence lingered.

Eirek finished his sandwich. "What were the other ones?"

Cronos studied him. "What do you want to know that for, boy?"

"To prepare for this one."

"You cannot prepare for the Curse of Pirini Lilapa. No one can. Not even the Ancients could..." Cronos went on to mutter something incomprehensible and then hoisted himself up on his staff and walked away.

"You upset him," Luvan said.

"I—"

"It is best not to bring up tose tings," Ethen said.

Eirek hung his head. "Alright."

"Are you finished eating?"

"Yes."

"Apologize to Cronos, and then we can leave."

"I was only—"

"Part of being a Guardian is knowing when to force an issue, when to not, and when to apologize. Ethen and I will pack the bags."

What's the point of having knowledge if you don't share it? Eirek grunted, got up, and walked over to Cronos. He stood on a path where the grass ended, looking up to the sky. His strength and vitality seemed to have returned to him, for he no longer needed his staff to hold him or a tree to lean on.

When at his side, Eirek said, "I'm sorry about earlier. May we continue?"

"At your lead." Cronos pushed the staff he carried out in front of him.

Past another stream, larger this time, and through a field of boulders, Eirek led them. Centaurs followed on the tops of bluffs overlooking their spot. Stone golems would sometimes stretch and yawn and look at the group with yellow eyes before going back to sleep. The heat didn't dissipate even the slightest until Eirek came to a wide, windy ravine with a 200-foot drop, and only a narrow stone bridge to walk across.

"The base lies right over this." Cronos pointed with his hand that carried the staff.

Eirek looked at the chasm once more, stalling time. *I can do this. Eska needs me to be strong.*

His first steps over the narrow stone bridge were awkward and included a misplaced step and a stumble, but he regained his balance by holding his arms out to the side. Rushing water from the side waterfalls made it hard to concentrate, but they did allow for a pleasant wisp of water on each gust that threatened to nudge him over into the blackness below.

He didn't know how long it took to get over. It felt like an hour. On the other side, an expansive alcove greeted him. The base of the mountain seemed immeasurable, and around it sat huge boulders that neared the size of Eska's estate. To the left, a path curved upwards around the mountain. The same sort of path was on the right but curved downwards. Hooves trotting around him made Eirek shift focus to the centaurs who watched him from the bluffs above, bows strapped across their chests.

"To go north, you must face the south," Eirek muttered.

Eirek looked at the path that descended deeper into the earth. *That must be what the riddle is referring to.* Eirek walked in that direction. It curved and curved the deeper they went, seemingly interminable. The soles of his shoes were getting worn from all the traveling he had done the past few days. Luckily, or unluckily, night would have little bearing if any for the next few days until Pirini Lilapa finished. That meant no need to worry about what may happen in the dark, but it also meant inadequate time for rest.

In an hour's time (or more, Eirek had lost track), he found himself sick of going downhill, so naturally when it leveled off, he looked around thinking he had solved the riddle. But then he noticed the large boulders and the bluffs. *Is this the same place? How is that possible?* Eirek stepped back toward the middle and looked at the direction they had just come from. It led upwards. *What?* Eirek put his fist underneath his chin and contemplated what just happened. *It must be Power.*

Perhaps if I go the other way. Eirek went to the left and up the mountainside. He climbed and his legs became weary, his shoulders sore and his hand sweaty from continually carrying the briefcase. Finally, he came to a plateau a few hours later.

It was the same plateau. With the same boulders. And the same bluffs.

By this time, the suns were receding with the planet's natural rotation, now just barely upon the horizon. Even though they didn't command the sky any longer, and the moon now hung where the great suns used to, the aurora the suns gave off didn't go away. Pockets of purple clung to the air, not black like what should accompany the start of night. Heat still hung about, not the coolness that would normally accompany nightfall. And light still lingered, making the moon seem rather inconsequential and useless for the moment.

The idea of a moon was silly, anyway. He had grown up without one all of his life. Its purpose now, in the wake of Pirini Lilapa, if any, was to show him how the centaurs waited on the bluffs, bows drawn. Out from the side of the cliffs, stone golems crept forward, their yellow eyes scanning them.

Cronos leaned into his ear. "You may want to hurry."

"I thought you said they wouldn't hurt us."

"I said they may not hurt us, assuming you can solve the riddle. They roam the bluffs right now, calculating your potential for success. The Meeting will be soon, and if you cannot make the Meeting, then it is pointless for you to be in the Sacred Passage." Cronos stepped around to face Eirek directly. His hooked, beak-like nose and his furrowed brows intensified his amber and blue gaze. "So, hurry."

Think, Eirek, think. Eirek sat on the ground.

"You shouldn't be—"

"I'm concentrating! Stop telling me what to do." Eirek cut Cronos off. The old man backed away. Eirek noticed a slight grin on the faces of the conseleigh.

Eirek stared up into the sky, past the centaurs. In one area of the sky, that the pockets of purple left unadulterated, Eirek made out the constellation Lady

Aprah showed him in Gar through the star Eshleeng. When he saw it, Eirek realized how far south he was. He continued spending moments looking at it and thinking of Lady Aprah and the northern city lights. He mouthed the riddle to himself, trying to sort out his thoughts. The tactic had helped him during the second trial back on the Core.

Volan lies ahead, but to travel north you must face the south
You will be fed answers only drizzled in drouth
Like the taste you won't, but that is the price paid
To reach the domain where gods lie and Ancients create

Then, an idea came to him; one he was upset about not considering earlier. He took out his sword and turned around so that he could no longer see the mountain. He held the sword up in front of him.

"What are you doing," Ethen asked.

Eirek ignored him. He looked into the smoky gray of his sword and saw nothing behind him, only a path with a slight incline to it. He turned around and there were the boulders again, blocking him. He looked once more into the reflection his sword offered. No boulder. *That's it. That's it!*

"Draw your weapons. Turn around and use your weapon's reflection. To go north, we must be facing south."

Luvan drew his oversized knife, Ethen his lance and Cronos positioned his staff.

Eirek moved backwards, and the others followed. Keeping their gaze on the reflection in their weapons, they inched backwards like caterpillars in the moonlight. And, as they did so, the centaurs turned away and the golems approached no further.

After the boulder, a short incline wound around the mountain with enough width for two people side by side. Eirek, with Luvan by his side, continued up the mountain.

"Let's make it to another plateau. We'll sleep there," Luvan said.

Eirek nodded. A few hours later, the ledge plateaued into an area spacious enough for all four of them.

"Tis will do," Ethen said.

"Make a fire, boy," Cronos said.

"That's what you say to me?" Eirek hadn't meant to actually voice it, but when he did, it felt good, confident and strong.

"What else is there to say?" Cronos furrowed his brows and leaned on his staff.

"I just solved the riddle. You could congratulate me."

"We are not at the top of the mountain yet, boy. You still haven't passed all of the Sacred Passage. Now, I'm going to bed. Make a fire so we don't freeze. Although it's not cold yet, it may be shortly. We are higher up, there is open wind, and the suns have finally disappeared." Cronos lay down on his side and clutched the staff close to him.

"Congratulations, Eirek." Ethen patted his back.

"Yes. Guardian Eska will be proud to hear that."

The compliments from the conseleigh put him in a decent enough mood for kindling a fire. Ethen gave him the pieces of wood and two stones from one of the travel packs. Using the stones around the area, he made a pit to contain it. This wasn't his first time starting a fire; he had learned to do it on Cresica from the Mourses. He utilized the skill every time he went to his spot near the mountains if the fireways hadn't been laid out yet.

"He seems weak again. Why?" Eirek whispered and nodded his head towards Cronos.

The fire cast an orange glow over the scars on Luvan's forearms as he held his hands over the fire. "Most likely because Eska has not given any word yet."

"Which means Pirini Lilapa has not yet occurred." Ethen stroked his conical beard.

"I thought... The suns converged, though..."

"Aye, t'ey converged Apprentice Mourse, but chaos 'asn't come yet. Tat is truly Pirini Lilapa."

"I do hope it happens soon so Eska can quit being tense," Luvan said.

"Do not 'ate 'is scolding, Luvan."

Eirek looked back and forth between the two conseleigh. He remained silent.

"How was I to know the necklace would be there?" Luvan raised his voice. Cronos stirred. Luvan continued, but this time in a whisper. "It was taken from there by the Pavos brothers. They died in the war that followed."

"They... they didn't die," Eirek spoke.

"What?" Luvan glanced at Eirek.

"They were in the labyrinth. I recall Prince Evber mentioning it to me. He was my partner in that trial of yours, and this man... this man with deranged black eyes... he... he came and attacked us out of nowhere. In the end... I... I killed Troy." Images of his first kill played back to him. Despite the fire, Eirek shivered. His hands tensed, and his body stiffened.

The conseleigh looked at each other. "Troy Pavos was in that labyrinth?"

Eirek nodded.

Luvan's posture fell to a slouch. He shook his head and rolled down the sleeves of his yellow tunic. "I... I need to lie down."

Ethen reached over and patted Luvan on the back. "Don't worry... It's fine. Eska won't be brash. Everyone makes mistakes."

Luvan mumbled something and put a hand on his forehead. Eirek couldn't hear it for at that same time Ethen turned to him and said, "You 'ave first watch, Eirek. Wake me in a few."

The conseleigh lain down and went to sleep.

In his solitude, Eirek laid on his back and looked at the stars. His was there. Somewhere. Angal had told him everyone had one, but only Blessed people could find it. Now that Eirek knew he was among those with the ability to use Power, he took another glance at the stars he had once abandoned. *They're beautiful.* Coppers and golds and blues looked back at him. *How does anyone find their star?* Angal once told him to watch the constellations and notice how the stars around them flicker or shine. Also, Angal encouraged Eirek to live life faithfully because that would only make his star shine more brightly, and eventually Eirek would know which was his. *Angal was always full of stories. It still seems impossible. I suppose the Ancients wouldn't want everyone casting a wish.* Eirek smiled, finally having the chance to reflect on his life in Cresica. The Mourses. His moments with Angal.

That time in his life seemed eons away, though it hadn't even been half a year. *What are the Mourses doing now? Does Angal still tell his stories? Of course he does, how stupid of me to think otherwise.* Then he remembered it was Linn's birthday soon, or now, he didn't know the exact date, but she had said it was around the suns' convergence the last time Eirek was in Syf. The time before the Trials. Before he was apprentice.

And then he thought about his own journey through the Trials and the training. *No one back home would even recognize me now. I don't even recognize me. Standing up to Cronos—what has gotten into me?* Eirek reveled in that brief moment. *If only Eska could see me now. If only he could have seen me solve the riddle.* Eirek let his eyelids close for a moment. And as he did so, he knew things were going to be alright, despite not knowing what else lay ahead of him on the mountain. Despite Cronos's contempt of him. And despite what the next days brought with them, he had the support of those close to him, and no supposed Curse could destroy that.

PART IV: PIRINI LILAPA

The suns have converged. Pirini Lilapa has begun. For the next week, a purple aurora will fill the sky with unparalleled beauty. However, it is only a matter of time before the Curse surely shows itself. But questions remain: Who will it affect? Where will it happen? When will it occur? And, most importantly, what will it be? As the system of Gladonus deals with this new, ominous, ubiquitous threat, the people that populate each nation turn their heads to the sky wondering what will befall them and if Guardian of the Core Edwyrd Eska and his apprentice will have the strength to save them...

CHAPTER 53

A STORY TO TELL

It was the day of her twenty-fifth birthday. Linn Clayse had awoken at dawn to see a purple aurora in the sky. There was no chaos or spectacle that so many people seemed to fear. Only beauty. And heat. There was much of that.

Although the heat was rather unfortunate, today would be the day when she would take her vows and be sworn in as the new Lady of Cresica if anything should happen to her mother. Even though all the various ladies and their families were supposed to be here to see her, many notified her mother that the voyage was too dangerous during a time such as Pirini Lilapa. And that it was hot. Linn agreed with them on the heat, but so far it had been nothing but beauty, and she loved looking into the purple aurora.

"Linn, darling, are you ready for the day to begin?"

Linn looked away from her open window to her mother at the threshold of her door behind her. "Yes, Mother. I put on the dress you wanted me to wear." She sat down on her bed.

"I noticed. It looks ravishing on you."

Linn straightened out the wrinkles of the full celadon silk skirt that extended from her waistline. Not nearly as large as her mother, she added a slim brown belt with a laced celadon flower applique above the waistline to help the gown fit properly. Hand-sewn buttons went up the back of her gown, making the detail even more intricate. White lace extending the full length of the upper bust went nearly unnoticed, for the brown, cropped jacket made from rayon did an excellent job in covering any exposed skin.

"Do you know where I got that dress from?" Linn's mother walked over and sat down next to Linn. She took her daughter by the hands. "It was my mother's, and she passed it down to me on this day as well."

Linn smiled. She wouldn't tell her mother that it was a little large for her. She had always been more petite than her mother. She wouldn't tell her that the shoulder jacket made her itch or that the dress was nearly unbearable in the heat. She wouldn't do that because Linn knew that even though it was her birthday, it was her mother's day, too. A day to watch the one she birthed and cared for all her adult life finally become a mature woman. A woman ready to take ladyship at any time.

"It is lovely."

"And hand-stitched. My mother made it herself." Linn's mother cupped her daughter's cheek in her hand. "Linn, you look beautiful."

Linn blushed. "Thank you, Mother."

"Follow me. We have much to do yet before the ceremony begins."

Linn followed her mother down the orthogonal halls to the courtyard. Much of the complex had no ceiling because her family preferred to let the suns always gaze upon the hallways' cobblestone beauty. Servants carried vases of flowers to and fro in the main yard, and a handful tended to the patch of lawn in the middle of the courtyard, making sure the trees were fully primed for the eyes of any guests.

"Roll the carpets out; it is nearly time."

Her mother called to no one in particular, but waited until two older gentlemen came back carrying a carpet of the lighter celadon and a carpet of brown. Once the servants finished rolling out the carpets, Linn's mother continued the prowl through the complex, checking on various activities.

At one point a female servant came up to her with a platter of food. "Care to try for quality, Lady Clayse?"

Linn's mother picked a cube of cheese and tested it. Then she plucked a slice of turkey off the platter and plopped it in her mouth. "Dry. Moisten up the meat. I will find my husband and have him inspect it."

"Yes, Lady Clayse." The maid bowed and left.

"Where is Father?" Linn kept her mother's stride.

"He is organizing the outdoors. I am managing the inside. Let's find him, shall we?" Linn nodded and followed but remained quiet. So quiet, in fact, that her mother took note of it. "Linn, there is no reason to be nervous."

"I—" Linn blushed. It wasn't so much her nerves, rather than her level of comfort. "Will Angal still be performing his story?"

"Yes, he will be. He performs right before dinner, after the midafternoon ceremony where you take your national vows."

"I'm sure he will have a story to tell. He always does."

"That is true."

"I wonder what story he will tell. Perhaps one on Pirini Lilapa."

Linn's mother waved off her daughter's proposition. "I am sure Angal could weave a fabulous story on why Pirini Lilapa happens, but would you really want that on your birthday?"

Linn's smile faded. "No, I suppose not." She paused. "Will Eirek be here?"

"No, he is too busy."

"How do you know? Did you ask?"

"No, I never sent an invitation to him."

Linn slumped her shoulders. "Why would you do that?" She stopped as her mother smelled a vase of flowers.

Her mother gave her a quick glance and then said, "Because he has yet to send us a thank you for not only our support at his Coronation, but also the gifts we sent him."

Did something bad happen? Why hasn't he sent one? Linn folded her hands in front of her, letting them come down to her waist. She continued walking with her mother to the front lawn.

"It doesn't matter, at any rate."

Linn stopped. "What doesn't?"

"I see how you've looked at him whenever that uncle of his brought him along. How you slumped your shoulders when I mentioned he wouldn't be coming. It would never work, Linn."

"I..." Linn followed after her. "Why?"

"Because he has vows now. Guardian vows. He can't just forsake those." Linn's mother turned to look back at her. "And, besides, Ezra Evengale is a respectable gentleman, from a respectable family, not just some family in Creim. You should really begin taking courting more seriously. Who knows how much longer I will be around..."

"Mother, do not say that. You are not even old yet."

"Well, I feel it. Maybe it's these damned suns." She put an arm to her forehead and looked up.

Shielding her eyes, Linn did the same. After a brief glance, Linn pointed. "There's Father!"

Linn's mother waved her arm. "Rybert, here."

Linn's father, a rotund man and slightly short for his size, left two guards and walked over to them. "What is it, Lynda?"

"You need to check on the servants in the kitchen. Make sure the food is presentable."

"Okay."

"What were you doing just now?" Linn asked.

"Telling all guards to be stationed at their posts and to report any strange activity. You can never be too careful, especially now, with the suns overhead and Pirini Lilapa upon us."

"We have yet to report anything to Guardian Eska or his conseleigh, Rybert."

"And that is a good thing. Hopefully, there will be nothing."

Her mother grunted. "To the kitchen. Now!"

Linn surveyed the landscape in front of her. Past the rolling greens lay the city of Syf. Their home was located on the crown of the large hill, and then the city was divided into three subsections: a lower level, a middle level and an upper level, each level rising by wealth and influence.

"You will rule over all of this one day, Linn," said her mother.

"I hope I will be ready." Linn continued looking outward.

"You will be. I think you are now." Linn's mother grabbed her daughter's shoulders and brought her closer and kissed her forehead.

"Lady Clayse, a word, please?"

Linn's mother looked back and saw a servant requesting her attention. "I will be there in just a second." She turned back to Linn. "Make sure you don't stay out in this heat too long. You don't want to ruin your face or fry your brain."

"Yes, Mother."

Her mother smiled and left. Even when she left, Linn stood there, looking down at the grassy fields and the city before her. In that moment, everything was serene. It was peaceful. It was quiet. She looked to the purple aurora in the sky and thought perhaps the Curse of Pirini Lilapa would spare Gladonus this time. Or, at the very least, Syf.

Off in the distance, she thought she saw a red and orange streak in the sky, almost like a comet. It came from the direction of Epoch, all the way on the other side of the planet. She thought it was getting bigger, but when she blinked, she noticed it still seemed like the same red and orange streak. Either it was moving towards them, or the heat was playing tricks on her eyes.

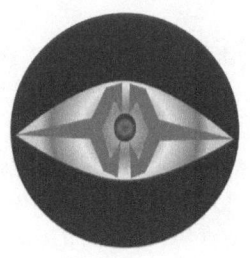

CHAPTER 54

HAPPENSTANCE

Fifty-two days had passed since Cadmar had last seen his father, his city, and the lady he wished to serve, Lady Aprah. That didn't mean, however, that he had spent those days in solitude and loneliness. In truth, his time had been far from that, as he had made two good companions during the Passage: Fayser and Garth. Five had set out to accomplish the Passage and become an elite, but the two others not with him didn't dare navigate Peril's Pass and decided to go around Eurador and White Cliff Village to eventually arrive at Iberene and secure a Goddess Flower for Lady Aprah. Garth had wanted to do the same, but Cadmar had convinced him otherwise and now they were a little more than halfway from completing their test if they went through Peril's Pass on their return. Now that didn't matter. All that mattered now is what lay above them.

"What be with the sky?" Fayser asked. "It be purple now."

"It be warm finally." Garth added.

Cadmar looked at his companions. Each of them had pulled up on the reins of their horses, shielded their eyes, and looked above. "I don't know it be either."

Cadmar undid the cloak of mammoth hide he had worn since entering Sereyan territory and then stretched open his woolrock sweater. Two necklaces hid underneath. He reached inside, feeling the warm, yet rather uncomfortable and stone-like material that made his shirt. He pulled out both necklaces. One of which was the eye that his mother had given him, the memento given to those who had served in the rebellion; it had been passed down in the family since his great grandfather Caerul Briggs. The other necklace was a fist-sized glass tube that housed his Goddess Flower. He examined the crystal petals, making sure the flower wasn't wilting or melting. He did not know what type of effect these suns and the increased heat would have on the flower's vitality, but he hoped it wouldn't wilt so that he could personally give it to Lady Aprah, join her elites, and make his father proud.

He turned to look at the others next to him, still enthralled by the suns overhead. "How be your Goddess Flower?"

Both men were elite of stature with broad shoulders and cut jaws and thickened skin, just like Garian were born to be. Fayser, though, was tall like Cadmar and Garth, short and stocky. Garth had no hair on his darker skin, and his eyebrows hung over his eyes, making the browns underneath almost like caves. Fayser had wavy hair and now touted a beard of seemingly equal length. Cadmar, however, had kept his hair cropped and his beard shaved. His father had told him to grow it out, but he ignored that advice, letting the activity of keeping the two in balance fill a part of his day on the otherwise arduous and mountainous trip.

Like Cadmar, they undid their mammoth cloaks and checked the condition of their own necklaces. Both were fine. With slight reassurance, they continued forward. Every so often Cadmar looked up to the sky, wondering what the eclipse meant. Did it bring with it fortune or foreboding? How long would it last? What was it named?

It was perhaps another hour of traveling before Cadmar found the answers he searched for. It did not come from experience, nor anyone's expertise in the matter, but rather, happenstance.

As the group made their way to the skirts of the Dune of White, leaving Iberene and the crystal fields on top of the snow plains where they had found the Goddess Flowers, Cadmar and the others halted as a hovercraft sped towards them. In their fifty-two days of traveling, they had yet to see anyone anywhere besides Eurador where they stopped to restock and purchase the mammoth hides they now wore, and those who lived in igloos just outside of Iberene's wooden gates.

The hovercraft sped by, hardly giving them a glance, or so it seemed, but as the humming of the anitron and the rushing of the wind passed out of dissonance, within a few minutes Cadmar heard it again, this time coming from behind.

"Who it be?" Garth asked.

Cadmar shook his head. "I don't be knowing. Keep ready."

At best, it would be a curious passerby not accustomed to seeing three men on horses that weren't snowhorses brave the Dunes of White (for most preferred to either stay in their city, or travel by hovercraft). At worst, it would be some sentry from one of the outposts checking for immigrants or those not of Sereyan blood. That would be a problem. Cadmar knew that. Ever since Gar became its own successful and sovereign nation, Cadmar was sure that Sereya resented the citizens they had once controlled.

The hovercraft stopped in front of them and landed softly on the snow.

Conseleigh Tundra Iycel stood up from the craft. Two men that Cadmar didn't know were with her. "Cadmar Briggs."

"Conseleigh Iycel?"

"You be knowing her?" Fayser asked.

"It be fine, men. Nothing to worry about." Cadmar kicked the sides of his horse and steered it towards the hovercraft, leaving the others behind. From horseback, he carried on his conversation with her.

"So Edwyrd's talk with Lady Aprah was successful I take it. You are doing the Passage?"

Cadmar nodded.

"You have come from Visis?"

"Moons ago. We be returning from Iberene now. We be returning to Visis with these." Cadmar showed her the Goddess Flower.

"Beautiful. I wish you a safe voyage back then."

"You not be at the Core? With Guardian Eska, with Eirek?"

"I am handling matters for Guardian Eska right now, and Apprentice Mourse is here in Gar."

"Eirek be here?"

Tundra nodded and recapped the events that led Eirek to Gar, and how he was on a journey of his own through a different passage to Mount Volan. When Cadmar heard the name of the mountain, he looked south. Even from this far away, the mountain loomed in the distance.

"I should be going. Farewell, Mr. Briggs. Now that the suns are out, take extra caution when you can."

"What be they?" Cadmar pointed upwards.

Tundra explained the suns, the eclipse, and what Pirini Lilapa meant. It seemed that the only good thing about the event was the heat, and that is only because he was in Sereya; Cadmar was sure further south, where his mother lived, things weren't as pleasant. Her cautionary tale caused Cadmar to bite his lip and crease his brows. He glanced back at his companions, wondering if they had heard any of what she said. They hadn't, as he doubted her voice carried to their position, still five horse lengths behind him.

A jump of wind caused Cadmar to turn back around; Tundra had powered on her hovercraft. She gave one final wave before leaving. Within minutes of her departure, the others joined him again. Cadmar regurgitated the information told as they continued forward, further into the Dunes of White.

Hours passed. Filled with wonderment, yet caution, they traversed the Dunes of White, a vast and open plain of Sereya that looked much like a white desert. With the heat now accompanying them, it only made the resemblance clearer. To the southwest Crestal's Tower slowly came into view, even more recognizable now with the purple backdrop making the crystalline tower a diamond beacon.

"Cadmar," Fayser whispered. "Cadmar."

Cadmar stopped his admiration of the Tower and turned to his friend, who had pulled alongside him. "What be it?"

"Up ahead. Look." Fayser pointed to a spot two hundred meters north.

Garth came next to Cadmar's other side. "Polar bears?"

After squinting, Cadmar's eyes widened. "Two of them." The journey had so far been free from any trouble. Both busied themselves eating a dead Clydesdale that lay between them. Cadmar hoped it would stay like that.

It didn't.

Soon after spotting the polar bears, Cadmar's telecommunicator rang. It was his father. "Pa?" In such an open expanse of white nothingness, the sound carried too well. As his telecommunicator rang, and as Cadmar took off his thick woolen gloves in order to answer it, the polar bears looked up from their carcass.

Cadmar denied the call.

His telecommunicator rang again.

"Cadmar, shut that thing—"

"I be..." The bears inched forward.

In his rush, Cadmar pushed accept. His father's face appeared in front of him.

"Cadmar, how it be?"

"Pa, I can't—"

His father didn't hear. "I just returned from delivering that Eirek friend of yours to the Sacred—"

The bears rushed them now. Cadmar ended the call, cutting his father's words short.

"What do we do?" Garth asked.

"We try to outrun them?"

"Maybe on different terrain. Not on the snow. These horses not be made for it."

"Then what?"

The polar bears were close now. Another minute or so and they would be upon them.

"We fight." Cadmar hopped off the saddle of the horse, axe in hand. "We protect the horses at all costs. They be how we return. Garth, create an ice wall around the horses. Fayser, with me."

The two men jumped off their horses. Cadmar rushed forward, creating distance between him and the horses behind him. Fifty meters away now. *Come on. Come on.* He held his zircha axe impatiently. From his peripherals, Cadmar saw Fayser by his side, bobbing in anticipation as well.

"Your plan?"

"Ice. It'll stun them and slow them. Then we act."

Twenty-five meters.

Twenty.

At fifteen, Cadmar raised his hand and said, "*Vesi.*" An ice shield shot up in front of him. He looked to the sides, expecting the polar bears to stop and maneuver around.

They didn't.

Unexpectedly, the ice wall shattered with their momentum. Ice blasted his face and informed his decision. *Shield.* Arm already raised to block the shattered ice chunks, his zircha axe changed to a shield within seconds of the incident. He fell backwards. Half a ton now crushed him. The unexpected shift in stance left him vulnerable. With the momentum and weight of the polar bear, the shield fell to the left, digging into his shoulder. Pop. Pain.

Cadmar's left arm jerked outward, fully exposed. The split sound of cut cloth faded into the tear of fresh flesh as the polar bear's paw tore open his left forearm and wrist. Adrenaline had now taken command, blocking him from pain momentarily and heightening his consciousness and survival instincts.

He pushed up with right arm with as much force as he could to tilt the bear even a little. "*Vesi.*" From underneath him, a slab of ice pushed him up, and the sudden change in height caught the bear off-balance and it tumbled off Cadmar to the ground below. Not wasting time, Cadmar slid off the slab and directed his attention to the polar bear, already on its feet again. Only a body's length separated them. *Come on. Come on.*

It pounced, paw raised.

Cadmar turned his torso away from the bear. *Lance.* He raised the shield, and within the brief seconds of the action, the shield turned to a lance, its tip catching the bear straight in its chest. He used both arms to hold the lance, but immediately regretted the decision, as pain shot up through his left shoulder again, agitated by the bear's weight. Cadmar crumbled to one knee. The follow-through of the bear's swipe caught Cadmar on the left shoulder, knocking him over backwards, lance escaping his grip, and falling to the snow.

Blood from the bear and from Cadmar now dotted the ground. His left arm now numb from pain, Cadmar tried using his right to try to stand, but he slipped and fell. The bear moved. Digging the heels of his boots into the snow, he bridged his torso and pushed up with his right arm. He took a step towards his lance, but it had vanished.

Fayser held it in his right hand. In his left, he held his own axe. He sprinted towards the bear. Pouncing, his comrade brought down both weapons on top of the bear's skull and neck, splitting it and pinning it to the snow. The bear collapsed.

For the first time, Cadmar felt his own heartbeat. He saw his breath in the air. Behind him, the other bear was already dead, Garth's sword stained with red.

Cadmar walked over to Fayser. "Thank you."

Fayser extracted both weapons from the bear's carcass. "Here." He returned Cadmar's zircha lance.

"*Vesi.*" Water washed away the blood covering the steel. *Axe.* The weapon changed. He sheathed it. "You okay?"

Fayser nodded. He headed over towards Garth. "We had the female. And there be two of us. We be fine."

Garth turned around. "Cadmar, your arm."

Instinctively, Cadmar looked to his left. Pain slowly replaced the adrenaline leaving his body. He tried moving it. He stopped. Pain. He bit his lip. "Broken. I will need a sling."

"We can make one out of the bearskin," Fayser suggested.

"Okay." Cadmar looked at the igloo. "The horses?"

Garth released the spell. The horses stood unharmed and docile.

"While Fayser be making the sling, cut up the meat from the bears. Stuff as much as you can into the saddles. We won't need to scavenge for food the rest of the Passage."

Garth nodded.

As the two worked, Cadmar called to Power's name and sat on a stool of ice. Cadmar successfully squeezed his wrist. His wounds would scar, certainly, but no muscles were torn. Things could have been worse.

Fayser sat down in front of Cadmar. He laid a long strip of white fur on his legs. "Your arm." Fayser cut off what remained of the left sleeve. He used it to bandage the gash. "I found this over there as well." Fayser showed Cadmar his telecommunicator.

A broken screen and a sliced wrist strap. The watch was unusable. "That be great." Cadmar tossed it to the ground.

"What did your Pa want?"

Cadmar shook his head. "I don't know. Of all the times to call..." Cadmar grimaced as Fayser took his arm and began working on the sling.

"You think what that woman be saying be true?"

"About Pirini Lilapa?"

"Yeah."

So they had heard?

Cadmar stayed silent as Fayser tied a knot around his wrist to keep the sling in place. The bear's fur would keep his exposed arm warm, and when they returned to Visis, he could get it checked out at the apothecary. That was around six or seven weeks away, though, depending on what other misfortunes may occur on the Passage. A lot could happen in that time. As Fayser finished tying and adjusting the final sling knot on his shoulder, Cadmar looked up to the poignant purple sky once more, not ever stopping to think if his father's call, accompanied by the polar bears assault, was truly the beginning of chaos and misfortune that followed Pirini Lilapa, or if it was truly just happenstance.

CHAPTER 55

SEARCHING FOR ANSWERS

The Dunes of White that Tundra passed on her way to Astor Grime's chalet weren't nearly as treacherous as she remembered them being. Mammoths that had used to roam the plain stayed hidden, and even the refreshing cold she had come to cherish after thirty-nine years living in Sereya didn't seem to greet her the same way either. That was fortunate for Cadmar Briggs, for now Pirini Lilapa controlled the sky, and many things, Tundra assumed, would change for the worse. It was rather nice to see the Garian again, not because she had any feelings for him or liked him in any way, but more so for the fact that he had acted upon Edwyrd's suggestion to Lady Aprah and elected to become an elite again. It pleased her to know that Edwyrd's influence amongst the community was strong and there were many who supported him. She hoped his reputation would stay like that, for she would feel somewhat culpable if it didn't.

As she steered her hovercraft towards the capital, Iberene, she caught herself looking up at the purple aurora. *What will it be now?* Although she hadn't even been born, nor had her parents been born when Pirini Lilapa last occurred, Edwyrd once let her wear his reimaje to see the chaos Deimos brought to the land. Tundra remembered thinking about the behemoth, taller and wider than Edwyrd's bonded dragon, Vesel. Tundra remembered its cruel black eyes, black eyes that Hydro may now have if his brother's statement was true. Tundra remembered its large hands, with earthen talons for claws. A tail that resembled a dragon's tail and its electric blue wings. And the voice. It had the deepest voice she had ever heard, as if the beast had been crafted from the material of the world, as if it spoke with the soul of the system or of some divine Power.

Deimos was certainly indelible. Hopefully, this Pirini Lilapa wouldn't be as memorable.

By the time she stopped thinking of the past event, she found herself within the city of Iberene, outside of a chalet guarded by thick wooden walls and towers. Two large double doors barred entrance to most everyone. Not her, though. She was one of Edwyrd's conseleigh.

"Halt. State your name and purpose." A guard in mammoth hide called from atop the wooden precipice.

"Conseleigh Iycel. I have come with two of Marquis Bernal's guards to speak with Lord Grime."

Tundra waited no longer than five minutes before being admitted into the compound. She parked the hovercraft in a large clearing to the left. There was a stone path for her to walk on, but she preferred the crunch of snow beneath her heel. She didn't know when she would return. From staying here before, she knew training courts were located in the back: one of stone, one of snow, and one of ice. Also, out front lay a frozen pond surrounded by benches made from snow to sit on. In all her years in Sereya, she never once utilized it.

As she and her two guards arrived at the wooden steps leading to the chalet's porch, Jel Paron greeted her. He was a man of short stature but large figure, with rosy cheeks, a double chin and nearly non-existent eyebrows on his albino skin. As all receivers did, he wore rings of different colors on his hands and a pin shaped like a clock on his lapel next to Astor Grime's sigil of the White Dunes.

"Conseleigh Iycel, this is a surprise pleasure. We were not expecting you, or company." Jel nodded to the two guards behind her in various leather paddings.

I know. That is the point, is what she could have said, but instead Tundra replied, "Things have been busy on the Core and in other nations. There was no time. Sorry for my intrusiveness. Hopefully I did not come and disrupt anything. These two have merely come along for company. Traveling the roads can be quite lonely." Tundra feigned a smile and followed Jel inside the chalet.

"The roads can be quite lonely, and your presence is never a disruption here in the North Lands." Jel smiled and let out a faint chuckle. Or was it a cough? Tundra couldn't tell.

"I am glad to hear it. Where is Lord Grime?"

"In the telecommunication chamber, finishing up a call."

"With whom?" Tundra stiffened.

"His son Canice. He is away at an adored academy in Therus now. I sure hope this heat doesn't dry him out."

"That would be most unfortunate." Tundra continued up the icy steps, keeping hold of the thick wooden railings.

The second level was a massive floor with two staircases—one that led to the left and one that led to the right. Both led to a divided third floor. The icy steps and the two staircases were a defense tactic in case someone ever tried to invade the chalet—again. Lady Aprah's parents, Visis and Autumn Aprah, and their troops already invaded it once. It was these trick staircases that slowed them down just enough for reinforcements to come and kill Autumn. They didn't succeed in stopping the revolt, though. Tundra was actually surprised Visis let Grime live after Autumn was killed. Tragic, too, considering Visis died on the way back to Gar carrying his wife's body. All on Grime's orders. A malicious man, that one was. *How filth takes over the pristine.*

"Follow me to our conference room. We will await his presence there."

"Very well." She turned to the guards accompanying her. "You both can wait outside the doors, understood?"

Both nodded and followed her lead to the leftward side of the second floor and up more stairs. She kept a hand on her icy scimitar at all times. She highly doubted Astor Grime would be stupid enough to try to assault her, nor could she think of a reason why he would want to. But Pirini Lilapa was in the air now, and the suns made people do crazy things. In her other hand she carried a glass flat-screen panel with an image and video of the issue she came here to discuss with Astor Grime—Zakk Shiren.

It was ten minutes before the lord walked in, leaning heavily on his cane, and his face looking paler and more wizened than usual. "Conseleigh Iycel, it is a pleasure."

"Aye. How was the chat with your son?"

"Canice is doing well. He is studying zircha and the ard compound found on Pyre."

"Interesting..." Tundra feigned. After the door closed, she wasted no time in laying the glass screen on the wooden table. She pushed it forward to Astor Grime across from her. Behind him, his receiver and advisor looked as well.

"What do you want me to make of this man?"

"Do you recognize him?"

"Should I?" Astor Grime stared back.

"No. Touch the image it should start to play a video scene."

She knew the video clip too well, for she and Edwyrd and the conseleigh watched it many times after the Trials concluded. Zakk Shiren, a man nearly identical in appearance to Zain, besides the braids that extended past his shoulders and a tattoo on his left arm, emerged from thin air to say something to Zain Berrese. And whatever he said must have been enough to tamper with Zain's mind and cause him to turn down the apprenticeship. And it may be the first step in an attempt to overthrow Edwyrd. But too much was unknown. And that is what she hoped to shed light upon—the persons behind Zakk's actions.

"I do not notice anything."

I'll give you another chance to come clean, you blind fool. "Play it again."

He did, and Tundra felt the vibrations as the screen shook to the volcano's intensity. Because of it, nothing much was audible. The noise of the grumbling volcano drowned out everything. The video stopped.

"Where was this taken?"

Do you see many volcanoes elsewhere? He should be more concerned with how Zakk managed to become invisible, or how he was invisible. Unless he has seen that technology before. She wanted to smirk, but she remained stoic.

"The fourth trial, on Vatu Volcano. His name is Zakk Shiren. He was one of the eight contestants Guardian Eska selected to attend his Trials."

"Then why does this footage seem so strange?"

Do you intend to play coy with me, Lord Grime? Tundra narrowed her eyes. "He never competed. In fact, he never made it to introductions." Tundra leaned forward and looked at Grime and then to his receiver and advisor. "Do you want to know why I show this to you?"

"Yes."

"Replay the video. Once more. Perhaps you will finally notice something, you blind fools."

All three took a closer look at the video. The advisor, Kalen Katarh, a man of a moderate frame and a grizzled beard that covered up all but a smidge of a scar on his face, spoke. "This Zakk just appears. Is that what you want us to take note of?"

"It is." Tundra nodded her head. "But there is something else. Something less noticeable. Play it again, once more. Look at Zakk's composure compared to the others."

The video played once more. Vibrations and rumbling and then silence. Astor Grime leaned over and stretched his thumb and index finger on the screen to zoom in. The advisor and receiver hunched over. All of them stared at it in mystery. *How long will it take for them to notice?*

"I do not see—"

"He isn't sweating," Kalen commented.

Tundra smirked when she saw the quick scowl on Grime's face. *Foolish man. I will never know how you obtained my position.* "Very good, Kalen." Tundra nodded towards the tense-necked advisor. "Yes, Zakk Shiren isn't sweating like the others."

"I... I do not see where you are going with this." Astor Grime narrowed his focus on her and clenched his cane.

Of course not, you old fool. You would much prefer to act ignorant. That is how you lost your hold on Gar. "When I was Lady of Sereya after my husband passed, you were the military commander on my council." With her left hand, Tundra started unraveling her crystal wristlace on her right wrist.

"Yes, I was, my lady, but—"

"Do you remember the Crystallizer Project?" Tundra raised an eyebrow and unwound another strand of her wristlace.

"Yes... yes... it was a project to form protective ice coatings over humans and make them into war machines."

"It was. Do you remember who initiated the Crystallizer Project?"

"The... the name escapes me. It has been so long."

Keep playing ignorant, you old fool. I will teach you ignorance is not bliss. It is pain. Tundra looked at him as she unwound another piece of her wristlace. Astor Grime's gaze shot to her forearm. "It was Dr. Genus Cere."

"I am not sure I see where the two connect, Conseleigh Iycel," Kalen spoke.

"Before the Crystallizer Project was initiated it was Dr. Cere who utilized the minerals of a snow crystal into the form of a ring that provided a cooling layer over the human body."

"I—" Kalen started.

"Let me finish." Tundra glared at the three of them, then focused her attention back to her wristlace and undid another strand. "Cere showed me this product and mass production started on it. Travelers and tourists who wanted to go to Pyre now could do so in comfort. That, I had no issue with. My issue is that he took the idea of the cooling ring and expanded it into a halo that encased its wearer in a full-fledged ice-suit protective coating. He named the halos *Crystallizers.*"

"He was the most brilliant man I have ever met. I do not even think Saeluste could match his wit," said Grime in a bemused tone.

"So you do remember the man, Astor?" She glared at the old man, who tensed his neck at the question. Tundra continued, "The man was brilliant, as you say. But, he was also twisted. It was too dangerous. We Sereyans are tolerant of the cold, not immune to it. Not like that."

"I do not see what this Crystallizer Project or this ring have to do with us here, Conseleigh Iycel," said Jel.

"I do not think anyone else is capable of designing something like this, Astor. How does a device that makes one invisible to even the Guardian of the Core exist? Why is it in the hands of Zakk Shiren and how did he get a hold of it? I need to know. Do you remain in contact with this man?" Tundra undid the final loop to her wristlace and held a leather grip in her left hand, letting the rest of her wristlace fall to the floor.

"No..." Astor cupped his hands together.

Tundra searched the dark blue eyes of Astor Grime. *He lies. I can tell.* "A pity..." Tundra flicked her left arm overhead and let her whip curl around his neck, the daggers of crystal piercing and suffocating him.

The receiver and advisor each pulled two knives. Tundra reached across her body with her right hand to the hilt of her ice scimitar. "I would not do anything if I were either of you. I am conseleigh, and what I do to Grime will be much more pleasant than what Edwyrd would do to any of you if he finds out I am hurt."

They still held onto their knives.

"Guards!" Tundra yelled. The two men who followed her entered. "Show these two gentlemen out. I would like a moment alone with Lord Grime."

If the guards were shocked at the scene, their faces hid it well. Both put hands on their hilts, which caused the other two to put away their knives. Before leaving, each gave Grime a look of concern and glared at Tundra. She ignored them.

The door closed. She smiled. "Now, where were we?" Tundra loosened her hold a little, just enough to let him speak. She could already see the rivulets of blood around his neck.

"What makes you think I have seen him? You banished him from here."

"I did. But I know you were in total support of the project. I also left it up to you to make sure he was properly banished. You were in charge of my military, after all. Was he?" Tundra pulled the whip forward, forcing him into an awkward, hunched position over the table.

"Yes... yes... he was." Astor Grime struggled, his bony fingers trying to loosen the hold.

"How certain are you he isn't still here on Sereya? Do you wish to inform me of anything now?"

"I... I don't know, Conseleigh Iycel."

"Tell me what you do know, then. Have you rejuvenated his Crystallizer Project since I left the throne to you? Do you keep in touch with this man?"

"No... no... Conseleigh Iycel I swear..." He said through labored breaths.

She looked into his dark blue eyes. They pleaded to let him go. Not that he didn't know what she was talking about. But she had no evidence to go on... yet. She yanked loose her whip, sat down and started nonchalantly curling it around her wrist again. "If you are lying, I will find out. And, if I do, I will make sure you are stripped of your rank and dealt with accordingly." She looked up halfway through her curling. "If that were to happen, you'd be the second person to lose reign over a nation in such a short span." Tundra gave a slight smirk and finished twirling.

"What do you mean?" Grime wheezed, rubbing his neck and smearing the red onto the pools of purple bruises.

"Aiton Paen now rules Acquava. His father passed away."

"Lord Paen passed? How? When?"

"He passed about a week and a half ago. Tell me, have you seen Hydro on Sereya?" Tundra stood expecting only silence.

"Yes... we have... Why?"

She turned her head at his answer. "What did you say? Do you have proof? Where is he?"

"Th—this way..." Astor Grime massaged his neck, continuing to smear the small drops of blood over his hand.

His advisor and receiver stood patiently outside. When they saw his presence, they followed him as he led her out of the room and into a chamber with electronic panels and screens that hung from the wooden chalet walls.

There were others in this chamber. Astor Grime motioned to one of them to get the image from the north port up on the screen. Tundra's pulse quickened as the man obeyed. *Has he found Hydro? How did he get here so fast in only a boat?*

Astor Grime walked back to stand next to her. "What does Hydro have to do with anything?"

"I'll tell you, if there is proof you have seen him."

"Here's the image, sir," a voice called.

"Put it up on the large screen in center." Astor Grime walked forward, raising the hand that gripped the cane toward the center screen.

Tundra walked with him. She felt slow, unsteady, nervous.

An image appeared. It was of a crowded line. There were men and women all ready to board a transport. She scanned it but couldn't find anything. As she was about to ask where Hydro was, she found him. He was near the front of the line, head turned over his shoulder, looking at a family and their infant behind him.

"Enlarge the image," Tundra commanded.

The man obeyed.

It is him. How? "Where was the transport headed to?"

"Myoli."

"Which nation?"

"It delivers to all three. You know how inter-system travel works..."

She tuned out the rest of Astor Grime's reply and fixated on the pair of black eyes in front of her. *So Aiton did speak the truth. What demon possesses you, Hydro Paen? What are you searching for on Myoli?*

"Print me this image."

Lord Grime nodded and gave a command to one of his men. "Now, what is this all about?" He handed her the print.

Tundra studied the picture, not wasting a second to glance at Astor Grime. "Hydro is the one who killed his father."

CHAPTER 56

THE SEA'S COMMANDER

It wasn't a red morning that Brisine Berrese had awoken to; it was one of purple and heat. The heat didn't affect her skin as much as it would the lighter-skinned people here. From her bed, past the beaded curtain, she saw a purple aurora in the sky. The sight was so magnificent that she almost missed lunch in order to view it.

"Has there been any contact from Gerald or Zain?" Brisine patted her lips with a silk linen as she tried to remain calm throughout a lunch that consisted of chicken broth soup, rolls, and shaved pork. She had been asking the same question every morning for the last month. They had last heard from Gerald a month and a half ago.

To her dismay, Lukas answered the same way every time. "None yet, so far."

Her heart plummeted.

"But that does not mean they are not safe," Abraham added. "We know Gerald is there with your son."

"You are just getting upset because of the heat," Lukas said.

"Our grandfather told us stories of what happened when those suns converged. Of course I am scared."

"None of those are true," Lukas said.

"Deimos certainly was," Brisine said.

"Even if Deimos escapes, he is contained in Chaon right now, and Guardian Eska will be able to beat him again," Abraham said.

That eased her worries a little, but she had heard so many awful things about Pirini Lilapa. Even Guardian Eska had contacted her brother and told him to keep on higher alert this week and to report anything unusual to him. Maybe it was the heat, but something had felt off to her ever since the purple preyed upon the blue two days before. As she pulled a piece of bread apart with her hands, she tried her best not to cry. *Is it so wrong to want the people you love back?*

A horn blew.

What is that? Brisine's head jerked to the sound.

Another horn.

"Are those the ship horns?" Lukas asked.

"They certainly are," Abraham said. "Brisine, wait!"

She didn't stop at her brother's words. In fact, by the time she had heard the second set of horns, she had thrown down her linen and sprinted to the door. *They're back. They're back. Maybe the Curse is just a folklore, after all.*

Brisine lifted the skirts of her burgundy dress down the steps of the courtyard and down a hill that led to the port. Air rushed past the cuts in the sleeves of the white blouse she wore. Her gait kept pace with her heart. Even though Zain said he wasn't going to be back on the voyage, she thought maybe he said that to surprise her. Maybe he had changed his mind? The least that could happen were tidings from overseas. Those would be welcomed.

Past the gates that barred the castle grounds and down another hill, somewhat steeper, and through a town that smelled of worms and sea and filth, she arrived on the dock. People who witnessed her run probably thought she was crazy, but she cared little about any of that. All she wanted was answers. Communication. Anything. There had been nothing so far, though. *Where is the ship?*

To the left, she saw the tail of the ship sailing past the city port to the bluffs. *Foolish me. They dock there.* Picking up her skirts, she ran through the city again, finding enough energy to make it to the cavern carved out of the bluff below the castle.

The *Sea's Commander* had docked, but the plank for disembarking hadn't been set out yet. She hoped that someone would peer over the massive hull, look down, and welcome her. Instead, only rumbling and groans and the sound of busy hands accompanied her as she paced.

A clank.

She torqued her head to the sound. She clasped her hands in front of her chest and drew in a steady breath.

A haughty man harrumphed down the plank, followed by a few others. The man in the lead carried a pack on his back and a letter in his hand. In fact, every man carried a pack on their back. *I suppose they did need provisions for such a long journey.*

When the man in front approached her, she noticed fingers missing from both hands and an ear was missing from his right side. *Oh no, something did happen.*

"Lady Berrese, how nice it feels to be back in Ka'Che."

"Is everything alright? You are Hector, correct?"

He nodded and then gave her a puzzled look. "Why... why wouldn't things be fine?"

"I... I see your hands... and your ear." Brisine blushed.

Hector guffawed. "I have carried these marks for a while now."

"Where is my son?"

"With Zigarda. Do you not remember when we informed you?"

"Yes... Of course... I'm... I'm sorry... it's... it's the heat..." Brisine smiled weakly. *My Zain and my Laron are not coming back to me yet.* Her shoulders slunk.

"It certainly is a scorcher." A tall man took a sip from a leather canteen. Droplets of red hit the pier deck. He wiped his mouth on a white sleeve, leaving a line of red.

"What kind of wine is that?" Brisine asked. The run down the hill and the heat had dried her throat.

"Bloodwine, my lady... Care to try?"

Brisine noticed Hector furrow his eyebrows and glower at the tall man, who held eyes of steel with a hint of amber. "No, I best not. I... I am just disappointed my son is not here. That's all..." Brisine fiddled with her hands.

"This is from Zain. He gave it to us before we left."

Brisine snatched it from Hector. "Thank... thank you..."

"If you excuse us, we will have your leave to enter the castle."

"Of course." She stepped aside and allowed the gentlemen to pass.

Once they were gone, she opened the letter and read it. It was sloppy, like Zain's handwriting, but it wasn't Zain. The dots over the *I*s were wrong. They were dots, not slashes. Brisine turned around, wanting to see if Hector was still on the pier, but he and the few with him had vanished. She reread the letter again, trying to convince herself it was Zain's. But it wasn't. Even the signature was off. *He always underlines his name. Why not this time?*

Her eyes spilled onto the pier, noticing the liquid that resembled blood more than wine. She turned her gaze towards the purple sky and the bands that cut it into quadrants. *What has happened to my son?*

CHAPTER 57

UPWARDS

E irek woke the next morning, groggy and sweaty. Aches ailed his body. The
ground wasn't exactly the most comfortable of places to sleep on. If all
went well, today they would reach the Palace of Power. At the conseleighs'
advice, Eirek changed into his Coronation outfit, a royal-blue dress shirt that
had cuffs crusted with rubies and the front dotted with golden buttons. A
stitching of a ruby-red sun flared brilliantly from the front of the shirt to the
shoulders, where two brooches in the shape of a dragon attached a cape of
silk. Hopefully, it would make a lasting impression on the Twelve. He would be
spending many years with them as Guardian of the Core, after all.

Shielding his eyes, he looked up at the interminable mountain. It hid its head
behind a blanket of clouds. "I do not see anything yet."

"You are not supposed to, boy. The Palace of Power lies high up on the
mountain, away from the gaze of those unworthy."

Eirek ignored the rudeness. "How do I become worthy?"

"You are about to find out." Cronos walked ahead of everyone. "Let us go."

Eirek caught up to Cronos and followed along as they circled the mountain,
but found it unusually difficult to keep stride with the old man. It was as if the
old man was anxious to get to the Meeting. The conseleigh couldn't even keep
the old man's pace. *He sure does have energy today. Did sleeping on the ground
not bother him at all?*

A while later, Cronos shouted back to them. "We're here."

Upon hearing this, Eirek quickened his gait, finding Cronos standing in the
middle of another plateau with both hands on his staff. A large bluff extended
upward until the clouds allowed him to see no more. Cronos stood there,
almost as if waiting for a door to open or for something to happen.

Eirek scratched his head. "Are we supposed to climb this?"

"In a fashion, yes. Now you must pass four tests to reach the Palace of Power. I will call the giants for you."

Giants! Eirek's eyes doubled in size. He heard Cronos speak a language he had never heard before. His voice lowered and his dialect became guttural and rigid, like the mountainside.

A rumbling occurred then, one Eirek hadn't heard since the moments before Vatu Volcano erupted during the fourth trial. Out from the mountainside a brown stone giant with black eyes appeared, with rough, cracked skin, like earth that had seen a drought. Its overwhelming size brought with it an earthy smell that even the freshest of breezes couldn't blow away. Another rumbling occurred on the upper part of the mountain and on three other cliff ledges. Similar giants stepped out from their homes in the mountainside of Volan. Each of their left hands rested upon a club the size of fully grown trees.

Eirek plugged his ears when the first giant spoke in a language he couldn't comprehend.

"To get to the Palace of Power, you must show us you can cast each element," Cronos translated. "Your first spell to cast is earth."

Earth—that is easy enough. Without much hesitation Eirek said, "*Maa.*"

A spire rose from the ground in front of Eirek and he pushed it up until it reached the giant's shins. Then he released the spell. The giant crouched and lowered his right hand on the ground, palm upward. The hand was as large as a home.

"We board." Cronos boarded the hand and waited for the others to follow.

After a brief cajoling from the Sage, the three stepped forward. The giant lifted them up overhead and held them at the feet of another giant and another ledge that jutted out from the large mountain.

Eirek almost fell down on the rocky hand when the next giant spoke. Afterwards, Cronos told him that his next spell was water.

Water. That one will prove a little more difficult. Eirek looked around while in the giant's hand but saw no water in sight. The only stream he passed was miles upon miles away at this point. He tried looking down but saw nothing. *The waterfalls are probably on the other side of the mountain.* Then Eirek remembered the canteens.

"I need a canteen."

Eirek put down the briefcase and accepted the canteen Ethen handed him. He undid the cap and turned the canteen upside down, pouring water out onto his hand. "*Vesi.*" The water circled around his hand, and he felt a temporary relief from the harsh heat of the suns. Almost so much relief that he forgot to enhance the spell's strength. After he had his moment's reprieve, he pushed the water from his hands to form a geyser the height of the giant's shins.

The giant bent down and placed his hand right next to the other giant's hand in midair. Cronos crossed with no worries, and so did the conseleigh. Eirek picked up his briefcase and took his time in crossing from one hand to the next.

At the feet of the third giant, Cronos translated the giant's words. "The next spell you must cast is fire."

Fire. The giant wants me to cast fire. Eirek looked to the suns in the sky. *Well, at least they're closer now.* Eirek held out his hand and looked at the brightness. *No, they are too far away. I can't draw from there. That would be suicide.* They studied him as he paced the giant's hand.

The rocks he had used earlier, he had left behind. Eirek scanned the ledge where the third giant stood. There was room for Eirek, too. *Can I leave the hand? Is that allowed?* The hand was close enough to the cliff to jump. He would need a running start, though.

Eirek backed up near the curve of the giant's palm and unlatched his cape. It would only slow him down. He set down his briefcase and took a deep breath. Focused, he looked ahead. Then he sprinted. At the last knuckle of the index finger, Eirek jumped and made it across the gap to the cliff. The giant on the ledge started moving around, causing massive tremors. The others shouted to him incoherently as he scrambled to find two flat stones. He found them quickly and put them in his pocket. As he ran to jump to the outstretched hand, an ill-timed tremor caused him to stumble instead of jump.

Eirek flailed in the air, half his body landing on the outstretched finger, half of it dangling off. He slipped. His fingers tried to dig into the giant's flesh, but it was too hard. Ethen and Luvan rushed towards him. They dived, trying to catch Eirek's hand before he fell. His fingers slipped through theirs. Eirek fell.

He tumbled through the air. Acting more on instinct than anything else, Eirek said, "*Maa.*"

From the side of the mountain, a spire shot out in the form of a ladle. Landing hard, Eirek coughed and rubbed the back of his head. *No blood. Good!*

Ignoring the tinnitus in his ear as beast as he could, he looked up. "I... I can't believe that worked," he muttered to himself. He stood, rubbed his neck, and shook his head. "*Maa.*" Eirek concentrated on making the handle of the ladle into a set of steps. Power obeyed him. The platform became wider and deeper, then cut itself into a staircase from which Eirek could climb. At the top of the steps, Eirek hopped back to the giant's outstretched hand.

"Are you mad?" Cronos scowled.

"The suns are too far away. I'll make fire faster than I can draw it." Eirek sat down and struck the two stones together. At first, he was unsuccessful.

"Eirek, how did you think to do that?"

Eirek looked up at Luvan. "I don't know. I... it just seemed natural to me. This is the largest mountain; drawing earth from it would be easy."

"Eska would be impressed, Apprentice Mourse." Ethen patted Eirek on the back.

"Thank you." Eirek returned his focus to the stones. On his fourth try a spark flashed. Upon seeing it, Eirek said, "*Palo.*" A purplish flame formed in his hand. He stretched his arm upward and let the fire flow fiercely from his fingertips. The sensation reminded him of the first night he cast Power.

The third giant's hand came down. Eirek grabbed his briefcase of jewels and cape and transitioned hands. Wind rushed past him as the third giant raised them even higher. How high they were now, Eirek didn't want to know. He avoided looking down. Even now, though, he couldn't see any part of the Palace of Power. *Which spell do I have left?*

Cronos nudged him after the guttural voice finished. "The final spell is lightning."

Eirek gulped. There wasn't a cloud in sight. There wasn't a fuse in sight. He was on a mountain, on a giant's hand. *How am I supposed to cast that?* The anxiousness of meeting the Twelve was now replaced by the need to cast the spell.

Think, Eirek, think. Eirek paced, trying to ignore the stares as best as possible. When he didn't want to feel Cronos's bright bi-colored eyes upon him any longer, he said, "Stop looking at me like that."

Cronos leaned on his staff. "Like what?"

"I will figure this out. Just give me time."

"Yes, well, I hope you do." He glanced at the suns for a moment and then back to Eirek. "We all have a Meeting to attend soon enough."

Eirek huffed and then spun around, turning his back from the others. He laid the briefcase down next to him and sat. He thought until his brain hurt from thinking, which after the predicament of the last spell wasn't very long. As he sat, he sweated in the suns' breath. *Stupid suns. I wish I had a shield for you.* Eirek tilted his head to the mountain. *A shield. A shield!*

Eirek spun around and stood up. "Conseleigh Katore, take off the pack. I need to check something inside."

Eirek rummaged through Luvan's pack and came across the box that Lady Aprah had given him. Her words ran through his mind: *it emits an electromagnetic pulse that collects all the particles in the air...* Eirek slid the ore band with a crystal crown onto his finger. Just as he was shown, he applied pressure to the quartz crown and said, "*Salama.*"

The shield formed in front of him on his right side. But on his left side, electricity crawled over his hand and wrist like centipedes, giving him tingles that jolted the rest of his body. *It worked.* Eirek beamed. He raised his hand up and let the electricity flow to the last giant's kneecap.

Soon enough, the last hand came down and raised them to the ledge. On the way up, Eirek readjusted his cape and picked up his briefcase. Once the hand stopped, Eirek stepped off to one remaining cliff. A palace now came into view, built into the mountain landscape. *The Palace of Power. This is it.* The palace was of white marble and it looked almost like a replica of Eska's palace on the Core. Where it differed, however, were the six pillars of gold on the bottom level that held up the second, the four pillars of silver on the second level that held up the third and finally two pillars of copper that held up the roof of the palace. On the gable at the very top of the palace were three large windows of stained glass. Eirek recognized Lyoen and Bane next to one another, depicted in their armor, but he had no idea who the third figure was on the very right. Underneath that figure's image was the saying, "*Ajid Volintasey Fuan.*" Eirek furrowed his eyebrows on the image. *Who is that?*

"You did well, boy. Very resourceful."

"I agree with Cronos as well, Eirek," Luvan said.

"Just don't go jumping off giants' 'ands again," Ethen said.

Eirek smiled. "I won't."

Cronos walked away. Waving his staff forward he said, "Come on, boy, let's see how well you really know the Twelve."

CHAPTER 58

THE PALACE OF POWER

Through the double doors was a long vestibule, nearly five times as tall as Eirek. On each side were six statues four times the size of Eirek, and underneath the statues were name plates in either copper or silver. Plated with gold and copper and silver tiles, the hallway continued its sparkling allure for another quarter mile. At the end, another set of double doors awaited them.

After this set of doors, the party came upon a large central room with silver tiles, golden pillars and a long rectangular pool of shallow water that spanned the length of the room, ceasing before two large staircases carpeted with red. Copper tiles lined the rectangular pool. The polished tiles reflected light from three giant chandeliers coming to rest halfway between the second and third floors above the pool. Eirek shielded his eyes at one point to accommodate for the brightness. *All this beauty and not a single—*

Humming in an adjacent hallway cut short his thoughts. Shortly after, a man with a limp on his left side strode into the hall carrying a golden platter. His skin was brown and leathery with age. The face seemed flattened, like he had taken one too many falls.

The man dropped his platter. "Hu... hu... humans!" He limped as fast as he could to the staircase.

Eirek found his attempt to flee comical. The voice and the clatter that echoed off the palace's interior brought different creatures to the hall within moments. Eirek saw them as creatures because they didn't look human. Quickly, his smile faded into a line of contemplation. *Are they the Twelve?* Eirek counted seven so far.

Poked in the back by Cronos's staff, Eirek led the way into the main part of the central chamber, followed by the others. *Don't be nervous. Don't be nervous.*

Clank upon clank clamored in the hall. Eirek stared in shock as a machine (at least that is what it looked like) strode forward from a hallway. Jets of fire escaped its large shoulders and behind a black helm hid eyes of fire. Black metal covered all of it, exposing no skin. It raised its arm and then slapped the limp-legged man across the face, sending him flailing to the ground. "Heph, you fool, I told you we were expecting guests." The gritty voice seemed louder than it should have been, echoing off the metal, embodying it and now definitely identifying it as a male. "I should throw you off the cliff again and break your other leg."

"Easy now, Fueoco, we have guests!" A woman with blue and white hair cropped upward like a rock of crystal called to the man of metal from across the pool. When she turned to look at them, Eirek noticed a crystalline face with eyes of a deeper blue than Tundra's. She winked at them. *Cronos said that they've taken on forms of their homes. Could that be Crestal?*

Fueoco grunted. "Run. Off with you." The steel hands pointed the way up the stairs for the limp-legged servant to follow.

"I know the Guardian of the Core wasn't to be expected, but I wasn't aware there would be four of you." A man of dark skin dropped down from the second level, spreading wings like a bat and landing directly in front of them. Amethyst lines ran up and down the blade of cloudy gray attached to the belt of his hip. His ears were drawn backwards. Upon landing, the wings folded back behind the man. Gray eyes examined all four of them, stopping on the conseleigh. "Luvan Katore and Ethen Rorum?"

Both conseleigh nodded and said, "Yes."

Luvan continued, "I am surprised you remember us, Luenar. We've only met once."

"Once is all a god needs." Luenar smirked. "Cronos, this is a pleasant surprise. It is nice to see you again."

"It has been a while. I am here as part of this one's training." Cronos gestured towards Eirek.

Luenar surveyed Eirek up and down. "And are you Eska's apprentice?"

Eirek glanced between the conseleigh and Cronos. Cronos smirked as if he expected Eirek to fail in his introductions. *I won't give him his satisfaction.* "Yes," he said.

"Your name?"

It's fine. Just like the introduction during the Trials. Find your strength. Eirek exhaled and said, "Eirek Mourse."

Luenar studied him more. "Mourse is your last name?"

Eirek would have answered, but Cronos spoke for him. "It is. Unless he has fooled us all."

Luenar shifted his gaze to Cronos. "He might have. The last name doesn't befit him." Luenar turned and walked away.

Who do I remind him of? Eirek couldn't think about that much longer for the other ten present flooded the scene to have a closer look at him and to introduce themselves personally. Each gaze dragged over Eirek, causing him to tap his fingers on his side. He stared back noticing, trying not to gawk at all the deformities.

"When does the Meeting begin tomorrow?" Cronos asked.

"There may not even be a meeting." Anemie, a woman clothed in light blue silk, scoffed. She tapped her trident on the ground. What Eirek found alluring about her, though, was that she was transparent. Literally. He found this out as she brushed her light blue hair. Or tried to; her hand went through her head.

"Pearl will show," Fueoco said. He stepped to face the transparent woman, his steel steps thudding on the floor.

"Yes, well, she hasn't yet."

"Well, look to your stars then, Anemie." A raspy voice came forth.

A man with yellow eyes spoke. He had introduced himself as Orekus, god of Abaddon. And certainly, he fit the part, for he was no longer a man, but a raptor with a split tongue like that of a snake that slid between purple lips. A black cloak dragged behind him but did not manage to cover a large tail that snaked after its master. Nor did it cover scrawny forearms with talons instead of fingers.

"I will take a look tonight once the suns die."

"That wench hasn't showed in Abaddon, yet." Orekus scoffed.

"Orekus, don't call her that!" Shouted Trema, a woman clad in earthy armor. Her breasts were little rocks and her face was lean, but dirty. Her cropped, grass-green hair matched the color of her eyes.

"Trema, you clump of sod, I can do what I please," Orekus hissed, exposing his split tongue again.

"Enough, both of you." Tomahawke, a man with a shaved pate, stepped forward in between them and unfolded wings that resembled those of an eagle. He no longer had hair, but had grown feathers on his chiseled chest and his muscular arms. On his belt were a sword and an axe. The god of war and death fixated his green eyes on Eirek, so much so that Eirek looked away when the skin on his forearms prickled.

"Thank you, Tomahawke," Cronos said. "Where are our rooms?"

"I will show you. Follow me."

Cronos nodded. Eirek followed in between the conseleigh and behind Cronos as they made their way through the crowd of gods and goddesses. While walking up the steps to the second floor, Ethen leaned into Eirek's ear and whispered, "Tomorrow's meeting will be long."

Tomahawke stopped and turned around. "Conseleigh Rorum, why do you say that?"

Cronos answered, "Because they always are."

It wasn't even dawn when Eirek was woken by Luvan and Ethen. His eyes adjusted slowly to the light and, if not for their voices, he would have thought they were blurs and shadows.

"I thought the meeting wasn't until after lunch." Eirek yawned and stretched. He blinked and made out a figure at the threshold of the room—Cronos.

"The gods are shouting. We need to stop the commotion."

Eirek jutted upright at a distant rumble echoing from the hallway. He dressed quickly into his outfit that he had worn the day before and followed the voices to the meeting room. A long table, divided into sections of gold, silver, and copper, sat in the middle, and around it were thrones. Each throne was different and unique to the god or goddess sitting in it. For example, Trema sat on a throne of earthen slabs covered in vines. Crestal on a throne of ice, and Fueoco a throne of fire. But most of them weren't sitting; they were standing and shouting and blaming. They failed to notice Eirek, Cronos, and the two conseleigh enter the room. Voices piled on top of voices hid any understanding Eirek hoped to achieve.

Eirek stared blankly at the situation. Luvan stepped forward and opened his mouth, but Cronos put his staff over the conseleigh's mouth, stopping him. "This is the apprentice's problem. Let him deal with it." Cronos glared at Eirek. The amber eye seemed to be at its brightest, holding the same intensity it had when Pirini Lilapa first occurred. The blue sparkled like a newly polished sapphire.

Luvan backed away from the Sage's staff. He exchanged a word with Ethen but did nothing more.

Find your strength. Find your strength. Voices battled for dominance. Eirek clenched his fists and looked around to see how he could get their attention. As he looked, he heard bits and pieces of the conversation, and one came clearer than the rest. "Pearl is dead." He didn't know who had said it, but the more he strained his ears, the more clearly he heard it. *Perhaps water will get their attention. She is the goddess of water, after all.*

To his luck, a golden pitcher sat on the table in the back of the room. Although he couldn't see its contents, he guessed it was water. "*Vesi.*"

It obeyed him. He remembered his training from Tundra and the conseleigh. He separated the strands of water and brought his hands back behind him, commanding streams to reach across the length of the table, acting like long mirrors. Both did an excellent job at becoming a barrier and muffling their voices. The noise stopped. The eleven gods looked at him and the others, finally cognizant of their presence and intrusion. Eirek gulped. He let the spell die.

"What is the meaning of this? Why are you fighting?"

Anemie pointed her trident towards the other side of the table. "One of those Heavol scums killed Pearl."

"How do you know she is dead?" Tomahawke asked.

"Two weeks ago, didn't you feel something? A jolt?"

"Yes, of course, but—"

"It was Pearl. At that time I didn't know what it was, but now that I see she still isn't here, I am sure it was the throes of death."

Theothe, a woman with eyes much too large for the glasses she wore, raised a feathered arm. She looked more like an owl than a woman, for she had a beak that curved backwards like Tomahawke's and feathers on the areas of her skin not covered by a toga. "I, too, felt something about a fortnight ago."

Myethos raised his hammer. "I felt it as well."

"As did I. I have never felt cold, but there was a moment two weeks ago where shivers ran through even me," said Crestal.

"Brothers, sisters. We all felt it. Her absence here confirms it, as if the stars shining less than before didn't already. It is them!" She jabbed her trident out towards the opposing tribe.

"We have done no such thing." Luenar slammed his fist on the table and spread his bat wings. "Why would we kill one of our own?"

"You Heavols had always been quick to reprimand us Evolics. Isn't that right?" Anemie crossed her arms over her chest, bringing her trident closer to her body.

Luenar scoffed. "Your assumptions are preposterous."

Theothe held up her hand. "On the contrary, Luenar, they are very much validated. Remember the Great War? Who was it that started it? We Evolics share blood of a sort. It would be only logical that we have felt something at Pearl's passing. You wouldn't feel anything. You don't have *our* blood."

Orekus stood and spat. "Blood."

Luenar waved his axe. "Orekus." The raptor sat back down. "Theothe, Anemie, what did this *pulse* feel like?"

"A ting," Theothe said.

"A tickle. But one that sent shivers through me. After, I looked at the sky and noticed the sky was darker. I am sure her star is now gone, wherever it may have been."

"Why?" Trema stood up.

"Sister, I know what you are about to say." Luenar glanced from Trema back to the other tribe. "If what you say is true about this pulse signaling Pearl's death, then I believe it is you who have done something more egregious." Luenar pointed his axe at all of them. "Just days ago, before I came here, I lurched over in my cave in Lurid. Even in the night, I couldn't see. For at least an hour I was blind."

"My flames went out from inside of me," Fueoco said.

"I grew old... I had been looking at myself in the mirror and my hair..." Saeluste grasped at her brown hair. "My hair was old and gray and tangled."

"Pray tell, how do you explain that, Theothe, oh goddess of wisdom? We Heavol are all still here, who is it that you killed to make us feel like that?"

Theothe stammered and looked at the others. They all remained silent.

Tomahawke eventually spoke for their tribe. "We killed none of yours. As you have said, no one is missing from your tribe."

"Oh, but there is. I am sure of it." Luenar fixated on Tomahawke. No longer did any of the Twelve care about Eirek and his party's presence.

"Speak your words then." Anemie jabbed with her trident.

Eirek turned his head to that. *Another death? Who is it now?*

"One of you killed Galan. I am sure of it now more than ever. I, too, watch the stars Anemie, and I have noticed they have grown especially dim ever since that shock to my system."

Gasps. Then more bickering. Eirek tried to comprehend the significance of what was just said. *Who is Galan? Why so much outrage over him?*

"Brother, are you sure? How are we to get to Gladima now?" Trema leaned over in her throne of vines and earth.

"*She* is still alive," Luenar pointed his blade towards the other side of the table. "Naydeia."

Who is Naydeia? Who is Galan? Why are they important?

"You do not think we killed Galan, do you?" Tomahawke spread his eagle wings and rose from his throne of bramble and sticks. "We needed him to return to Gladima, same as you!"

"Yes, but you still have her! You plan on getting rid of these bodies yourself. Without us!" Crestal raised her voice.

Theothe stood and crossed her arms over her chest. "You forget we cannot hunt Naydeia down. Just like we could not find Galan."

Eirek stepped forward. "Who are these two?"

Orekus torqued his head to Eirek. The others of the Twelve did the same, finally noticing his party's presence again. "This is the apprentice Eska sends?" Orekus used talon-like fingers to remove his brown hood. Underneath the hood hid a raptor face and piercing yellow eyes. His large tail swung forward to tap his neck. "His judgment has lacked as of late."

Eirek did his best not to cower. "I just... If I know who they are, maybe I can help."

"The only one who can help is this wench here." He pointed a talon finger towards Anemie.

"What makes you think I can help?"

"Your sister. That's how you tracked down Galan in the first place, I reckon. You used her to get to him and then killed him to get back at whatever missteps you think we did to Pearl."

"Orekus, you know I cannot find my sister, nor my niece."

"I don't know that. Maybe you are lying."

"Both have blocked me. Besides, it's too dangerous to return there, anyway. You know what waits for us if we go back." She jabbed her trident now.

Just because they have First Blood doesn't make them better. Stay strong. He collected himself and focused on the conversation. He needed to ease the tension in the room.

Orekus gave a wide smirk. It was clear he meant to upset her. "Desmós? Its master? The Third One is gone. Your sister and niece are paranoid. And even if they weren't, the black dragon cannot return to form without the necklace."

Eirek tensed. *Who is Desmós? Who is the Third one?* Eirek resisted the temptation to look at the conseleigh and Cronos behind him. Instead, he focused on the conversation, trying to figure out some way to pull it together and end it.

"Yes, but the necklace still survives. Somewhere. And my sister is not going to risk her life nor Naydeia's life if there is a possibility of the dragon's return and thus the full-return of the Third One."

"Are they talking of the Zas Necklace?" Eirek muttered and put a finger to his lips.

"What was that, apprentice?"

Neck tightened, Eirek looked up as if he had just been caught in a lie. Tomahawke glared at him.

Oh no. All eleven of the heads turned towards him. *What did I do?* "I—"

"What do you know about the Zas Necklace?" Tomahawke spread his wings.

Eirek looked back to the conseleigh. Their postures were rigid. Hands idle their weapons. Neither would approach. Cronos merely looked on, curiosity in his eyes. The look prickled Eirek's skin.

Eirek gulped. "I know who has it."

"Who?" Luenar opened up his bat wings as well.

Shock and fright stilled him.

"Out with it, boy!" Myethos pounded a hammer on the table, cracking off a part of it to the floor. His body was cloaked in orange fire and his eyes were white flames. His body flared, making it appear twice the size it was normally.

The uncertainty of what to say made it so that he didn't say anything.

"Are you making a mockery of us?" Luenar's wings flapped.

Eirek shook his head.

"Well then, out with it!" The god with the hammer approached closer.

Cronos stepped forward, almost meeting the god face-to-face. "Myethos, enough. Prince Hydro Paen has it."

The gods changed their glance to him now. "How is it this necklace came to be found?"

"Ethen, I'm fine." Luvan stepped forward. "It was I. I created a trial. It was found during it."

Eirek's heart rate steadied. The tension in his neck ceased. He could breathe again.

"You did not think to tell us this?" Luenar flapped his wings and rose himself in the air. He flew in front of all of them.

"The matter is under control. It is under the Guardian's jurisdiction now." Luvan didn't cower at the sight of Luenar.

"The Guardian has no jurisdiction over us. We are the Twelve." Orekus jumped up on the table, his large tail knocking over plates and glasses.

"He..." When Eirek began speaking, all eyes turned towards him. "And he is the Guardian of the Core. Of Gladonus. You gave him your Power."

Luenar turned his back to them, facing his fellow Twelve. "Now we want it back." He turned around and swung the blade wielded in his right hand at Eirek.

On instinct, Eirek crouched and touched the crown on his ring. The shield appeared in an instant and did much to slow and redirect the blade but it could not stop it. When the shield broke due to the sheer force of the Luenar's strength, it redirected the trajectory towards Eirek's left hand and sliced the telecommunicator from his wrist. Any lower and it would have claimed skin.

Seeing that he missed, Luenar swung again. This time the blade was caught in mid-air by Cronos's staff. Cronos looked at the conseleigh and then to Eirek. "Run! I will hold them off." Cronos pushed back with his staff and made Luenar tumble backwards to the table. Orekus flew off the table, trying to pounce on Cronos, but he merely put up his staff and flung him to the side.

Eirek didn't have time to examine the beginning of the fight any longer, for Ethen dragged him out of the room, following Luvan in front of him. Yells. Commands for Power. And the clang of steel.

"Will he be alright?"

"I have never seen Cronos like this." Ethen crouched as pieces of rubble exploded out of the wall.

Walls shattered all around them as the brute force of the Twelve revealed itself. The palace shook as the whole mountain rumbled to their ire.

"We need to get outside." Luvan pointed to the double doors as they were at the top of the steps.

Water overflowed from the central area. Pillars were almost breaking. One of the chandeliers had already broken itself upon the pool, sharding the surrounding area. They hurried down the stairs as fast as possible. It wasn't fast enough. Tomahawke and Myethos had caught up with them. As they traveled past the overflowing pool, Myethos leaped from the second floor to the bottom and swung his hammer at a nearby column. It broke and came down. Tomahawke dived into the column, pushing it towards the humans. Still, they managed to make it past, but when the column came down, it crashed into another part of the pool, sending a torrent of debris and water into the air. On impact, Ethen tripped, and a large slab of stone landed on his leg. He screamed in pain.

Wetness clung to Eirek. It was a hot wetness, laced with blood and sweat. Eirek wiped his eyes to clear his vision from the deluge. Tomahawke and Myethos approached slowly and confidently.

"Eirek, go! Now. Get outside! Contact Guardian Eska and tell him to get here immediately!" Luvan yelled over Ethen's shrills.

Myethos smirked. "Your Guardian won't save you now." He leaped in the air.

"No, he won't." Tomahawke flew towards them.

Luvan grabbed his knife and twirled it on his fingers. "Leave, Eirek."

Eirek turned and sprinted. Voices yelled after him. Never looking back, he ran as fast as he had ever run before, trying to drown out the shouts and screams and steel with his footsteps.

Past the double doors, the large statues rocked back and forth. Halfway through, another figure burst through the door. The god of war and suffering held a look that befit his title. He flapped towards Eirek and spiraled downwards. Out of instinct, Eirek hopped up on one of the sides and used the wobbling statue to catch his balance. It broke off and made a short barrier behind Eirek, which Tomahawke had to fly under in order to escape slamming into the wall ahead of him. He flew upwards and spiraled out of sight, hands over his hawk-like face.

Once outside, Eirek ran to the steps. Glass shards falling from above halted his advance. Tomahawke flew into the air, stopping with outstretched wings, a dark silhouette in the purple aurora skyline.

Eirek hid behind one of the columns. The cliff shook. He looked down at his arm. His telecommunicator was gone. *How am I—* Eirek paused in mid-thought. He would need to use telepathy to contact Eska. But the distance. The vibrations. And the noise. Could he do it?

Eirek peeked out from the column. Tomahawke had vanished. *Where is—*

"Looking for me?" Tomahawke appeared upside-down in front of him. He swung his cloudy gray axe with veins of amethyst towards Eirek's head.

Eirek ducked. The axe went right through the column, and Eirek scurried out from under it. Tomahawke chased him. His talons knocked Eirek to the ground. Scrambling, Eirek turned around. He reached for the sword at his belt and withdrew it just in time, as Tomahawke's axe was preparing to cleave him in two. The steel clanged. Eirek lost grip of the sword, and it fell to the cliff next to him.

Tomahawke's eyes widened. His wings flapped. "An Ether Weapon?" Tomahawke picked him up with one arm and carried him in the air. "Who are you really, Apprentice Mourse?" His eyes scanned over him. After a moment, they widened. "You're his—"

A caw escaped his beaked mouth, and he let Eirek tumble to the cliff. Eirek looked back. Luvan carried Ethen out from the palace, right arm extended. Tomahawke flapped his wings and spiraled away. A knife clanged on the ground in front of Eirek. Luvan picked it up.

"Thank you."

"My duty, Apprentice Mourse. No..."

Luvan's voice tapered off. Eirek gulped. He turned around to see what had stopped the conseleigh from finishing his sentence. A fight had erupted into a war on the mountainside. A war in which every single person was his own champion. Or perhaps it was divided. Eirek couldn't tell through the tiffs of tumult that took place. He saw Cronos on the balcony of the third floor.

I need to contact Eska. Eirek searched in his mind, now that the battle had suspended their attention for a little while. He found pulses. Multiple pulses. He assumed it was the conseleigh by his side. But there was one that was faint. *Eska.* Eirek focused and blocked out the din and distress around him and focused on the pulse. When it was close, he latched on.

Guardian Eska.

Eirek, what's wrong? You seem rushed.

The Twelve. They are fighting. They tried to kill us. The whole mountain is shaking. Eirek looked up to the sky and noticed Luenar's batwings outstretched, hands overhead.

Eirek, what is happening? Communicate with me.

Eirek trembled. What he saw wasn't possible. It shouldn't be possible. Couldn't be possible. The other two conseleigh looked up in fright as well. Cronos had vanished from view.

Eirek, what is happening?

Luenar, he, he... It seems he is bringing the moon towards the mountain.

Silence.

I'll be there shortly.

He didn't allow his gaze to fixate on the moon, preferring bliss to bedlam. Instead, he lowered his eyes and scanned the glass gable he had first noticed when he arrived. Two of the frames had broken, leaving the third. The one he didn't know. The remaining frame looked outwards into the ball of heat that was the two suns, into the purple aurora of the sky, immune, for the moment, to the Curse and the chaos and cacophony that came with it.

CHAPTER 59

PIRINI LILAPA

The line of telepathy cut. *They're in trouble. The Twelve are fighting.* Eska stepped out onto the balcony of the estate and looked up into the purple aurora that populated the sky. He hadn't seen it for 150 years. *The situation in Syf will have to wait.* He clicked his tongue. Only an hour before, he had gotten reports of a different tragedy. *The Curse has begun. Will there be more?*

When last it occurred, the first reports of Deimos had come from Pyre, but soon Onkh, Agrost, and Myoli all witnessed its rampage. The beast had been able to warp, to rip open the very fabric of sky and jump through it. Something only Ancients had ever done. How that was possible? To this day Eska didn't know, although he had his suspicions.

Gripping the balustrade, he spent moments breathing in the tranquility here, feeling the breeze caress his cheek and Vesel's presence soaring overhead. He needed to take this moment in because it could be his last.

Vesel landed on the roof of the estate and let out a roar.

I know, old friend. It's happening. Eska exhaled, pushing his breath out into the heinous heat, letting his patience die. *That's enough. It is time to deal with this.* He opened his eyes. *Riagan, come to my chamber now.*

On my way, Guardian Eska.

He needed to make sure Riagan knew his role to play in how the next events would play out. The others were unfit to help in this situation. Eirek was unfit to handle the situation. Although he had a mind on him—made evidently clear by his ability to reach him through telepathy from a different planet—he did not have the physical prowess of a Guardian yet. Eska would take time to revel in the small accomplishment for his apprentice later, but he didn't have time now. Only he and Vesel could handle the Twelve.

The door opened and closed behind him.

"Riagan, the Twelve are fighting amongst themselves. I think they have turned on Eirek and the others."

"Are they alright?"

"Eirek is alive. For now. But the Twelve are ripping Mount Volan apart."

"What caused this?"

With his mind, Eska followed Riagan's presence, but never turned to look at his youngest conseleigh. Instead, he continued looking up at the domineering purple sky. Never did he enjoy dealing with the Curse of Pirini Lilapa. In his muse, he tried thinking of a way out. He still wanted one. But Gladonus wouldn't afford him one. Duty couldn't afford him one.

"We will find out later. All I know now is that chaos is erupting on Mount Volan and Onkh's moon draws closer with every idle minute."

"You are certain of this?"

Eska took his gaze away from the skyline to look into Riagan's orange eyes. "No. But I cannot take that chance. Mount Volan symbolizes hope. If that is taken away, will Klaff be next? If the moon is moved out of orbit more than it already is, Onkh will be affected as a planet. Acquava will drown itself in the sea. And that, that, may lead to an unsettling time."

"What do you intend to do?"

"Stop them. All of them."

"How?"

Eska's only answer was his loosening of the darknether glove he wore on his left hand. When he yanked it off, the white light underneath spread to openness. Slowly, his eyes became acquainted with the influx of light. The Power of the Guardians was ready. With both hands, he reached behind his head and unbound the knot of his reimaje. *This will need to come off.* The black cloth stretched to his height as it fluttered in the wind. Eska threw it off the balcony and muttered under his breath. The reimaje caught in midair. It hardened in the stale air. Wind no longer roamed this place. Not anymore.

"Guardian... Eska... I... I am having... trouble... breathing." Riagan clutched his throat.

"Stagger your breathing, Riagan. You will live through this."

Eska squeezed his left hand into a fist, containing the white light. Then he raised and unclenched his hand. The light shot out onto the reimaje, and Eska drew an oval large enough for himself. All Power, even a Guardian's, drew upon strength of mind—what he thought is what he would do, so he let Mount Volan and the Palace of Power enter his mind.

Forged from the ether of space, the reimaje allowed him to view the stars on its black surface, keeping track of his along with others. It allowed him to view the events of other Guardians. But mostly, combined with the Power that hid underneath his darknether glove, it allowed him access to his own wormhole. It was the sole reason he had been able to keep pace with Deimos as it jumped through space. Now he would use it to get to Volan quickly.

As Eska continued thinking about the Palace of Power, a mural painted itself on the canvas of the reimaje. The painting trembled and shook, rippling like disrupted waves on a placid pond. *They really are fighting.* Eska straightened his shoulders. The longsword, Adonis, was in its sheath on his back. There, he hoped it would stay. Eska turned around and looked upwards towards his dragon. Vesel beat his wings back and forth. *Are you ready?*

Vesel roared.

Good. He turned his focus to his conseleigh. "Riagan, you are to take a ship to Onkh. Hopefully you will arrive by the time I sort out this disaster. I may not have enough energy left to transport myself back here."

"What of the Core? We will leave it defenseless?"

"Use the telecom chamber below the estate. Inform Hown of the situation before your departure."

"I understand, my Guardian."

"Then leave now. I will handle things from here."

Riagan nodded and left.

Once Eska heard the doors close behind him, he turned his head back to the portal in front of him. "*Tuuli.*" The wind listened to Eska's command. Besides Zeph, he was the only other person who could control the wind. An element that was always present. An element that could never be halted. An element that was more powerful than the rest. A fifth element.

Vesel, follow behind me.

His dragon roared.

Next, Eska closed his eyes. He levitated himself. When jolts traveled down his body, when his limbs and skin seemed to stretch and twist, when his skin prickled, Eska knew he had entered the reimaje. The tranquility he knew on the Core became replaced with the dissonance of cursing and shouting and screaming. The next sight he took in was the Palace of Power. He had arrived.

Eirek held the ring over his head, hoping Lady Aprah's shield would protect the incoming strike from Tomahawke. To his surprise, the blow never landed. The other member of the Twelve whom Luvan had been combating was also nowhere to be seen. Instead, in the matter of a blink, Eska stood in the spot Tomahawke had been, his fists clenched. There was a crash off in the distance. Eirek spotted two large craters in the mountainside.

On one knee now, Eska panted.

A roar cut through the cacophony of the air. Eirek's eyes bulged. *Is that...* Eirek returned his gaze to Eska. His chest sank and rose in such fervor. With a grunt, he raised his left hand. A light shot out from his palm and pulled the black bandanna—the reimaje—back to him.

"How—" Eirek started.

Eska cut him off. "We will talk later." His head tilted.

A thud.

Eirek braced himself as Eska's dragon landed on the ground next to him. Lurched forward on all legs, wings outstretched, it shielded Eirek and the two conseleigh close to him from the heat of the suns.

The fighting on the mountainside continued, Eska's sudden apparition not worthy enough of their attention. Eska analyzed the situation and then turned back to the group on the cliff. His eyes glazed over Eirek, fell upon Ethen's leg for a brief moment, and then lingered upon Luvan. "Where is Cronos?"

Luvan took a heavy inhale. "We lost track of him in the palace... He stalled them enough for us to escape."

"How did this—"

"Guardian Eska!" Cronos came out of the double doors, staff clutched in his hand.

Eirek was surprised the old man had not died or become injured during his bout with the Twelve. In fact, the old man, must have had some innate prowess in him and the mettle to match, for it seemed as if there was no form of exhaustion in him, save for the robe cloaked in sweat, but that very well could have been from the overbearing heat of the suns.

Eska furrowed his brows at the Sage. "What happened in there?"

Cronos detailed in brief what had happened—the necklace's resurgence, Galan dying, and their need to return to Gladima.

Eska glowered at Luvan. Then his eyes crawled over Eirek for a moment before returning to the sky. Bedlam and banter and discord still ruled above. But not for long. Tomahawke and Myethos now directed each of the Twelve to Eska and Vesel's presence below.

Eirek gulped.

"We cannot allow them to disrupt Mount Volan anymore. Their force brings the moon closer. If it gets any closer, Onkh and all of its citizens will suffer."

"What are you thinking of doing?" Cronos asked.

"I need to stop them. Somehow." Eska reached behind him for the hilt of his Guardian's blade, Adonis.

"You are not thinking of killing them."

Eska let go of the hilt and pointed at Luvan. "I would not need to do such a drastic thing if not for your blasted trial." He never lowered his arm.

Luvan stayed silent and Ethen took up his voice. "But your Power will be siphoned."

Lost in his thoughts, Eirek looked to the detritus on the ground. *Siphoned? Does Eska need the Twelve to retain his Power? It would make sense with everything I've been taught about bonding.* What Cronos had told him on the journey about the necklace and the girl sealed inside came back to him. Why Eska had been so on edge came back to him as fragments, but fragments he put together. *Could that be a solution?*

When he tuned into the conversation again, Eska was saying, "... Power diminished every second I am away so—"

"What if we were to bind them?" Eirek cut in.

"What do you mean?"

"Do the same thing you did with Deimos."

"There are too many of them."

"Then, what about sealing them? Separately. In different objects. They would live, and you would retain your strength."

Eska folded his arms over his chest. "What objects? This mountain is sacred."

The smell of blood and sweat soon overtook the waning shouts and yells and metal that once had clamored for dominance. The Twelve had become attracted to the newcomer—Guardian Eska.

"So, you come." Wings slightly flapping, Luenar hovered in mid-air in front of the rest of the Twelve.

Eska turned his head to the voice. "You threaten my apprentice and my aides. You are destroying yourselves and with you, all of Onkh as well. How can I let this continue?"

"You are destroying us by not letting us return to Gladima."

Eska cupped his hands behind his back. "Letting no one return to that place is the task you charged the Guardians with when you created our position. You wanted no one to return to Gladima so that you could live like gods."

"That was before now."

"You know why you cannot return there. If you return, there is a chance the Third One will bring back Desmós and return to His former glory."

"Now, the necklace has resurfaced. Once we find it, we can get back to the Core. Naydeia will help us."

"What makes you believe she will help you? You disown the Ancients."

Howls and roars were the response.

Vesel roared back, drowning out theirs.

Cronos tugged on Eirek's outfit. Barely audible through Vesel's roar, Cronos whispered, "Boy, where are those jewels you received? I have had a thought."

Looking away from the standstill, Eirek turned back to the Sage. *Of course.* Eirek's eyes widened.

Cronos gleamed. "You know? It just came to me."

Eirek nodded hurriedly and then turned around to tug Eska's cape. "Guardian Eska, what of the jewels I received from Lord Zigarda? How about those?"

Eska didn't reject them. While continuing to focus on the Twelve in front of him, Eska muttered, "Where are they?"

"Inside." Eirek pointed to the palace.

"We will make Naydeia help us. Once we find her."

"Those matters are strictly under my jurisdiction, Luenar. Do not be angry with me for the boundaries you outlined centuries past."

"Times have changed, and we have become desperate. Our bodies cannot afford any more deformity."

"You will need to kill me before I retire my duties."

"That can be arranged." Luenar looked back at the rest of the Twelve. "Brothers and sisters, to arms. It is time to take back our Power."

"Get them. Hurry." Eska pulled Adonis from its sheath on his back. "Vesel and I will buy you some time."

Eirek's eyes widened. "What if they overwhelm you?" Eirek asked. "Deimos... Gladonus..."

"That is why you must hurry." Eska rushed forward, ready for battle.

You cannot be serious right now, my Guardian.

Luvan, there is no other way. This is the only option. Eska used Adonis to swat away the hammer Myethos used as he approached. It flew back into the mountain, making a little crater. Momentarily shocked, Vesel used his tail to whip Myethos into the mountainside as well, making another crater alongside his hammer. *We are not killing them.*

You are killing everyone who believes in the Twelve.

They did this to themselves. Eska did not like using telepathy while in battle, but it was something he had trained for. In this instance, his training proved useful. *Tell Cronos to have the jewels laid out.*

I will not support you in this. You are consolidating your Power. It isn't right.

Guardian Eska dodged two of the Twelve and noticed Orekus jump at him from a mountain cliff, two sais in his hand. If Eska had ever been angrier at one of his aides, he wouldn't have known when. He pulled back and came through clean with Adonis on one of the god's arms. With his free hand, he punched Orekus in the face, sending him flying into the Palace of Power.

I am saving Onkh. That is my task.

The ground split beneath him. He jumped to one side of the fissure. Vines crawled from the crack and wrapped their way around Eska's ankles. Using Adonis, he slashed the vines. He toppled backwards. Crestal now sat on top of him, daggers of ice plunged into his chest. Well, they would have pierced Eska, for they made contact, if not for Eska's darknether jerkin and mythril chainmail underneath that. Both materials were extremely proficient in stopping anything besides an Ether Weapon. When she realized that her attempt failed, she brought the dagger down to Eska's face. Eska bobbed to the left. Before the next strike could land, Eska opened his left hand. "*Voima.*" A shot of light punched Crestal and sent her flying backwards into a cliff, losing grip of her ice daggers in the process.

No longer on top of her, Eska saw Vesel in the sky dealing with Luenar, Tomahawke, and Anemie. Out of all the Twelve, they were the most danger-ous—they held Ether Weapons. One wrong move for Vesel could prove fatal. For both the dragon and Eska.

Eska stood. Eyes still on Vesel, Eska thought. *Luvan, where is your propri-ety?*

It vanished when I realized you didn't obey your own propriety.

Vesel unleashed silver flames to encompass the trio he was fighting; Luenar and Tomahawke folded their wings in front of their body, bracing for the attack. Anemie, on the other hand, did nothing. She let the fire pass right through her transparent body and lunged at Vesel with her trident, stabbing him right in the belly. The trident couldn't penetrate his mythril underbelly, but noticing that his fire hadn't worked on her, Vesel snatched the trident out of her hands with his mouth and bit down, breaking the staff in half.

"Vesel! To me."

Vesel spat out the staff and flew down to Eska's side. Eska hopped onto his dragon's back and looked at Luvan. *What do you mean?*

You know whom I refer to.

Eska, Eirek is back.

At Ethen's voice, Eska flicked his gaze to his apprentice, darting back through the rubble. *Tell Cronos to get the jewels prepared. I will seal them myself.*

Aye, my Guardian.

Eska patted Vesel's neck. They took off into the sky, fighting the Twelve mostly through Power or long ranged assaults, as many were intimidated to get close to Eska's dragon. Hoping to capitalize on the aerial assault distraction by Tomahawke and Luenar, Fueoco jumped up towards Vesel from below, hoping to skewer his belly. Eska recognized the tactic when both of the aerial Twelve glanced down for the briefest of moments. Eska patted his dragon's neck. *Below.* Vesel flapped his wings and pushed himself upwards, somersaulted in the air, and whipped its tail straight into Fueoco's metal body, sending him crashing into another one of the Twelve on the mountainside. Vesel roared, causing Luenar and Tomahawke to fly back a few paces. The impact rocked the mountainside, giving Eska the briefest of reprieves from the onslaught he and Vesel endured. Through the reprieve, he noticed his second-most trusted aide stare at him, arms crossed against his chest, silent.

I will need to deal with that later.

Eirek had found the jewels relatively easily. It was climbing through the debris that had slowed him down. But he was back now, and with his footsteps, everyone seemed drawn to his presence. Everyone but Luvan, who remained fixated on the fight above.

"Bring them here." Cronos pointed to a spot near his feet. "Open them."

"Eska will throw each of the Twelve to you individually, so 'is strength isn't shocked by te sudden flux of it," Ethen said, through gritted teeth. His hand still rested on his leg. "Through his Power tey will be sealed."

"Tell him I am ready."

The glow in Ethen's eyes only lasted a few seconds.

When telepathy finished, Eirek noticed Eska jump off of Vesel and command the mountainside to meet his feet. He rode it down like an elevator to where Orekus lay bloodied and without hands. He sheathed his sword, picked up the crippled god with one hand, and threw him towards Cronos, who then tossed up a jewel. When the two collided, Eska shot a beam of light from his left hand. The god vanished. The jewel fell to the ground. *Is this the Guardian's Power? Is this what I will be able to do someday?* Eirek looked at his hands in contemplation.

Vesel kept Luenar and Tomahawke engaged up above, freeing Eska to deal with the members of the Twelve who couldn't fly. First, Eska focused on outliers of the battle who had done nothing much but watch as the others fought, Saeluste, Theothe, and Lucine. Before being taken, each had mounted some minute defense, whether a verbal plea or an ill-attempt at combat, but all succumbed to Eska's strength as he threw them towards Cronos and the jewels. Screams of injustice accompanied each toss followed by the clank of the jewel as it hit the mountainside. Eirek fetched each jewel and put it back inside the briefcase at Cronos's feet. In between it all, Eirek watched the battle in the sky and mountainside, trying not to blink. Too much was happening. Too much was at stake.

Myethos charged Eska with his hammer. Eska withdrew Adonis just in time. The large hammer and the longsword made a steel song that shimmied down to the onlookers. When Myethos misjudged a lunge and a sweep, Eska punched him to the ground with a free hand. But the move seemed to infuriate the god only more, for he quickly regained his composure. A hammer came down from overhead, attempting to crush Eska, but Eska leaped back and, putting his foot on the hammer, brought his shoulder into Myethos's chest, causing him to lose grip of his hammer just slightly, just enough that Eska tossed him towards Cronos to join his sealed kin.

Vesel roared.

Eska keeled over and torqued his neck upwards. Patters of blood fell to the ground below. Luenar's Ether Sword had found Vesel's body, and Tomahawke's Ether Axe had found a section of its right wing. Vesel brought his wings in closer and spun like a tornado, whipping both of the Twelve backwards into opposite mountainsides.

The momentary falter by Eska as he regained his strength allowed Fueoco to slam into Eska with speed Eirek didn't think was capable in such heavy armor. Eska crashed into a mountain cliff. Fire spewed from cannons located on the forearms of his black armor. It hurled its way towards Eska and engulfed him, and the rubble on top of him, in an inferno.

"Eska!"

The rubble crumbled. Flames danced around Eska but never harmed him. He stood and dashed towards the plated man, not bothering to dodge the spews of flames that came from jets located on Fueoco's armor.

"How is that possible?" Eirek asked.

"His bond with Vesel. Fire doesn't affect him any longer," Cronos answered.

Sheathing Adonis once again, Eska dodged punches in order to dart around the large man and grab him by the plated collar of his armor. He tossed him overhead and Vesel batted him with his tail towards Cronos. Before Fueoco could clang to the ground, the god vanished into a ruby. Vesel settled down next to Eska, nuzzling his master. Despite the tough, invulnerable façade of the duo, Eska panted. Vesel's underbelly breathed in and out as if he, too, sucked in air as greedily as his master. Blood dripped out from him. From both of them. But they still stood as renegades to their duty.

"Brothers! Sisters! We must attack him in unison." Anemie rushed towards Eska. "After my lead."

Try as he might to stop Anemie, Eska couldn't. The tendrils of Power he had tried to trap her with went right through her. Before he knew it, Anemie closed in on Eska and for a brief moment made herself corporeal and punched Eska in the stomach, catapulting him into the mountainside. She hopped upwards, passing through the dragon as it tried to clamp down on her, and then reappearing again on the other side, kicking its head, sending the dragon skidding back into one of the columns holding up the Palace of Power, far away from Eska. Half of the building collapsed onto Vesel. But before the Guardian had time to think about any of that or recover, Tomahawke dragged Eska from the mountain cavity, holding his arms behind his back. Tomahawke bit down onto his neck with his beak.

Luenar flew in front of Eska. Blood dripped from his batlike wings. "You do not have Power here, Guardian Eska. You nor your pet. Tomahawke, hold him still. He won't be needing Adonis anymore." Luenar closed in on Eska.

Fear and terror crawled into Eska's eyes. "The Guardian's blade is not yours to have." Eska leaped back and crushed Tomahawke and himself into a mountain cliff. With the hold weaker, Eska spun Tomahawke over top of his shoulder, ricocheting him off Luenar into Crestal.

Eska leaped into the air. He levitated himself. Hovering there, in the mixture of moonlight and sunlight, the remaining deities looked to him as the common enemy—an enemy they would need to kill to stay alive and in power. An enemy that had halted their duel. An enemy they loathed.

The remaining six of the Twelve jumped towards him then. A gale caught them all in midair, halting their advance. Each looked at one another dumbfounded, locked in their invisible chains.

Eirek choked and tightened his neck. "What... what is... going on?"

"Cronos, the rest of the jewels. Toss them to me."

Cronos struggled as well, but tossed each of the remaining jewels to Eska. As each one was tossed to him, Eska shot out a light from his left palm and tossed a deity into it. A batch of light encumbered each transaction, resulting in six jewels falling to the mountainside below, clanging about on impact. Eirek forced himself forward, trudging through the invisible chains that he felt on his body as well, almost as if he were in a vacuum of space.

I can't... Eirek choked. He grabbed an opal.

Eska tried floating seamlessly back to the ground but collapsed ten feet from it. The chains binding Eirek loosened. He sucked in air. He hurried over to Guardian Eska. Sweat pelted his face, and his hands shook as much as his voice.

"Eirek... Eirek... go... find ard leaves... in pal... palace. Hurry."

Eirek left them then, hoping to find the leaves that would save his Guardian's life.

Eska heard Eirek's feet clatter across the rubble. *My body cannot...* His chest heaved. *Cannot handle that again. Eirek needs to hurry.* Eska knew the palace kept some ard leaves. They always had, to slow down the progression of their deformity. But now he needed some to regain his strength.

"Vesel... where is..."

"Don't speak, my Guardian. Conserve your strength." Ethen leaned on Luvan. Both conseleigh looked down at him, blocking his view of the sky.

Exasperated breaths made Eska shift his focus behind him. Hands on his knees, Cronos panted. The clouds of his Ether Staff swirled. Eska remembered talking to Cronos about how he received it from the Pavos family as a present when he declared Troy a Blessed. Supposedly the lord's great-great-grandfather had killed a Smith and had taken it from him. He said it was called Foresight because it could predict the future, but Eska believed none of it. He had only ever met Zeph, who held a certain clairvoyance about her. *I will... need to see her again.*

Eska grimaced. The energy in his body was deteriorating. The tightness of his skin loosened. Strands of hair fell to the ground. *This is not supposed to happen yet.*

Footsteps.

Soon enough, Eirek hovered over him, a bag of leaves in his hand. Eska reached for the bag and ate five of them. He collapsed then and waited for the energy and nutrients to course through his veins. He placed a hand on his neck and felt the wound Tomahawke had given him. It started to bleed again. *At least my blood flow is back.* Eska examined his hand; it had been a while since he saw his own blood. *I will need to spend some time in the apothecary myself.* Eska hoisted himself up and strapped on his glove, no longer needing the Power underneath.

"Where's Vesel? Vesel?"

A rumble occurred by the Palace. Debris shifted. Vesel shot up into the air. At least, he tried to, but crashed shortly after his attempted escape from the debris pile.

Eska's eyes widened. He ran over to his dragon. Patting his head, Eska looked over Vesel's body, noticing wounds on his belly and his right wing. Eska put his hand on the dragon's underbelly and pushed his head into the dragon's nose. *We will get these looked at when we return to the Core.* Eska was thankful the cut on the underbelly wasn't deeper than what it was. Normally, it would have probably been strong enough to kill a dragon, at least bleed it out, but since they were bonded, Eska's strength was also Vesel's strength, and now that Eska regained a majority of his strength, he noticed that Vesel's wound was already stitching itself back together.

Knowing Vesel was safe, Eska surveyed the wreckage. The palatial palace now lay partially pulverized in the mountainside. Columns were missing and half of the second floor had collapsed to the ground level. An axe with purple veins and the recognizable cloudy gray steeling caught his eye. He strolled over to the Ether Weapon and picked it up. *The man who wielded you last could hurt Deimos with you. Why couldn't Tomahawke use it to its full extent? Do you hold a secret, or is the secret only blood?*

"My Guardian?" Ethen called out.

"We take the Ether Weapons with us." He ignored the temptation to look back and examine them after his declaration. Instead, he walked amongst the wreckage and picked up Myethos's hammer and Luenar's sword as well.

"What do you intend to do with those?"

The Sage's question surprised Guardian Eska, as he would have expected it from Luvan. Instead, his conseleigh had crossed his chest, glowering at Eska as he returned with the three Ether Weapons cradled in his arms. Eska ignored Luvan and answered Cronos's question. "Research and training. The Twelve will no longer need them."

"Neither do you. You have Adonis."

There it is. Eska shot a glance to his conseleigh. "Aye, I have Adonis, Luvan. But these weapons are too valuable to fall into the wrong hands."

"Hands that would need to pass many tests in order to reach them here. Perhaps those are the most competent hands?"

"Deadly hands if they are able to make it this far on Mount Volan. It is better I take them to where they are safe. On the Core. Ethen, your thoughts as my master on weapons instruction?"

"Here, together, we possess six of te Eleven. It can only be a boon to te Guardian's position tat he knows the locations of the most powerful weapons in Gladonus. If tis is te reason for taking tem, tis is fine."

"We are through here then," Eska said, not waiting to hear a retort from the politician so well trained in refutation. "Eirek, bring the briefcase. Gather around. Vesel, can you fly with us all?"

The dragon roared.

Certainly ambitious old friend, but it won't be for so much longer. I will help you slightly if you need it.

Dragon roared and spewed silver flames into the sky.

Okay. Okay. I understand. I will leave it to you then. Eska smirked at his dragon's insistence. Ever since he had shown Vesel that he no longer needed him to fly, his dragon had been jealous. Now it was his turn to show Eska his Power and strength. Eska liked that in Vesel, and despite what the bonding had cost him, was happy to have such a loyal and brave bonded animal.

"Everyone, gather onto Vesel."

Eska sat up by the neck of Vesel. Eirek directly behind him with the briefcase. The others took spots on the dragon's spine, making sure to equally distribute their weight on his frame. When everyone boarded Vesel, the dragon leaped into the air, more graceful this time, and transported them away from the Palace of Power, away from the Sacred Passage, to the ground below.

CHAPTER 60

SEPARATE PATHS

A few hours later, the thriving metropolis of Visis came into view. *To think Gar would become this after their secession.* It gave Eska hope. He hated war of any kind. But oppression was worse.

A league outside the city, Eska saw Riagan's ship descending on the outskirts of the city. *So he took the tankard? Smart.* It was the only type of ship in Eska's fleet that would be able to transport Vesel, and Eska knew his dragon didn't have the strength to make another jump through the reimaje.

He leaned closer to Vesel and pointed. *There!*

Vesel snorted and changed course to the ship. For being injured by two Ether Weapons, and carrying more weight than usual, Eska was surprised by his dragon's strength. It was a testament to their bond. A bond that had helped him win his own Trials, and now a bond that had helped me through another Pirini Lilapa. After the carnage and destruction on Pyre from Deimos, Guardian Eska made sure his dragon wasn't in the rest of the fray and left him on that planet with his other kindred. There, at least if Eska died, he would have strength perhaps to manage the severed ties. But seeing that Deimos could rip open space, seeing the size of the beast, and knowing that the Twelve were inclined to help cage the beast, he thought it best for Vesel to remain idle for the last battle. One jump through the reimaje was already taxing enough on the body, and Eska could only imagine what multiple jumps and fighting a beast such as Deimos would have done to his dragon. Now, though, he was glad to have him as an ally to grant him the strength necessary to overcome the Twelve. That and his necklace. But he would talk to her about that later.

Vesel touched down near Riagan's ship. The conseleigh was already waiting for them outside the ship. Eirek and Luvan slid off first, helping Ethen to slide off Vesel afterwards. Then Cronos left, and Eska then jumped off and approached Riagan.

"Riagan, be quick and take these to the ship, then help Eirek carry Ethen up to the ship. The adored in the apothecary will take a look at his leg when we arrive back on the Core. Cronos accompany them as well." Eska handed the three Ether Weapons over to his youngest conseleigh.

His eyes bulged upon seeing the newly acquired steel. "What happened?" He switched his gaze to Ethen. "Are you okay?"

"The Twelve happened."

"I be fine, Riagan. Tis not'in."

Riagan rushed to put the Ether Weapons away. Ethen let Eirek take hold of him around the back, draping his arm over Eirek's shoulders.

When Luvan tried to help as well, Eska called him to his side. "A moment with you alone, Luvan."

Ethen and Eirek looked back and when they met Eska's glare, they quickly turned back around and hobbled as fast as they could towards the ship. Once Riagan came back, both men took Ethen under a shoulder and helped him move faster. Eska continued watching them for a couple of minutes in silence and then redirected his attention to Luvan.

"Your badge." Eska held out his gloved hand and stared from the golden C on his vest to the eyes of his conseleigh.

"My... my... What?"

"Your badge," Eska restated.

"Are you... are you dismissing me?" Luvan's face contorted into a look of bewilderment.

"I cannot allow you to be a member of my conseleigh any further." Eska remained stern and stoic, like his master Matthau Crevon had taught him.

"For what exactly?"

"You did not follow my orders on Mount Volan. You questioned my authority *twice*."

"I did not agree with your decisions. You seal the Twelve and then take their Ether Weapons? You are doing nothing but consolidating your Power!"

"Think what you may, but I make my decisions on what is best for Gladonus as a whole, not for me. Tundra did not agree with my decision following the fallout of the second trial, but she remained loyal."

"That is because she is your loyal lover." Luvan glared at him.

Eska's eyes bulged. *He does know.*

"Do you think I never noticed how you look at her? How you call her privately to you at times? How you favor her company to ours?"

Eska's lips snarled slightly. *Control yourself.* He regained composure. "My relationship with Tundra is not the issue here. It is the mess you have made for me now that Hydro wears the necklace."

"And I am at fault for what he wears?"

"You designed the trial."

"How was I to know the necklace would turn up in the very labyrinth it was taken from?"

"Surely there are other labyrinths? You knew of its history."

Luvan fidgeted with his eyes, looking to the ground, then back to Guardian Eska. "Yes, I admit, I chose the location based on its history. You wanted a competent apprentice, and I strived to give you that! You wanted the contestants pushed past their breaking points, and I strived to give you that as well. I gave you everything you wanted when you outlined the Trials for me."

"No. What I got from your recommendations was a contestant who didn't show, a prince who didn't win a single trial, and an apprentice who needed much refinement."

"But an apprentice all the same! Eirek Mourse passed the Trials. You cannot blame me for Zain's failure to accept your position. I have told you that I do not remember giving such confidence to Eirek Mourse, but he won regardless; he is more competent now."

"Yes, *now* he is, but it is from the actions of Tundra that the boy has grown. If not for her, he would still be as incompetent as the day you picked him and he still has a long way to go."

"I—"

It was clear Luvan had no retort. "Your badge, Luvan." Eska held out his gloved hand once again.

Silence.

"Do you think it is wise for my dismissal? Now? Amongst all of this?" Luvan raised his arms.

"I think it is more unwise to stay on the current trajectory that you have put me on." Eska didn't falter when Luvan searched his eyes.

With a grunt, his conseleigh plucked the golden badge off of his chest and laid it in Eska's hand. "You will regret not having me by your side."

Once there, Eska clutched his hand and reached into a satchel with his other hand. "Here are some spells and bonds for your travels."

Luvan spat on the ground. "I do not need your money. You forget that long before I was your conseleigh I was a politician. I have plenty money of my own."

"And you were a brilliant one. I hope you give good counsel to someone else in the future."

"I was supposed to give counsel to you!" A redness began to enter into Luvan's eyes.

"Not anymore, Luvan. I am sorry."

Luvan flicked a glance at Vesel and one more at Eska. He snorted and walked away. Eska's rigid figure slumped. This was his first dismissal. Hopefully, it would be his last. Luvan had left him with no other choice. Vesel's nose nuzzled Eska's head. Warm breath tickled his ear.

Duty is such a hard master to obey. Keeping his eyes on Luvan's skulking figure, Eska grabbed Vesel underneath the chin and rubbed his nose. *It'll be alright, old friend. He'll get through this. He is strong.*

Vesel snorted.

I don't know what he will do now, but I'm sure whatever it is, he will be great at it. He has an aptitude for it. I can sense it in him. Eska turned around to look his dragon in the eyes. Only for the briefest of moments. If he stared too long into those eyes, he would see his sister, and melancholy would take hold of him once more.

Vesel snorted. Twice this time.

Eska smiled. *Let us go back home.*

Eska walked around his dragon and towards the ship's large cargo area. He walked up the ramp and Vesel did the same, although he needed to retract his wings and duck his head to fit. Sitting down, he curled his tail around him. The ship's cargo hold closed. Eska went through another door that lead to the main chamber of the ship, where the others waited.

Noticing Eska entering alone, Ethen asked, "Where is Luvan?"

"He will not be returning with us."

"Why is tat?" Ethen spat.

"We can discuss such things later. Riagan, we head to Iberene to pick up Conseleigh Iycel. I received word from her that she has finished talking with Lord Grime. From there we return to the Core."

"Yes, my Guardian."

The engine started. The ship hummed. Eska closed his eyes, but even there he could not escape the stares of those around him.

Although Tundra wanted answers from Eska when she boarded outside of Iberene, his silence told her not to press the matter, and she knew him well enough not to do so. Eska was thankful for that. He would tell them all when they reached the Core in the comfort of his chambers.

They landed on the Core a little after midnight. On instinct, Eska looked up to the stars. Veins of purple still roamed the air, but the Curse had finished. Well, he suspected, anyway. So far it seemed only Onkh and Agrost were its victims. He would need to find a way to tell Eirek later, but knowing what he knew now, he looked up to the stars. Perhaps it was his eyes deceiving him, but it was true that the stars looked less luminous than before. Many souls were lost during Pirini Lilapa. Eska bit his lip, wondering what unforeseen repercussions would come from his actions and the fate that befell Galan and wherever he had been hiding.

Eska walked to his estate. Once inside, he extended his hand. "Eirek, the briefcase." Eirek gave him the briefcase. "Go take Ethen to the apothecary and then come to my chambers. Tell Adored Amiti to look at Vesel when he is finished with Ethen."

Eirek nodded and hobbled with Ethen to the staircase and then slowly began their ascent.

In his chambers, Eska hadn't even stepped over the threshold before Tundra asked questions.

"Why didn't Luvan board?"

Eska didn't answer right away. Instead, he went over to his desk and laid all three Ether Weapons on top of it. He let his gloved hand run over the metal of all three weapons, preferring a talk with them, then the one he was about to have.

Tundra raised her voice again.

"I heard you the first time, Tundra." He turned back around, exchanging glances with all three of them before taking a deep breath. "Luvan is no longer a conseleigh."

"Edwyrd—"

"Tundra, he refused my orders while on Mount Volan. He has questioned my authority on multiple counts. His actions have been careless, and those actions have resulted in numerous lives lost. I will need to tend to these misfortunes now."

"I see..." She lowered her head.

"I stick by my Guardian," Riagan said.

Eska acknowledged his youngest conseleigh's obedience. Eska was sure that Riagan knew, with Luvan gone and Ethen injured, that he was needed to take on more responsibility.

Cronos remained silent, however. During the silence, Eirek entered the room. When the door closed behind him, Cronos asked, "What do you plan on doing with the gems?"

Eska turned to Cronos. The glow in Cronos's eyes allured him, but he figured it was due to his First Blood and the suns' convergence. Surely they would return to the normal blue and amber in the next day or so.

"Scatter them. Which brings me to my request. Riagan..."

"Yes, my Guardian?"

Eska walked towards the briefcase and unlatched the hinges. He looked at the twelve jewels. Only the beryl did not have a god encased inside. His hand hovered over all of them, but he chose the carbuncle and picked it up.

"This is for you." He handed the gem to Riagan.

"I... I do not understand."

"You are to take this and leave the Core. Go somewhere. Do not tell me where."

"My... my—"

"Edwyrd—"

"Tundra, these gems contain gods. Very angry gods. Their fury has only been multiplied by my actions. Because these jewels were bound together, they need to be unbound all together as well. If we scatter them, there is less chance of that happening."

"But, here, the Core is safe. Hown protects us. You, yourself, are here."

"Aye. But what if Hown falls? I am one man, two with Vesel, but what if someone bests me? I fear having them all in one location, so I will keep one here, in my guard. The others will scatter as you will." Eska looked deep into Riagan's orange eyes, then he thought of something. He turned back to his desk and examined the three Ether Weapons. He picked up the hammer and turned around. "You will take this with you as well."

"My Guardian? I am unfit to wield such a weapon."

"Your absence from your station here will allow you time to train. It will also help you protect the jewel. You must do so at all costs."

Riagan gave a nervous glance to the hammer at first, but after a brief second his eyes focused on the weapon and he took it from Eska's hand. "Thank you, my Guardian. I will protect both with my life."

"You will make contact with me once per month through telepathy, but you will never reveal your location to me. Is that understood?"

A hint of reluctance hung in the air before Riagan said, "It is, my Guardian."

"Good. Pack your things. Before you leave, I will give you a small vial of my blood. Perform the bonding ceremony at the end of each month when you feel my presence leaving you. Understood?"

Riagan nodded.

"Then see me when you are ready to leave." Eska turned his attention to Eirek. "Eirek, you impressed me on Volan."

Eirek smiled and nodded. "Thank you, my Guardian."

"But that is not why I called you in here."

Eirek's face contorted in confusion.

"Shortly before the incident on Mount Volan we received reports that Lady Clayse died in a horrible fire in her palace in Syf."

"What? Is Linn okay? Did it spread to Creim?"

"I cannot answer those questions for you. It is better if you find those answers for yourself."

"What are you—"

"Do you mean to send him there by himself?" Tundra asked.

"No. You will go with him since Ethen is still recovering."

"What about the boy's training?" Cronos asked.

"Postponed."

"Why?"

"I have a feeling the contestants who competed in the Trials have been targeted."

"Targeted? For what? By whom?" Cronos massaged the upper shaft of his staff.

"I do not know why, or by whom yet, but my suspicions began on Vatu Volcano with the appearance of Zakk Shiren."

Eirek tilted his head downwards.

"I believe he said something to convince Zain not to accept apprenticeship."

Eska acknowledged Eirek's longing gaze, then continued. "With the reports of Hydro on Acquava, and now Syf on Cresica, it makes me wonder if any of the other contestants have been targeted in some way."

"Acquava happened because of the necklace," Tundra said.

"But there is his disappearance before he returned home. Perhaps someone during that time came into contact with Hydro."

"So, what will you have us do while we are gone?"

"You will first investigate the incident on Syf, then travel to Epoch and check with Prince Evber. After, you will go to Myoli and find out the status of Zain Berrese and Gabrielle Ravwey."

Eirek remained silent.

"Where will you be during this time?"

Eska furrowed his brows. "I will be taking the jewels and scattering them. I will tell Ethen of the arrangements. Now, go gather your things, for we leave tomorrow."

All of them left. All except Eirek. He waited while others walked. If it were any other time, Eska would have forced him to leave the room, preferring his solace after events such as these. But he felt Eirek's devastation. It was his duty as Guardian to support him. Because of Eirek, he had been able to find an appropriate solution to the chaos on Mount Volan.

"Eirek, I am sorry about the news. I could not break it to you any other way."

"I... I know. I hope everyone is alright."

"It seems that Lynda's daughter, Linn, is alive and well.

"Did she speak of any other casualties?"

"She would not. Nor did I ask."

Eirek released a heavy exhale. Eska let silence speak for him. He thought that would let Eirek know that Eska didn't have any answers. But his apprentice continued standing around.

"Is there something else, Eirek?"

Eirek fidgeted with his thumbs. He nodded quickly. "How... how did you appear on Mount Volan like that?"

Eska chuckled. "It was my reimaje. You will learn about it in time. Your training requires it."

"How come you don't use it all the time like that?"

Eska came over to Eirek and put a hand on his shoulder. "Just because you have the Power to do something, doesn't mean that it is right to do so."

"What do you mean?" Eirek looked up at him.

"That Power, my ability to warp through space, is a Power only the Ancients ever had. Every time I do it, my strength diminishes. I have the Power of the Twelve, not Ancient Power. Every time I use it, I take a chance with my life. I am strong, Eirek, but I am no match for an Ancient. And I'm cautious about the stress I put on Vesel as well. He is as much a part of my strength as is the reimaje I wear or this glove." Eska held up his fist donned in darknether.

"How did you even get the reimaje in the first place?"

"The Twelve. From what I have learned through the memories of the other Guardians that live in this." Eska pointed to the cloth on his head. "They stole it from Gladima during the Great War, before the Core covered it from view."

"And they gave it to the Guardians?"

"They did. There is only one of it in existence and there are Twelve deities. If one would have kept it for themselves, another war would have ensued, and after what they had just witnessed with the Ancients, that was meant to be avoided. That is also how our position came to be on the Core."

Eirek turned to leave, but then stopped. He turned around and asked, "Who is the Third One?"

"What?"

"Who is he? I heard mentions of him from the Twelve. Along with Galan and Naydeia. The, well, the Twelve thought I wasn't worthy because I didn't know who they were, but you never told me about them."

So he's found out. I suppose earlier is better, considering what happened. "Eirek, I never mentioned those names to you because they are ghosts. No one has been able to track them down, and since they are nothing finite, they are nothing worth learning about."

"But, who are they?"

Eska sighed. "Galan and Naydeia are the supposed offspring from both ancients Lyoen and Bane. They married one another, and it is rumored to have created a bloodline, with not First Blood, Eirek, but with Ancient Blood."

"How does the Third One come into play?"

"The Third One is the Third Ancient; there hasn't only just been Bane and Lyoen. I believe the Third One erased his name from the history books so that people would forget about him. But, he, too, had a son, but it wasn't any human son."

"It was Desmós. Wasn't it?"

The boy is bright. That is for sure. "Yes, he created every animal you see in existence, but none will be as special to him as the first one he created, the black dragon you refer to as Desmós. In fact, he bonded with Desmós."

"But what do they have to do with Galan and Naydeia?"

"The Great War started when Desmós was slain by Zas Banegul in Bane's attempt to solve the problem of peopled becoming Denied. This is the very necklace Hydro now wears. It is said that Zas sliced off a section of the necklace from Desmós. Partially flayed it, if you will. Lyoen and Bane's tribes turned on one another and fought to exhaustion. It is rumored that the Third One sealed them away in retribution for slaying his son. And only Ancient Blood can break an Ancient's seal."

"That is why the Third One wants Galan and Naydeia dead."

"Correct. So they can have no chance of undoing his seal on Lyoen and Bane, the only two capable of stopping him if he ever regained his full strength."

"How would that happen?"

"If Desmós were to get resurrected. That necklace, Eirek, is the key to its resurrection. In order to be alive again, it must be whole again. It must be perfect, because it was the Other's most perfect creation. The section of scales Zas took from Desmós severed its bond with its master. That is why they have never been able to find one another since." Eska turned to face the windows, hand clasped behind his cape.

"How did Desmós even die in the—"

"Because, Desmós wasn't an Ancient—an Ancient can never die—he was merely the animal that had bonded with an Ancient. So, the dragon could die and when it died—"

"The Ancient nearly died with it." Eirek finished Eska's sentence, putting it all together now.

"That is correct." Eska turned back around, hands still behind his back. "And that is why it is pertinent we find Hydro. Before the wrong person does."

CHAPTER 61

RUMORS

When the vibrations first started, Aiton found himself in his room, sitting on top of his bed, the cup of Mount Klaff in his hand. Since his family's funeral, he had looked at it whenever he felt alone, which was often every night. In truth, he knew he shouldn't look at it, for it brought back memories that were better left suppressed; memories that would have been best, buried like his father or taken away like the body of his mother. *Brother...*

When the vibrations continued shaking the castle foundations, Aiton set the cup down, and crawled on all fours towards the window at his bed. The blinds were down so that he could have gotten sleep, but that was the last thing he had wanted for the past few weeks. Whenever sleep came, nightmares followed, and when the nightmares followed, only depression and loneliness remained. Aiton had just finished pulling the blinds up when he was taken underneath the stomach and carried out of the room by Korth. Down one flight of steps and then another, they went and into a hangar built within the castle walls meant to withstand even the strongest earthquakes. Elias and Darien had joined him and the other acqua guards there, while many had to fend for themselves within the castle complex.

And when the vibrations finally finished after hours, Aiton went out of the room to the stone court despite heeding from Korth, his other acqua guards, Elias and Darien. He was a lord now, after all, and he needed to examine any potential damage and fatalities that may have occurred within the castle. Korth and Kent walked alongside Aiton while he surveyed the outer area. Besides portraits on walls knocked down, and the occasional broken vase, the inside of the estate seemed to hold up remarkably well to whatever circumstance had just triggered the tremors. Aiton examined the courtyard and noticed the granite water basin had toppled over and cracked on the ground. East Wall had held up well, and so had the battlements of the West Wall for that matter, but when Aiton had finally wandered to the west side of the castle courtyard, he noticed the bethel in shambles.

"The bethel..." He muttered to himself.

The wooden bethel behind the small pond had collapsed. Wooden boards now blanketed the four pews and the blue rug that had made up the inside of the bethel. Some of the wooden foundation had found its way into the pond in front of it.

"We can rebuild it, my lord," said Kent.

"I..." Aiton looked from Kent to the ruins of the bethel. Korth's hand came to rest upon his shoulder.

"It would not be difficult to do, my lord."

"Aiton, please." He looked at both of his guards.

Kent and Korth looked at each other but would acquiesce to his demands. Although he was lord now, the title still reminded him of his father, and when reminded of his father, his brother and mother, and that awful night slowly slid in, never too far behind like a shadow.

"If you like, we can have workers get started on rebuilding it right away, Aiton," Kent said.

"Okay. Thank you."

"I will go give the command then." Kent nodded and left.

Aiton left the bethel behind and wandered back to the courtyard, this time making sure to meander through the hedge labyrinth. At its center, he stopped and took a seat on one of the marble benches around the fountain. The dolphin centerpiece had remained intact. Water continued to shoot up from the dolphin's lips into the sky, only to fall and be recycled in the pool below. It was after a moment of silence here that Korth spoke to him.

"We cannot continue to call you by your first name forever, Aiton."

Aiton slouched his shoulders and blew air upwards, trying to see if it could reach his brown hair, growing a little too long for his taste. "I know. Darien told me the same thing."

"And you should listen to Darien as much as you can while you and he search for an advisor to fill Len's role."

Darien had explained to him that a title brought with it power. If none of his soldiers or servants called him by his title, it weakened his authority. That is something a new lord could not have happen. Aiton never fought back against Darien's insistence on calling him by his title, but he knew he could persuade Korth. Korth liked him more than just for duty's sake. That much Aiton could tell.

"What if you only call me *my lord* around others?" Aiton looked towards Korth.

"That would be acceptable, Aiton." Korth brought Aiton closer and rubbed his hand, letting out a little laugh in the process.

Aiton laughed as well. He gazed at the dolphin statue in front of him. He tapped his knees, trying to determine the best way to ask the question. Thinking of no nonchalant way of asking, he turned to Korth. "Do you know much about my sister?"

Korth shifted. "Your sister?"

"Anya."

"Oh." Korth inhaled deeply. "For her age, she was beautiful. Very much like her mother."

"Tell me about her. Please?" Aiton folded his hands on his lap, looking up to his trainer.

"Well, I had the pleasure of working a little with your sister in combat. She was a swan on water. Her real forte, though, was her ability to use Power. That was the word around the castle. I saw her cast Power during her sessions with Professor Haruko, but I am not one to tell you how complex or extraordinary it was. You would need to ask the professor that for he specialized in that section of training with her."

"Will I ever be as gifted as her or my brother?"

"They say third is the best, don't they?" Korth nudged Aiton with his elbow.

"That's second," Aiton corrected.

"Hmmm, then third is the one with the treasure chest. Perhaps you'll end up owning or finding something greater than both of them." A few moments of silence passed. "Shall we go back inside?"

Aiton sighed. "Okay."

They had just only exited the labyrinth when Professor Haruko came scurrying from the barracks of East Wall. It wasn't only him, however; it was Darien, as well as Elias.

"Have you seen it? Have you seen it?"

The guards stepped in front of Aiton. "Seen what?" they both asked simultaneously.

Haruko and the others stopped a body's length away from them, bent over and panting. "The moon. The moon." He pointed upwards, but then withdrew his finger. "You cannot see it from inside the castle. We must go outside. Follow me."

Aiton did the best he could to keep up with the long strides of the adults in front of him, but every so often he found himself needing to enter a slight jog in order to keep on their heels. The guards on the parapets, Aiton noticed, now all turned in a singular direction towards the west. He wanted to see too, but the West Wall wouldn't afford him that privilege.

Once outside the complex, they hustled around the compound until they cleared the castle's visage. It was then Aiton saw what Haruko must have wanted them to see. A large white moon sat in the air, closer than usual. So close, in fact, that it seemed the wisps of clouds lingering in the sky from the sun's convergence could touch it. So close that it almost seemed like a white stone along its ebony counterpart on a palette of purple.

"When did you first see this, Ignis?" Darien turned to Professor Haruko.

"It began happening when the vibrations happened. I left Symeria a few nights ago. Last night I spent in Sepul to make it here, now. This happened right before I made it to Alar."

"My lord." Darien turned to him now. "You may want to prepare to give a statement. Ignis and I can write it, but you must be the one to deliver it. It's your duty now."

"But Acquava had nothing to do with this."

"No, it did not. Perhaps it is something dealing with the Curse. If that is the case, perhaps the Guardian of the Core will lend us more information, but I mention the statement to you just in case if civilians start wondering. You need to act confident and competent now. The people will need you."

Aiton gulped. He nodded. He knew he could deliver the speech, but could he follow and fulfill what he outlined? Words were water. Actions were ice. Could he prove to be the latter? With the suns overhead and the suppressive heat still clutching the air even at night, Aiton sometimes doubted how solid he could make his actions.

"When you traveled through Alar, did you see many casualties, Professor Haruko?" Aiton asked, trying to sound more like a lord in front of Darien.

"I admit that I wasn't looking, my lord. The moon distracted me as has other news."

"Other news?" Darien asked this time, a hand under his elbow and the other hand under his chin.

"From Symeria." He nodded to Darien and then turned to face Aiton. "I went there to peruse the libraries at *Finesse* as you know, but while—"

"And did you find anything to help my brother?" Aiton stepped forward, chin up.

"Your brother's situation is interesting. While I found texts on the necklace that he now wears, none of those texts mention black eyes." He paused for a little while and when it was clear that Aiton yearned for more knowledge, he continued. "As you are well aware, my lord, our eyes are the gateway to our soul. That is why we do not cry here on Acquava. If Hydro's eyes are truly black than I believe that this issue is deeper than just a virus or disease. I... I feel as though it may be a sycophant controlling or leading Hydro to do things..."

"Sycophant?"

"Ah, yes, parasite if you will. It has taken over his body, or is in the process of taking over his body."

Aiton's eyes bulged. "What can we do?"

"Now, nothing. But perhaps if we can find him again Elias could make a drought to rid his body of the syco... of the parasite. Elias?"

"The type of problem you are talking about, Ignis, is very severe. I will check my texts, and if I cannot find something, I will contact the Academy in Qotia."

"What if this is one of those rare cases of possession? I heard about one in Hart Isles growing up as a kid."

"The case you mention, Korth, happened thirty or more years ago. The clergy dealt with that. We can reach out to them, too, I suppose, but the fact still remains that we need Hydro here in front of us if we are to cure him." Elias leaned on his staff.

Aiton looked to the ground and clenched his fists. *Brother...* He slunk away from the group.

"Let him be... Was there something else you wanted to mention, Ignis?"

"Yes, while in Symeria I heard rumors of a wedding."

"A wedding. Between who?"

Aiton didn't care enough to hear the rest of the conversation. Weddings were happy, and enough things had happened in the past few weeks that it seemed happiness had abandoned him. Whoever was getting married didn't matter. The only thing that mattered to Aiton was seeing his brother again and somehow getting him to come back to the castle so that he could be saved. But then a thought crossed his mind. What if he couldn't be saved? What if they tried potions or these clergymen and nothing worked? Then would Hydro die? Would Aiton have to execute his own brother? Even if they did work, would the outcome be the same for the sins Hydro committed against his family, whether he was aware of his actions or not? The predicament made Aiton's head hurt enough that he sat down, cross-legged, on the grass outside the castle. He put his arms behind him, using them as pillars to look towards the sky.

Even though the suns had converged, Aiton didn't know what that meant besides the name *Pirini Lilapa.* Even though the moon had descended upon Onkh, Aiton didn't know why it happened or the repercussions that would come with. And even though Haruko had returned and brought news of his brother's plight, Aiton didn't know what could be done about the situation. It seemed that, even though Aiton was a lord, he still felt clueless and powerless and hopeless—lost now, like his brother.

CHAPTER 62

RUINS

S ilent.

The ride had been silent. His newfound knowledge about a third Ancient left him speechless. Nervousness aided disbelief in silencing him, as well.
Ever since Eirek had found out that Syf had been attacked and that Lady Clayse,
and maybe others had been killed, Eirek had been as tense as Eska had seemed
in the weeks before Pirini Lilapa.

Tundra landed the ship deep within the Sages' Valley in the nation of Epoch
under Cronos's instruction. Cronos must have been in a hurry to leave, for
when he left, the Sage spared but a second's glance at Eirek and exchanged
not a word of goodbyes before walking out to the large alcove they had landed
on. The shimmer in his amber eye had dulled. Cronos crossed the alcove to a
forest path with a stone bridge that accommodated for the river cutting through
before Eirek lost sight of the old man. The path, Eirek observed, led to a large
golden house that Eirek could barely see through the foliage.

A few hours later, Eirek and Tundra arrived in Syf. Eirek wasted no time
in stepping off the ship and into the heat. The purple aurora that had once
decorated the skies had faded into its usual blue. Like worms in the rain, his
stomach crawled. Even though he hadn't visited for a while, nor had he ever
lived there, he knew something was wrong. Ash lingered like dust in the air,
choking his nostrils and squeezing his lungs. Nerves ostracized Eirek from
any feeling of normality. He didn't know what awaited him at the top of the
multi-level capital. All he knew was that he needed to know who caused this
and who was affected. Syf had practically been his second home, and now it
had come to this. Ruins.

Standing outside of Syf's city gates, Eirek exhaled. He looked back, past Tundra, eastward to where Creim was. *Did Creim get attacked? Are the Mourses safe?*

"Are you ready, Apprentice Mourse?"

Eirek turned back to the city. He would focus on his home later. "Yes."

The first section of town—a squalid section with brothels, bums, and beggars—hardly acknowledged their presence. Instead, the inhabitants rummaged through the broken and beaten houses of the slums. Tears ran wells on the dusty and dirty faces of the poor. Eirek couldn't tell if soot or ash covered their clothes.

Eirek walked over to an older man clothed in dirt. Eyes glazed over, he lay oblivious to his surroundings. "What happened here?"

"It came from the sky." He pointed a dirty finger eastward.

"We will not get many answers until we reach the top."

"Let's go."

He continued uphill. The second section echoed the first. Broken windows, houses ravaged with burn marks, and the smell of decay ruled over this level in tyranny as well. He figured it had been present in the former section, but the filth of the place had made it seem organic. Even Syf's most iconic statue, located in the second section, known as the Three Maidens—three separate statues shaped to represent maidens in the colors of copper, silver, and gold—was damaged. Only the gold maiden still stood free of black scars.

"What do you think happened?" Eirek asked.

"A firestorm of some sort, it looks like. It would make sense considering the man's story from the squalid section." Tundra crouched and looked over the two of the Three Maidens toppled in the water fountain.

"What could cause something like that?"

"The Curse of Pirini Lilapa."

She stood up and turned back to Eirek. The usual vitality had returned to her eyes. "I admit it is interesting how some of the town remains unscathed."

"Luck, I suppose."

Tundra surveyed the ruins of the second section. "Mhm, perhaps. Let us continue."

A part of him didn't want to believe that the third section was in ruins as well. He figured if some parts went unscathed, maybe the third section had. Surely, at least, his uncle's place had survived the firestorm? As he attempted to deviate from the course, Tundra put a hand on his shoulder and steered him straight. "Remember why we are here, Apprentice Mourse."

"Yes, Conseleigh Iycel." He gave a furtive glance at the broken section to his left. *He has to be safe. He has to be.* With few thoughts, he continued forward.

One more section and they arrived at a gate and ruins of a palace. Some of the white walls were now caved in certain places. Most of the white had been blackened with soot, as if the whole place had been engulfed in fire. Workers and soldiers busied themselves cleaning the rubble of the aftermath.

A man with a greatwood shield and leather padding stopped them at the gate. "You—" He noticed the *C* on Tundra's chest.

"We are here to see the Clayses," Tundra said.

"Yes, of course. I'll notify them that you're here. Your names?"

"Tundra Iycel."

"Eirek Mourse."

The gates opened, and Eirek and Tundra ascended to the palace courtyard. He found it strange that even with his fancier clothes and title of apprentice, people didn't recognize him. Then Eirek remembered what Lady Aprah had told him about needing to lead your people by example. *Perhaps that is what I am missing.* He grinned a little. *She is a wise leader.*

In a matter of minutes, he saw Linn rushing from the palace courtyard. Trees that had once guided him to the inside chambers were either cut at the stem or burned. A few of the courtyard pillars had crumbled into pieces. Compared to the rest of the palace, though, the courtyard seemed fairly intact. Her father strode out behind her with a calmer gait, but the same redness to his cheeks as Linn.

Linn hugged Eirek immediately. Wetness dammed her eyes.

Eirek was about to speak when Tundra spoke before him. "I am sorry for your loss."

Linn nodded. Lord Clayse had joined the group by this point.

"What happened here?" Eirek asked. "Did anyone else die?"

"Eirek... I..." Linn looked to her father and then back to Eirek. She breathed and tightened her grip on Eirek's arms. She stared into his eyes with her own eyes of sapphire. "Angal is dead."

Eirek shook his head. "What?"

"Your uncle died in the same assault that killed my wife," Lord Clayse said.

Eirek collapsed. His hands went straight to his face. *Angal...* Shock overwhelmed him enough to dam the tears, but it only worked for a few minutes. When the shaking came from the realization that Angal would never be in his life again, the tears came as well. And they came in floods and deluges that moistened the burned grass below. *How did it happen? Why was he killed? No. No. No. He can't be dead. Linn must be lying.*

Eirek wiped his forearm across his eyes. "Where is he?" He sniffled.

Eirek couldn't stand yet. When hands fell on his shoulders, he twisted his head. Once again, he got lost in the agony of Linn's eyes.

"He isn't here."

"What do you mean he isn't here?"

"The... the..." Linn looked at her father. "This thing that attacked Syf took his body when it killed him."

"What do you mean thing?" Tundra asked.

"I... I do not know how to explain it. It..." Linn looked to the ground and then up again. "It was plated in all gold. It held eyes like lava behind its visor and it had the most magnificent wings I have ever seen and of the warmest colors. It looked like an angel, but it only brought death."

Eirek and Tundra looked at one another and then back to Linn.

"Angal saved us. Well," Linn looked to her father. "Most of us."

"What do you mean?" Eirek asked. "What did my uncle do?"

"This... this creature brought with it flames and it caused the damage you see around you. But Angal, Eirek, Angal raised a watery defense around us that rippled with jolts of electricity through it. I never knew he could cast Power. Never had he ever cast Power when telling us stories in the castle."

"I..." *Angal can cast Power?* Eirek bit his lip. "Go on."

"The beast, whatever it was, tried again and again to get to us, but it could never break through the shield. Instead, it forced us to listen to the wails of our fellow butlers and maids and soldiers getting impaled. Angal knew that he needed to go on the offensive to save those in the castle, so before he released the spell, he asked others in helping him create a new one. It was a fake shield of Power, similar to his own, but much weaker, but it would give him a chance to regain energy and to think of a plan to combat the threat. He said that he also needed to contact someone..."

"Who?" Tundra cut in.

"The name escapes me. I'm sorry. She came briefly to collect his body, but I told her there was nothing for her to collect," Lord Clayse said. "But she showed us her ring, and it was identical to the ring that Angal had. That is the only thing we could give her."

The wife Angal would never speak of. Eirek turned to Linn.

"It escapes me as well. I am... I am sorry." Linn looked down and brushed the wrinkles out of her blouse and skirt of celadon and brown. "But... before he died, Angal did leave you this." Linn averted his gaze and extended her hand.

Eirek reached out for the note. "What is it?"

"He scribbled something. I could not make any sense of it."

Eirek turned over the piece of parchment and saw a scribble of three letters—*A V F*. Eirek nearly dropped the note when he saw it. *The dream.* The eidetic dream came to him after his first kill. *Perhaps it had been a premonition.*

"Do you know what it means?"

"I... I have to go."

Eirek turned and sprinted down the hill. He needed to be alone. Out past the gates, Eirek turned right on the city's third section. He ran and ran, determined to find his uncle's home. And he found it. After his burst of energy died, he stood before an estate that had once belonged to his uncle, but now was owned by ash and dust and detritus. The only way Eirek had identified the house was by the granite hawks at the entrance that still remained intact. Remnants from old books were strewn about, tables broken or turned over. The pillars that had held up the second level had all but crumbled—only one remained intact. Eirek walked through it all, falling down multiple times in the dilapidated dwelling.

He yelled then, long and hard. He screamed to the skies and pounded his hands onto the wooden boards he had collapsed upon. Tears came to him as easily as the dirt and the dust that overwhelmed his nose, causing him to sneeze. The snot and the sobs mixed together to form a larger mess of regret and heartache. Through the tears, he took another glance at the note. *A V F. What am I supposed to glean from that?* He used the sleeves of his shirt to dry his eyes and wipe the snot from his nose.

Boards cracked behind him.

"Are you alright?"

"I..." Hearing Linn's voice, Eirek sighed. "I'm not sure. I just..." He breathed. "Can I tell you the worst of it all?"

"What is it?"

As she sat beside him, he continued looking blankly outward. "I never got to say goodbye."

"Eirek, you can't—"

"No. I... I was writing a letter to him during my training. But, I never sent it. I..." Water welled in his eyes. "What was I thinking?"

"Eirek, how were you supposed to know?" Linn rubbed his back.

"I just wish there was more time."

Linn took her hand off his back and put it on her knees. "I know what you mean."

Eyes wide, Eirek looked out from the ruins around him. *She lost her mom. Stop being so selfish, Eirek. Angal wouldn't want that.* Well, that he wasn't sure of. Angal had been selfish in his decision to choose his career over fostering Eirek, but the Mourses wouldn't want that. He knew that with certainty.

"Linn, I'm sorry."

"I... I know how tough it is to lose someone..." Linn sniffled. "My mother..."

Eirek felt her brush up against him. Her arm wrapped around his waist. She leaned her head onto his shoulder.

"It was my mother and Ezra Evengale who joined forces to make the shield while Angal recuperated. It worked for a little while. I remember it stalking about the courtyard, waiting for the defenses to fail... Before the spell broke, Angal tried to find an Ether Weapon. An Ether Weapon, Eirek. Why? A weapon such as that hasn't been in Cresica's possession since Syf ruled. What *was* that creature?"

Eirek held onto silence. *An Ether Weapon? My Ether Weapon? Would Angal have still been alive if he hadn't given me this?* His right hand moved up and down the sheath. *Did Angal give it to me for protection?* Linn's hand stopped his. He looked at her.

"It was then that the spell broke and my mother and Ezra Evengale went up in flames. To hear the noise she made..." Linn pulled his hand from the weapon and rested it on her lap. She sighed. "I... I am unsure anyone should ever hear that noise. Already weakened from earlier, Angal didn't last long without a proper weapon to fight..." Linn paused, struggling for the right word until she properly decided on *it*. "As *it* skewered his body, Angal looked at me and mouthed his apologies. I..." Linn leaned over, hugged Eirek, and cried into his chest. Through sobs she said, "I have seen things that no person should see. I have heard things no person should hear. I feel things now, that no one should feel so young. I..." She readjusted her posture to stare Eirek directly in his eyes. "Eirek, it took your uncle's body away when it killed him. Why would it do that? There are so many things that don't make sense."

Again, Eirek sat in silence. He held no words for Linn. There was no advice he could give to comfort her. Not now. Not that he knew. All he could do was lend an ear while she spoke.

Linn sniffled. "And now... now I am twenty-five... I... I am Lady of Cresica... Everyone wants me to raise our banners... declare war... but war on *what*? On *whom*?" Linn threw her arms into the air. She turned to Eirek and hugged him. The embrace that lasted only minutes felt like hours.

She was brave to speak. Pain and shock still denied him that ability. Ruminating on her words, though, he found similarities. He, too, struggled for attention and acceptance in his new role as apprentice. Unlike her, however, Tundra had been there to help mold him with her advice and suggestions. So had Lady Aprah. And even Cronos, in his own way. But Linn didn't have any of those people. Here, in this moment, all she had was him. And he would do his best.

He turned to Linn and massaged her hands with his thumbs. He searched her eyes. "I don't know what you should do. But, whatever it is, work alongside the people you represent... whatever the course."

Linn pulled away from his eyes. When she did look at him again, she raised her eyebrows. "Even if that is war?"

Eirek wanted so desperately to say no, but is that would Lady Aprah would have said? "Yes," he said.

"But..." Linn stopped her thought. "You've grown, Eirek. You have. I'm impressed."

Eirek forced a smile. They sat there in silence, looking at one another. Longing entered him. And she knew it as well. She must have, for she leaned into him, lips pursed. Eirek pulled away and stood up. *I can't get attached. Not now. We both just lost someone. It wouldn't be right.*

"Eirek, I'm sorry."

"It's not you. It's just..." He needed to change the subject. Pacing over the ruins, he asked. "Why did you come here? Was it to tell me how Angal died?"

"No..." She stood up as well.

"Then why?"

"I... I remembered the name of the woman who came for Angal days ago... She... she didn't have a last name... or not one that she would give me."

"Who was it?" Eirek stiffened and looked at Linn.

"Her name was Naydeia."

CHAPTER 63

SCATTERED

E ska breathed in what little air lingered in the floating isle cavern upon the skies of Agrost, upon mist and clouds that could never be cleared away. His soles clapped against the aventurine floors as he walked a brisk pace, carrying ten jewels by his side. Past the jade pillars and the narrow hallway with lighted blue moss was the only woman he wished to talk to after Pirini Lilapa—Zeph, wife to Ancient Bane, mother of Naydeia, sister to Anemie.

The narrow path that Eska had traveled only a handful of times opened up to a cavernous hole with five spinning blue walls. She stood in its center, but her back wasn't turned to him this time. This time she faced him as if not surprised by his presence.

The first time Eska had been summoned he had asked, "How does a place like this exist?"

She had replied, "There used to be one on every planet. There still may be. They were made by the Smiths themselves so they could carry Power's word across the planets to anger the Ancients that banished them from Gladima."

Now she looked towards the briefcase he carried and then into his eyes. "So, you come."

"You should know I would."

"No... I never know... I just have a feeling... Fate is never set in stone, merely molded in clay."

"I do not believe you. You knew my necklace would help me with this Curse, didn't you? How did you know?"

"I just assumed you would need my help once more, Edwyrd. Ever since the Burning and the Branding of the first Pirini Lilapa, each one has gotten worse. The last one was Deimos, and it helped you greatly there."

"And this one I fought against the Twelve. Against my vows." Eska exhaled deeply.

"Not only the Twelve suffered. Galan died as well."

He flicked his eyes to her ever-knowing gaze. He bit his lower lip, curiosity gnawing at him to ask. He obliged. "You told me this is how my fate would start." Using his gloved hand, he pulled the necklace from underneath his black, darknether jerkin.

"I did say that."

Eska lowered his chin. He contemplated to himself whether he should ask a question that had been nagging him ever since he met with her last. When curiosity overran him, he asked, "You said my name is fit for fate. What fate am I fit for?"

"I believe the prophecy is being fulfilled."

Eska stiffened. *How is that possible?* Eska turned away from the blue, all-knowing eyes that made even him tremble.

"You do not see how it is possible?"

"No..." Eska turned around to face her.

Zeph recited the prophecy:

> *Chosen will be blood from all five domains.*
> *Hope they will bring through chaos, anger, and pain.*
> *Twelve will lose favor, four will regain form.*
> *Bringing with them more death than the Great War.*

The words prickled Eska's skin. He hadn't heard it spoken for so long, and when she spoke it, she added a coldness to it, a foreboding about it that he wished she didn't.

"Like I was taught, I only invited residents of three domains... not five... I... I—"

"Did not want to be the one to set the cogs of fate in motion? Funny how fate works." She paused, then stepped towards him, walking on the air around him. "Even the most conscious of choices play into its hand."

"But... that would mean blood of Gladima and Pyre were chosen." Eska strummed the patch of stubble on his chin.

"And they were, Edwyrd, they were."

"But... who?"

"Ask yourself that. You will find the answers."

Eska thought back to everything. To the process of selecting contestants. There were no applicants from Gladima, of course, but he looked at the merits of the others and remembered choosing Peter Koluma over a lady from Pyre to avoid any chance of a prophecy being fulfilled. What a mistake that had been. Peter hadn't even shown. Zain, Zakk, and Gabrielle were from the domain of Myoli. Cadmar and Prince Paen were from the domain of Onkh. Eirek, Peter and Prince Evber from the domain of Agrost.

He thought back to each contestant during the Trials. He stopped on Eirek, the man who had an Ether Weapon; Eska was sure he possessed one when he examined each contestant's weapon before the weapons tournament that was the third trial. *Is that why Luvan and Tundra had trouble tracing him after the Blood Bonding ceremony?* His eyes widened.

"You are starting to see now?"

"Eirek... Eirek Mourse... is... is from Gladima?"

"If what I have learned about him is true, it makes him a descendant of Galan and Naydeia."

"How do you know?"

"The wind talks, Edwyrd. And it talks to me about many things."

"But... his name?"

"Mourse isn't his true last name. You know this. You should finally accept it."

Eska bit his lip. *Did the Twelve know? Could it have possibly led to their disagreement?* Eska set down the briefcase and tied it around his head once more. "What of Pyre?"

"Look for the clues. You should already know..."

Eska didn't, though. There weren't any that he observed. He opened the briefcase and opened them, hoping the jewels would speak to him. They didn't.

"You understand why then it is important to keep Eirek alive?"

"You say it as if it is only his blood that matters. Naydeia is still alive. You are still alive."

"My blood does not matter in returning to Gladima. Only the blood of an Ancient's descendant matters, for it was their fight that sealed their home. There may be other reasons for you, but none matter more than what his blood means."

"I will not forget."

"It is best you don't. Now that Galan is dead, Naydeia is being hunted. They have been hunted since the Great War concluded. I am unsure how Galan was able to be found, but it brings the Third One closer to his goal."

"Will Eirek be targeted as well?"

"The Third One may already know, and is waiting."

"Waiting for what?"

"Chaos, anger and pain, if you believe the prophecy."

"It says hope will be brought."

"Hope is fickle. It is a matter of perspective."

"But why now?"

"The necklace's resurgence. It is what causes my daughter to seek Zas now."

"How do you know about the necklace? You know where she is? She has been in contact with you?"

"She has only mentioned Myoli to me. She first contacted me shortly after she found out about the necklace."

Hydro. Eska got lost in his reverie. It was clear to him now where he had gone while in Chaon. Whom he'd seen. *How did he manage to find her when others couldn't? Is that why he returns to Myoli now?* Then he thought about something else. Was he being targeted? Even though Hydro wasn't linked to any threats against him being guardian, it didn't mean there wasn't any. *It will be interesting to hear Tundra and Eirek's findings.*

"You say she first contacted you... There has been another time?"

"Yes. Very recently, a few days ago. She told me the Third One has Galan's body. You know what that means, don't you?"

Eska furrowed his brows. His skin prickled. "I do."

"If the Third One obtains her, as well, he can reopen Gladima. And if Gladima is reopened, Desmós may return, and with the dragon, the Third One to his former glory. She will be even harder to find now."

Hydro or Naydeia, it would be a contest to find either of them now. If Hydro was found, the necklace could be destroyed. If Naydeia was found, she could be kept under better protection.

"If you hear from her again, will you tell her that I am looking for her? She can stay on the Core."

"If she reaches out to me, I will tell her." Zeph nodded towards the briefcase. "Do you know which one is hers?"

Eska shook his head. "I cannot say." Eska crouched down and opened the briefcase. He scanned over the jewels; there were ten left, but only nine contained deities. He plucked the beryl from its hollowed cushion and stood up. "This is for you."

"You are entrusting me with one of the jewels?"

"I am. It is as safe here as the other places we discussed before my arrival. No one but me and my conseleigh know of this place."

Eska felt a slight guilt about giving her a hollow shell. Although he trusted her, he still knew to be wary of her Power as being with First Blood, and one who had been married to an Ancient. If anyone could know of a way to release the Twelve individually, it would be her: the only other person who knew of wind's true name. The real reason he left one with her, though, is he knew that she would make a formidable guard to anyone who may try to seek out the jewels should their locations become known.

"Scatter the rest of these then to the places I suggested."

"I will use the portals and the wind."

"Excellent."

"They will go their separate paths, just as we will go after we are finished here."

"I will not see you again?"

"Not in this lifetime, Edwyrd."

"Are you certain?"

"I am never certain, Edwyrd. But you will be busy training a young apprentice soon, will you not?"

Eska hung his head. "Yes, I will be."

He closed his eyes for a moment, then opened them. The jewels hovered in midair. With a push of fingers, each jewel shot out like an exploding star to four of the five portals on the wall, denying the center one which led to the Central Core. The walls spun faster now, and the jewels sunk into them. As they did so, he turned around and walked out of the cave, past the narrowed hallway with lighted blue moss, and across the aventurine floors, anxious to see where this new trajectory of fate may lead.

CHAPTER 64

A SPECIAL SPOT

"**Y**ou said *Naydeia?*"

"Yes. Do you know her?"

"I'm sorry. I need to leave."

"Eirek, what's happening?"

"I... I wish I knew too. Can we... can we not talk about this?" Eirek stood.

Linn stood to match him. "Sure. Let's get back."

At the palace, Tundra still stood outside talking to Linn's father and Linn's receiver and advisor. "Apprentice Mourse, are you ready to leave?"

"You will not stay for my mother's funeral?" Linn asked.

"Castle Thoth calls us elsewhere."

"Yes... no... I mean..."

Tundra arched her eyebrows.

"Can we go to Amon Forest?... There.... there is a spot I need to see."

"How long will it be? It is already nearing dinner."

"A few hours. Tell the Evbers we will meet with them tomorrow. We can stay at... at my parents' house." It felt odd saying that now that his only true family was gone.

"Okay..." Tundra smiled.

"Thank you." Eirek turned to Linn. "Take care."

"Bye, Eirek, Conseleigh Iycel." Linn nodded her head.

Eirek and Tundra left Syf. In request of this new destination, Tundra advised Eirek to sit up in the cockpit. She launched the ship in the air and they were off. During the eastward journey to Creim, when all was silent besides the hum of the engines fueled by the anitron in the cockpit container, Tundra said, "It is never easy losing someone, Apprentice Mourse. I am sorry about your uncle."

"Why did it have to happen? Why here?"

Eirek noticed Tundra's glance, but then she pivoted her gaze ahead again. "Death is only natural. All must die eventually."

"But not like this!"

"No, not like this. You are right."

Eirek rode the rest of the way in silence. Once at the forest, Eirek excused himself, telling Tundra to stay in the ship. If she had had a retort, Eirek couldn't hear it, for he was out of the cockpit area before she even opened her mouth.

At the skirts of the forest, Eirek took a deep breath before entering. After a few strides, he remembered his whereabouts and the path he always took in the forest. It had been months since he last visited his spot, but he knew he needed to. It was one of the few places he could think clearly.

In a half hour, he found his spot—still the same old clearing he had left it. The waterfall that came out from the mouth of the Spera Mountains soothed his senses. The mountain didn't seem quite so large now that he had climbed Mount Volan. Now that he had time to think, he did.

Naydeia. Her name was Naydeia. The woman that Angal would never reveal to him, the woman whom he left to live with Eirek, the woman whom Angal had loved. *Galan... Angal...* Eirek saw the switch in the letters. *Is that why he talked in riddles? Even his name was one. Were those real stores that he lived through that he told?* What did that make Eirek now?

Eirek's mind spun so fast he lurched into the middle of the hollowed-out stump next to him. Slowly, his senses returned to him. Then, he thought back about his experience with those of First Blood. Cronos had seemed to recognize him right from the start. The Twelve did too. Was Angal more than just an uncle? Was he even an uncle? Who else knew of his heritage? Actually knew?

Eirek took out the note and stared at it. *A V F.* "A V F," Eirek said it out loud. He looked to the sky and asked it, "What are you trying to tell me, Angal?"

Maybe Naydeia knows. Surely she would. But how to find her? *Is this fiery thing after her too? Is it after me? What is it?*

Frustrated, he threw a stone in the little lake that flowed from the waterfall.

"I take that as a sign that you are ready to leave, Apprentice Mourse?"

Eirek spun around. "How did you—"

"It has been more than a few hours. I thought you may have gotten lost. So, I traced your presence; you forget we are bonded now. Although you were rather difficult to find."

"I..." Eirek let his thought trail off and he turned back to the still-distorted lake.

"Darkness is falling upon this place. How much longer will you want to stay?"

"We can leave. I... I won't figure out much more."

Tundra waited for Eirek to join her near the edge of the clearing. Once he did she said, "Do not be so sour."

I just lost my uncle. Why is she—

"You know, Apprentice Mourse, I lost my husband before joining Edwyrd's conseleigh. He was killed during a mammoth hunt. A mammoth had hidden under one of the Dunes of White in Sereya. My husband's hunting party came across it. They had no idea a snowstorm had just blown through, and thus the mammoths had taken cover. Upon being awakened, they were startled and my husband was trampled to death. My... *heart* has never been the same since then. His death left me with all the duties of Sereya... I performed them for five years and every month I would turn down suitors for me, preferring to focus on my duty. Because of it, I was able to grow more as a person and eventually ice the pain." They made it to the edge of the forest. "Where do your parents live?"

"Close. We can continue walking. I want to finish hearing your story."

"Very well, we can walk. When I had accomplished enough, I learned that it was the combination of time passing and the rigorous schedule of my duties and affairs that allowed me to cope with my husband's death. It allowed me to conceal my hurt and pain behind a wall of ice, and even though I learned not to cry, I couldn't bear seeing the Dunes of White, or living in the place that my husband and I had lived while we were together. That is what ultimately led to my decision of resigning my position and seeking employment under Guardian Eska."

Eirek noted the crude metal fencing that eventually guided them back to his home. "Why did you tell me all of that?"

"I was..." Tundra struggled for a word. "Insensitive earlier. I have never been good with comfort and support. But I wanted you to know, Apprentice Mourse, that what you feel right now, the loss for your uncle, it will get better. The training ahead of you will be arduous and long and soon your busyness will help you forget, as mine did. And although we cannot change the past, we can certainly choose to not let it affect our future."

Eirek spotted the Mourses' burgundy house. The broken screen door still had yet to be fixed. "This is it." Eirek pointed.

Tundra stepped in front of him. "Do you understand me?"

Eirek looked into Tundra's eyes. They were the normal blue again, but they didn't chill him like usual. There was an openness to them now. He nodded. "Thank you."

"You are welcome. Sheryin and Gerald are the names of your parents, correct?"

Eirek was surprised she remembered, but he supposed it was her duty to take an interest in him, now that he was Eska's apprentice. "Correct. I have a brother too, though. His name is Jahn."

"Yes. Of course. After you." Tundra ushered Eirek forward.

Eirek walked up the porch steps. The creaks failed at silencing the ruckus inside. There were arguments and screaming. A plate shattered.

"Do you hear that?"

Tundra nodded.

He gave a nervous glance to Tundra and, hand on his hilt, burst through the screen door. As fast as he could, he made it through the hallways and into the kitchen. Jahn's mother was on the floor sobbing, broken ceramic plates near her. Jerald sat at the head of the table, looking at Jahn, who was back by a little desk in the corner, arms crossed.

"Is everything—" Eirek looked around and noticed no intruder. It was them. Just them. "What happened here?"

"Eirek? What, what are you doing here?" Sheryin got to her feet. "You... I thought you had training." Sheryin sniffled and wiped the tears from her face. Her eyes were red.

He looked to Jerald and then Jahn, almost forgetting that he had yet to answer the question. "I, I am, but during part of it I was notified of the attack on Syf. I, I wanted to make sure all of you were okay. What happened here?"

"Nothing. I was just clumsy." Sheryin tidied her hands on her apron.

"Ma, they need to know."

Sheryin turned around and glared at Jahn.

Tundra stepped beside Eirek, arms crossed. "Need to know what?"

"It is a family matter."

"And Eirek's family," Jahn argued.

"Jahn, what is going on?" Eirek noticed Jerald's gaze distant on the table in front of him, Sheryin ignored the rest of the family. Only Jahn looked at him.

With an inflated chest, he showed the upper body strength he received from working in the forge with his father all his life. He smiled and pointed at himself. "I'm going to be a solider, Eirek. Cresica has called their banners."

CHAPTER 65

CASTLE THOTH

T he smell of lilies, scarlet pimpernels, fire pinks, liverworts, and blue-eyed grass invaded Cain's nostrils as he flipped through an anthology of short stories called *The Bard's Tales*. He sat in the upper garden of Castle Thoth, thoughts floating through his mind like the scents in the air. Freyr and Lugh felt good on his skin, but the light did give off a glare from his glasses that made reading more difficult than usual. But he wouldn't read inside, not on a day such as this.

The story he had just read titled *The Price of* Bravery told of different men who acted with valor, something he wished he would have done once. It spoke of men hailed as heroes, casted as cowards, or those who dealt with death. Other stories had told fantastical things like the origins of the system. Life in other systems. And even talks of uprising. While the writer remained anonymous, Cain could certainly feel the man had an imagination on him that could match the greatest thinkers of this very castle. In fact, one of the stories had even detailed the Pavos Brothers, but he skipped that tale, not wanting to be reminded of the horrors that took place inside the Zas Labyrinth.

He flipped another page, landing on the new names of a couple and their story, Flint and his wife Lule. The man had red hair and was tall. The picture in the book showed a necklace but not in distinguishable detail. The man held a lance of some sort in one hand and stood on a rock, raising it up to a sky full of orange. The story told of the First King of Pyre who challenged the creatures who threatened to destroy his village. The tale ended tragically with his death and the destruction of the village, but his wife and her unborn baby being saved provided some redeeming grace. The thing that intrigued Cain most about the story, however, was the name of the village—Vatu. He wondered if it had any connection to the volcano.

"Prince Evber."

Cain tilted his head up, leaving the rest of his reading for a servant of a portly build with freckles and balding hair. "Yes?"

"Conseleigh Iycel and Apprentice Mourse have just landed outside the castle walls. Finnian is retrieving them now."

"Good." Cain closed the book and set it on the wooden bench.

Cain stood and brushed the wrinkles free from his apple-green vest that overlay a brown, long-sleeved shirt. He fidgeted with the emerald owl-cut ring on his left hand and walked into the upper portion of the castle. The stonewalls were heavy and fortified; his family had inhabited these walls for over 600 years, and the number of portraits that hung to them spoke true of that.

Cain descended the stairs that hugged the leftmost wall. At the bottom, he went straight down a few corridors meant to be the soldiers' and servants' barracks and eventually out double doors of heavy ironwood. Outside, an open area of trimmed grass bordered a stone walkway that led to a large granite carving of an owl. Past the owl lay a drawbridge that acted as the only way in or out of the castle, for a moat surrounded it otherwise. Past the moat, a dirt road traveled a slight declined hill that eventually tapered off to a forest trail connecting the closest town, Erinhod. The forest trees hid the entire town except the town's bell tower.

Cain strode up next to his father's receiver, Finnian Lugus, and saw from the forest a few lowships, shaped in the form of owls, carrying Eirek and Conseleigh Iycel.

"Did your father tell you why they come?"

Cain readjusted his glasses. "They are here to check on me. Guardian Eska believes there have been calculated attacks on the participants of the Trials or their nations."

"Good thing Castle Thoth remains free of such things."

"Yes, it is."

The lowships stopped feet from Cain and Finnian but did not shut off. Instead, Eirek and Conseleigh Iycel hopped off the back of each ship, and once they did, the ships turned around, ready to go survey the city again.

"Apprentice Mourse, it is nice to see you again." Cain extended his hand.

"Eirek, please."

"Okay then, Eirek." Cain repeated the gesture. "You as well, Conseleigh Iycel."

"Yes, we are happy to have you in our company," Finnian said.

"We are glad to be here," Conseleigh Iycel said.

Eirek had remained silent. He seemed different than in the Trials. His face bespoke confusion. *I wonder what ails him. I will need to have a talk with him later.*

"Lord Evber wishes to see you both. Follow." Finnian turned on his heel.

Cain walked in stride with Finnian back across the moat, past the granite owl statue, but instead of going upstairs, they went downstairs. There were two levels of downstairs, the basement and the dungeon. They went to the former, which housed the telecommunication chamber and the war room. Cain knew his father was in the telecommunication chamber communicating with Edym Langol of Ambit, who reported more activity in the firelands of Kane since Pirini Lilapa. As marquis, Langol looked over the older cities of Epoch: Ambit, Lorian, and Dadger.

"Lord Evber, the two are here."

Cain's father raised a hand concealed in a white glove, acknowledging he heard.

"Let me know if any other happenings occur."

"Yes, Lord Evber."

"Bye."

Cain watched his father, who stood a foot shorter than he did, punch a button on the screen and turn around. "Conseleigh Iycel and Apprentice Mourse, how pleasant to have you in our company."

"It is nice of you to accept a visit from us."

"Well, I must admit, when you were the ones who wanted to see me, I was confused. Typically, I treat with Conseleigh Katore."

Cain saw the slight exchange of glances that occurred between Eirek and the conseleigh. While Eirek remained silent, Conseleigh Iycel said, "Luvan has been reassigned a different task."

"As in he is busy, so it is you who have come to see me?"

"As in he is no longer a conseleigh."

Cain shook his head. *That is news. I wonder what happened.* He looked to Eirek, who looked at the ground.

"I did not know such a position could go dismissed." Cain's father furrowed his eyebrows.

"It usually isn't," she clarified.

"Then why—"

"We did not come here to discuss the actions or reasons of Guardian Eska. We came here to talk with you and your son."

If Cain's father had been offended by the conseleigh's bluntness, he only showed it by the slight pause before talking again. "Most interesting. What may I help you with then, Conseleigh Iycel?"

The conseleigh didn't speak. Instead, she prodded Eirek to speak. "Have you noticed anything unusual around Castle Thoth or Epoch recently?"

"The activity in Kane is picking up again, but nothing inside our borders. Cain?" His father turned to him.

"I have nothing to report either."

"Why do you ask, Apprentice Mourse?" Cain's father asked.

Conseleigh Iycel spoke for Eirek. "There is reason to believe that contestants who participated in the Trials or their nations are being targeted."

His father fidgeted with his fingers and glanced at Cain. "Yes, my son mentioned something of this to me. Would you care to provide an example?"

Conseleigh Iycel relayed shocking information about the tragedy that had befallen Acquava. Cain couldn't stop wondering if it was the necklace Hydro had taken. *Would the same fate have befallen me if I had taken it?* Cain scratched an invisible itch on his neck. She talked about Zain Berrese and a mysterious man whose identity Cain knew not. But, for it to be the reason that Zain did not take apprenticeship, the man must have been important. Then, as she began to speak of another incident, Eirek cut her off.

"There has been an attack on the capital of Cresica. Lady Lynda Clayse is now dead."

"Most unfortunate. We did not yet hear of such—"

"Did you do it?" Eirek asked.

"Are you accusing us, Apprentice Mourse?"

Cain heard the annoyance in his father's voice. It appalled him as well. *Why would we start a war for no reason?*

"I'm... I'm sorry. I shouldn't have."

Conseleigh Iycel spoke as soon as Eirek stopped. "Forgive us for the accusation. We just merely want to understand. From my talk with those close to the new Lady of Cresica, they are urging her to call their banners against you."

"Why us? We have no business with Cresica. They thrive off of our wood trade, and we survive off their farms and pastures."

"Yes. But the firelands of Kane lie mostly within your territory and you regulate the activity there."

"The matters you bring give me cause for concern." Cain's father held his chin with his left hand and the left elbow with his right hand. "We will make sure to keep an eye out for—"

A door opened, and Nathan Alaois, the advisor, rushed into the room. The chubby man with two chins, large ears and beady eyes would have been ugly if not for the most magnificent and mesmerizing gray eyes Cain had ever seen. There was a hint of amber to them. Nathan put a hand on his chest and tried calming his staggered breath.

"What is it, Nathan?"

Cain raised an eyebrow. *Why weren't you down here earlier?* To Cain the man seemed incompetent—always late or something, but his father listened to the man's word like he was family. He hadn't always been that way, perhaps only changing within the past year, when Cain noticed the man drinking more. After the last advisor died a few years back to old age and mindloss, Cain's father and mother had gathered a group of politicians in Epoch and picked Nathan out of them. Cain wondered if his father regretted the decision now.

"My lord, Cresica has called their banners."

Cain's father sharpened his neck and his stare. "How many houses?"

"All of them."

His father turned around and stood motionless, now contemplating the proper course of action. War. He had never fought in one, but surely his father would want him to ride alongside him. Cain swiped his hands on his pants.

"Let them come. They will crash upon our lands like every other army has." Cain noticed the quick glance his father gave him when he turned forward. "It is time we call our banners."

"Daven, a quick word?" Conseleigh Iycel asked.

Everyone rushed his father. Cain thought this the perfect opportunity to steal Eirek away and find out more, so he took Eirek by the elbow and walked with him to the upper garden. The smell of flowers in the open air made bearable this time of certain unease.

"What other contestants do you have yet to visit?"

"Tundra says we head for Myoli next to visit Zain and then Gabrielle."

Cain's heart fluttered. "Gabrielle?"

"Yes."

"I do hope nothing ill has befallen her. Or Zain."

They walked upon the short rows of many varieties of flowers the upper garden offered until Cain came upon the perfect flower—an iris called blue-eyed grass. It was a plant with long, linear, grass-like leaves and a flat stem that opened up to six petal-like segments notched twice at the tip, with a longer central point. They were in bloom, and the violet leaves spread to reveal a yellow center. It had kind of reminded Cain of the purple aurora in a fashion of sorts. Cain plucked it from the ground and twirled it in between his thumb and index fingers.

Cain turned to Eirek and showed him the flower. With his free hand, he bent down to the ground and from a basket withdrew a small glass case kept available for servants to pluck flowers as garnish for food plates when they dined with other families of Power. He opened it and put the blue-eyed grass inside. He extended the glass to Eirek and said, "Give this to Gabrielle. Tell her that I think of her often and that she should float to my castle like pollen in the air and sweeten and drink away my senses."

Eirek refused. "Did you hear anything that has just happened?"

Cain took a step back at Eirek's raised voice. He pulled the flower close to his chest. "My father is going to war."

"Yes. He is. Doesn't that mean anything to you?"

"Cresica will crash upon our lance and sword as they have done in the past." Cain turned away from Eirek.

"That means you will have to fight."

"I am not afraid of a fight." To hide the snarl on his lips, Cain looked at the flower.

"You may die!" Eirek threw his arms in the air.

Cain tucked his head back. He turned around and walked away. *Who is he to lecture me?*

"Cain... I'm sorry... I didn't mean to yell."

Cain stopped and turned around. "I..." Cain noticed the bench he had been sitting on earlier. He sat down and pushed the book over to the side to allow Eirek a seat. "Would you like to sit?"

Eirek sat next to him.

"I have never been good with death or dying, Eirek. It is..." Cain shifted his eyes. "A personal weakness of mine. I'd rather think about the fight than the consequences of what should happen if I were to lose." Cain put down the glass-encased flower in his lap. He remembered the book and began speaking again. "To fight, I envision myself as a hero from a story. Heroes never die in the stories."

"This isn't a story, Cain. This is really happening. Epoch is going to war."

Cain inhaled, taking in the flowers around him. "I understand that, Eirek. Quite clearly. What I meant is simply that even if heroes do die, they live on in their words and actions." Cain looked to Eirek and grinned. "I want to be a hero someday."

Silence. Save for the birds that flew from ginkgo tree to ginkgo tree that sprouted from the lower level garden.

"My uncle was a hero."

"Was he, now?" Cain caught Eirek's eye.

Eirek nodded. "He died, though, in Syf. That's... that's why I was on edge earlier. I'm sorry."

"It is hard to lose someone, Eirek. Especially a great man like your uncle surely must have been."

"He was a great man."

"And I want to be as well. But, that first means I need to apologize. So will you take this flower to Gabrielle and tell her?" Cain offered the flower to Eirek once more.

Eirek looked to Cain and smiled. "Cain, of course. I will tell her." Eirek took the flower and held the glass case gingerly in his gloved hand.

"Eirek, we are finished here."

Cain stretched back around, same as Eirek, to see his father with Conseleigh Iycel. She had her arms crossed and hip slightly out. *Father never backs away from a challenge. She should have known she could not sway him.*

Cain turned back to Eirek. "Bye, Eirek. And thank you."

"I... I pray you become the man you want to become."

"I can start with your help."

Eirek nodded. He stood up from the bench and then left. Cain continued sitting on the bench, enjoying the open air. It was almost as if the heat of the suns called to him, for during the summer months and, now, during Pirini Lilapa, he had never wanted to be indoors. Hands came to rest on his shoulder. He looked up. His father stared down at him.

"Are you going to remain out here, Cain?"

"Yes, Father."

"Very well. Once more will not hurt, I suppose. But do not forget your training. A war is coming."

"I can smell it on the air."

"And soon we will taste it on our tongues. Together." Cain's father smiled at him and squeezed his shoulders once more before walking away.

Cain closed his eyes to his father's muffled footsteps on the grass. He continued listening to the birds chirp, feeling the wind brush against his cheeks, and inhaling the sweet scent of flowers. All the while he thought, *Yes, soon, I will become great. I will become a hero.*

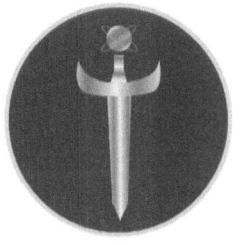

CHAPTER 66

ABANDONED

A long lay of land that rather bored Eirek gave him cause to look elsewhere as they flew to the capital of Ka'Che. Lugh was just beginning to dip in the east behind the watery horizon that Tundra had explained to him was the Krine Sea, which separated Ka'Che from Empora. Freyr wouldn't be long after. In the days after Pirini Lilapa, the two slowly separated from one another, and eventually, they would retain their normal distance and separate zeniths.

Eventually, a castle overlooking a port town came into view. The castle sat near a white bluff. The pier docked many ships, some more extravagant than others, but Eirek found all the traveling and the new sights surreal. *This is what I will be doing when my training continues.*

Tundra landed the ship on the grass near a path that led upward towards the heavily fortified stone castle. They were here because Zain's home in Konmer was abandoned. Thick double doors opened and two hovercrafts came to meet them on the hillside.

"You cannot—" The man quit talking into the amplifying device once he saw the *C* on Tundra's chest and Eirek beside her as they exited the ship.

Eirek chuckled slightly at the scene.

"Where is Conseleigh Rorum?"

"Injured. I am Conseleigh Iycel. We have come to see Zain Berrese and Lord Vangle."

"Lord Vangle eats supper now. I just notified Receiver Mansen of your presence. He is on his way to gather you."

"Excellent. We will meet him inside the castle walls."

"My duty, yes."

Eirek and Tundra boarded the hovercraft and were taken up the hill past the double doors, where a man with a long jaw and large forehead met them. Green eyes glanced from Eirek to Tundra and he fiddled with the cuffs of his burgundy sweater that tried hiding, although rather unsuccessfully, the potbelly the man had acquired. Why he wore a sweater when heat still clung to the air, Eirek didn't know, but who was he to judge?

"Conseleigh Iycel and..."

"This is Guardian Eska's apprentice, Eirek Mourse. I suggest you remember it."

The man's grin flattened. "How could I not have known? Of course. Apprentice Mourse, how fantastic to receive your presence. Follow me, please."

Eirek followed the man up a short series of steps and across a courtyard full of stone arches that connected to multiple towers. Grass grew where there weren't stone paths. It was a far walk, but not a long one, for the receiver had a gait to him that felt like more of a jog.

In the dining room, Eirek noticed the grandness of it first. It was large, more expansive than Eska's. It could easily fit five times as many guests. Soldiers were talking amongst one another when they arrived. At the dais, a table large enough for ten only had seven sitting. Upon seeing Mansen enter with Tundra and Eirek, Lord Vangle wiped his mouth with a brown linen, then stood up.

Lord Vangle walked around the table to meet them in front of the dais. "My apologies for how crude such a meeting must look, Conseleigh Iycel, Apprentice Mourse."

"We traveled from Epoch today. And Cresica before that. A meal would serve us well. Thank you," said Tundra.

"My servants are preparing something for you now. We will talk afterwards?"

"Yes."

"Follow me to the throne room, then, once we are finished here."

When they received their food, Eirek wasted little time eating. It was a variety of sea-caught animals. The squid took time to cut and chew, but Eirek found it rather tasty, something he thought never to admit.

"Zain isn't here," Eirek said in a hushed voice.

"Yes, I noticed that as well."

"Where do you think he is? Do you think something happened to him?"

"We will find out once we talk to the family. After the incidents on Agrost between Cresica and Epoch, I dare to find out what they have to say. So, enjoy this food. It may be the only good thing about this visit." Tundra plucked the meat from an oyster and put it in her mouth.

She was right. Eirek knew she was. He hoped better news would come from Zain, but without him here, the chances of it didn't seem likely. Following

Tundra's lead, he ate more of his seafood. And as his mouth adjusted to the need to chew longer, it gave him time to think. But all he could think about was Zain and why he wasn't there.

After supper had concluded, Lord Vangle led a group consisting of two females, a stocky guard with a shaved pate, his receiver and advisor, and both Eirek and Tundra to his throne room. The group formed an oval with Lord Vangle at the head of it and Tundra and Eirek at the tail, directly across.

"Conseleigh Iycel, Mansen tells us that Conseleigh Rorum is injured and that is why you are here instead of him?"

"Correct, Lord Vangle. He was injured while attending the Meeting of the Twelve."

"I hope it is nothing serious."

"He will recover. Ethen has lived through worse." Tundra grinned.

"That is good news. What is this meeting about? You wanted to see me?"

"Yes. We have reason to believe the contestants in Eska's Trials have been somehow targeted. Incidents on Acquava and Cresica and even one with Zain, require us to check in on every contestant who participated."

"My son. What has happened to my son?"

"You are his mother?" Tundra directed her gaze at the woman who had spoken. She had blue eyes and a scarf wrapped around her neck. Long black hair, streaked with blonde, fell past her shoulders.

The woman nodded. "Yes. Brisine."

"In the fourth trial he was visited by Zakk Shiren. Do you know of him? He trained at Gazo's with Zain."

"Yes. Yes. We took Zakk in when he was a little boy, after we found out he was parentless. His parents were killed in the Konmer Killings when he was young."

The pause in Tundra's continuance told Eirek of her shock. If he had known more about who this *Zakk* was, he probably would have been just as shocked.

"There is footage of Zakk communicating with Zain during the fourth trial. The conseleigh and Guardian Eska agree that whatever Zakk said to Zain affected the outcome of the Trials. Did Zain tell you anything when he returned home?"

Brisine looked around the room. She wiped her hands on her black gown. "Yes, he did. I, I don't remember the exact words, but Zain said that Zakk had threatened my life. That he came back to protect me. But, but I don't see how that would affect the Trials."

"Zain never told you?" Eirek spoke this time.

"Tell me what? What didn't Zain tell me?" Brisine stepped forward.

"Mrs. Berrese, your son, well, he won."

Brisine arched her eyebrows. "Excuse me?"

"Guardian Eska chose him to be apprentice. But... but he denied it. That's, that's why I'm here."

The expression on the faces around the room made certain that no one had known about Zain's success. *Why did he keep it such a secret?*

"Brisine, your boy won."

"My Zain. My..." Hands covered her open mouth. Brisine fell to her knees.

Lord Vangle and the stocky man helped her to stand again. Tears formed in her eyes.

"I am sorry that Zain didn't tell you earlier. It was not my intention to upset you, Mrs. Berrese."

"No. No. I'm just... confused."

"As are we, which is why it is important to tell us what you can. Did anything else happen when you returned home?" Tundra asked.

"No. No. We, we just came here."

"Why not stay at your home in Konmer?"

Brisine scanned the room. "We... I... was attacked. Zain thought it best to stay here. This, this is my scar." Brisine unwound the scarf around her neck and pointed to a long line across her throat.

"Attacked, by whom?"

"A shape..." Brisine's voice trailed off. She looked around the room, her gaze grazing to and fro. "A shapeless man, I'm afraid. My memory is fading." She smiled weakly.

Eirek narrowed his focus. *Is she not telling something?* "Why were you attacked?"

Brisine told the story of a man who stole documents out of a safe they kept hidden. She told them that Zain had wanted to find this man, that he was convinced that he worked for Lord Zigarda and that is why he left.

"Where is he currently?"

"He is still in Empora visiting with his father in Mendeck," Lord Vangle said.

"What was Zain's father doing in Empora?" Tundra crossed her arms.

"Jewel work for Lord Zigarda," Brisine said.

"How many jewels was he doing work on?" Eirek asked.

"Twelve."

Eirek exchanged a quick glance with Tundra, then returned focus on Zain's mother. "How long has he been gone?"

"Laron for a little over eight months now. Zain for only a couple of months."

"Has contact with them been steady?" Tundra asked.

"No. Our last contact with them was a little less than two months ago, although our ship that we sent over came back just a few days ago with a little over half of the original crew." Lord Vangle said.

"What happened to the other half?"

"They remain with Zain and his father in Empora, as safety precautions," the stocky man said.

"Any suspicion of foul play?" Tundra asked.

"No. To do so would cause war. Even Zigarda knows that would be foolish. The falcon always watches," said the stocky guard.

Eirek noticed Zain's mother open her mouth but then shut it once Lord Vangle started speaking. She looked down the whole time while he talked, fidgeting with her fingers. *What is she—*

"Lukas, what if that is exactly what he wants?"

"Then you'd be another planet bent on war," Tundra said.

There was remorse in her voice. Worry even. Eirek sensed it. He had spent enough time with her these past couple of days to notice.

"What do you mean, Conseleigh Iycel?"

It was then she reported on the happenings of Agrost.

"That is grave news indeed," Lord Vangle said. "We are lucky that no ill has befallen Ka'Che as of yet."

"Let us hope luck continues to fare you well. Tomorrow we will go to Empora and check on Zain. Gabrielle Ravwey, another contestant, lives in Empora. We will see if Zain has tried reaching out to her at all. But it is late. We will need to stay here for the night."

"That will be fine. Mansen..." Lord Vangle turned to the receiver. "Show these two to the guest chambers."

"Of course, my lord."

While out on the veranda of his room, Eirek looked up into the night. Bands cut across it, dividing it into quadrants. Although he couldn't see it, he knew a star was missing from the starlit sky. His uncle's star. Angal's. Galan's. He dropped his gaze to the city lights of Pelopon and to the Krine Sea that lay beyond that.

Splotches of light sat on the placid murky waters of the sea, remnants from the city at its front.

Over the sea, Zain was with his father. He had left the apprenticeship to pursue his mother, and his mother to pursue his father. But he did it in good intentions. Did Angal abandon Eirek for the same reason? Angal must have known the Third One would kill him if he was ever found. Was abandoning Eirek a way of protecting him? Was giving him the Ether Weapon? He wanted to tackle these thoughts more, but a knock came to his door.

Who could it be? Tundra? Eirek walked over and opened the door. "Mrs. Berrese?"

"I need to speak with you, Apprentice Mourse."

Eirek stood there, dumbfounded for a second. "Yes, of course. Come in."

Brisine entered and shut the door behind her.

"How may I help you?"

"I... I wanted to tell you something more about my son." Brisine fidgeted with her thumbs.

"What is it?"

"I'm afraid I wasn't completely honest during our meeting after supper. On two counts."

"The first?"

She breathed in deeply, then exhaled. "It concerns the man who stole the documents from my house. I told Conseleigh Iycel that I didn't know the man. Well..." Her eyes browsed back and forth between both of his. "Well, that was only half true."

"What do you mean?"

"I knew the man who stole those documents."

"Who was it?"

"It was Zain." Brisine clutched her hands to her chest. Eirek was about to say something, but Brisine must have anticipated his confusion, for she continued speaking. "It was someone who looked exactly identical to Zain."

"Are you certain?"

"Most. This... this... is the part that may confuse you."

"What is it?"

"The man had been Zain, but then he changed to someone else. A... a man with leathery skin and a drooping, porous face. His eyes were amber. I know what it sounds like, but I'm not crazy. The man, the man had been a shapeshifter."

"A shapeshifter?"

"I know how ridiculous it sounds, but my eyes have always been sharp. I swear he was my Zain one moment, and a different individual in another."

Eirek bit his lower lip and tilted his head. *I have never even heard of a shapeshifter. Maybe Tundra or Guardian Eska would know? I will need to ask them. Still, I need to appear competent to her... I replaced her son. She needs confidence.* Trying to think of something an apprentice would say in a situation that he knew nothing about, Eirek asked a question that would only require a simple answer. "Have you told the others?"

"I did. They... they do not believe me." Brisine let her vision fall from her hands to her lap.

"Why?"

"Because shapeshifters haven't been seen since the Conquest and that was four-hundred-and-fifty years ago."

That is something. Eirek resisted the urge to ask about the incident. He would look it up when he returned to the Core. He put his hands behind his back, not willing to reveal his fidgeting fingers. While thinking of something to say, he remembered she was here for two reasons. "The second?"

"It... it concerns Zain."

"What about him?"

"When Conseleigh Iycel asked about the suspicion of foul play, I... I wasn't sure if I should mention anything, but I think my Zain is in trouble. I, I haven't mentioned anything so far because my brothers think I'm crazy for believing in shapeshifters, but, but something isn't right and I know it."

"What do you mean?"

"I was given a letter by one of the men who returned without Zain. It was a letter from Zain."

"What did it say? Did you share it with the others?"

"I haven't told anyone else. Zain said he was fine and so was his father."

"Well, that is good news then."

"It wasn't Zain's handwriting. I would know. I'm his mother."

"What do you think has happened to Zain?"

"I... I don't know. I want to believe my older brother Lukas about Zigarda not wanting to start war, but the tale Conseleigh Iycel told me about your home planet has given me cause for concern. That is why I come to you now."

"I'm not sure what I can do about this, Mrs. Berrese."

"When you see Zain tomorrow, please make sure you request to see him. I want to make sure one of those, those things hasn't morphed into him again."

"How will I know?"

"You won't be able to tell... He will look exactly the same... At least, I haven't been able to tell how to distinguish them yet. But, but perhaps look at any items that may give him away."

"Like what?"

"Well, before he left, I gave him a golden feather. It was left for him in his father's will. I, I think Zain is wearing it as a necklace. I saw it on him during one of our telecommunications while he was at sea... before they stopped coming."

"Is there anything else?" Eirek asked.

"He took his sword on the trip as well. Neither of those things can be replicated."

Eirek didn't have a good idea of what his sword looked like, but a golden feather necklace, he could look for that easily enough.

"Is there anything else?"

"Be careful when dealing with Zigarda. I, I never have liked him, in truth. Compared to my brother Abraham, he treats his people horribly."

"I will be as careful as I can be. Zigarda will not be foolish enough to try anything on Eska's apprentice or his most-trusted aide."

"I hope you are right." She smiled weakly. "Thank you, Apprentice Mourse. Goodnight." She walked out the door, closing it gently behind her.

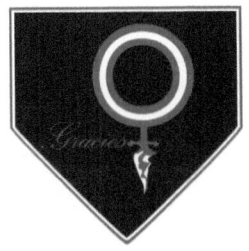

CHAPTER 67

GRACIE'S ACADEMY

"**A**ncients, I pray to you on behalf of Gracie's Academy, which taught me to be thankful for our minds, free to think." Malysen placed the palm of her left hand to her forehead. "For our bodies, aahh..." Malysen paused, trying to remember the prayer. "For our bodies, free to..." Malysen looked down at her little black heels. "I forgot, Miss Gabrielle."

Gabrielle sat cross-legged across from her trainee and smiled. "It goes like zis, Malysen." Gabrielle tucked a strand of black hair behind her ear. "Ancients, I pray to you on behalf of Gracie's Academy, which taught me to be zankful for our minds, free to zink." Gabrielle placed the palm of her left hand to her forehead. "For our bodies, free to fight." She clenched her right hand and placed it over her heart. "And for our souls, free to bind." She then combined her two hands at her lips and kissed them.

During the whole time she recited the prayer, Gabrielle kept her eyes open, studying her trainee, seven years of age. She was a girl with blonde hair curled to her shoulders, green eyes, and a freckly face. She had been Gabrielle's most recent assignment since coming back from the Trials. Although she didn't win, the women of Gracie's still respected her, even more so now that she had been accepted to compete. And, when she told her headmistress, Carla Sonetta, she had beaten Zain Berrese from Gazo's Academy in a weapons tournament, an announcement rang throughout the academy. Cheers and praise came abundant enough to make Gabrielle flush a deep purple.

"Try again."

Malysen tried again. She performed the prayer correctly, although nearly forgetting the last line.

"Very good, Malysen. Now, do you remember za next prayer?"

"No," Malysen sighed. "Why do we need to learn these prayers, anyway? I just want to be a fighter like you."

"Our Power derives from prayer, Malysen. Faith and skill make Gracie's za best weapons academy. Now, repeat after me."

Gabrielle recited the prayer that was said by Grace Sabore in the times of her abusive relationship. She paused every once in a while to make sure Malysen repeated it correctly. At the end Gabrielle said, "Now it isn't enough to only say it. You must believe it, too. If you don't, zere will never be any true Power in zese words."

"How will I know if prayers work?"

"You will." Gabrielle smiled. "Here. I will show you." Gabrielle extended her hand to her young trainee, got up from her cross-legged position, and led her out of the room and down a hallway of Gracie's Academy.

Not only did the Academy function as a classroom facility for women's learning and training, but a section of it housed quarters for the females who didn't want to commute every day or couldn't. Gabrielle knew of one girl a few years younger than she who had lived here for years while in school because her parents were from Lurid. That girl had albino skin and amber hair, like her eyes.

She flounced down the purple and white tiled hallways, passing by classes in session and welcoming the eyes of other students she hoped to be an inspiration for. Grabbing Malysen by the hand, she led her down a flight of stairs and outside behind the Academy. There were several brick courts around for practice of sparring, but that wasn't what Gabrielle wanted to show her. She wanted to show Malysen proof that prayers worked. She would take the Walk.

"Where are we going, Miss Gabrielle?"

Gabrielle looked down and smiled at her. "Over there, Malysen." She pointed to a small pond not fifty paces from the Academy. At the edge of the pond, she turned to Malysen and crouched on her heels. "Watch closely, for you'll have to do zis someday."

"Okay."

She let go of Malysen's hand and, out of habit, brushed her hair behind her shoulders. Gabrielle looked to the suns and sky and said, "Ancients, hear my prayer. My mind is yours, free to zink as you zought. My body is naked and pure, free to fight even za darkness of night. Take my soul, uncovered and untainted, free to bind. Never let us forget zat you give za air we breaze; never let it grow stale. Never let us forget zat you drench us in za flames of Freyr and Lugh to keep us warm, even when zings seem cold. Never let us forget zat you make solid za water, which helps us stand. Never let us forget zat you feed us, spiritually and physically, wiz your words and grains zat you give us."

Then Gabrielle walked forward. But when she reached the water she continued walking, not sinking. She walked on top of the water as if it were land. Gabrielle turned around to look at a stupefied little girl. "When you believe in za Power of prayer and supplication, Malysen, anyzing is possible." Gabrielle smiled at her young student.

"I want to be like you, Miss Gabrielle."

She walked back towards her and once she reached her, crouched down and held her hands again. "One day you will have za courage and faiz needed to take za Walk, Malysen. Zis is za ultimate test for a student here. But you need to pray and train first."

Gabrielle tucked a strand of her trainee's blonde hair back behind her ear. She loved seeing girls invigorated to learn. It reminded Gabrielle of herself when she saw Carla Sonetta do the same thing after Gabrielle had only been at Gracie's two months. From that moment on it made Gabrielle train longer, pray daily, and fighter harder to forget about the past years of abuse from her father. Sometimes, when she looked to the Red Cloud, she wondered if he had died in the cell he was supposedly rotting in—yet, a man like that shouldn't even be allowed to live.

"Gabrielle."

Gabrielle jerked her head to the sound of her name. Carla Sonetta stood with her arms crossed at the top of a slight hill. Even though heat still clung to the air, Carla wore a purple scarf. Her hair was as white now as the dress she wore, but Gabrielle had seen pictures of her younger years when blonde hair and young blue eyes made her attractive to any man. Even in her old age she looked ravishing, and her figure held well despite seventy years.

"What is it, Lady Sonetta?"

Gabrielle was the only student at the Academy that could call her Lady instead of Headmistress.

"You have two visitors. A woman and a man."

"Visitors?"

"Yes. They are waiting for you in the lobby. I told them I would find you."

"Zank you."

"Of course." Lady Sonetta smiled and walked away to the stone courts, ready to observe students spar.

Gabrielle turned her attention back to Malysen. "I need to go now, but your homework for zis week will be to memorize zose prayers."

"Alright."

"Perfect." Gabrielle smiled. She stood and took Malysen by the hand and walked her back to the Academy.

Once inside, Malysen darted upstairs, ready to make use of what free time she had left. Gabrielle, on the other hand, walked forward, her heels clacking against the tiled ground. *Visitors?* She hadn't one of those since her ex-boyfriend had come to visit her years ago. Last she heard, he was in Soeco in an underground rebellion formed to stand against Victor Zigarda's southern oppression. Gabrielle had told him that if he joined, she wouldn't be able to continue on their relationship, but he joined anyway. *Stupid men*, she had thought. She hated Victor Zigarda as much as anyone, but to openly express it, especially as the star student she was at Gracie's, put the Academy in danger of defunding and military retaliation. Carla Sonetta explained it all to her years back.

That is why she would put on a fake smile for Victor Zigarda when she visited him in a few days' time. To look good in the eyes of the senate and citizens, he invited her for dinner in his Web and scheduled an interview to compare and contrast his own Trials that he had participated in to Gabrielle's. Gabrielle had not wanted to go, but Carla Sonetta convinced her that it would give the school further prestige and that Gabrielle could unknowingly change the lives of those who watched the interview when it aired. Her chance to help others and give them a new life is why she agreed to go. She remembered what it felt to be hopeless, in pain, and think things were futile. That was a different life, though.

Gabrielle turned a corner, and her eyes widened. "Eirek?" Gabrielle cleared her throat. "I mean, Apprentice Mourse." She turned her head. "And Conseleigh Iycel?"

"Eirek is fine." The man smiled.

Since the Trials conclusion, he had acquired a little muscle and more confidence. The pair of traits donned him nicely.

"Miss Ravwey, I hope we didn't come at a bad time."

"I was merely training one of za younger students. What brings boz of you here?"

"We need to speak to you."

"Zen let's talk."

"A place more private, perhaps?"

"My room. We can talk in zere."

Gabrielle led them up three flights of stairs and down two hallways before arriving at a corner room. One set of windows faced towards the west. Another set of windows in the main compartment of her living quarters faced north towards the Red Cloud. She had a larger room than most other students due to her popularity and her seniority. She even had her own bathroom. Gabrielle loved that. She remembered so many times as a younger student when she would have to fight for mirrors with other girls in the Academy. When students were young, they roomed with other students as a way to get to know each other and push each other to train harder. Gabrielle's first roommate, Perrine Victorie, was still one of her good friends.

"What may I do for you boz?" Gabrielle closed the door behind her and then sat down with them on a purple couch in her main living quarters.

"Have you noticed anything strange as of late?" Eirek asked.

"Nozing out of za usual. No." Gabrielle shrugged her shoulders. "Should I have?"

"We have reason to believe the nations and participants of the Trials have been targeted in some way."

"Nozing has happened here. What makes you zink zat?"

Eirek explained everything that had happened regarding Acquava and Cresica. Her heart panged when she heard of Eirek's loss. He shouldn't have to go through that; he was a decent guy. In terms of Acquava, to say Gabrielle was shocked was an understatement. *Hydro killed his parents. What is zat necklace he is wearing?* She remembered the night he showed it to her, believing she knew something about it. She didn't. She really didn't. But it did speak to her. It told her that if she wore it, she could make up for her past. It told her it would take away that pain. It told her she could have revenge on the father who was so cruel to her. The voice, whatever it was, had sounded like a girl's. It had been enthralling.

As Eirek talked, she noticed one person still missing from his updates—Zain. The man who had risked his life to save her from death on the volcano, a man she had wanted to give her heart to, but a man who had made no effort in stealing it. "What of Zain? Have you talked wiz him yet?"

"He left his uncle's castle in Ka'Che to travel to Empora and visit his father in Mendeck. We are to go there after here."

Zain was in Empora and didn't visit? Gabrielle looked out her north-facing window towards the Red Cloud. She stroked her wrist, running her fingers past her bracelets.

"The matter of Zain stems from the fourth trial, Miss Ravwey."

Gabrielle cocked her head and looked away from the window. "What do you mean?"

Conseleigh Iycel went on to explain the appearance of Zakk Shiren and asked for information about him. Gabrielle explained that she knew him, but she didn't know all that had happened. She mentioned that Zain and he had fought before the Trials even began, and that Gabrielle had watched the fight unfold from the hangar of the ship. Zain had been the reason Zakk wasn't on that ship. How he had managed to reappear on the volcano, she didn't know. Conseleigh Iycel's countenance changed, as well as Eirek's, when she explained that initial duel. They looked at each other, causing Gabrielle to feel the need to interject.

"All of zat should explain to you zat zeir rivals. Zey always have been and always will be."

"It does more than that, Miss Ravwey. It potentially gives us another reason as to why Zain turned down the apprenticeship." Conseleigh Iycel put her finger and her thumb under her chin. "Do you remember anything from the fourth trial specifically?"

Gabrielle admitted that her vision had been blurry from the heat, and with the volcano grumbling, it was hard to hear what they talked about. But there was one piece of information that she relayed that caught her by surprise—the description of the ship Zakk had gotten on. A ship that looked like a purple bubble.

Conseleigh Iycel furrowed her brows in thought. "Thank you for the information."

"I wish I could help more."

"You've done enough. We will look into the lead." Conseleigh Iycel turned to Eirek. "Are you ready to leave, Apprentice Mourse?"

"I will catch up with you in a little. Wait outside."

Gabrielle arched her eyebrows and turned her attention to Eirek.

"Okay." Conseleigh Iycel left, closing the door behind her.

"What do you want?"

"When I visited Cain... well, he spoke of you."

"Cain did?" Gabrielle put her hand on her chest.

"Yes."

"What did he say?"

"He told me to tell you that he thinks of you often. And that, well, he apologizes for not coming down." Eirek reached into a pocket in his pants. "Also, he gave me this gift to give to you." He extended a sleek glass case tied with a purple ribbon.

Even though Gabrielle could see the flower from outside the case, she still unwound the ribbon and opened it anyway. She picked up the purple flower with six petals and brought it to her nose, letting the scent overwhelm her senses. *Cain.* Her eyes began to tear.

"Cain is going off to war?"

"I... I do not know... but I know war is about to occur."

Gabrielle smelled the flower again. "Zank you, Eirek."

"You're welcome, Gabrielle. Contact me if anything does happen."

"Alright." She smiled, gave him a hug, and led him out the door.

She closed the door and walked back to her purple couch. She sat down and stared out the window to Mendeck, the Red Cloud. The flower twirled between her thumb and index finger. Once more, she brought it to her nose and inhaled. *Zain comes to Empora but doesn't even see me? Cain sends me zis?* A tear slid down her cheek and fell to her lap below. It wasn't right for men to play with a woman's heart. It wasn't right at all.

CHAPTER 68

BLOOD SAMPLES

"Y ou're gonna leave me, just like zat?" Jasmyn propped herself up on her elbows. She blew curly brown hair out of her face.

Zakk stared down at her nakedness while he pulled up his pants. "I gave you what you wanted."

"I want more zough." She whimpered and pursed her lips. Using her right index finger, she touched herself. After a long second, she brought the finger to her mouth and licked it clean. "Don't you have more to give me?"

Zakk bit his lips, devouring her in his thoughts.

His telecommunicator beeped. Again. His meeting would happen soon.

"No. I don't," he lied.

She crawled towards Zakk. Chocolate-colored eyes melted over him, dripping down his body until they spotted his midsection. She reached out and tugged on his pants, trying to bring him back to bed.

He brushed her hand away and stepped back. "I have business to attend to."

She fell back on the bed, folding her arms across her breasts. "Business zat you can never tell me about."

He rezipped his pants and buckled his belt. "Correct."

"Why can't you ever tell me?"

"It would be bad for us. Here." Zakk flicked two golden bonds onto the burgundy sheets.

She swiped the coins and brought them closer to her face. "Why you do zat to me?"

"We have an agreement."

"I zought we were past zat."

In truth, they were past that. It had been almost a month since they began their liaisons. Zakk no longer regarded her with the same objective mentality he did so when they began. She was no longer just a hole for his attention; they had been intimate enough to call each other by name now. But he would still pay her. It was his way of safeguarding himself and her. The more they could pretend they didn't care about one another, the easier it would be to keep the secret. And to be fair, although she warmed him in some regards, he never felt completely full with her. She wasn't his one. But she would do for now.

They had met the day after Zain had tried to kill himself to save his troops. A noble act, but stupid. His near death forced his father's actions and so upon completion of the jewels, a huge celebration occurred. Drinks were plenty. Women were many. If any one of Zigarda's closest confidants did not have a woman with them that night, Zakk would have believed they were lying. The foot soldiers had rounded them up and brought them to the Web. There, in a stupor of debauchery and drunkenness, Zakk had met her, along with hundreds of other streetwalkers.

Their paths had crossed again during Pirini Lilapa. He had traveled outside the city to see the eclipse and on his way back had noticed her along the street in an argument with a man, a fellow soldier of Zigarda, much lower in rank and green. Zakk had told the man to leave her alone, and when the man responded with a quick quip implying their relationship, Zakk killed him. Disrespect is one thing Zakk didn't tolerate.

For saving her, she allowed him to give her his seed again. So he did. After, they had properly exchanged names. But he wouldn't not pay her. Zigarda took care of his needs at the Web; he had given him a home and coin, yes, but most importantly, Zigarda had given Zakk a family and purpose: the things he had lost in Ka'Che. Both of those things had started to come into question as of late, however, and perhaps that is why he continued speaking with Jasmyn. A part of him wanted more, and he knew that she surely wanted more as well. Who would be content with living her lifestyle? That is why he paid her. If she was smart, she could escape her situation someday.

"We will see each other again." Zakk threw on his tunic stitched with the spider on a web, Zigarda's sigil. "Goodbye, Jasmyn."

Jasmyn huffed. "Bye."

He left the rather dilapidated apartment complex and turned out onto the main road that lead further into the city and straight to the Web. He was a mere thirty-minute walk away from Zigarda's compound, but the meeting wouldn't happen there. It would happen in an alleyway near one of the city's parks.

Vibration came to his wrist.

Edwyn?

Zakk didn't accept the call right away. Instead, he looked around for the nearest indistinct alleyway he could find. It greeted him with the rancid smell of rotten rats that had been leftovers for stray cats. Rubbish littered the ground, spilling over from the black garbage dump piled past its brim.

His wrist vibrated again.

Zakk positioned himself in front of a ladder and took the call. "Yes?"

"Where are you currently?"

"Waiting for the meeting to occur."

"Good. Stay there and do not return for a while. Reports from Ka'Che have been confirmed. Eska's apprentice and conseleigh have finally showed in Mendeck."

Zakk looked at Edwyn's chubby, curly-haired face. A part of him wanted to go back now and view Eska's standards. If the new apprentice was as poor of a choice as Zain had been, Zakk was sure to be unimpressed.

"Notify me when I can return."

"Will do. Good luck with your meeting."

The connection ended. He left the alleyway and continued walking towards where the actual meeting would take place. Ten more minutes of walking through side streets and avoiding the main road, Zakk stood in an alleyway glued in grime. There, back turned, was an obese man, half the size of the dumpster next to him. Upon hearing Zakk's footsteps, the man tucked in his elbows, squeezing the briefcase underneath his left armpit, and turned around.

Senator Numos strolled forward, his cane in his right hand. "You? I thought I would be meeting with Lord Zigarda."

"Yes, well, there has been a slight change to plans. Lord Zigarda is currently meeting with Eska's apprentice and conseleigh."

"So Eska has caught on to your plan, has he?"

"I assure you he has latched onto nothing."

"Eska isn't a fool. Why else would he be sending his conseleigh and apprentice?"

"He is a fool," Zakk spat. *He chose Zain for apprenticeship. How much more foolish can he be?* "There is nothing to latch onto yet, for you carry with you the device." Zakk pointed to the briefcase still underneath Numos's armpit.

"Yes, I do. But this interference gives me pause for concern." He let the briefcase fall into his left hand. After he looked at it quaintly, he turned his attention to Zakk. "Zigarda realizes what happens should this plan fail, does he not?"

"Its success depends on your clout, Senator. Now, the briefcase?"

Numos clicked his tongue. "Yes. Here." Numos leaned forward on his cane and gave the briefcase over to Zakk.

Zakk took it and unlatched the small locks. In cool, velvet cushions sat four tests of blood, all labeled: Hydro Paen, Cadmar Briggs, Eirek Mourse, and Gabrielle Ravwey. They had been collected after each of the contestants successfully completed a trial. Numos had told them it was merely for identification purposes, but it was for this reason all along—to put their plan in motion. Zakk smirked. *Perfect.*

"Now, when will my payment come?" Senator Numos asked.

"You will be Lord of Mistral soon enough."

"Yes, well, I want more than that. I want Lady Liliana's head tossed over the floating isles and watch it fall to the ground below." Senator Numos guffawed.

Zakk let out a slight chuckle. "What did she do, bruise your ego?"

Numos furrowed his nonexistent brows and leaned forward on his cane. He tsked. "Something like that. *That* matter is my own. Knowledge is power, after all, correct?"

Zakk thought about slicing off the fat swine's head then. Or even putting a knife up to his throat until he cowered or pissed himself. But out of courtesy, he merely snarled. He didn't believe in killing the innocent, after all, and Numos had done nothing wrong so far. His snarl turned into a quick smirk. "Correct."

"When should I start the next phase of the plan?" Numos glanced down at his gloved hand, looking at the watch on his wrist.

"Immediately. The shifters are already in place."

"I am glad Victor is hurrying this along. I am not sure how much longer he will live."

Zakk paused. He scanned Numos. "What do you mean?"

"Victor is more than two-hundred years old. How much longer do you think he can really live without his youthwater from Lord Paen? I'm sure he has heard what has happened over there."

"We have. And we are currently looking for his son."

"Everyone is. Rather awful turn of events there."

He didn't say anything. He didn't know what to say. Zakk didn't care about that. People went crazy every day. His parents were killed by deranged people.

"Although, it does seem to fit well with our plan. Albeit in a rather—"

A beep came from his telecommunicator. Zakk pushed the crown, connecting with Edwyn, tuning out the rest of Numos's words.

"They left. You are free to return. How did the meeting go?"

"We are finishing now."

"I will see you soon, then."

The connection ended, and Zakk stared at Senator Numos. "Until next time."

"Until next time, then." Senator Numos tapped his cane and left.

Zakk followed after him for a little while as he bustled through the crowd gathering in the park, but then Zakk took side streets back to the Web, leaving the Senator on his own. When Zakk entered the building, Zigarda stood present with his advisor and receiver.

"I have the device." Zakk hoisted the recorder in the air.

"Good. Give it here." Doctor Cere offered his hand.

Zakk gave away the briefcase.

"Go get Zain and his father from the dungeon. Make sure they get to the Blood Chambers."

"Why them?" Zakk looked at Zigarda.

"Because Eska's apprentice demanded we release them." Zigarda smirked. "And release them we shall."

Zakk's face grimaced a little, but he hid it well. He never liked the Blood Chambers. It smelled of metallic rot. "I will gather them, then."

Zakk walked from the room down a few hallways to the elevator shaft. When he found Zain, he was in his usual position, leaning against the wall with his head tilted back. He twirled one of the four jewels in his hand, always looking at it. Zakk had never seen Zain as sad as when he lost his sword; it was as if he lost a part of him. *Serves him right*, Zakk had thought, but a part of him regretted what he did to Zain; he would never have wanted to lose his sword to the fires, but Zain had needed to know the loss of a loved one. It was only fair.

"Get him up." Zakk motioned to the guard that sat by the cells.

Zain raised an eyebrow and put down the jewel. Guards in black snakeskin suits unlocked his cellar door and the chains to the wall. They hoisted him up, grabbing each arm so he couldn't escape, not like he tried to, anyway. He was defeated.

Once brought out into the red light that filtered through the cells, Zakk looked upon Zain's clean countenance despite his internment. He knew that Zain had been cleaned up weekly so that the shifters could steal his identity if situations like the one that just happened arrived. When Zain said nothing to him, Zakk spat, making sure to hit Zain's shoe. Zain merely looked at him, lost animosity in his eyes. He wanted Zain's passion back; he wanted Zain's ire to return. A part of him had died, but he shouldn't have given up yet. He was a Gazo's student after all. "Both of you are about to go home."

Zain's brows furrowed. "Home?"

Zakk smirked. "Isn't that what you wanted?" He flicked his eyes over to Zain's father, now escorted by two guards.

"What is this about?" he asked.

"The apprentice came and said we had to release you."

"Eirek is here?"

Zakk ignored his question. "Take them away." He nodded to the guards that had been accompanying him.

Halfway out of the dungeon Zain yelled and struggled. "Wait my jewels!"

"You'll get them later," one of the guards said.

They left.

Zakk flicked his gaze from the exit to the floor of Zain's cell. He tapped his right foot on the ground, hands akimbo. He spat on the ground next to the cell, then went inside and picked one of them up, the blue topaz, and twirled it in his fingers. The cut was exquisite. It truly was a gift from his father. The same thing his father had completed for Zigarda.

"Hey, how much longer vill I be in zis cell?"

The man brought Zakk's focus back. He ignored him. He didn't know Zigarda's plans for the man, just as he didn't know why the completion of the jewels was cause for celebration. Or why they had to be completed before Pirini Lilapa.

A beep came to his wrist: *Zigarda.*

He dropped the jewel and stood up.

Why Zigarda was calling him back to the Throne Room so early, Zakk didn't know.

It seemed as though he had been left in the dark in a cell of his own.

CHAPTER 69

THE RED CLOUD

They had made it through the city of Mendeck without any cause for concern. They had even entered Zigarda's keep with little to no hesitation. The anticipation Eirek had felt on the way over, built upon by Zain's mother, had subsided. Now, Zigarda was having his receiver, Yuan Shimes, fetch Zain.

It was a long and awkward ten minutes before the man came back with Zain. He stood three body lengths away, back with the advisor, receiver, and Victor Zigarda.

"Eirek, nice to see you again. Conseleigh Iycel." Zain nodded.

"We were looking for you in Ka'Che but found no one at your house. Your mother said you were here," Tundra said, arms across her chest.

"Visiting my dad, yeah."

Eirek looked at Zain. Everything appeared normal. He wore a long-sleeved, v-neck shirt in the colors of Lord Vangle and the sigil stitched on the upper right of the chest. On the left side of his hip, his sword hung attached to a belt. *There's no necklace. Perhaps he took it off? Would he?* Eirek needed to find a way to bring up the necklace without being accusatory. Since he didn't have a plan on how to do that, he asked, "How is he?"

"Good."

"You and your father are to return to Ka'Che. Lord Zigarda will provide the transportation," Tundra said, her fingers playing with a wristlet on her right wrist.

"I will have them prepare their things today, then, so that they may leave by tomorrow," Zigarda said. "You leave at noon."

"Your mom will be glad to see you." Eirek smiled.

"It will be nice to see her again as well." Zain returned the gesture.

This could be my opening. "She wanted me to make sure you don't leave anything behind. You still have the feather necklace, right?"

A pause.

Zain felt at his neck. "It's in my room. I take it off when I go to bed. I must have forgotten to put it on this morning."

"Make sure you bring it back."

"Of course. I wouldn't want to leave a gift of hers here." Zain turned to Zigarda. "Can I tell my dad about our departure?"

Zigarda nodded. "You may."

Zain turned back to face them. "It was nice to see you, Eirek, Conseleigh Iycel."

"You as well, Zain."

Eirek watched Zain leave through the door he had entered.

"Are you satisfied?" Zigarda asked.

"We are," Conseleigh Iycel said. "Good day."

Eirek followed Tundra out the door. They passed the gates and made their way into the bustle of the city. The tall buildings reminded Eirek of Gar's capital, Visis, but the red mist that lingered above did not.

Far enough away, near a street filled with various vendors, Tundra turned to him. "Did Zain act differently to you?"

He had, but Eirek didn't know Tundra had been evaluating him as well. Curious, he asked, "What seemed off about him to you?"

"He didn't seem himself. And, his sword."

"His sword?"

"The one at his hip. It isn't his."

Eirek hadn't even noticed that. "How do you know?"

"During the Trials, Edwyrd called Zain to his chambers to examine a gift his brother left for him after the second trial. The gift happened to be a sword, one that he used in the third trial. It was a longsword, with four jewels."

"Zain's sword was in its scabbard. We never saw it."

"It was a longsword, Apprentice Mourse. He had a special scabbard for it, one that hung over his back. The sword Zain had on today was not his; it was on his hip."

"Conseleigh Iycel, there is something that Zain's mother told me before we left."

"What is that?"

"She said that a shapeshifter took Zain's form and that it was he who attacked her."

"A shapeshifter? They haven't been seen since the Conquest."

"She told me to notice items on Zain. He wore a golden feather necklace on his voyage over. He didn't have one on just now. And, Zain said it was from his mother, but Zain received it as a gift from his father."

"You think that the Zain in there was a shifter?"

"It would make sense, right? With how strangely you thought he was acting."

Tundra turned around and looked towards the street vendors. "It would."

"Let's go in there, then, and get the real Zain."

"We can't, Apprentice Mourse, without Edwyrd's orders. We do—"

Tundra paused and tilted her head forward. She began walking down the street. Eirek tried to glance and see what she saw, but too many people swaggered through the city street. He caught up with her and noticed that she was slowly unraveling her wristlet. One loop. Two loops. Three. She paused.

"Do you see him?" She pointed in the direction of a nearby vendor. A Chaon vendor, from the looks of it, for it had the lord's sigil on its awning.

Eirek looked over to where she pointed. Black hair. Longsword by his side. Traveled and tattered clothes. But Eirek would know that figure from anywhere: Hydro.

"What do we do?"

"We go after him."

Tundra continued walking forward, making her way through the crowd. Eirek stood in shock for a moment before realizing what was happening. She was going to confront him. Here.

He gulped. He inched forward, following Tundra's lead.

Hydro was in conversation with the vendor, making signals as if he wanted directions to some place.

Tundra was five paces from him now. Then four. Three.

He looked her way. Noticed her. But it was too late. Tundra's crystal whip was already in the air. It curled around his neck. His black eyes bulged. "Hydro Paen, you are coming back with us."

His eyes scanned over from Tundra to Eirek and snickered. He drew his longsword. People around the street gasped. Tundra drew a large ice scimitar. The crowd scattered.

Hydro swung. But he didn't aim to strike her. He severed a section of the crystal whip. Then he ran.

Sword out in front, Hydro bustled through the crowd, cutting through the traffic. Screams erupted in the throng of madness. Soon enough, people scrambled over one another, not wanting to fall victim to the madness that tyrannized the city streets. Eirek tried keeping his pace. He pushed. Shoved. Jostled. He didn't have time for the injured now; he needed to capture Hydro.

I'm losing him. I need to contain him.

Ahead, two torches set the ambiance for a tent of candles at the end of the street. *Perfect.* "*Palo!*" Eirek thought about creating two levels of the spell and successfully did so. He pulled walls of fire across the end of the street, blocking Hydro's escape.

Hydro stopped for a brief second. He turned around and studied Eirek through his black eyes. Eirek shivered at the intensity of the stare. Blood dripped from his sword down onto the cobblestone. Hydro smirked, ignored Eirek, and continued towards the wall of fire. Water came from Hydro's his right hand, drowning out the flames. And from his left, electricity laced the watery wall with electrical centipedes.

How is that...

Hydro ran through.

Possible?

Eirek stopped and stood there, staring at the spell. Dual elements, water and electricity, working together, in unison. Could such a thing exist? He looked around, trying to find the source Hydro pulled from. There wasn't any. Eirek felt the presence of onlookers, but all he thought about was the wall before him and its formation. *I was so close.*

He tapped his feet on the ground and felt something. Lifting his shoe, Eirek found a golden bond. He picked it up and ran his index finger over the serpent that snaked its way around the back of the coin's circumference. *Ajid Volintasey Fuan.* Then he noticed something. *A V F. Is this what Angal was trying to tell me?*

"Where is Hydro?"

Tundra's voice cut through his thoughts. Eirek stuffed the coin into his pocket and looked at the conseleigh. "I lost him. He created that." Eirek pointed to the wall in front of them. "He's gone."

"I'll notify Edwyrd." She turned away from him.

Eirek flipped the coin between his fingers while his hand was in his pocket. He stood there, oblivious to anything else Tundra might have said. Oblivious to any of the traffic around him. Oblivious to anything but the piece of gold in his pocket. *Ajid Volintasey Fuan. May we find each other again...*

EPILOGUE

Year: 719 AGW (After Great War)

The air was dry, so when the wind blew, it scratched across every part of Luvan's exposed skin. The small village he traveled to, hidden behind a maze of trees and a sea of brown, held something he needed to know—knowledge. A larger man of dark skin and even darker tattoos that molested his body had led him here, but now he stayed outside. Now, it would be only between Luvan and her, this three-eyed prophetess.

Luvan swiped away the beaded curtain and saw a woman with fair skin and hair that fell to her shoulders. Her hair was streaked with more blue than gray. Her eyes matched the blue in her hair, but there was a slight purple to them as well. She wore a ring, one of copper and silver, on the ring finger of her left hand.

"Luvan Katore."

"Yes, that is I." Luvan was fidgety. If what he had heard was true, she knew things, queer things, things that could change him. Luvan thought to himself, Do I really want to do this? Yes, I must.

"I hear you want answers."

"And I hear you give the best of them." Luvan tried regaining his confidence. He was a politician, after all. He knew how to speak elegantly, persuasively, or even have a verbal joust if needed.

"They are not always the best. But, they are some of the most precise." She pulled a cloth off of the table to reveal a cloudy gray crystal ball tinted with amethyst. "Sit."

Luvan sat across from her and watched as her fingers massaged the orb. She eyed him and said, "Tell me, what do you want me to look for?"

"Well, Poland Gryf of Eska's conseleigh recently died, and there is an opening..."

"And you want to know if you will be the one to fill that spot?"

Luvan nodded.

"And what makes you want to be Guardian Eska's conseleigh?" Her fingers continued massaging the orb. It was glowing now.

"It has been a dream of mine to see the Core."

She laughed. *"There is nothing much there now."*

"How do you know that?"

"I know many things. Let us see what your name has in store for you, Luvan Katore. Are you ready?"

"Yes."

She tilted her head and blankly gazed into her crystal ball. While continuing to massage the orb, she spoke to him. *"Luvan Katore... I see why you come to me... You have a fear of rejection..."* She leaned closer. *"But, there is no need for that... You have a strong name, Luvan Katore, a name given for greatness..."*

Given for greatness, *Luvan thought.* He clenched his fists. *"Does that mean I will become Guardian Eska's conseleigh?"*

"Yes..."

"What other things am I meant for?"

She stopped massaging the orb on the table and looked at him. *"Insight cannot tell me that. Only its brother staff Foresight could."*

"Where is that?"

"Not here. But my guess is that it will be something to do with your time as a conseleigh." She went back to looking at her orb. Her eyes widened. She gulped.

"What is it? What did you see?"

"I cannot see clearly. But what is clear that you have a name given for greatness, Luvan Katore. But every greatness costs a price."

"What price will I have to pay?"

"You will..."

A knock came to his door, snapping Luvan Katore out of his reverie from thirty-one years prior. A time before he knew what being conseleigh was like. A time before he knew about heartbreak. Only nerves. Nerves Eska had replaced with trust. At least, he thought.

"Luvan, who is it?" His wife called to him from upstairs.

"I will get it. Don't worry." Luvan called back and went to the door.

"Senator Numos?" Luvan stepped back a little when he saw the man.

"Conseleigh Katore..."

After returning to the floating isles of Mistral since Eska's dismissal, Luvan had crossed paths with Numos during a meeting in the senate. He had told him then, but since that time, he had no contact with the man.

"You know I'm not one of Eska's aides anymore."

"Sorry. It was merely habit from the Trials." Numos readjusted his eyepiece. "Can I come in?"

Luvan stepped back and let him enter. He led Numos to where he had been sitting and offered him a chair at the table he had been sitting at. Luvan took a spot at the table perpendicular to Numos.

"What may I do for you?"

"I find it interesting that you still have Eska's portrait hanging up." Numos nodded his head towards a portrait of Guardian Eska above the fireplace and directly in front of Luvan.

"Yes... Well, I still have unfinished business with him..."

"Don't we all." Senator Numos chuckled.

"Be quick with your point." Luvan drew the large knife from the notch at his belt and became disinterested in Numos, preferring to look at the knife in his hands.

"Do you still communicate with Eska?"

"No, he's blocked communication with me."

"But, he can still trace you."

"Only perhaps for a few more weeks if he chooses."

"Interesting..." Numos looked around the estate, tapping his cane gently on the tiled floor. "Tell me if I am reaching too far for this, conseleigh, but—"

"I am not his conseleigh anymore."

Numos smirked. "Yes, sorry. Old habit, I assure you. Let me start over. Tell me if I am reaching too far for this Luvan, but you do think that how Eska treated you was unjust, correct?"

"Yes. I was merely doing my duty to him as a conseleigh."

"Duty. The death of us all. Is it not?"

Luvan let a slight chuckle escape.

"Well, how would you like to see a... hmm, how do I put this... a *change* in power?"

Luvan's brows perked. "By what do you mean?"

"I have caught wind of a plan to potentially overthrow Guardian Eska."

Luvan chuckled. His chuckling became a chortle, and then he guffawed and leaned back in his chair and nearly fell over with laughter.

"What is so funny?"

"That is a foolish plan. Edwyrd is too powerful. Whoever thought of this plan has no brains. He can do things of Power with that reimaje of his that you wouldn't even believe. And he is bonded to a dragon. If he could overpower the Twelve, what makes you think you have any hope for success? Your plan will fail." Now completely disinterested in Numos's words, he threw the knife up in the air and watched it twirl.

"Who said anything about fighting Eska?"

"Then how will you—" Luvan extended his hand upwards, sparring a moment to glance at Numos.

"There is more than one way to overthrow a Guardian."

Luvan caught the knife and thought about the senator's words for a moment. "What do you mean?"

"I'm afraid I cannot tell you that." Senator Numos stood. "If you change your mind, you know where to find me."

Luvan let the sentence sink in for a second. He looked away from his knife, up to Eska's portrait, and said, "Why is it that you want to overthrow Guardian Eska, anyway?"

"Change. It is always a good thing, I feel. Gladonus needs it now, more than ever..."

Luvan heard thumping for another few feet and then the senator left, closing the door behind him. He returned his gaze to his knife. He tossed it into the air, caught it, tossed it again, and repeated the process as he thought about everything that happened. *What could he be planning?*

Luvan caught the knife and squeezed the handle. He thought back to his daydream about the time when he was eager to be Eska's conseleigh, not scorned for doing something that he needed to do. *She was wrong. She said my name was given for greatness. She told me. She told me. Surely I have not achieved it yet!* He slammed the butt of the knife on the wooden table in front of him.

I needed to make a trial. How dare he punish me for that! Luvan stared blankly ahead at Guardian Eska's portrait that clung to the wall in front of him. Luvan snarled. *I gave him good counsel. I gave him the best counsel.*

Luvan tilted his chair back and tossed the knife into the air again. He caught it and repeated the process, counting how many times it would spin before landing in his hand again. His father, a hunter, had given him the hunting knife—he had been born in Epoch in a town by a forest. He had taught Luvan how to throw a knife, how to catch one, and the basics of survival. He had been a strong man, a confident man, but mostly, he would be disappointed in knowing that Luvan was no longer conseleigh to Eska. That's where Luvan had gotten his fear of rejection from. His ability to use words came from his mother and had helped him secure a beautiful wife who had given him two children who were now teenagers boarded up at Pauana Academy. He still hadn't told any of them about his dismissal—only that Eska wouldn't need him to help train his apprentice until later.

Change. Gladonus needs it now, more than ever. The senator's last words came to him then. *Eska is too stubborn to listen to me if I told him of what's coming. Not that I think he can be overthrown, anyway. Not without the Twelve. But if he doesn't need me anymore, then I don't need him.*

Luvan reached up for the knife and misjudged its distance. The large knife cut open his hand and dropped to the floor. Luvan clutched his hand and pounded a fist onto the table again. He looked at the knife on the ground, now coated in blood. He picked it up. And then he looked at his hand and saw how the blood soaked his palm. It reminded him of Blood Bonding, of a bond he wanted to forget.

"Aargh." He yelled and threw it forward.

It struck the portrait in the center of Eska's forehead with a twang and quiver. The blood that had coated the steel slowly slid down Eska's face. *He will not be Guardian without me as his conseleigh. He won't.* A thought came to him then, quick and short and brilliant. Luvan smirked. *Numos is right. There is more than one way to overthrow a Guardian.*

"Luvan, are you okay?"

His wife's voice shook him from his thoughts. He heard clattering on the marble flooring. Quickly, he covered his bloody hand and looked up at his wife, who had come down from upstairs. She had blonde hair, cropped to the ears, and golden earrings. Her eyes dazzled green, and she wore a white gown with lacing around the sleeves.

"It's nothing, Lucine." Luvan stood up. "I merely dropped something. You can continue tidying upstairs."

"Are you certain?"

"Yes. Don't worry. I'm going out now. Business calls."

She smiled the same smile that he fell in love with. "I will have supper ready for you, then, when you return home." She went back upstairs.

Luvan's smile quickly faded, and he cursed his clumsiness. He grabbed a rag and wrapped it around his hand, then he strode over to the portrait of Guardian Eska and pulled his knife out from Eska's forehead. He put the knife in the sheath on his belt and walked out the door of his home.

He flew his hovercraft to Senator Numos's house. What he had said intrigued him. No more than fifteen minutes later, he arrived at the senator's home and knocked on the door with his undamaged hand. Senator Numos answered.

"Luvan Katore... A surprise. What brings you here?"

"We have unfinished business to discuss."

Numos removed his eyeglass and blinked. "I was hoping you would say that. Come in."

Luvan followed the senator inside to a place less grandiose than his, but it had an ambiance all its own. Black couches were gathered next to a wooden table. In front of them was a black chimney that had wood, unlit, in the pit. A holder for various wines lined the right side of the room, and before Senator Numos sat, he grabbed a bottle and brought it and two stemmed glasses with him.

"Wine?"

Luvan nodded. He took the glass and watched as Numos poured a dark red wine halfway. "I know your plan."

Numos finished pouring his own glass and sat down across from Luvan. "Do you now?"

"I do. You will need my help if you want Eska overthrown."

Numos sipped his wine and smirked. "Why the sudden change of heart?"

Luvan studied his wine and swirled it. He looked to Numos. "Because there is a greatness in my name. I will not let Eska deter me from that."

"You know what it may cost you?" Numos set his wineglass down on the table.

"Better than you, I do."

Numos sat there, both hands on his lap, studying him. After a brief moment of silence he said, "You interest me, Luvan Katore."

Luvan took a sip of wine. It was bitter. And dry. And warm. The taste reminded him of too many things he wished to forget. He put the glass down, looked at Numos, and smirked. "By the time we are through here, senator, you are only bound to become more interested."

Hi readers,

Just as quickly as the Curse came it has gone. But, what happens now? What will the fallout and aftermath of the Curse of Pirini Lilapa look like? Will Hydro be caught? Will Zain escape the dreaded Blood Chambers? And what will become of Eirek now that Guardian Eska knows his lineage? To find out, make sure you check out the next book in the series, The Hunt for Lost Souls.

If you enjoyed the book, I would be thrilled for a review on Amazon or on Goodreads. They are of tremendous importance to authors, and we are always hugely appreciative.

Take care and happy reading.

Michael E. Thies

MAPS

T he following pages are the maps of each of the domains the characters travel throughout the book. These are to guide you in understanding their journey and to bring to life more of this stellar system that is Gladonus.

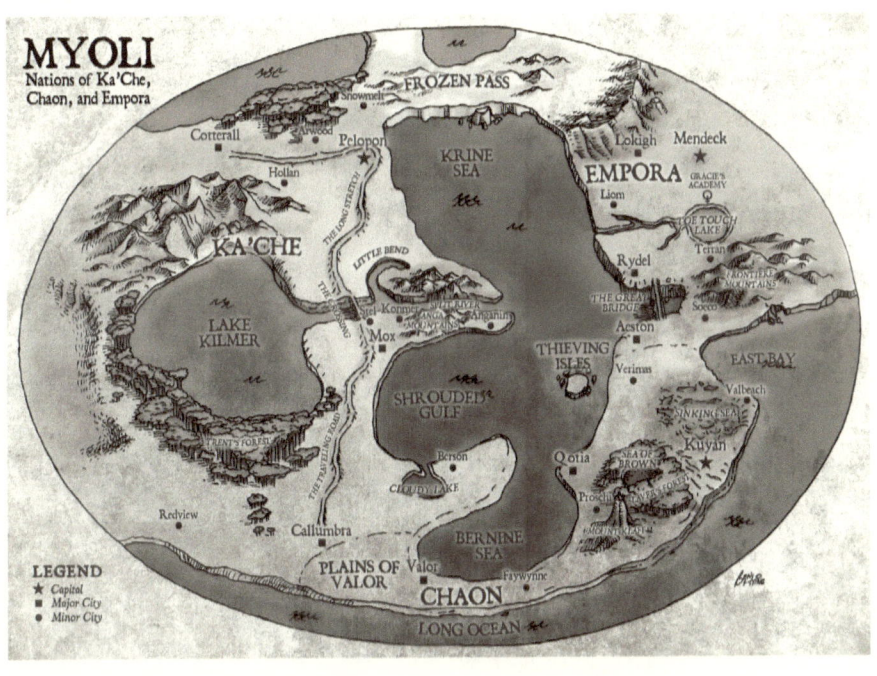

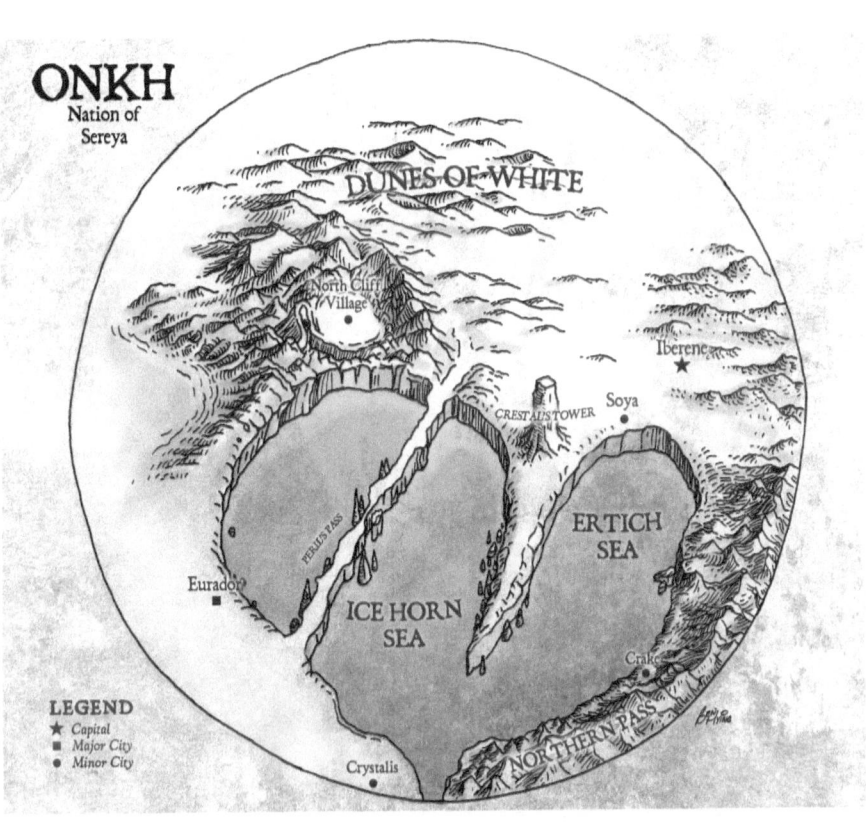

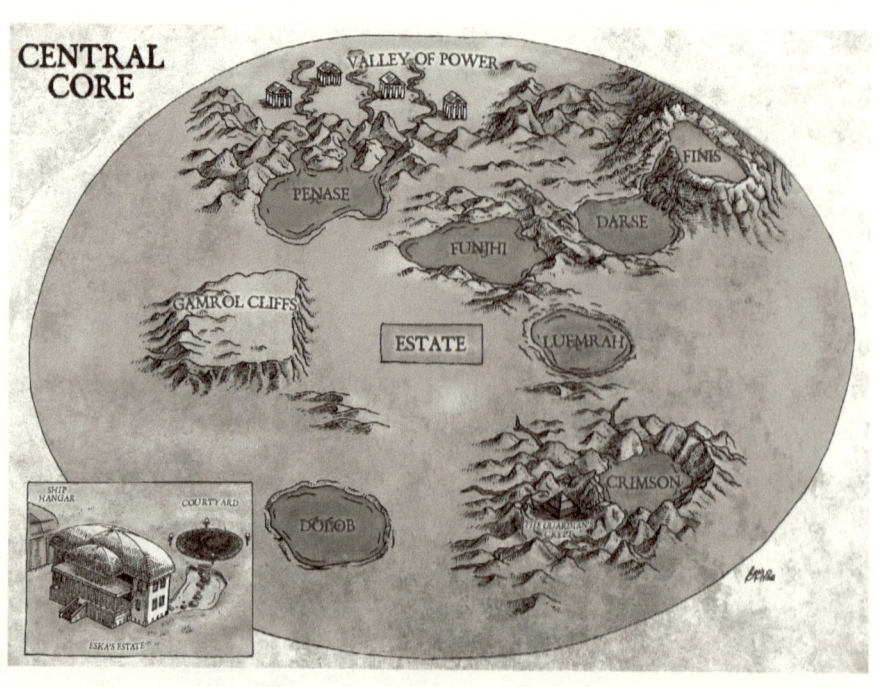

CHARACTER TREES

This section of the novel is designed to give readers a sense of reference for the characters in the novel. Each nation will be displayed along with the ruling house and their sigil. Those who make up that house will be noted below. In certain cases, some characters in the story will not be directly related to the house, in that instance, their relationship to the house will be explained on the page. It's important to note that I only listed the houses that are pertinent to this novel so as not to overwhelm you more than necessary.

After making your way through the nations of importance and the families in power, a few pages will be taken to detail the two prominent academies in the story and those who attend them, along with a few of their sayings and beliefs. Finally, a brief history on how the Twelve came to be and a list of their attributes will be shown at the end.

Thank you for reading and I hope this helps you as you make your way through the book.

THE CENTRAL CORE

GUARDIAN EDWYRD ESKA, Guardian of the Core for 185 years. Bonded to a dragon named, VESEL. Has one sister, ALICIA, deceased. Was sponsored to participate in his own Trials by LORD GARRETT OMYON from Nova. Has four respective aides called his conseleigh:

- TUNDRA IYCEL, conseleigh of the planet Onkh. Before being an aide for Guardian Eska, she was Lady of Sereya. He has been in Eska's service for thirty-five years.

- LUVAN KATORE, conseleigh of the planet Agrost. Before being an aide for Guardian Eska, he was a politician for the nation of Mistral. He has been in Eska's service for thirty years. He is now currently dismissed from his duties for disobeying the Guardian's orders.

- ETHEN RORUM, conseleigh of the planet Myoli. Before being an aide for Guardian Eska, he was a weapons' instructor and trainer for the Lord of Chaon, Zalos Kapache. He has been in Eska's service for fourteen years.

- RIAGAN INFERNO, conseleigh of the planet Pyre. Before being an aide for Guardian Eska, he was Lord of Therus. He has been in Eska's service for eight years.

- CRONOS, one of the four Sages, and is the only one who speaks. Is of First Blood and helps train the apprentice after Coronation. Very versed in the language of Power.

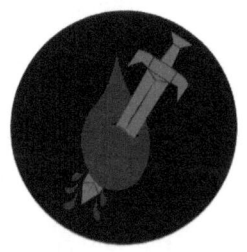

Nation of Acquava

HYDRO PAEN, Lord of Acquava. Only son of AYLAN and LORYEL. Married to ATESIA. Father of three children:

- HYDRO THE SECOND, heir to Acquavan throne and also participated in Guardian Eska's Trials.

- ANYA, deceased.

- AITON, youngest child, going on nine years old.

Figures of Import:
- DARIEN DORNELL, receiver to Lord Paen.

- LEN POSAIR, advisor to Lord Paen.

- ELIAS WARD, lead adored to Lord Paen.

- KORTH CENTELL, head acqua guard, from the Hart Isles.

- YUNVA YIGYR, one of Lord Paen's acqua guards.

- KENT POIL, one of Lord Paen's aqua guards.

- CASSIUS FRAUSTER, one of Lord Paen's acqua guards, deceased.

- HOLDEN HAUGHTER, one of Lord Paen's acqua guards.

- PROFESSOR IGNIS HARUKO, private Power instructor for the family.

Marquises of the Lesser Houses in Acquava:

- ROY TITYLE, marquis of the Katarh province.

- MARQISS PUWL, marquis of the Rhemu province.

- HEKTER SIGURD, marquis of the Roil province.

- ALYN BLOCTER, marquis of the Summer Isles.

- CADELL PERIWINKLE, marquis of the Hart Isles.

- SETH AXYEL, marquis of the Talyn province.

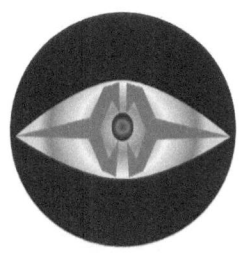

NATION OF GAR

O LIVIA APRAH, Lady of Gar. Only daughter of the deceased VISIS and AUTUMN APRAH.

Figures of Import:
- HORM DUBHALEN, head elite for Lady Aprah

- CORRIGAN BRIGGS, second in command to Lady Aprah's Father of CADMAR BRIGGS, a contestant who participated in Guardian Eska's Trials currently completing The Passage.

- Jöðurr ELDREDGE, advisor to Lady Aprah.

- Gøti LANAM, receiver to Lady Aprah.

Marquises of the Lesser Houses in Gar:
- ROWAN BERNAL, marquis of the major city of Nore.

- WILLIAM CREAZON, marquis of the major city of Brockstun.

- ROGER LUTEN, baron of the minor city of Roan.

Nation of Sereya

ASTOR GRIME, Lord of Sereya. Had two wives, both deceased. First wife was named NEVA gave birth to WHITTIKER, currently a weapons instructor at the academy of Storm Academy. Second wife, WYNTER gave birth to CANICE, currently studying the Adored Arts on Pyre.

Figures of Import:
- KALEN KATARH, advisor to Lord Grime.

- JEL PARON, receiver to Lord Grime.

Marquises of the Lesser Houses in Sereya:
- NICHOLAS COLDEN, marquis of Eurador.

- CONNER ERTICH, baron of the minor city of Soya.

NATION OF CRESICA

L YNDA CLAYSE, Lady of Cresica. Lives in the capital, Syf. Married to RYBERT. Has one daughter, LINN.

Figures of Import:
- AERYN SHIREWOOD, advisor to Lady Clayse.

- EMBRY KNOSSOL, receiver to Lady Clayse.

- ANGAL, a well-received and well-traveled bard who has strung his chords in favor of the royal family and plays for them often, telling stories of mystery and wonder. Has a nephew, EIREK MOURSE who is a contestant that partakes in Guardian Eska's Trials. Angal gave him to the to the MOURSE family at the age of seven which consists of parents: SHERYIN AND GERALD and their son, JAHN.

Marchionesses of the Lesser Houses in Cresica:
- ALBONY EVENGALE, marchioness of the major city, Stynt. Has two children OSWYN (older) and EZRA (younger).

- MARA SURG, marchioness of the major city, Lisyn.

- TIPHANE TALHEND, marchioness of the major city, Cruxe.

- MELODON SHEER, marchioness of the Triangle Islands.

Nation of Epoch

D AVEN EVBER, Lord of Epoch. Lives in Castle Thoth, in city it was named after, Thoth. Married to DAWN. Has one son, CAIN, who participated in Guardian Eska's Trials.

Figures of Import:
- NATHAN ALAOIS, advisor to Lord Evber.

- FINNIAN LUGUS, receiver to Lord Evber.

- CASTOR LEELAN, head of the owl guards.

Marquises of Lesser Houses in Epoch:
- EDYM LANGOL, marquis of the major city, Ambit. Has one son, JOSHUA.

- CHRISTOPHER SOLLEN, marquis of the major city, Briarwood.

- SOREN MESH, marquis of the major city, Vale.

- ROGER YOUNG, baron of the minor city, Lorian.

Nation of Empora

V ICTOR ZIGARDA, Lord of Empora. Lives in Mendeck. Never married. Had one younger brother, RENAUL, now deceased. Renaul's legacy was carried on by three children:

- HAYDEN

- SELBY

- MEADE

Figures of Import:
- EDWYN LYZE, advisor to Zigarda.

- YUAN SHIMES, receiver to Zigarda.

- DR. GENUS CERE, lead scientist for Zigarda.

- ZAKK SHIREN, lead bodyguard for Zigarda.

Marquises of Lesser Houses in Empora:
- PILLIAN DESMIER, marquis of the major city, Lokigh.

- SHEAMOUS STRONGHAND, marquis of the major city, Soeco.

- MYCKEL CRUNE, marquis of the major city, Rydel.

Nation of Ka'che

A BRAHAM VANGLE, Lord of Ka'Che. Son of TYON. Lives in Pelopon, the capital. Married to SHAYNA. Has four children: KYLAN of twenty, TREV of fifteen, and LIQUA and LEDLA who are twins at twelve.

Abraham has three other siblings:

- LUKAS, an older brother who is Denied.

- ELORINE SESSO who is married to RAMSEY.

- BRISINE BERRESE, the youngest, married to LARON. Have two children and one adopted child:

- JAMAAL, oldest son. Married to REINE. Has two children, AMAYA, four years old, and KALANI, six years old.

- ZAIN, a student at Gazo's Academy. Also, a contestant who participated in Guardian Eska's Trials.

- ZAKK SHIREN, adopted son of Brisine and Laron. Family murdered at the age of six. Taken in at the age of twelve. Another contestant who was accepted to attend Guardian Eska's Trials but never ended up participating.

Figures of Import:

- ERRION VESK, advisor to Lord Vangle. Nicknamed ERIE and the LORD'S EAR.

- OWLEN MANSEN, receiver to Lord Vangle.

- AENEAS KHREOS, captain of the Sea's Commander.

- BERN DENARDI, first captain of the Sea's Commander.

- GERALD STARSHINE, a royal guard in service to Lord Vangle, deceased.

Marquises of Lesser Houses of Ka'Che:

- RAMSEY SESSO, marquis of the major city, Cotterall.

- BRRYN ROPIS, marquis of the major city, Callumbra.

- DARAN MOXXIE, marquis of the major city, Mox.

THE TWELVE

T he gestalt that is the Twelve are the warriors who survived the Great War and managed to escape before Gladima sealed itself away. Born on Gladima and endowed with First Blood, the Twelve used their Power and authority of birthright to claim home to the other planets as their home had now vanished. By showcasing their strength and ability, many citizens view them with awe and wonder and have surmised that they are deities sent to rule over Gladonus in the absence of the Ancients. Those belonging to the Heavol Tribe were created by Ancient Lyoen. Those belonging to the Evolic Tribe were created by Ancient Bane.

Rivals towards one another, and tensions still high after the Great War, a constant feud ended with them needing to quell the events of the first Pirini Lilapa (year 150 AGW) together. What's more, a prophecy floated upon the air that spoke of the Twelve's loss of Power. The considerable effort it took to stop Pirini Lilapa and the vulnerability that it exposed them to, along with their heightened sense of paranoia due to the prophecy, made them realize they would need to create a role to handle such an occurrence if it should happen again. The first Guardian of the Core, Jorey Raule, fulfilled that role in the year 165 AGW (After Great War).

The Heavol Tribe
- Fueoco = God of heat and fire.

- Orekus = God of underworld.

- Myethos = God of the suns and day.

- Saeluste = Goddess of mental health, wisdom, and intelligence.

- Trema = Goddess of the lands and harvest.

- Lucine = Goddess of birth and peace.

The Evolic Tribe

- Pearl = Goddess of water, seas, and oceans.

- Anemie = Goddess of the sky, lightning, and Axiumé.

- Luenar = God of the moons, night.

- Theothe = God of physical health and beauty.

- Crestal = Goddess of cold winds and winter seasons.

- Tomahawke = God of war and death and suffering.

About the Author

Michael E. Thies is an English educator and Holistic Health Coach currently living in Suzhou, China. He is a child of God and is a proud member of the Church of God Ministry Jesus Christ International (CGMJCI) and draws much of his inspiration from the Bible.